HEAVEN'S GOLD

HEAVEN'S GOLD

GILES TIPPETTE

A TOM DOHERTY ASSOCIATES BOOK
NEW YORK

This is a work of fiction. All the characters and events portrayed in this novel are either fictitious or are used fictitiously.

HEAVEN'S GOLD

This book is printed on acid-free paper.

A Forge Book
Published by Tom Doherty Associates, Inc.
175 Fifth Avenue
New York, N.Y. 10010

Forge® is a registered trademark of Tom Doherty Associates, Inc.

Library of Congress Cataloging-in-Publication Data
Tippette, Giles.
        Heaven's gold / Giles Tippette.
            p.   cm.
        "A Tom Doherty Associates book."
        ISBN 0-312-86047-1
        I. Title.
    PS3570.I6H43 1996
    813'.54—dc20   96-8895
                                              CIP

First Edition: December 1996

Printed in the United States of America

0   9   8   7   6   5   4   3   2   1

To Betsyanne,

As always

HEAVEN'S
GOLD

CHAPTER
1

I WASN'T exactly sure when I had come to the firm resolve to rob the Federal Reserve Bank in San Antonio of the quarter of a million dollars' worth of gold bullion the United States government was going to put on display there. It could have been as soon as I read about the coming event in the San Antonio newspaper, though I had to doubt that. The story in the newspaper had made me mad as hell, but it is a long stretch between getting angry and organizing a robbery, especially at a big bank in a big city. Given the impression I presented at first glance, there were folks who probably thought I was a man given to sudden actions and desperate chances. Nothing could have been farther from the truth. I might have appeared hell-bent and reckless but that was just for show. I was a man who gave careful thought and planning to any effort more elaborate than going down to breakfast. If I had been as wild and headstrong as most folks thought, I doubted I'd have survived for fifty-eight years, not considering the kind of career I'd had beginning at about the age of fifteen.

But, of course, *when* I'd decided about robbing that Federal Reserve gold wasn't near as important as when I was going to get around to telling my wife, Lauren, of my intentions. I could come to all the conclusions I wanted to, but they were just so much West Texas dust in a high wind unless she and I reached agreement on that conclusion. Just swirling, swirling brown smoke without firm form or direction. It had been that way ever since I had married her some twenty-one years previous. And that had been the next thing to a running gunfight. She was from Virginia and I had written her I was coming up to claim her hand and bring her back to Texas and marry her. What I'd considered to be a quick errand had turned into one of the longest trips I'd ever made and we'd ended up getting married in Virginia and then, and only then, was she willing to come back to Texas.

She was sixteen years my junior and it was a sad commentary on me that a forty-two-year-old woman who didn't weigh more than one hundred ten pounds with her makeup on and a jeweled comb in her blond hair could get the Indian sign on me, but she could. I was fifty-eight in that year of 1916, but some thirty years past I had been the most feared bank robber in most of Texas and some parts of other states. I'd given the law such fits that the governor had finally offered me a full pardon to come in off the owlhoot trail and give the law officers a rest. Since that retirement from the business of taking people's money at the point of a gun I'd drifted into the enterprise of operating a saloon and casino down along the Mexican border in the town of Del Rio, Texas. It achieved about the same results as bank robbing, only it was legal and you didn't need a gun. But even though I had left the outlaw game I was still known as a man you didn't want to push too far. Even at my age I was still pretty fit and the hundred ninety pounds I carried still fit my six-foot frame pretty well. I wasn't scared of anything, mounted or afoot, or any kind of critter that could be stopped with the traveling end of a revolver cartridge. I no longer wore a gun at my side. Now it was carried in a shoulder holster hidden under the light linen coats that Lauren made me wear. Seeing me dressed for my day's rounds, you'd have figured I was near on to civilized— even though Lauren had not been able to force me to wear a necktie. And I damn near was. Or as civilized as I was likely to get.

But that business about the Federal Reserve gold had made me angry and the idea of doing something about it just kept whirling around in my brain. All that was needed to spur me into making some sort of decisive plan was the courage to bring up the subject with Lauren. The day the lightning rod salesman had come calling had damn near give me the push I was looking for. The reason that gold had me so angry was that I considered it just one more example of the direction the country was heading, a direction I didn't care for one little bit. And the lightning rod salesman, him and his goods, was a prime example of what I saw as a weakening and a dependency that was afloat in the country and was being encouraged to grow and spread. Whether I'd have felt that way if our boy, our son Willis, hadn't been over in Europe in a war we oughtn't to have had any part of, I could not honestly say. I reckoned it did have its effect on my thinking, but there were other factors as well. I had not made a practice of talking about them out loud, not even with Lauren, but they were quietly boiling away in my head.

The lightning rod drummer had shown up at our door no more than two days after I'd got back from San Antonio. I was sitting in a little morning room that we sometimes used to sit and read the paper in or have that extra cup of coffee after breakfast, when the knock came. The room is situated close on to the front door and I heard Lauren call to the housekeeper that she would get it since she was handy. I heard a low buzz of voices, but didn't pay it much mind until I heard a man say, louder than I wanted folks talking to my wife, "Madam, I do not see how you can risk the lives of your family and loved ones by living in a house not protected by the Little Giant guaranteed, never-fail, galvanized, and copper-plated lightning rods!"

It sounded like he was talking in words about the size of a newspaper headline when there is big news to report. I glanced out the front window by my chair at the road that ran by. What I saw was a damn infernal gasoline-burning tin lizzy pulled up on the little gravel semicircular driveway that ran up to our front porch. The vehicle was more what they called a carryall truck than it was a passenger automobile, but that didn't make any difference. I had done everything short of putting up a sign to discourage folks from bringing those damn rattling, noisy, smelly contraptions onto my property. That sight and the sound of the man's voice were enough to get me out of my chair and started for the front door. I didn't doubt Lauren's ability to deal with such a nincompoop but I wanted to get my own licks in.

As I came down the short front hallway she was standing there with the door open and holding the screen door out as she listened to the salesman. When she heard my footsteps she glanced around and gave me an apprehensive look. I had my linen jacket off, and the .42-caliber revolver built on a .44-caliber frame was clearly visible in its holder under my left armpit. As politely as I could I slid in between her and the screen door, backing her out of the way and coming face to face with the peddler. The sight of him was near enough to make me want to draw my revolver and shoot the sonofabitch, and never mind the presumption of him setting that hellish machine within smelling distance of my front door.

The man himself wasn't so unnatural looking that he ought to have been kept off the street, but his clothes just set my teeth on edge. It was early summer and he was wearing a straw boater—which was irritating enough of itself—with a red hatband around it. He had on a white shirt with a celluloid collar and was wearing a red bow tie, which I didn't care for in either shape or color. But his gravest error was a pair of the widest, reddest galluses I'd ever seen. On top of that the sonofabitch was complected like a freckled horse and had a red, pencil-thin mustache. I figured him to be in his thirties, at least old enough to make an honest living without calling unannounced at people's doors. In his hands he had a couple of iron rods about four feet long that were tipped at one end by a copper arrow, with some kind of electrical wires coming off the other.

When he saw that I had taken over my wife's position he brightened up considerably. "Why, hello!" he said. "Looks like I am now dealing with the man of the house. Always glad to speak with a man who can see the scientific angle and understands the lifesaving electrical conduction principles of the lightning rod, and not just any lightning rod but the Little Giant lightning rod, manufactured in St. Louis, Missouri, and sold on an exclusive basis to demanding clientele." He put out his hand. "Name is Pike, George Pike. You'd be . . . ?"

I ignored his hand and reached out and took the lightning rods out of his other. "So this is the famous Little Giant lightning rod I've heard so much about. I tell you, ain't a day goes by that one or the other of my neighbors don't mention this little item and how much safer they feel since they've had them installed on their roofs. Yes, sir, there's a widow lady here in town claims that this very object has not only saved her life on more than one occasion but has given her so much confidence that she is thinking of remarrying." I was pretending to give the rods a good looking over, but I could see his cunning little face brighten up at the prospect of loading up such a hick as I was presenting myself as.

He said, "Why, there you go, sir! By golly, I taken me one gander at you and knowed you was a high-steppin' forward thinker. A real goin' Jessie! Yes, sir! And you is holdin' in your hands the very latest in scientific forward thinkin', guaranteed to keep you and your loved ones safe from the awful dread of lightning strikes that can not only set your house afire, but strike you dead right there in yore own bed! Yes, sir, the safety of your own bed! Why, lightning strikes your house and runs down a wall and acrost the floor and, next thing you know, it has jumped right in bed with you and killed all that is there! A horrible prospect."

Innocently I said, "How many of these highly scientific items would you reckon I'd need on my house to be absolutely safe from the dreaded prospect of a lightning strike? Two?"

Looking serious and businesslike, he stepped back and gazed up at the house. It was our town house, the one we lived in when we weren't out at one of our horse ranches. It was two stories even though Lauren and I didn't use half of it, but a two-story house was cooler and that was what you were after down along the border. Sounding as if he knew what he was talking about, he said, "Well, you've got a mighty high structure here, Mr. . . . Mr. . . . ? I didn't quite get your name?"

"I am most anxious to know how many of these wizard instruments I need."

"Weell, I'll tell you. High as your place is—highest point around here, I'd reckon—I'd say you need four. Reason I say that is that your lightning can come at you from any of the four corners of the sky. Yes, sir, that's a fact. That's why we at the Little Giant company recommend you cover all the major points of the compass. It's the surest way. And you save money by buying four. They would cost you eleven dollars apiece, but if you taken four I could let—"

"Oh, money ain't no object," I said. "Not with the dread of a lightning strike hanging over our heads. Maybe frying us in our beds."

Behind me Lauren said, "Will! Now stop it."

Lauren was dead set against me chousing people even when they had it coming. I said, "Honey, I'm trying to do a little business. You heard the drummer here, this is men's business. We are the only ones can understand this scientific concern."

The little dandified drummer was so busy calculating how much he was going to clip the rube for that he didn't hear her. He got out a pencil and a little notebook. "Well, I can see you are a man don't believe in doing a job halfway." He wet the end of the pencil and started scratching out some figures. "Now, to be really safe, and I am talking about copper-bottomed, silver-lined safe, I'd recommend you maybe put six of the Little Giants in place on your roof. You never know when a thundercloud is likely to come out of nowhere and catch you halfway between lightning rods. It has happened. Oh, yes, sir! I'd hate to tell you how many times I've had the sad duty of surveying the ruins of a house that perished with all aboard just for the need of one more scientifically engineered Little Giant lightning safeguard. Yes, sir!"

"Six, hell!" I said. "If six is good, eight is better!" Behind me I heard Lauren give a little sigh, but she didn't say anything. But my words just set the drummer to scribbling faster and faster. I reckoned by then he figured he knew he had a live one and was going to live pretty well the rest of the month just on this one sucker.

He said, "Now, there is thinking for you! Been this kind of thinkin' 'round years before, we'd've had the automobile fifty years earlier! That is the kind of thinking that gets the get-up-and-go to gettin' up and goin'!"

He'd made a mistake with his remark about the automobile, but I never let on. Instead I suddenly snapped my fingers as if I'd had an idea. "Say, we got a windmill out back that's near as tall as the house. Might even be taller. Hadn't we ought to put a clutch of these scientific gadgets up on it? Say four of them?"

"Oh, my, yes!" he said. "Lightning will strike that highest point, you know." He went to scratching out his figures and writing in new ones. "Yes, sir, yes, sir. Now, that would make an even dozen, as I figure it."

"Hold on!" I said. "Not so fast. When I believe in something I take right to it. I got a carriage house and a small barn out back. Got a corral with horses in it. Some of them is special racing horses and worth quite a bit of money. You shore just the high places ought to be protected? Might not that lightning swoop down and maybe kill a couple of them horses? Some of them are worth upwards of a thousand dollars."

I thought he was going to faint. "Oh, my, oh, my! Yes, sir, Mr.—Mr. . . . ? I never did get your name."

"What about the barn and the corral and the carriage house? Can they be struck?"

He lowered his little notebook and reached in his back pocket and got out a red bandanna and mopped his face. "Oh, yes, sir! If they is one thang you can't put no assurance in, it is lightning! Why, them thunderbolts is as likely to strike the ground right under your feet as the church steeple! No, sir. When it comes to lightning, the more protection the better."

I let a little edge come into my voice. "Well, that being the case, I'm wondering if I ought not to take some extra steps here. Why don't I send to town and get a crew out here and have them build me a wooden tower that is just higher than anything around here. I mean build that sucker way on up yonder." I lifted my arms and waved my hands toward the heavens. "I mean really high! And we could stick them Little Giants plumb all over it! A dozen of 'em. Maybe more. Just invite that lightning to come on and do its durndest. What do you think of that?"

I couldn't tell if it was my voice or the way I was waving my arms around that got his attention. Certainly lifting my arms had made the revolver more obvious where it was hanging under my arm. I saw his eyes cut over to it. He was standing on the porch about two or three feet from me. Now he took a step backward. "Uh, what did you say your name was, sir? I don't reckon I caught it."

I said, "You ain't writing them new numbers down. You ought

to keep up while I'm reeling them off. Hate to forget them. By the way, the name is Wilson Young."

He was old enough to have heard of me from the bad, wild days. But even if he wasn't, there were still stories circulating that had grown and changed like a bastard stepchild. If I'd robbed as many banks and killed as many men as some of those stories claimed, I'd have had to be as fast as Mr. Pike's lightning strikes and about ten times more dangerous.

I saw the name register in his mind and then begin to sink in. He took another step backward, heading for the porch steps behind him. "Uh, maybe I ought to just check out here in my truck. See if I got enough Little Giant rods on hand to fill your needs."

I reached out and snagged him by one of his red suspenders. "Hold on there, Mr. Pike, I ain't done figuring yet." I took a step toward him, still holding him by a gallus, though he was stretching it a bit as he leaned toward the porch steps. "You know what I been thinking about? I been thinking about old Ben Franklin. Now, there was a man knew about lightning. Listen, this matter is clear as a bell. All I need to do is build me a great big kite. We get a damn good wind around here blows all the time. I'll build me a kite, big as a barn door. Get me a spool of smooth wire, say a thousand foot of it, and get me a bunch of Mexicans to fly it. We could stick a half a dozen of them Little Giants on it, and, why, we'd be as safe as if we were in a big copper kettle. What do you think of that, Mr. Pike?"

He was looking very uncomfortable. He glanced over my shoulder, no doubt appealing to Lauren to do something before the crazy man shot him, but if I knew Lauren she was laughing inside in spite of herself. He finally stammered out, "Why, why, Mr. Young, that is a first-rate idea. Mighty fine, yes, sir, mighty fine."

"Is it a going Jessie? I mean, I could get enough Mexicans they could fly that big kite right around the clock, twenty-four hours a day. This is the border and they is a lot of Mexicans around here. Lot of them out of work, too. They'd be glad to get on a crew flying a kite twenty-four hours a day. Did you say it was a going Jessie?"

He nodded vigorously. "Yes, sir, yes, sir. It's a going Jessie."

"Is it get-ahead, get-going, forward thinking?"

He started stammering worse. "Why, why, yes, yes, yes—yes, sir." With a little twitch he jerked his suspender loose and began backing down the steps. "I'll jus—I'll jus—I'll just slip on out here to my truck if you don't mind, Mr. Young."

He had reached the yard and was halfway to his truck. I started down the steps, and then suddenly snapped my fingers. "Say! I got the best idea yet! Hold on there, Mr. Pike. Wait'll you hear this. I got the best idea of all. Here, hold up a minute."

But he was too busy spinning the crank on his tin lizzy to listen to me. I heard the engine catch with a rattle and saw a cloud of venomous blue smoke belch out the back of the machine. As Mr. Pike ran around to the door of his jalopy I started toward him. Speaking louder and louder on account of the engine noise, I said, "Here now, Mr. Pike. Wait a minute. Hear my idea. Listen, you run inside and get our bed and put it in the back of your horseless buckboard and then you *can drive me and my wife around the country at such a speed that we'll outrun the lightning! Wait a minute!*"

He wasn't waiting. Without a backward look he got his machine going and bolted down my gravel drive. Once he must have goosed it too hard or not hard enough because it backfired like a cannon and the smoke turned black. I yelled, "Hey! *Hey! It could be your life's work! Driving us around!*" Then I realized that I was still holding the two Little Giant lightning rods in my hand. I waved them over my head. *"Pike! Pike! You forgot your Little Giants worth eleven dollars each! That's twenty-two dollars!"*

But he didn't seem inclined to stop. I stuck them into the ground by their arrow-shaped heads and started back to the house, laughing to myself. As I came up the steps I saw that Lauren had quit the doorway. I opened the screen door and stepped in. She was waiting for me at the end of the entrance hall, looking severe, her arms folded under her bosom. By nature Lauren was as sweet and loving and good-humored a person as I reckoned was alive in the world. Certainly it took an extraordinary woman to put up with a man of my whimsy. But on occasion, when she considered it necessary, she could spot a hell-and-brimstone preacher or an old maid schoolteacher a week to get their faces set and still whip them hands down on looking severe. I was a respecter of that look so I run the laughter out of my system as quick as I could and let out a sigh as I got up to her. "All right," I said. "Now what have I done and how long is it going to take to get that look off your face?"

"Wilson Young, you ought to be ashamed of yourself, treating that poor man like that. And all he was doing was trying to make a living. Shame on you for that little act you pulled."

I went on past her and through the dining room and into the small room next to the kitchen where we had breakfast. I sat down at one of the chairs around the wooden table. I kept a bottle of whiskey on that table as well as some extra glasses. Lauren had never quite taken to the idea of having a bottle of spirits, as she called it, on the breakfast table, but she'd finally given in on that one. She'd known I drank before we married and she'd also understood I didn't drink by the clock. As far as I was concerned there was no difference between whiskey in your coffee at six in the morning or whiskey in a tumbler at six in the evening. Besides, she'd take a drink now and again herself, though she generally wanted some kind of sweet nonsense like a julep or watered-down brandy or a French wine.

Before I answered her I reached over and uncorked the whiskey and poured myself a little. Before the drummer had come I'd been about to go down and see how my businesses were operating. Not that I paid them that much attention. I had a good manager for the casino and one for the saloon, and I'd hired them to run the places, so that was what I let them do. I took a drink of whiskey and let it roll around in my mouth before I swallowed it. It was eight-year-old bonded sour mash and about as smooth as whiskey was allowed to get. It was the best that money could buy, but then I was a long way from being poor. I'd come out of the bank-robbing business with a pretty healthy stake and all it had done was grow, as I'd converted the money into legitimate ways to steal. I'd even owned a Mexican whorehouse until Lauren and I had gotten married. I'd actually owned it until she found out that I was in that line of work along with the saloon and the casino. Hadn't taken me very long to get shut of the whorehouse. On recollection, I figured I'd managed to sell it just before she got finished packing.

She had followed me into the breakfast room and sat down. "Well? At least have the good grace to make some excuse."

I glanced sideways at her. She was struggling to hold on to the severe look. I said, "Your face is going to freeze like that one of these days. Then you'll be sorry."

She said dryly, "I nearly kicked the slats out of my cradle the first time I heard that from my mother."

"Surely you are not taking the side of that drummer? Just making a living? Yeah, off widows and orphans and the seriously ignorant. Hell, Lauren, the damn man was selling a fraud and at an outrageous price, too. I will give him credit for that. If you are going to sell a fraud, put a high price on it."

"You still didn't have to treat him like that. Heckling him in that deadpan way of yours. And then raising your arms to show him the revolver you insist on carrying. My goodness, Wilson, the country is settled. Or haven't you noticed? And that sly way you let him know who you were just at the right time. I swear, Wilson, sometimes I think you enjoy tormenting folks."

"You better keep your voice down or Mrs. Bridesdale is going to hear you. She's probably right inside the kitchen listening at that swinging door."

"Mrs. Bridesdale is hanging out wash."

"Then Mr. Bridesdale will hear you."

"Mr. Bridesdale is working in the kitchen garden. Besides, Mr. Bridesdale is half deaf, as you well know."

The Bridesdales were the couple that kept up our town place. We had several other hired people that tended to our ranch outside of town and the ranch we had in Mexico just across the river.

"Besides," she said, "I'm not saying anything I'm ashamed of. *You're* the one should be ashamed. Running that poor man off like that. Get a kite and fly it! You ought to be ashamed of yourself. Build a tower!"

A little smile was trying to tug at her mouth, but she was fighting it. I said, "Lauren, quit calling that poor huckster a poor man. He was a fraud. Did you get a look at that red hatband and that red bow tie? And them red suspenders? Lord, I nearly shot him on their account, let alone him pulling that mechanical monstrosity up next to the house. That sonofabitch! I'm getting mad again just thinking about it."

"Now, Will, don't swear. At least don't swear in the house."

That was familiar ground. "I wasn't swearing, I was cussing. Swearing is what you do when you testify in a court of law."

She gave me a look. "You know what I mean."

"How many times we had this little exchange?"

"Every time you swear."

"Cuss. Listen, Lauren, I know you ain't seriously sticking up for that drummer. Hell, the man is a crook. Preying on folks' ignorance. Why, he don't know no more about lightning or science than a pig knows about ball gowns. First he says lightning strikes the highest object around. Then I mention the horse corrals and, yeah, they ought to have a set. Hell, if we'd had a cellar he'd have tried to sell me a set of rods for there. Nobody knows where lightning strikes or why. Them Little Giants of his are just like about a thousand other items on the market—just something to get you to spend your money on that you ain't got no more need for than a rabbit needs a wrestling jacket."

She blinked and gave me a slow flicker of a smile. "A what?"

"Nothing. Just something that popped into my head so I said it. Same way I asked you to marry me."

"I see," she said.

I sat there a moment admiring her. She was wearing a kind of jade-green house dress that was made out of silk and had big floppy arms but was cut pretty tight around her waist and hips. With the sun coming in through the window behind her and lighting her hair up I didn't figure there was a much better-looking woman to be found anywhere. She might have been forty-two years old, but you'd never guess it, with or without her clothes on. The only woman I knew who had a figure that could match hers was her sister Laura. Laura was four years older and married to a close friend of mine in the horse-breeding business. The two of them favored greatly though Lauren, I thought, had a much gentler and more beautiful face. Their hair was nearly a match, that buttery color until right near the tips where it looked like somebody had touched it up with strawberry juice. I reckoned that every man had a right to think he was married to the best-looking woman on earth. All I knew was that I was well satisfied with what I'd drawn as my lot.

But we had a serious area of disagreement. I thought the country was going to hell with the politicians leaning into the traces to help it along, and she didn't. Lauren and her sister favored physically, but they weren't much alike in attitude and personality. Laura had a good streak of wildcat in her and could be as dangerous as a loaded gun when she thought something wasn't right. Lauren was that way herself, except she took a much gentler and calmer approach. Not that she wouldn't get mad; she would. But it was the kind of calm, reasoned anger that nearly drove me nuts. She seldom raised her voice, and if she had ever screamed, I had never heard it. Her big mistake was she thought everyone was as good as she was, and nothing I could say would dissuade her from such a fool idea. She didn't just believe in giving folks a second chance, she gave them third and fourth and fifth chances. Early in our marriage we had a maid working for us that was quietly taking most of our portable possessions back to Mexico with her every night. I'd catch her at the theft and bring her before Lauren, since the house was her business, for a good tongue-lashing or the threat of jail or discharge from our employment. Time after time Lauren let her off, telling me that the girl wasn't really a thief, she was just needy and trying to help her family. Once I caught her giving the girl a hundred dollars as reward for trying to make off with a good part of Lauren's wardrobe. When I jumped her about it she explained that the girl had taken the dresses to sell because she needed the money. Lauren's solution was to cut out the middleman and give her the cash up front. But, as I remembered it, I don't think she ever got her dresses back. And that girl was just one instance. There was nobody bad in the world; they were just "misguided." Well, I couldn't complain very much because it was those very qualities that had made me want her as my wife. The fact that she was beautiful and as satisfying as a man could want in other ways was just frosting on the cake.

But through the years her naïve approach to the world had frustrated and baffled me to the point of trying to drive her toward a more clear-eyed look at reality. It had not worked. One time I had asked her if I'd just been "misguided" during the fifteen or sixteen years I'd spent taking other people's money at the point of a gun. She had replied that every flock has a few lost sheep but, in time, they return to the flock. I had looked at her in disbelief and said, "A soft answer turneth away wrath." She'd been surprised at me quoting from the Bible. Oh, yes, I knew considerably more about the Bible than most folks would have thought. I'd had it hammered into my head by an old sour-faced aunt I'd been farmed out to when my folks had died early. I hadn't, however, found much use for the knowledge.

As I've mentioned, Lauren did not share my dim view of the direction the country was headed in. She said that I was set in my ways and resisting progress. But she didn't seem to mind that I would not buy an automobile or have a telephone or electric lights installed. If that was the way I felt, then it was fine and she'd go along with it.

I took a drink of my whiskey and said, "Did you hear that yahoo call me a get-going, forward-thinking, going Jessie? Did you hear him say that I appreciated progress when I saw it? Did you hear all that?"

"Yes, dear."

"You ain't surprised I didn't strangle him with my bare hands?"

"Oh, I know you, Will. What's that code of yours? You never kick a cripple? Or fight someone who hasn't got a chance against you? Well, Mr. Pike was safe. Though I do think you should have bought some lightning rods from him. Suppose he has a family to support."

I looked at her in amazement. "Buy some—I'll be damned, Lauren. Sometimes I don't think you hear a word I say. Don't you understand that the goddamn government and them damn eastern industrialists are trying to invent new gadgets just so we'll have something to buy that we don't need? This damn country is going soft and small and I'm beginning to think I'm the only one can see it. I showed you that article in the paper I brought back from San Antonio. The one about the display of gold bullion at the Federal Reserve Bank in San Antonio. Don't that make you mad as hell?"

She shrugged. "Wilson, I don't really see why you get so upset about that. The way I read it, it is a program by the government to show people that the country has ample gold reserves. I don't understand it as I probably should, but aren't we on something called the gold standard?"

I looked away and shook my head. I started to reach in my

pocket for a little cigarillo but stayed my hand. If I lit one, Lauren would get up and fetch me an ashtray for fear I'd use my whiskey glass or something else for the purpose. That woman was nearly death on cigarillo ashes being put in the wrong places. I said, "Lauren, that is what the government wants you to think. But the real purpose is to encourage people to spend paper money, specie, and for other folks to take it in like it was gold. It is just more of the government's purpose to get people to spending so the manufacturers can make more goods and trinkets to sell so they can buy them and so the manufacturers can make more. And so on and so on."

She wrinkled her brow, which was still as smooth and silky as when I had first set out to court her. "Why would the government want to do that? A dollar is a dollar whether it is gold or paper."

I nodded. "I know that and you know that, but there are still a hell of a lot of people in the South and the Southwest, stuck back in the sticks, that don't trust paper money. They won't take it for debts and they won't put their savings in it. Gold and silver is all they understand. And it is hard to get them to part with it. But once you get folks to believing in paper, why, it's nothing to them. It's like it ain't real money."

She shook her head. "I don't think so."

"Damnit, Lauren, listen to me. A lot of casinos, over in Louisiana especially, use chips instead of money. They won't let you play with real money. Make you buy chips when you come in. Their theory, and it is a good one, is that it makes people more reckless. After a while they forget they paid out money for their chips. They are just little wooden chips, no matter how gaudy they are painted. Folks gamble a lot looser when they ain't using money."

She stood up. "I suppose so, Wilson, but I wish you wouldn't get yourself so upset about such matters. It hasn't got anything to do with us."

"The hell it doesn't!" I said with a little heat. "In the first place it is an insult to my intelligence. And in the second, I hate to see any-body run a con and get away with it. Especially my own damn gov-ernment. They remind me of that damn lightning rod salesman."

She walked past me. "I had better get Mrs. Bridesdale started on lunch and you had better go on downtown if you are going, oth-erwise you'll be late getting home."

I watched her disappear through the swinging kitchen door. It was a good thing, I thought. If she'd stayed I was well on my way to broaching my plans for robbing the quarter of a million dollars in bullion.

CHAPTER

2

It was a little after ten when I put on my linen jacket and left the house to go down to my places of business. It was Monday morning and I always went into the office to take a look at the books with my two managers and see how we'd done the previous week.

It was a nice day, so I just walked. Not that walking was still a habit for me or any other horseman. But I'd quit wearing high-heeled boots, except when I was going to ride a snorty bronc. They'd got to where they hurt me in the back. Now I wore what they called cavalry boots, which had a heel on them about like a shoe. Not that it was that far to downtown. No more than half a mile. There wasn't anyplace very far from anyplace else in Del Rio. What with the transit trade and the fugitives from the law passing both ways on the International Bridge, it was a little difficult to get an accurate census on the anchored citizens, but I figured the place for about five or six thousand. My businesses, of course, were supported more by the transient gentry than the home folks, and that was the way I wanted it.

I actually had two saloons and one casino. My main saloon was not attached to the casino and was run as a completely separate operation. The casino itself had a bar in it so I guess you could say I did have two saloons. The reason I had it set up like that was that I was mighty particular about who I let in the casino. To get in my casino you had to be old enough and sober enough and gentleman enough and well off enough to be able to lose and not leave the place crying or blow your brains out on the front sidewalk. And I didn't want any wives coming down the next day to plead that their husband had just blown his whole payday and the baby didn't have any milk. It was well known among the circle of gamblers that you had better not come in my place unless you could afford to lose. You better not lose and start crying because I wasn't going to cry when you won.

Of course, gambling was illegal in Texas just as it supposedly was in the rest of the United States, but Del Rio was on the border and the border was a different place. There was some cause to believe it was a separate country all to itself, neither the United States nor Mexico. There were other casinos in town, but they weren't much. You got a fair play at my gambling house. The games were restricted to blackjack and faro and roulette. We didn't play poker because that is a difficult game for the house to control and I wasn't about to have any dice table in my establishment. Dice players got out of hand. They went to hollering and screaming and just generally getting carried away. I was of the opinion that gambling ought to be quiet and relaxing.

My casino manager was an old Mississippi River gambler who knew every trick in the trade. He styled himself as Captain Phillip Service of Wilmington, North Carolina. I never bothered to inquire as to his real name. Maybe that was it and maybe he really was a captain; I didn't care. When I'd hired him I'd told him that I wasn't going to look over his shoulder. I'd said, "I hire you, I got to trust you. It is yours to operate unless you let me down." He'd simply replied that he wouldn't cheat me and he'd see nobody else did. But I was more interested in making certain that my customers got a square play. Service hired and trained all the dealers and housemen. He made them to understand that if they cheated the house they'd get fired, but if they cheated a customer they were going to jail, and jail anywhere along the border was to be avoided.

These days, my saloon was run by a man in his early thirties, named J. J. Jones. He was quick and smart and had had training at several good hotels in big towns. I didn't know what he was doing in a place like Del Rio, but that was his business. So long as he done me a good job his other affairs were his own.

My saloon wasn't the normal kind you'd find in a border town. We served a good lunch and you could find nearly any kind of whiskey or liquor as was produced anywhere. We kept the beer cold and the prices right and didn't allow no gambling or any kind of rough horseplay. I had several men on duty at all times in both my saloon and the casino whose job it was to spot trouble before it could start and then make sure it didn't.

Both the saloon and the casino were nicely decorated. Lauren had seen to that. She had an eye for such business. We also had entertainment in the saloon. Sometimes it was a singer or a line of dancing girls or, now and again, we'd get a cabaret out of Monterrey or Mexico City, and that always drew well.

Both places were named The First State—The First State Saloon and The First State Casino. A lot of people thought I was referring to Texas, but actually they were named after the first bank I'd robbed, The First State Bank in the little town of Cuero, Texas. Only a few people knew that.

So I had a good life. I had as much wife as any man ought to want and I had two good businesses, either one of which would have supported a man in very grand style. I cleared about five hundred dollars a week off the casino and a little more than half of that from the saloon. And that was net after I'd paid a percentage of the profits to my two managers. I made close on two, three thousand dollars a month, month in and month out, and that didn't count my investments, which threw off nearly an equal amount. I guess the fact that I would even entertain the idea of chancing all that on the highly risky prospect of robbing government gold went to show that I was either losing my mind or I felt more than just a little strong about the robbery as a gesture. I didn't, however, feel either strong enough or sure enough about my beliefs to up and blurt it out to Lauren. That was a contradiction that I couldn't quite explain to myself.

Not everything I was involved in was a money producer. There was my string of thoroughbred and quarterhorse racing stock. You didn't make much money in the horse-racing trade unless you were my brother-in-law, Warner Grayson. He could not only make racehorses bring home the bacon, but train them to cook and serve you at the table.

I walked on through the pleasant morning, nodding to this person or that as I reached the downtown. I turned in at my saloon and went on back to my office, waving to a few of the regulars who were having their first of the day. You could drink all you wanted in my joint—you just couldn't get drunk. I couldn't abide drunks, young or old, male or female. If you let yourself get into a condition where you didn't know what you were doing, I didn't want you around.

Hell of an attitude for a man who was beginning to seriously think about stealing a heavily guarded gold bullion shipment.

My two managers were waiting for me in my office, and for the next half hour I busied myself with the figures they presented me with. Finally I nodded and closed the books. "Looks like everything is going about right. I ain't got no complaints. Any from y'all?"

They both hesitated, and then J. J. Jones said, "Mr. Young, I wonder if you've heard that they are about to reopen Camp Verde."

I glanced at him. He was sitting across from my desk wearing a four-button-up-the-front suit with a Beau Brummell tie. He wasn't a dandy, but he thought his position required that he wear a business suit. On the other hand, I think Service had been born in a frock coat and foulard tie. I said, "Where'd you hear that?"

Camp Verde had been a cavalry fort that had been used, on and off, by the U.S. Army. It was about six miles north of Del Rio. He said, "Got it from a clerk over in city hall. They say the army is going to set it up for a training post. Infantry."

I frowned. The country, the army, and the prospects of our getting into the war in Europe were not thoughts that pleased me. "I hope to hell not," I said. "What about it?"

J.J. looked at the captain. The captain cleared his throat and said, in his lightly accented southern voice, "Will, me and J.J. was jus' wonderin' how you'd feel about them soldier boys coming in the two places. They will have money to spend, but some of them will be a touch on the young side."

"No," I said. I didn't even have to stop and think about it, and it had nothing to do with my own son, for whatever his reasons, being a member of some kind of aeroplane flying outfit in the French Army. I had understood from Lauren, who'd had letters from him, that he was about to complete his training and would be going into combat. But it was a subject I did not care to discuss, and those who knew me knew to steer around it.

J.J. frowned. "Boss, those young men are going to be mighty thirsty of a Saturday night. They'll drink someplace."

I knew what J.J. was thinking. Both my managers got ten percent of the profits and J.J. hated to see all that whiskey and beer money getting away from him. I said, "Yes, they will be keen to drink. They will also be keen to get drunk and keen to fight and raise hell. Not in this saloon." I glanced over at Captain Service. "Besides, you know I'm not going to let them in the casino. You think it would be fair to the captain to let you get their custom and not him?"

J.J. smiled ruefully. "Don't hurt to ask."

"You know the rules," I said. "Nobody comes in any of my places unless he or she can afford it and behaves themselves. Won't be me watching the door. However, I will be in from time to time."

J.J. nodded. "I'll keep a close eye on the door."

The captain said, "And have you heard from young Willis?"

He was not asking me about my son the soldier, which he knew better than to do. He was asking about Willis the person. He was fond of the boy. There was a difference. I said, "His mother says he is getting along fine. He sent a picture in his last letter. He's got up in some kind of French uniform. Looks kind of silly to me."

The captain said dryly, "Willis is a fine young man. I doubt he could look silly in any uniform. Though I would to the heavens that he would not mess about with those flying machines. Goes against nature."

I got out a cigarillo, deliberately ignoring his words. "Books look fine, gentlemen. Only problem is that my wife is getting that charity look on her face again. I'm fearful I am about to make a sizable contribution to the Mexican economy." I struck a match and lit the little cigar. "Last time she and her church group went over there and gave her kind of picnic, it cost me nearly two thousand dollars."

"Reckon I better go to watering the whiskey again?" J.J. asked.

"And I," the captain said, "will give the roulette wheel a house tilt."

They were both kidding. I got up. "Well, I better get home and get something to eat before she trucks it all across the border."

I left and walked back home. I tried not to think of Willis but was not entirely successful.

Willis was not the name I had intended we call our son by. We had christened him Leslie Willis Young with the intention of call-ing him Les. The "Leslie" had come from an old comrade of mine, Leslie Richter. I found, however, that it was too painful to call the boy after Les Richter, so we had ended up calling him Willis. Les Richter had been, until his untimely death, the best man I had ever known. He continued to be so in my thoughts. He and his cousin Todd—as sorry a man as Les was noble—had joined me early on in the outlaw pursuit. They were both of an age with me, about sev-enteen if I remembered correctly, and as broke and homeless as I was. Todd came naturally to thievery and violence. I did much less so, even though I proceeded grimly with the job at hand because robbing and gun work, once started, are a more powerful addic-tion than alcohol and harder to quit than a freight train going at breakneck speed. The normal end for such a career is a bullet or the hangman's noose or the walls of a prison. Of the three of us only I had survived. Todd had died during a bank robbery when a final bit of foolishness had gotten him killed. Les had been killed by two deputy sheriffs who had illegally pursued him into Mexico and taken him in ambush. I had later evened the score, but there was never a day went by that I did not, in some way, miss the presence of Les Richter. He had no more belonged in the outlaw trade than I was meant for the ministry. As in my own case, circumstances had driven him there. And even then he was reluctant and unwilling. Stealing agonized his conscience until he could barely support it. And I never saw a man more reluctant to fire a bullet at another human being. The few times he did, it was only as a last resort and was done more to save others than to save himself. He was a good man. He was wise and he was funny and he knew the meaning of friendship. It wasn't just a word with him. I was never as comfort-able with another human being until I married Lauren. She knew about him, of course. You don't give your son a name and then not call him by it without giving your wife some explanation. But I had told her about him before, about the thirteen or fourteen years we'd ridden together. She'd said it didn't sound as if he was meant to be an outlaw, and I'd been glad to hear her say it. Explaining Les was a difficult proposition; explaining Les as an outlaw was impossible. You couldn't talk about a kind, generous, thoughtful man and then add, "Oh, yes, we used to rob banks together until he got shot down in Nuevo Laredo."

I was thinking about Les as I walked home because I knew I needed someone to talk to about the Federal Reserve gold, someone besides Lauren. I needed an outside opinion, and for that I needed a man who'd been in and out of some scrapes with me. Les would have fit the bill perfectly but he just wasn't there. Thinking about it, though, I feared that he would most likely have advised me against any sudden actions, especially ones calculated to bring me into conflict with the law or my fellow citizens. I always had the uneasy feeling that the only reason Les stayed on the owlhoot trail was to watch over me. It wasn't anything we ever discussed— men didn't talk about such things—but he was in the right place at the right time to my benefit with eerie regularity. I think he would have been just as happy in some honest pursuit even if it paid a whole hell of a lot less money. But he was gone and couldn't help me, not even to stay out of trouble.

The two men, living, that I had the highest regard for were Warner Grayson, my brother-in-law and the horse breeder and trainer, and a rancher up near the coast in Matagorda County, a man named Justa Williams. I had known Warner considerably longer than I had Justa. I had known Warner long before he became my brother-in-law by at least some twenty years. In fact it was through Warner, or rather his wife, that I had met Lauren when she had come to Texas for a visit with her sister Laura.

My first meeting with Warner had taken place about two years after I'd commenced robbing banks. I had pretty much confined my outlaw exploits to the part of the country I knew best, South Texas and the coastal plains area. As a result I was pretty well known in a short time, not only for the boldness of my efforts but because I went well out of my way, given an occasion, to cause as much trouble as I could for the Yankee Reconstructionists and those of their ilk who were profiting by the rape of the South and the Southwest. Make no mistake—as long as the money would spend I didn't much mind who I took it off of; but since, during that period, the Reconstructionists controlled most of the banks, they were usually the ones I robbed. In some small way it made me a sort of hero to some elements of Texas society who were being bent and broken under the cruel yoke of Yankee greed.

I met Warner within the confines of his own horse yard. His grandfather had lately died and he had come into possession of the place as the natural heir. The place was just outside the little town of Seguin, Texas, and Warner must have been all of seventeen years old. I would have been about nineteen, but I was a considerably more experienced man than he, having been on my own for four years. My gang and I were fleeing from a bank robbery we had just committed in the town of Bourne and were hotfooting it for the border when my horse went lame on me. We limped into Warner's horseyard with a catch party no more than a couple of hours behind us, and out came this skinny kid to inquire if we were looking to do some horse business. In memory it almost made me want to laugh. There we were, four rough-looking outlaws, just bristling with guns and knives, and here comes this kid setting up to do some horse-trading. I dismounted and told him that, yes, I had a lame horse and needed a replacement in something of a hurry. He took the time to examine the injured foot of my horse and then said it was nothing but a bruise of the frog (the soft part on the inner underside of a horse's hoof) and that if I'd take it slow the horse would be fine in a few days. That got a laugh all the way around. I had a black Mexican riding with me then named Chulo who was about as mean and ugly looking as it was possible to be. He said, "Seeñor Weelson, chu want me to choot the leetle sonofabeetch?"

Warner never turned a hair. He just looked at me steadily and said, "I knowed who you was minute you rode into the yard. You here to trade for a horse or just steal one?"

Les said softly, "Watch it, sonny. Ain't no call to get insulting."

I said to Warner, "You got anything with good staying power and a little speed? I'm a little pressed for time right now."

He nodded slowly. "I would reckon you are, Mr. Wilson Young. Ain't you generally?"

Todd, who could never keep his mouth shut, said, "Hell, Will, take a horse and let's get the hell out of here."

I looked around at him. I couldn't stand the damn fool. "Don't call me Will," I said. "I ain't going to tell you again. The reason we ain't in better shape is because of that fool stunt you pulled with that lady teller. You keep your mouth shut or I'll turn Chulo loose on you."

And Warner had the gall to stick his oar in. "Y'all squabbling amongst y'all's selves?"

I said, "Shut up, kid. Send a grown-up out. I need a horse."

"I'm the sole proprietor of this here establishment and I'm as growed up as you are. Now, then, I got such a horse as you are looking for, but he is a hundred-dollar better horse than yours."

I looked at him in amazement. "Hell, kid, I paid a hundred and fifty dollars for this horse in San Antonio. Not six months ago. At the horse auction there."

He took a moment to look inside the horse's mouth and then to walk around the animal, patting him with his hand. Even then he had a wonderful touch with horses. He said, "Well, you paid fifty dollars too much and I don't care where you bought him. The most I could sell this horse for once I get him back in shape is a hundred and a quarter. I got a five-year-old bay that you'll have a hell of a time finding the bottom of. He's quarterhorse Morgan bred back into Morgan. He'll go two hundred yards as fast as anything you've ever had between your legs and he'll make sixty miles in a day if you don't abuse him. The best I'll do is let you have him for eighty dollars' difference."

We had just robbed a bank and probably had close to five thousand dollars distributed around in our saddlebags, and here I was arguing over twenty-five dollars with a posse not that far behind us. But that is horse-trading. I said, "I'll give you sixty difference."

He shook his head. "Naw. I'm down as low as I can go. Only reason I'm making you that price is who you are and the hurry you are in. My grandfather spoke well of you before he died. I can get two-fifty for that horse within a month."

I said, "Say seventy-five difference."

Behind me Les said, a little alarm in his voice, "Will, what in hell are you doing? This ain't trades day. We got business on down the road. Give him the money."

I ignored him. "Say seventy-five. That's a nice round amount and your conscience won't hurt you tonight."

"You an expert on my conscience? If you are you'd know it would gnaw at me all night if I let this horse out of here for less than eighty-five difference."

"Wait a minute, wait a minute. You just said eighty."

"Did I? Well, if I said eighty I'll stick to it."

Les said urgently, "Kid, lead the damn bay out here and get the saddle on him. You stall around much longer and you're going to have a gunfight in your front yard."

I figured I'd met my match in the horse-trading business and was glad to get my saddle on the slick-looking bay and get up astride him. Les counted out the extra money to the kid and then I asked his name and he told me. I said, "Well, Mr. Grayson, if this horse ain't everything you've said he is, I am liable to find myself in trouble and I will lay it at your door. If that happens you can depend I will be back to collect some difference in a different coin than gold."

He stood there and looked up at me just as cool as you please and said, "You'll be back, Mr. Young, but it will be to get another horse. If you get in trouble it will be your own doing, not the horse's. I know the horse."

About then Todd decided to pull another one of his fool stunts. "By damn, I've had all I'm gonna take off this smart aleck," he said. And he pulled out his revolver. Les slapped his gun hand into the air and I backhanded him across the mouth.

That was Todd for you. When things got settled down again I said to Warner, "You're pretty sure of yourself."

He spit in the dust and then stirred it around with the toe of his boot. "When it comes to horses I'm damn certain. Maybe not about much else, but horses, yes." Then he looked up at me with as certain an expression as I'd ever seen on a man's face unless he was holding a fistful of aces.

I laughed and we rode out, heading for the border and some spending time in Mexico. The bay was everything he'd said and I rode the animal for a year, finally giving him a rest in a pasture in Mexico from the hard life of an outlaw's mount. And Warner had been right about what I'd be back for. As near as I could recollect, since that time I bought every horse I ever owned from him and was glad to get them. There was one thing a man in the bank-robbing business had to have and that was a fast, dependable mount with a ton of bottom. That was the kind of horse Warner Grayson bred and trained and sold. Every animal I had at either one of my ranches, at least the racing stock, I bought from him in some fashion or another.

But I wasn't going to go see Warner to have a talk. For one thing he had located his thoroughbred farm way the hell up in northeast Texas in Smith County near the town of Tyler. Hell, he was damn near in Louisiana. But that was where he'd had to go to find the kind of pasturage that would nourish and grow thoroughbred colts when you turned them out to play and grow up to their legs. Before that he'd had a breeding ranch for quarterhorses near Corpus Christi, which was my old stomping grounds, the country I'd grown up in.

The main reason, however, that I wasn't going to Warner was that he was my brother-in-law. That meant that Laura would be around, and if there was any woman that could sneak out a secret it was Laura. And I wasn't about to take the chance of her getting on to my thinking. I might as well go tell Lauren straight out rather than make the long trip to northeast Texas.

Now, I had met and become friends with Justa Williams some twenty-odd years before. We had met at a horse race right in the very town I had selected as my home. Back then Del Rio was the horse-racing capital of the southwest country. We had a mile track out at the fairgrounds and it was the only one to be found. Now, of course, they have big tracks at Houston and San Antonio and New Orleans and even Galveston, but back then Del Rio was the place the big money got bet. I had been of some little help to Justa back then in a situation that had not been of his making. As a result we had found a foundation for a friendship and it had grown from there. Justa was also about my age, and he and his two brothers ran, acre for acre, the finest cattle operation to be found in Texas. The Half-Moon Ranch it was called, and it had been started by their daddy back in the 1840s. The old man had had some rough times but he had come through until an ambusher's bullet nicked his lungs and weakened him so that he could not take the strain of the big operation. As a consequence, Justa, at the ripe old age of nineteen, had been thrust in charge of an enterprise that counted its cattle in the thousands and its acreage in square miles. The grass that the ranch was founded on was as green as printed money and, cured off, the color of gold. Justa had taken an operation based on the old mossy-horned, man-killing, horse-killing, all-bone, and all-fight long-horned cattle and began a breeding program with Herefords and whiteface and shorthorn stock that soon had him producing some of the best beef and the easiest managed cattle in the country.

Justa Williams was a man with as level a head as anyone I knew. He was a born organizer. If he'd been in the military he'd've been a general in about a week and a half. As it was he ran that ranch and his two brothers as smoothly as could be done. He had made his family wealthy and, in the process, hadn't done so bad for himself. But you would never know it to be around him. He was as solid and as down to earth as a man could be. Me and him had engaged in a few scrapes together and I didn't reckon I knew a living soul I'd rather have beside me when matters went beyond the talking stage.

But I guess the biggest reason I wanted to talk to Justa was that he had an only son, just as I did. His boy J.D. was several years older than Willis, but he was standing in the line of fire as surely as my boy was.

Besides, it wasn't that hard a trip to where Justa was. Ride the train to Victoria, make a change, and about two hours later you were in the little town of Blessing. It wasn't but about seven more miles to his ranch. I could make the trip up and back in no more than three days.

There was a final reason, though. The thought of robbing that Federal Reserve gold bullion had no more than leapt into my head than it was followed almost immediately by another thought. That idea was that my wife and friends were going to instantly consider that I wanted to commit the theft either because I was senile or because I wanted to prove I hadn't gotten too old. I couldn't blame them. At fifty-eight, a man starts looking back down through the years with longing. Maybe he wants one last fling with a young maiden, maybe he wants to gamble with his money or life, maybe he wants to board a ship and see all those far-off places he missed as a youth. Maybe, if he's an ex-bank robber, he wants to rob just one more bank to see if he has still got it.

Nothing could have been farther from the truth. I considered the government's putting that gold on display an insult and an affront to the intelligence of the ordinary citizen. They were the same as saying, "Look, sonny, we don't think you got sense enough to know your ass from a saddle horn so we are going to teach you about money and, after that, you run along and be a good boy and just spend the hell out of that paper currency."

Hell, I wasn't keen to make the attempt. It looked damn dangerous to me, and if somebody else had come forward and said they'd do it, I'd've applauded them and bought a round of drinks and even proposed to underwrite the expedition.

But I'd heard no such stirrings among the citizenry. In fact, the few people I'd mentioned the business to had seemed uncaring, not realizing the sleight of hand the government was pulling. I couldn't believe I was the only one who recognized the slippery hand of danger, but for some time I had felt an air of complacency abroad in the country that damn near amounted to a stupor. Folks didn't seem so much interested in getting ahead as getting things, every gadget somebody's brain could think up. And they didn't seem so eager to make progress as they were to accept change and call it progress.

By the time I reached home from my office I had determined that Justa Williams was the man for me to see. He might not agree with me on such a drastic measure but he wouldn't insult me by hinting that I was putting myself to the test because I was getting old. Justa Williams was a thinking man and the kind of thinking man who would hear all that was to be heard before he gave an opinion. All I had to do now was think up some reason to give Lauren as to why I was going to see Justa and she couldn't come along. The main problem with going to see Justa was that his wife, Nora, and

Lauren were great friends. I expected Lauren to be damn curious as to why she couldn't accompany me.

MRS. BRIDESDALE gave us breaded veal cutlets and garden vegetables for lunch. One advantage, and maybe the only one for most folks, of living on the border was you could have a year-round garden. As a result, Lauren was able to make certain that I didn't eat meat and potatoes as a steady diet. But she wasn't working no hardship on me with garden truck on the diet. As it happened I liked fresh vegetables and fruits. What I hated was that canned junk that tasted like lead.

Lauren asked me how the books had looked and I told her we'd come up on the deficit side this week, as we had the week before and the week before that, and she was going to have to curtail some of her charity work. She only nodded absently. She'd heard it all before. She said, "I wish you'd have five hundred dollars put in my account, dear. Our medical society is arranging for a doctor and a pair of nurses to accompany us to Chileta. Wilson, there are some children down there who are in urgent need of medical attention. Some of them haven't even been vaccinated against smallpox."

I grimaced. Knowing it was useless, I said, "Lauren, I don't mind the money, but I do mind you going to hellholes like that. You don't have any idea the risks you are running yourself. I'll double the five hundred if you won't go."

She stopped eating and put her hand on my arm. "Oh, honey, that's so sweet. Then you'll be putting a thousand in my account?"

"If you'll stay the hell on this side of the border, yes. Lauren, I don't like you going down in those pigsties in Mexico. Even if you do have the faith of ten thousand, or however many it is, it ain't a fitting place for a woman like you."

She smiled. "Will, you really should stop trying to quote from the Bible. You always get it mixed up. Honey, I have to go. The other ladies are. It's my duty."

I sighed. My wife was full of a faith that I could neither hear nor see nor feel. Oh, I'd had an introduction early on to it. First by my mother, but that had come so early it was but a dim memory. Mostly what I remembered was my sour-faced old aunt, like I mentioned, who'd presented the idea of Christianity as a medicine you were supposed to take whether you liked it or not. It was fire and brimstone, it was the straight and narrow, it was grim-faced and threatening. I had rebelled.

Lauren had never said much to me about the subject. As soon as she saw that I was not going to ridicule her or her faith or stand in her way, we'd had peace on the matter. Sometimes, however, I did feel she'd try to slip a little lesson past me now and again.

I said, "All right, I'll see that you get five hundred put in your account."

She made a pouty face and stuck out her lower lip. "You said a thousand."

"Damnit, woman, if you stayed out of them damn hellholes over on the other side."

She gave me a calm look. "Wilson, I go there because that's where the sick and hungry are. Didn't you once tell me you were famous because you never robbed the poor? Which you said made you laugh because the poor didn't have any money so why should you want to rob them? Well, there's no use in my going to the healthy and the well fed."

I put up my hands and crossed my fingers as if warding off evil spirits. "All right, all right. A thousand. That maid we had wasn't enough. You are gradually transporting every dollar I make into Mexico. Pretty soon we'll have to move over there because we'll be too poor to live in Texas."

She patted my arm. "You're a nice man, Wilson Young. And if

Mrs. Bridesdale wasn't upstairs cleaning I'd take you right up there and give you a nice surprise."

I suddenly came alert and started out of my chair. "I think Mrs. Bridesdale suddenly got the afternoon off."

The only benefit to the matter had been that Lauren wouldn't be available to go see Justa Williams. Her medical society work would keep her busy for a week. She was disappointed, however, that I was going and she couldn't. She wondered if I couldn't delay the visit. I told her some lie about having business with the bank that Justa's family owned and that it was fairly urgent. She took it with good grace, though she said she expected to miss me while I was gone. She said she'd pray for my safe trip, which I politely thanked her for. Being of the turn of mind I was, I had to add that, for a thousand dollars, I expected a pretty first-class prayer with maybe a little luck thrown in if me and Justa got to gambling or making some sort of deal.

She told me sweetly that prayers were not for sale and that luck had nothing to do with it. She was something, my Lauren, and sometimes it gave me pause when I considered the sweetness of her character and her strength and where she said it came from. But, no, believing wasn't for me. Outside of preachers and such it was mostly women who went in for all that church stuff. I believed in what I could see and touch. I could do that with a Bible or with a church, but they had been made by men and didn't prove nothing to me. I could see and touch a revolver and a horse, or a deck of playing cards, and they too had been made by the hand of man. I found the latter to be of greater value.

Lauren had straightened me out on one point early on. She had not always been of a spiritual bent. In fact, when we got married, she pretty much looked at such matters as I did, with a kind of amused tolerance for folks who went in for such stuff. But once she got what she called "converted," she was a regular bearcat about the matter. One time I made the mistake of talking about her being religious and she straightened me out on that point right quick. She said, "Religious is something you do with regularity or a sense of duty. It could be said, for instance, that you used to rob banks religiously. I am a Christian; I am not religious. There is a difference. Although I am religious about my Christianity."

I said, "Sounds like you're splitting hairs to me. What do you call somebody that goes to church every time they open the doors?"

She gave me a look. "A churchgoer. What else?"

Sometimes I wondered why she didn't put a little more spade work in on my soul. I'd always thought that them as were in the fold was supposed to be out working in the vineyards or some such thing. I wondered if she considered me beyond saving or if she thought I might make fun of her or she couldn't be bothered. Sometimes I was almost tempted to ask her if she didn't love me enough to make a stab at my soul.

But I reckoned it was the same with a lot of men whose wives cluttered up the church. I figured it was something women were more drawn to. I could, however, have done with a little less of her charity work. I didn't mind the money, not a bit. She could spend every dime I made and I'd never complain, but I sure as hell hated to have her sloshing around in all that poverty and disease over in Mexico. But I couldn't argue with her when she said that was where the need was. Some of them folks was so poor they needed a cash loan just to work their way up to destitute. I idly wondered if Lauren would approve of me stealing the gold if I gave it to her and her ladies' societies to use for good works across the border. I didn't, however, figure on asking her anytime soon.

I TOOK the newspaper on the train with me in case Justa hadn't seen the article. As the train rocked and jerked over the flat roadbed of South Texas I got it out and read it again for the twentieth time. The article began by saying that as a gesture to reassure the general populace of the United States' continuing strong position as one of the major gold holders in the world, a display of a glittering quarter of a million dollars in bullion would be put on display at selected cities throughout the South and Southwest.

I found the itinerary very interesting. The display would begin in Jacksonville, Florida, move on to Tallahassee, and then jump over to Mobile, Alabama, and then to Jackson, Mississippi. From there it would go to Shreveport, Louisiana, and then into Texas at Beaumont and on to San Antonio and finally into El Paso. After El Paso the gold would be displayed in Albuquerque, New Mexico, and then whip on to Phoenix and Tucson in Arizona. Its last stop would be in the California city of San Diego. What made the selection of cities so interesting was that they were all in the southern parts of their states, back where the hicks and the rubes lived. They were also not particularly big cities. They weren't going to display the gold in Atlanta, for instance, or New Orleans or Houston or Birmingham or Mobile. It didn't take a United States senator to figure out that they were going for the highest percentage of hayseeds that they could hit at every stop, the rubes that still didn't trust paper money as much as they did the coin of the realm, which was gold and silver. But if they could get that sharecropper used to the idea of flinging dollar bills around he'd pretty soon get to the point where he wouldn't realize what he was doing until it came time to pay the grocery bill and he discovered all his money had gone for trinkets and foolishness.

Ah, but according to the newspapers, prosperity was just around the bend and a man wouldn't be able to spend all the money he could make. At least that was what all the experts were saying. I once set out to find out exactly what an "expert" was, and the closest I could come to it was a man who didn't stand to lose nothing by his advice and opinions.

I had also heard, through another source, that the government was in the very act of reducing the size of the dollar bill (and other denominations) to make it easier to carry around. They said it had been sized in accordance with the dimensions of the most popular wallet. I did not doubt for a second that the government would be guided by such criteria. Lauren had once reproached me for running down politicians. She'd said, "Why, Will, you ought to be grateful that there is a body of men more wicked than you and your fellow bank robbers."

At least I had been shot at. And hit several times. A newspaper man, after I'd been pardoned, had once asked me if I'd ever been shot. When I told him I had, he asked, with his pencil posed to write down the answer, if any of my wounds had been fatal.

Thus far, I was able to assure him, I had not been fatally shot. But the more I thought on the idea of trying to steal that gold the more it sent little shivers up my spine. The way the whole proposition set up it looked dangerous as hell and a long way from a sure thing. In the first place, according to the paper, there was a twenty-one-man detachment of soldiers escorting the gold. I didn't know how good soldiers would be in a gunfight, but they were carrying Springfield bolt-action rifles, and the fact that there were twenty-one of them was in itself a force to be reckoned with. There'd have to be a few in the bunch that could shoot. I didn't know much about army soldiers, but they'd surely had some training.

But to my mind and my eye the terrain and the location were the biggest problems. I knew San Antonio as well as I knew any town. Right in the big middle of it was a huge plaza, probably four hundred yards across and about six hundred long. It was called the Military Plaza because, in the days when San Antonio was under Spanish rule and then Mexican, that had been the parade ground for the cavalry that was stationed there. The plaza had since been turned into a park. It had been bricked over and they had planted trees here and there and scattered some benches and fountains around and it had become a popular place for lovers and loungers and folks just wanting to stretch their legs. Government House was still located there, though now it was a big building crammed full of bureaucrats of different colors and stripes. Of course, the whole plaza was surrounded by various kinds of businesses on all four sides, across the ample avenues that bordered the place. The Federal Reserve Bank, where the gold would be displayed, was on the southwestern corner. The train depot was one block off the plaza to the northeast. The soldiers would take the gold off the train there, take it the one block to the plaza, and then trundle it the six or seven hundred yards to the bank. The whole way they would be right out in the open, and you could bet, as many rubberneckers as lived in Texas, there would be one hell of a crowd lining their way as they proceeded to the bank. Depending on how much of a commotion they made about it, my best guess was there would be at least three or four thousand spectators out to see their government showing them their own money. It was going to be a hell of a place for a stickup. I didn't care if you went in there with a hundred experienced gunmen, you'd still be way outnumbered between the soldiers and those in the crowd who were carrying a gun. And, of course, you couldn't depend on people minding their own business and saying, "Well, those fellows are robbing that gold. Ain't none of our affair. Reckon we ought to get on down the road." Oh, no. That wouldn't happen. First one and then the other would want to get involved, and before you knew it, you'd have more folks interfering than you could say grace over.

Then there was the matter of how much the gold weighed. The paper called it a "half ton worth of gold." That was a thousand pounds. It might or might not have been accurate. It could have been a newspaper making talk like newspapers would. It wasn't necessary for the government to build up their case with phrases like "a ton of gold." It was enough money as it was. It was a powerful lot of money. It was a king's ransom in gold. I had read in a newspaper that the average workman made something like a dollar and a quarter a day, and here was his government parading a quarter of a million dollars in front of him to give him the idea that times were good and riches untold were just around the corner. Spend what you got now because there is plenty more where that came from.

I knew what the government was up to and I was ashamed for them.

But there it was, and it was about as poor a situation for a robbery as I had ever seen. First off, you had twenty-one armed guards. That wasn't all that serious. Ten good men, or even less, could get the drop on them and they'd be helpless. But there was that long crossing in all that space and with all that crowd. That was a real stinger. Even if you could get the gold you would have one hell of a time making a getaway even if you were willing—which I wasn't— to shoot innocent bystanders.

And there was the weight of the bullion. Even if you distributed it among ten horses you'd still be loading them down to where they'd play out within five miles. I doubted even if you had one of those runabout flivvers like the lightning rod salesman that it would carry such a load. Not that I'd ever use such a contraption. I'd do prison time before I'd ever let such a gillywhiz near me, much less ride in one. And I'd never spent a day in jail, at least not behind bars. I reckoned that folks thought I was an old stick in the mud to hold such views, but that was the way I felt. I was horse loyal and damn proud of it.

But none of that had anything to do with the problem of separating the government from their gold bullion. It was a knotty little problem and I didn't have all that much time to figure out how to do it. The gold was due to be displayed for five business days in each of the cities. They had already commenced their show in Florida and would be heading west any day. As best I could figure they were due to arrive in San Antonio in about six weeks, give or take a day or two due to travel or other snags. The item in the San Antonio newspaper had promised to keep the reader apprised of the great gold bullion extravaganza as it progressed west and neared the Alamo city. I wondered how my own mood would progress as the gold and the time for decision neared. I had a pretty good life and I wasn't all that sure I was willing to risk it on a principle that really didn't have that much to do with me. Hell, Willis was already over in France, and it wouldn't be long before he'd be sailing around in the air with shells bursting all about him.

But as we neared the town of Blessing I put all thoughts behind me. There'd be a period of visiting with Justa and Nora before I brought the matter up with my old friend. Maybe, just maybe, he'd say something that would save me the trouble of getting myself killed. Maybe he'd ask me the question I'd been asking myself: "Where the hell you going to get the nerve to pull a stunt you ain't got the nerve to tell your wife about?"

That was a fine riddle. I was going to have to discuss it with Lauren sometime.

CHAPTER
3

JUSTA WILLIAMS said, "Well, Will, I got to tell you, that was a mighty nice surprise when I got your telegram that you were coming for a visit. Tickled me and Nora to death. Hell, what's it been, two or better years since we had a get-together?"

I took a moment to light a cigar Justa had given me. "I ciphered it out coming up on the train. Be two years in about a month. You and Nora came down to Del Rio for the big race meet we had there over the Fourth of July."

"Oh, yeah. And Warner and Laura come also. Yeah."

I nodded over my cigar. "Yes, Mr. Grayson graced us with his presence and made a number of edifying remarks about our knowledge of horseflesh. Warner never was one to hide his light under a bushel basket."

Justa looked rueful and rubbed his hand along the side of his jeans. "Problem is the old sonofabitch always knows what he's talking about. If I remember right he won every race he entered with them few thoroughbreds he brought down with him."

"Cleaned the table. Swept up all the money and stuck it in his pocket. I had bought a couple of horses from him just for that meet and them suckers ran second to his horses the whole meet. I asked him to explain the why of that since they were supposed to have been as good as anything he had in the breeding line. You know what the sonofabitch said? He give me an astonished look and reminded me that those horses had been under *my* care for a full year while *he* had been training their cousins and half brothers, the ones that had beat my horses. He said, giving me this real sincere look— you know how he can get—he said, 'You don't really reckon horses that you've had a hand in are gonna beat anything *I've* trained, do you?'" I shook my head. "Warner is a pistol. He says he knows more about horse breeding than any man alive, and I can't argue with the sonofabitch."

"Maybe it is just as well that he and Laura never could have any kids," Justa said. "If he'd had a son I ain't sure there'd be a horse business to pass down to him. Looks like the automobile is off and running."

I let that pass because I was not ready to talk of such matters at that moment. We had finished supper and had come into Justa's office to have a drink and a talk. I had sat in that office on many an occasion, some happy occasions, some not so. It was a big square room full of well-worn furniture, a man's kind of room. I doubted if Nora or a maid got into the place much and then just with a hurried broom or a dust cloth. At one time a little room had been walled off at one end for the head of clan, the father of Justa and his two brothers, Ben and Norris. When Justa was about seventeen his father had taken that bullet through the chest that had nicked his lungs. As a consequence he had become something of an invalid, and a very young Justa had taken over the running of the huge Half-

Moon Ranch. He had been equal to the task. But the old man had still liked to be where the business was going on, so they'd made a little partition and fixed him up a little day room with a bed and a big, comfortable chair so that when he got tired he could take a rest and still feel a part of the ranch's activity.

Like many of the old homesteads that had grown as their owners had prospered, the room we were sitting in, which was the original cabin, was buried deep within the big, rambling house that you saw as you approached the headquarters of the Half-Moon Ranch. From where I was sitting I could still see a little patch of hand-hewn logs that had once formed the walls of the cabin. Someone had squared the timbers with an ax and an adze and chinked them with a mortar of limestone and clay. I reckon Justa left that one wall bared to remind all of them just how far they'd come. Of course, the timbers had come a considerable distance themselves. Somebody had to have hauled them a hundred miles or more. Matagorda County and its environs was wealthy in grass but flat broke when it came to a tree of a size enough to be called such.

I looked around me. I knew the place well from long-past memory. Outside you'd see a beautiful two-story frame house painted white with a big porch running three-quarters of the way around the front and sides, but it had begun where Justa and I were sitting. As prosperity had come, so had the additions to the house. I could remember my mother's excitement when my father was finally able to build her a kitchen onto our little cabin. And then— I think I was about eight at the time—my father managed to have a good year and add on a bedroom for him and my mother. Lord, with all that it had seemed like we'd had room to burn.

I knew what old Mr. Williams had gone through because I'd watched my father do the same thing. They'd both started their ranches in the late 1840s when it was just them and their grit and determination and a string of good cow horses and a branding iron and a prairie full of the orneriest critter in the world, the longhorn. I knew they earned every head of beef they could get their brand on. I knew they worked from can to can't and that would sometimes be so long after dark my dad would use the moon to guide him home.

If he had lived, I reckon he would have ended up with a house for my mother something like I was sitting in. But what the Comanche Indians and the Mexican *bandidos* and the cattle thieves and the droughts and the countless other catastrophes that can befall the lone man on the big prairie couldn't do, the scalawags and the Yankee carpetbaggers did with a stroke of the pen. They got control of all the banks, and once they had that power they had the Texans and the other southerners right where they wanted them. They started in chipping away at the holdings my father had built with his courage and sweat and, little by little, they took it all. Took it legal, at least by their laws. Of course they were the ones that had made the laws, so they could make them read any way they wanted. My daddy had been a prime target because he had been a captain of cavalry in a Texas brigade that was charged with defending the frontier from any intruder, Indian, Mexican, or bandit. He never fired a shot against the Yankees, but that didn't matter. He had been a Confederate officer and that was enough for the Yankee Reconstructionists. The fact that my father had been nearly fifty years old, and knew nothing about the military never made them no difference. Here was a Confederate officer that needed Reconstructing and they were going to do it if they had to kill him in the process.

He didn't last long after they took away his ranch. He just died. My mother joined him shortly thereafter. That was in 1870, when I was eleven or twelve years old. My daddy had a half sister in Corpus Christi who grudgingly took me in. I guess it was a good thing for me because I got sent to school and got some book learning, which I figured stood by me the rest of my life. But I also got sent to my aunt's church every time they opened the doors, and walloped with the Bible in between. I didn't know what Bible she was using, but it wasn't the one my mother had read out of so lovingly. My parents hadn't got to church much, isolated as we were out on the prairie, but I couldn't figure it was anything like that sour-apple bunch my aunt sent me around. Her religion was grim and harsh and full of do-nots. Sometimes I thought of the difference between what Lauren had, which made her happy, and the religion of my aunt, which didn't seem to contain even a speck of joy.

I left as quick as I could, which was at fifteen. I had my daddy's old Navy Colt revolver and about six cartridges and maybe a dollar and a half. On the way out of town I stole a horse and then, some fifteen miles later, I held up a rancher and his wife as they were coming down a country lane. I took fourteen dollars off the man and was so ashamed an hour later that I turned the horse loose to find his way home and hid the money and took off on foot. It was the banks I was angry at, the Yankee-controlled banks that had been Reconstructed. Not too long after that I met the Richter cousins and we went into the business of taking some of that Reconstructed money back and putting it to use by Texans, which we happened to be. I tried every way I could think of to get that fourteen dollars back to that rancher but I was never able to. Even forty-odd years later it still shamed me. I never again robbed an individual or took a working man's money. Todd never understood my principles, if a robber can be said to have any, but Les did. I never really had to explain it to him. He'd helped me try to find that rancher to return the money and had seemed as disappointed as I was at my failure.

I said to Justa, "How are your brothers?"

Justa had a brother two years younger that handled the business end of their affairs, the banking and the investing and such. That was Norris, and he had had a good education at the university in

Austin. The youngest brother, Ben, had gotten his education in the bed of every woman he could get in with and in every saloon between Houston and Mexico City. He was a good hand with a gun or a horse, but he was wild as a March hare.

Justa said, "Well, you know Norris has got his office in Houston." He shook his head. "I'm not sure where Ben headquarters. Some whorehouse, I would reckon."

"He ever going to settle down?"

Justa shook his head. "He was wild at sixteen and he ain't changed in all the years that have passed. Why some woman's husband ain't killed him is more than I can figure."

"Has he quit tomcatting around?"

Justa said dryly, "He ain't quit nothing that I know of. Except work. This ranch and Norris and his trades just keep on making money and Ben takes his share and tries to see how fast he can spend it."

J.D. was Justa and Nora's only child. They'd lost a daughter in childbirth and, after that, Nora couldn't have any more children. I asked after the young man. "J.D. would be what, twenty-four or so now?"

"He turned twenty-four last month."

"He doing all right?"

A little frown flickered over Justa's face. "He's industrious. I can't fault him for that. But he seems more interested in his uncle Norris's end of the business than running the ranch. I keep asking him who does he expect me to turn it over to if he's going to be in stocks and bonds with Norris. He claims he can handle both." He paused and then said hesitantly, "What about Willis? What do you hear from him?"

My face set. "I reckon you'd have to ask my wife about that. Me and the boy ain't exactly regular correspondents."

Justa and I were having a sociable drink of whiskey. I figured it was going on for ten o'clock. Nora had visited with us for a time in the parlor after supper, but then she'd excused herself, and me and Justa had come in the office to catch up on matters. Now he took a pretty good swig out of his glass and said, "Will, this ain't none of my business, but I'm going to ask anyway. Willis is over there amongst all that shot and shell flying around. This seems like one hell of a time for y'all to have a falling-out. Is it anything you can tell me about?"

I heaved a breath. It was not a subject I cared to discuss, but Justa and I had been friends for a long time. I reckoned I owed him an explanation. "Well, he is over there amidst that shot and shell by his own choice. I done everything I could to keep him out of it, including telling him he'd never see another nickel from me if he insisted on going, whether it broke his mother's heart or not."

Justa looked pained. "Hell, Will, he's got some wild oats to sow. This country has settled down and growed up so much a boy ain't got that kind of a chance here. Hell, you ought to be the last one to deny him that."

I lifted my chin. "Justa, if that had been the case he'd have gone with my blessings. If he'd told me he wanted to go over there to learn how to drive one of them aeroplanes I'd have said, 'Go get 'em.' If he'd said, 'Dad, there's some shooting going on over there and I want to get in on it, find out what kind of a man I am,' I'd've said, 'Son, I'll help you pack.' But it wasn't neither one of them things. It was the damnedest silly reason I ever heard of."

"What?"

I had to take a drink before I could answer him. I kind of spit the words out. "Duty. Justice. Or his version of it. Ever since that war started back in 1914 Willis followed it in the paper like I imagine Norris follows the stock market quotes. I tell you, he was down on them Germans, especially when they did what they did in Belgium, wherever that is. But then when they taken to sinking all those ships with their U-boats, those submarines that fire torpedoes, well, he was was nearly jumping up and down. Said it was every man's duty to put a stop to such meanness. Said they ought to be stopped just like the school bully needed his nose bloodied. That kind of talk."

Justa looked perplexed. "You mean even though it didn't have anything to do with us?"

I made a disgusted sound. "Yes, and don't think I didn't point that out to him several times. He asked me one time if I'd stand by and watch a helpless man get beat up just because the man was a stranger or lived somewhere else." I snorted and drained my glass. The office had two big desks set up against each other. In days gone by Justa had sat at one and run the cattle business and Norris had sat at the other fooling around with his bank numbers and such. I was sitting in Justa's swivel chair. He was across the room sitting on a divan up against the wall that showed the hewn timbers. The whiskey was on the desk so I helped myself and then got up and walked over and poured Justa a little more. I said, "That was the kind of thinking I was up against. His mother said he was an idealist, whatever in hell that is."

"I think it means taking up for what you believe in."

I sat back down. "Yeah. That's fine. But I never been much of a one for going and looking for a fight. There's been more than enough have found me."

Justa shook his head. "So he just up and took off?"

"Well, more or less. One day last year he come home from that Baptist college up in Waco Lauren insisted he go to. It had been in the paper that the *Lusitania* had been sunk. It was a British ship but I believe there was something like a hundred fifty Americans got killed when it was blown up by the Germans. Anyway, Willis come in and said he wasn't going to stand for it no more and that he, by damn, was going over and get in the scrap." I raised my eyebrows. "And him all of nineteen years old."

"I suppose you tried to talk him out of it."

I shrugged. "Me and Lauren went at him in shifts. Never done a bit of good. He said he was going and that was it. Said he had money, had the desire, and was over six foot tall. I couldn't argue with him no more."

Justa said softly, "I hope he makes out all right, Will."

"Well, you know as well as I do that when the bullets start flying, luck enters into it. Lauren don't agree with that, though. She believes in prayer."

Justa smiled slightly. "There's something to be said for that, too."

I glanced at him quickly. "Don't tell me that Nora has got you helping sweep up the church and pass the plate."

"Might be more to life than what you can see, Will. But let's don't get off into that."

"No, let's don't." I took a drink. After a second I had to smile. "The hell of the whole deal is I think the little sonofabitch is going to turn out right about one thing."

"What's that?"

I was starting to get around to what I wanted to talk to Justa about. "He told me all he was doing was beating the rush. He said the United States would be in the war within a year or so, but by the time the rest of the yahoos got over there he'd already have the prettiest women tied up and know where the best food and whiskey was. Said he was just getting a jump on the crowd."

Justa had been about to take a drink. He lowered his hand. "You don't believe that, do you? Hell, it ain't our war. Ain't got a damn thing to do with us."

At that moment I got out the article about the gold and walked over and handed it to him. "I was in San Antonio a little over a week ago. Come across that. Have you seen it yet?"

He got his reading glasses out of his pocket and put them on and took a quick look at the article. He handed it back to me. "Yeah, I seen it. They printed it in the local paper. Got a lot of folks excited. Quarter of a million dollars' worth of gold bullion, that's a sight. Folks around here are scheming some way to get a gander at that display."

I went back to the swivel chair and leaned back. "What do you reckon the government is up to with that?"

He thought for a moment and then shrugged. "Hell, I don't know. Nothing, I guess."

"Go to all that trouble? Haul that gold around to eight or nine cities and not have something in mind? Come on, Justa, you didn't ride in on the morning freight."

He looked puzzled. "Only thing I can think of is to give the citizens a chance to see what's behind their dollar."

"That's it exactly," I said. "But why? Why would they give a damn? Ain't ever done it before."

"Well, times have been kind of hard lately. Maybe it's the government's way of saying that things are about to look up."

I smiled grimly. "You mean prosperity is a-comin'? Yeah, I've heard that enough. I'll tell you what's a-comin' in a minute, but first I want to sound you out about what I think."

He laughed. "Nobody ever accused you of not having an opinion, Wilson. I bet it irritates the hell out of you to see so much of you coming out in Willis. You wonder why you couldn't change his mind." He took a sip of whiskey. "All right, tell me what you think about that bullion."

"I've been giving this a good bit of thought and—"

"Why?" He gestured toward my shirt pocket where I'd replaced the article. "That's pretty straightforward. What's to think about?"

"It just struck me funny," I said. "It seemed like such a stupid thing for the government to do. We all know they got a wagonload of gold in that Fort Knox. They don't have to come out and parade it around. I got to thinking about that."

"Why shouldn't they show the people they got the gold?"

"You got a hell of a bunch of cattle. When was the last time you drove them through town just so people would know you had cattle?"

He rolled his eyes. "All right, tell me. What are they up to?"

As best I could I explained my feeling that the government was showing the gold in an attempt to get folks to feel better about greenbacks and therefore be more loose in their spending. "Justa, the government of this country wants to give the impression of prosperity so that folks will spend more, thinking they'll have more coming in. Up north they got plants and factories turning out trinkets and gadgets just as fast as can be done. The more stuff folks buy, the more them industrial plants are going to turn out so there'll be more to buy. It's a damn circle."

Warner looked skeptical. "Will, if it was anybody besides you telling me this I'd figure they'd fallen on their head. Why would the government be doing that?"

"Because of what is sure to be a-comin'."

"Prosperity?"

I shook my head. "War. As a man told me up north, the best way to get prosperity is to have a war. But the war comes first."

He threw his head back and stared at me over his cheekbones. "Well, I will say it. Wilson, you are crazy as hell. This country don't want war. Why, eighty percent of the people in this country are isolationists. We ain't got no business in that European war. How in hell do you figure showing a display of gold around is going to lead to war?"

I leaned forward. "You ever been up north? Especially to one of them big cities?"

He shrugged. "Well, me and Nora had a little look around a couple of years ago. Rode the train all over the place."

"You ever see so many factories and plants and assembly places in all your life? Air over them towns is just black with the smoke coming out of the chimneys of those big factories. Last year Lauren and I rode to New York with Willis, hoping to talk him out of going. We were still talking right up to the time he got on that boat for France. But meanwhile I had a chance to look around and ask a few questions. I went over to the Colt factory, which they say is in another state, but it ain't no further from New York than Blessing is from Bay City. I wanted to see how they made them revolvers I been depending on so long. Well, they wasn't making revolvers. They were making machine guns, Maxim machine guns on license from the British government."

Justa relit his cigar. While he twirled it in the flame I studied him. He'd weathered the years pretty well. Other than an extra ten pounds he didn't have much use for and a good deal of gray around his temples, he didn't look all that much different. He still dressed like a working rancher in denim jeans and a cotton shirt. Of course his boots were the best-quality shop made, but even the poorest cowhand made certain of good boots, even if he had to go without whiskey. I hadn't grayed, for some reason. My hair was still dark brown and I reckon I'd shrunk down half an inch. And, like Justa, my face had gone to kind of sagging. That was all right except that it made shaving harder. I could remember the days when my face was all flat planes and I could whisk a straight razor over it in jiffy time and never fear a cut or burn. Now I had to shave carefully as hell and pull the skin tight with my off hand.

Justa said, "Wilson, you ain't going to convince me that this country is going to war because the Colt company is making a few machine guns for the British. Woodrow Wilson ran on a peace platform and folks would lynch him now if he was to get us in a war. The country wouldn't stand for it. What business would we have in that damn war?"

"It's big business, Justa, big, big, business. I tell you, it took me a long time to work it out, but finally all the pieces started to fit. Answer me this: Right now there is a bill in Congress calling for conscription. If they ain't going to be a war how come they are going to start drafting men into the army?"

Justa frowned. "You sure about that? I ain't heard nothing to that effect. Besides, what makes you think it will pass?"

I stood up and leaned toward him. "Because the goddamn peace president was the one got certain congressmen to put the bill up. And it will pass. I will bet on that, and you know I don't gamble on anything but sure things. So name your price and I'll take the bet."

He rubbed his hand over his face and looked worried. Then he said, "Aw, hell, Will, I've already heard you on the subject of how the country is changing and not for the better. I ain't going to listen to a man who thinks the automobile is the work of the devil and that the telephone will never take the place of a telegram. Hell, Wilson, you want things to stay the same as when we were young men. Well, they ain't, and you might as well make up your mind to that."

I was still standing up. "You want to know the reason I don't have an automobile or a telephone or won't have electricity in the house?"

"Because you're an old drag ass, that's why."

"No. That ain't the reason. Tell me, Justa, how many automobiles get manufactured down here in the South and Southwest? And how many telephone companies we got hiring local folks?"

A shadow flickered over his face. But he said, "Hell, Will, all the manufacturing is up north."

"That's right. And ain't a one of them sonsofbitches come in my places of business and bought a whiskey or risked a dollar in my casino. My customers are men who make their living with cattle and horses. You think I'm going to put a dollar in some damn Yankee pocket? Not very damn likely. And, by the way, it was big business that elected that scrawny little Princeton professor and it is big business that will tell him to get in the war. Right now the business at hand is to convince the people we ought to be at war. Find a damn good reason so folks like you will get on the bandwagon. Well, I'm here to tell you that we will be going to war for one reason and one reason only: money. They might say different in the newspapers, but that's what the idiot son of mine with all his sense of right and wrong is fighting for. So don't be so damn sure you know why I take a stand about this or about that. The reason might not be what you think."

He got up and walked over to the desk and refilled his glass. Going back, he said, "I hope to hell you're wrong, Wilson. I got a boy just the right age for conscription."

"While we were in New York I made it my business to get around and see what was going on in such a place," I said. "Went around to a lot of small factories and plants. For instance, I went to one outfit where they were stamping out copper cooking pots. The manager told me, give him a week and he could be geared up to turn out casings for artillery shells. And said he was confident it wouldn't be much longer before he was doing that very thing and making triple the money he was on pots."

Justa sipped at his whiskey. "What'd you come down here for? A visit or to worry me to death?"

I ignored his question. "You know what I saw being made up there? Tractors. Turning them out like licorice whips. A tractor is a gasoline-engined machine that—"

"I know what the hell a tractor is, Will. Did you know they also got cultivators and mechanical corn shuckers and cotton gins and big combines that will pick your cotton or harvest your wheat or whatever you want it to do? They say some of those machines will take the place of ten men. Pay for themselves in a year."

I said quietly, "And where are all those men going to work, Justa?"

He looked blank. Finally he furrowed his brow. "Hell, I don't know, Wilson. Somewhere."

I leaned forward. "In the war plants, that's where. It's all another piece in the puzzle. Just like the gold."

He sat and looked at me for a long time. Finally he shook his head. "Naw, naw. You got this one wrong, Will. You are one of the smartest men I ever met and about as slick an operator as ever come down the pike. But you are talking through your hat right now."

I pointed off in what I hoped was a westerly direction. "Then tell me what General Pershing is doing down in Mexico with a hundred thousand men chasing Pancho Villa?"

"Well, that's easy. Villa come over and raided Columbus, New Mexico. Now we are going to give him a whipping."

I had not meant to get off on a side trail with all the war talk. All I'd wanted to do was see if I couldn't get Justa to understand why I felt an obligation to make the government look damn silly by taking their gold away from them. But, once started, I couldn't see to turn off the tap. "If you were going after Villa in Sonora, which has got to be some of the worst land outside of northern Arizona, would you go clattering in there with a clutch of trucks and big artillery pieces and aeroplanes? Would you take after him with a hundred thousand soldiers and damn few of them on horseback? Hell, Villa ain't never got more than twenty or thirty regular men around him. You'd get yourself a small posse of cavalry and run him to ground."

"Then what in hell are they doing if they ain't after Villa?"

"Practicing! I think the army calls it maneuvers or something. I'll make you another bet and for any amount. I'll bet you they never get within ten miles of Villa, much less catch him."

He pulled a face. What I was saying was starting to have an effect on him. "Hell," he said, "Villa's got an army. He attacked Juárez with a hell of a bunch of men."

I nodded. "Yeah, he picks them up as he goes along, as he needs them. When they ain't fighting for Villa they go back to being peons and peasants and vaqueros or whatever. It's what I did when I was robbing banks. The core of the outfit was just me and the two Richter cousins and then later Chulo. But sometimes I'd have ten men in on a job."

He sighed. "You are making my head hurt. As I understand it they are going to display a bunch of gold to get folks to spend money so they can get industry up and running so they can declare war so they can make more money. And meanwhile our main general is running around northern Mexico practicing to fight the Germans. That about it?"

"Yeah, except I read in the paper the other day that we have already shipped over three billion dollars in goods and arms to England. *Billions*. Hell, Justa, I don't even know how much a billion is."

He said absently, "I think it's a thousand million or a hundred thousand million."

"Whatever it is, it's a pile of money. Only most of it got sunk and a lot of it was on credit. So if we don't go over there and help whip the Germans, the big banks are going to be left holding the bag, and I know for a fact that banks don't like to end up on the losing end."

Justa put his hand to his forehead. "Hell, Wilson, let's get off the damn subject. You are about to give me a headache. Talk about something else. How is your casino doing?"

"It's doing about the same." I paused. "But I think I'm fixing to make a change in my life. I'm giving serious thought to robbing that Federal Reserve bullion."

Justa slowly took his hand away from his head and lifted his eyes up to mine. "You're joking." He stared at me for a half moment. "You're not joking. Wilson, have you lost your mind?"

"No. I've been giving this a lot of thought. This is what I come up to talk to you about."

"Oh, hell," he sighed. Then he held his glass out. "I was thinking about going to bed, but I reckon you better pour us out another drink. I got an idea this will take some telling."

CHAPTER 4

NEXT MORNING, after breakfast, Justa and I took seats out on his big front porch, sitting in whitewashed wicker chairs and looking out over the gingerbread railing at the front part of his ranch. It was a pretty sight, all green and dotted with his cattle. Here and there a cowboy could be seen working, spreading seedcake or putting down salt licks out of a buckboard.

Of course, it was fenced now. The days of the open range were over. Fear and greed had caused men to fence their neighbor off from water, from the best pastures, from ingress and egress from his land. Some men had even tried to fence off the government land that belonged to all. Justa said that of all the fights he'd had to make to keep the Half-Moon operating, the fencing wars had been the worst. His family only owned about two hundred thousand acres but they needed four or five times that to handle their cattle operation. It had been a costly battle for Justa to buy and lease the extra land he'd held in common with his neighbors for so long. The Half-Moon had not started the fencing, nor had it been initiated by Justa's neighbors. No. Newcomers, seeing a good thing, had come in and bought up small, well-located parcels of land and kicked off a rumpus that took ten years to settle. But that had been at the turn of the century and was now almost forgotten.

We sat there sipping our coffee and smoking and thinking our own thoughts.

Justa said, "You trying to get yourself killed, Will?"

I shook my head. "No. That ain't never been my style."

"Well, the way this robbery you're talking about plays out I don't see any way you can pull it off and not get killed."

I nodded. "Now, there I agree with you. Of course, I haven't given it much thought yet."

"Didn't you tell me one time that the reason you never got caught or killed was that you never went in on a job without you had an advantage on your side?"

"That is true. I have never seen the sense to taking unnecessary risks. Let the other man put on a brave face and expose himself. I believe in cover."

Justa shook his head and set his empty cup down on the floor of the porch. "And all this just to give the federal government a black eye. The laugh is liable to be on you, Mr. Young. You could be resting your bones in a federal prison with no war going on and a whole bunch of peace on earth and goodwill to men breaking out."

I smiled slightly and said, "You Christians say peace on earth, goodwill to men, but history says otherwise."

He didn't say anything for a moment, just frowned. Finally he said, "You say 'you Christians' like we were a completely different breed of cow than you. I can't understand how you can live with Lauren for twenty-some years and not have a little of that goodness rub off on you."

I shrugged. There wasn't much I could say. "Maybe it ain't meant for everyone. Maybe I got hold of the wrong end of the stick at an early age and got a bad taste in my mouth. Hell, Justa, the Lord don't want me. My soul is blacker than the ace of spades. The only reason I haven't broke more than ten Commandments is that is all there is. If there were fifteen, I reckon I'd have put a fracture in them other five, too."

Justa tilted his chair back and put his boots up on the porch railing. "That is near as big a bunch of bullshit as I ever heard. I got a feeling you don't want to give God's way a chance because you are scared you couldn't hack it."

I gave him a look. "You preaching this Sunday? You warming up on me?"

He let his chair to the floor with a thump. "If I thought it would do any good talking you out of this fool idea, I'd set in to preaching and keep at it until you outrun me."

I spit out across the railing. I had got to chewing on my cigarillo and had a mouth full of tobacco juice. "Justa, I don't like the way this world is headed. At least this country. Folks are getting soft. Was a day when we judged a man by what he could do. You'd say about a man that he was good with cattle or that he'd give you an honest day's work. Now it seems like we judge people by what they got. By the things they own. Seems like everybody is rushing around trying to see how many whirligigs they can stack up in the living room."

Justa raised his eyebrows. "It appears you are intent on getting the whole country straightened up. I hope to hell you don't start on me."

I looked around at him. Here we were, two old men with nothing left to argue about but matters we couldn't do a damn thing about. "I'll give you an example," I said. "The other day a man was pointed out to me on the street by an acquaintance of mine. My acquaintance said, like it was big news, that the man had a Cadillac. Said it with a kind of awe. Well, hell, I didn't know what a Cadillac was. I thought it was some kind of disease, maybe like a goiter or something. So I asked what the man was doing about it. My friend looked at me like I wasn't hearing too good. He said that the man was driving it around. Of course, I found out that a Cadillac was an expensive motorcar that cost nearly as much as a damn good racehorse. But the point is that this friend thought—"

"I know what he thought. All right. Wilson, I don't like the change in the country any better than you do. I see men getting weaker. I see folks looking for the easy way. I see dishonesty every day. I know a man's word ain't what it used to be. I see all that, too, Will, but they ain't a damn thing I can do about it except be glad I'm as old as I am and won't have to watch it get much worse."

I gave him a shadowy smile. "You could go in on that robbery with me. That would be a start."

He snorted. "Listen, Mr. Wilson Young, I ain't never had no desire to be a famous outlaw." He paused and gave me a hard glare. "Now, that wouldn't be the reason you're contemplating this adventure, would it? Was a time you was as well known as canned peaches. But that was a long time ago. You sure you ain't thinking about past glories? You sure you ain't thinking about proving you can still do it, that you're still as good a man as you ever was?"

I stared at the green pastures. I was disappointed, to say the least. "Well, I come to talk with you and to get an answer. I reckon you just gave it to me." I made to get to my feet, but Justa put out a hand to stay me.

"Where the hell you going?"

"There's a train at one o'clock heading south. It's nearly ten now. I thought I'd better start getting ready."

"But you said you were staying two nights."

I turned a sad face on him. "Like I said, I come to have a discussion with you about this gold bullion business. I figured to get some level-headed thinking out of you. But you've already decided why I want to try this harebrained scheme, so there ain't no use stay-ing another day."

He looked puzzled. "Because I asked you if you didn't have it a little in mind to try and capture past glories? Is that what has got you all stiffened up?"

"Hell, I could have got that answer anywhere. I didn't need to come all this way. If I'd told Lauren what I was thinking she'd've accused me of being an old man wanting to have one last gamble. Damn, Justa, I thought you had a little more bottom to you than to jump on what appears to be the obvious."

"Listen," he said, "I never meant—"

"For your information and the information of anyone else, I don't figure I got a damn thing to prove. I am not considering that robbery to enhance my reputation. It might surprise you to know that I ain't proud of my reputation as a bank robber and I ain't got no interest in getting it stirred up again. You say at one time I was as famous as canned peaches. Well, the fact is the stories ain't stopped yet. I wish I had a dollar for every story I hear about what I done in them bad old days. If I did, I'd have as much money as you. What irritates the hell out of me is I spent the biggest part of last night laying out what I thought were good and sensible rea-sons why I could do the people of this country a service by expos-ing the goddamn federal government's hole card. Maybe make them aware of the way we are being led down the primrose path to war. But if one of my best friends can't understand it I sure as hell ain't got no chance of getting other folks to savvy what I'm up to."

He was sitting there with his mouth open. When I finally ran down he said, with surprise in his voice, "Damn, Will, you're mad. You're mad as hell. I didn't think you ever got angry."

With some heat I said, "I ain't angry, I'm surprised. I never thought you'd be one to reach out and grab the nearest potato just because it was handy, never mind if it was roasted or not."

He looked down at his boots. "All right, fair enough. But what would you have thought if you'd heard the same proposition from somebody like you?"

"If I'd been listening to what they had to say for half the night I might have figured they had reasons other than to act like a jackass. It might have escaped your notice, but it has been damn near twenty-six years since I robbed a bank. If I was a drunk you'd say that was a pretty good spell to lay off the bottle. But I guess once a bank robber, always a bank robber. Or maybe it's there's no fool like an old fool."

He straightened up and put his hand out. "All right, all right. I got the message. You ain't doing it for one last fling."

"You said it was suicide and I damn near agree. You call that a fling?"

"Damnit, Wilson, get off your high horse. Actually, I really thought it was for another reason but I was scairt to say."

"What?"

He looked away. "You are kind of touchy about the subject."

"What, damnit!"

"Well, Willis. I thought maybe you was doing it for Willis. Or was thinking of doing it for him."

I wrinkled up my brow. "What in hell are you talking about? What the hell has Willis got to do with it?"

He hesitated, frowning. "Well, you were kind of talking about stealing the bullion to expose the federal government as trying to lead us into a war. I never quite understood how you figured to do that, but that was the impression I got."

"But what the hell has that got to do with Willis? Willis is already in the war."

"You said he went out of some sense of justice or duty or some such. I thought you maybe figured to show him how his own government was conniving to go to war and get him to see that all governments connived and that his sense of fair play was plain wasted."

I looked at him hard, and said flatly, "That is the craziest god-damn idea I ever heard."

He reared his head back and showed me a lot of the whites of his eyes. "It ain't a damn bit crazier than you trying to steal a thousand pounds of gold in front of five thousand people and twenty-one soldiers with rifles."

"It didn't say a thousand pounds. It said *near* half a ton."

"Oh, yeah. Like that is going to make a big difference when you got twenty holes in you."

"Maybe I ought to take up the church so I'd be bulletproof like the rest of you Christians," I said sarcastically.

"Sssh!" He looked away. "Now you are talking plain foolishness. You ain't going to get at me that way, Wilson, digging at my faith. You might get at yourself, though."

"We wouldn't be talking like this if you'd paid the least bit of attention to me last night," I said. "I thought I made a pretty damn logical argument for the government wanting to get in the war for economic reasons. There's a ton of factories up north about to run out of gimcracks and gewgaws to make. They are pretty soon going to have to start making something else, and I think it's going to be guns and bullets and uniforms. You don't see it down here in the South because we ain't got no factories or industries. The North wouldn't let us have them after the war and the Reconstruction."

Justa flexed his shoulders like he was shucking a load. "All right, maybe you did have some good points. And of course I agree that the North is way ahead of us industrially and has got to keep them plants busy. I can see that. Hell."

I fixed him with an eye. "They want it to work out so they supply the guns and the South supplies the men. You didn't want to listen because you were thinking about J.D."

His eyes flared. "Don't start that talk."

"If it was me I'd send him down to South America to buy cattle and keep him down there until this was over with."

He got out of his chair and leaned against the railing and looked out over his land. "Will, do you realize that this is the first time in all the years we've knowed each other that we've come near hard words?" He swung around and looked at me. "And for what? For nothing. We may well get into that damn European war, but I doubt it. I ain't denying, though, that you've made a pretty good case for what the government is up to, especially that part about John Pershing down there in Mexico chasing Pancho Villa all over the state of Sonora with trucks and motorcycles and aeroplanes and I don't know what all."

"And what about all them goods and armaments we been shipping to the British that the Germans have been sinking? How long you reckon them big shots are going to put up with that? Listen, I've had a taste of one war and I didn't care for it. But one thing I learned was that it's the politicians that start and end them and the young men who do the dying in between."

"But all that don't mean nothing, Will. We can talk till we turn blue in the face and it is not going to change one damn thing."

I said grimly, "I'm giving serious thought to doing more than talking."

He shook his head. "No you ain't. Not unless you have gone loco. You ain't got no more chance of stealing that gold than a government mule. You could go and get yourself killed, but that wouldn't serve your purpose. So we really ain't got nothing to argue about. And I, for my part, am sorry I got carried away and put the spurs to you a little bit." He smiled. "You are generally a man who makes good sense. You took me unawares. And I will admit that war talk does make me kind of nervous about J.D."

I sat back in my chair. "You are giving it as your opinion that it would be impossible to steal that gold?"

He turned away from the railing and sat back down. "I ain't saying it's impossible. If you had about five hundred men I reckon it would be a piece of pie. Of course, you'd get a hell of a lot of folks killed in the doing, but I reckon you'd have the gold. What you'd do with it I don't know. And where you'd get five hundred fools to throw in with you I don't know. But even if you got the gold and made the government look foolish and gave a bunch of newspaper interviews as to just why you done it and what the government was up to, I don't think it would make a tinker's damn."

"I'm not giving up on it that easily," I said stubbornly. "There has to be a way."

He studied me. "Have you given any thought to Lauren in all this? You go and get yourself killed, what will become of her?"

I didn't answer him.

"Hell, you ain't even got nerve enough to tell your wife." He gave me a crooked smile. "You ain't discussed this with her, have you? I bet you ain't said a word. Tell the truth, now. Have you?"

"Not only ain't I told her or even hinted at it, but I wouldn't give you a nickel for the life of the man that takes it upon himself to put her wise."

He laughed. "Boy, you are a pistol. Talk big about holding up some big government gold shipment, but you are scairt to death of a woman don't weigh more than a hundred pounds, maybe a hundred and ten."

I leaned toward him. In a confidential voice I said, "Be all right if I go in and tell Nora about some of the moonshines you and I got up to in Mexico? Reckon she'd like to know about that side of you?"

He colored under his tan. "Damn you, Wilson Young, you can cut that kind of talk out right now! You better not start no telling-the-wives contest with me. You are liable to lose. I'll rope Warner Grayson in on my side and we'll swamp you."

"Yeah, well, who started it, mister? You want to be careful about such matters. I wish to hell I was talking to Warner instead of you. I don't reckon he would think I was so crazy. Of course, he's got considerable more sand in his craw than you do."

"Hell, why didn't you go see Warner? I could have done with-out the honor of listening to your nonsense for half the night. I've come of an age where I need my rest. I don't need to be sitting up half the night drinking whiskey and watching a friend go out of his mind."

I got out a cigarillo and lit it. "Warner lives too damn far away. Besides, that hellcat sister-in-law of mine would find out what we were talking about and then Lauren would know about it ten min-utes later."

He got up, standing over me. "Well, then, let's go in there and telephone him up. Won't be no way Laura can hear."

I knew Justa had a telephone and I didn't really blame him for it. Their business went so far beyond the ranch that Norris, when he was in residence, had to be in contact with all kinds of places. They'd got one just as soon as a central exchange had been set up in Blessing. I hated to think what it had cost Justa to have a line run out the seven miles from town.

But I didn't much think that Warner would have one of the damned things. He was a horse man and as resistant as I was to what some folks chose to call progress. I said, "In the first place, Warner Grayson ain't got no damn telephone, and—"

"Yes, he does. Had it about six months. Hasn't been two weeks since we ordered some breeding stock from him, Morgans and quarterhorse mixed. Herd is getting a little narrow-eyed."

I glared at him. "Even if he has got a telephone, I don't use them. If I want to talk to somebody I either go where they are or ask them to come to me. Remember that, Justa? Used to be called visiting. You ain't forgot, have you?"

"All right," he said. "You won't call Warner and you won't take my word for it that you are thinking loco. What say we hunt up Ben and—" He stopped. He realized what he had just proposed. He knew that I had been Ben's hero since he'd been a teenager. Un-fortunately, he'd learned all the wrong sides of me, the bad sides.

He'd grown up thinking a gun could settle anything, never knowing how many times I kept mine in my holster and walked around
trouble. Or how many times trouble had stayed out of my way. That
is one advantage to having a reputation with a gun—not many folks
want to bet their lives to find out if it's true or not. All that penny
pulp fiction written by lamebrains like Ned Buntline was just a
bunch of bullshit. I reckoned I hadn't seen five out-and-out pistol
duels in all my life, but them penny-thriller gunslingers appeared
to have about that many on a page.

I said, "So you reckon we better not go hunt Ben up?"

"I remembered he ain't around," Justa said. "He's in Houston
contracting for some large shipments of feed."

I laughed. "Sure he is. Don't worry, Justa. I wouldn't get Ben involved in this harebrained scheme of mine. Not for his sake, but
for mine."

"All right, you won't listen to me. Let's get another opinion. You
will agree that my wife has got a right level head on her shoulders.
She thinks pretty good for a woman, don't she?"

I whistled. "Boy, I'm glad for your sake she didn't hear you say
that. 'Thinks pretty good for a *woman.*' I might have to let that slip
out at lunch."

He gave me a stern eye. "You keep making remarks like that and
I'm liable to see that you eat your lunch out of a sack on that one
o'clock train. You know what I mean, Wilson. She can see the possibility of a thing. She has been a hell of a help to me in running
this ranch."

I shook my head. "No, thanks, Justa. I'm not going to talk to Nora
about this. I value her good opinion of me too much to let on I
might be going back to stealing."

"I bet if your old running mate, Les Richter, was here, he'd put
the stops on this idea. From what I heard he was the one done the
thinking that kept your bunch from getting killed or ending up in
prison."

The hair rose on the back of my neck. I was suddenly overcome by the strangest feeling. I looked up quickly at Justa. "Why did you mention his name?"

"What?"

"Les Richter. What caused you to suddenly mention his name?"

He looked at me curiously. "Will, you ought to see your face. If you wasn't so tan I'd swear you'd gone pale. What about Les Richter? It just popped into my head, that's all. Is something the matter?"

"No, no." I looked away. It was curious was all, him mentioning Les on top of what had happened. The day before, while I was changing trains in Victoria, I had caught sight of a man who looked and walked and acted as Les Richter had. I'd been on the station platform and there was quite a crowd, what with Victoria being a switching point for a lot of other destinations. There had been considerable people between me and the man and I really hadn't gotten a clear view of him. As I'd tried to work my way nearer, the man had vanished. I'd known, of course, that it was only someone who bore a slight resemblance to Les and that the reason I'd seen so much similarity was that I'd been thinking so much about my old friend of late. But also, the Richters were from Victoria, which was only about eighty miles from where I'd been raised near Corpus Christi. It had been not more than fifteen miles from the very train station I was standing in that we had met up and formed our partnership.

Justa was still looking at me. Awkwardly he said, "Y'all were pretty close, weren't you?"

"Yeah." I got up. "Listen, it's well on into the day and I ain't had a drink of whiskey yet. My constitution can't stand such deprivation. You're a hell of a host."

"Well, hell, let's get on in there and get you drunk. I'd like to see Nora crawling on somebody besides me about the evils of liquor."

We didn't talk any more the balance of the day about the gold or the war or any other such somber subjects. Instead, at lunch, I had to try to answer Nora's questions about Del Rio society and what all the ladies were wearing and if there'd been any acting companies come to town and everything there was to tell about Lauren.

Nora had been a schoolteacher and, if Justa was to be believed, a no-nonsense one. But I found that hard to believe. She was getting a little plump and her light brown hair had picked up some gray, but she was as lively and sparkling and pretty as the first day I'd ever met her. And also relentless. I was hard-pressed to answer all her questions and, on a few occasions, thought I was about to get a ruler across the back of my hands for being laggardly. Maybe Justa had been telling the truth about their courtship and how she'd sometimes forget that he wasn't one of her pupils.

But he'd been a reluctant bridegroom, so I'd heard the story. Finally, it was said, Miss Nora announced that she was tired of waiting and was going off to St. Louis to marry a drummer who traveled in yard goods. Justa was supposed to have wired ahead to have the train stopped and then pursued her in a locomotive he'd hired from the railroad. Supposedly he yanked her off the train and drug her back to Blessing and a wedding. I doubted the truth of all the details, but it made a good story.

That night at dinner Nora told me proudly that she was going to get an electric refrigerator and that they were going to have electric lights, too. She said Justa had arranged to have a line run out and now half their food wouldn't spoil for lack of refrigeration. Justa told me it was a huge contraption made by General Electric for hotel restaurants, and not generally available to the public. I turned and gave him a look, but he wouldn't meet my eyes. Nora said she reckoned that Lauren already had all the conveniences, us living in town as we did. That made Justa choke on a bite of steak but he had the good grace not to make comment.

Justa and I rounded out our visit by going back down to his office to talk for a while before bedtime. Neither one of us wanted to whip a tired old horse so we stayed off my thinking about why I wanted to steal the gold. But Justa did draw out, on a square of paper, the location of the railroad station where the gold would be coming in, and where the bank was and then all that open space between the two, most of which was represented by the Military Plaza. He said, "Now, I don't claim to be no bank robber, but this looks like a fighting problem and I am familiar with them, as many scuffles as we've had around here. I don't see how you can try and hold them up at the train, because that is where they're going to be extra wary. And when they are en route to the bank you are going to be exposed as hell. You try it inside the bank and you're going to have yourself bottled up." He pitched the pencil down on the desk. "So tell me, Jesse James, where you planning on doing this?"

I had been standing by the desk watching him draw the layout and then make his points. Now I sat down and shook my head. "I haven't given it a moment's thought, Justa. Not the how of it, anyway."

He blinked at me and then sat down in the chair that accommodated the facing desk. He took a moment to pour himself out a little whiskey. "With not much more than a month to go, you're telling me you ain't given no thought to how you plan to rob that gold?"

I shook my head slowly. "No, why should I?"

"I'd guess," he said dryly, "to figure out a way to keep from getting killed more than two or three times."

I half stood and reached my glass out to him. He poured it about half full. "First things first, Justa. I got to make up my mind to plan on trying it. What's the use of making a plan and then not using it?"

"Strikes me that it's a hell of a lot better to have a plan and not use it than to try it without no plan."

I shrugged and sat back down. "There's plenty of time for that. I've thought of plans, good plans, in less than five minutes before. I'd need to go back and study the terrain with an eye toward the robbery. I've never looked at that locale as the site of a robbery before."

He was looking at me curiously, a slight smile tugging at his mouth.

"What?" I said.

He shook his head. "You'd just get mad if I told you."

"Hell, you can't make me no more angry than you already done. You and your telephone and electric refrigerator. Damn. Now, what?"

"Aw," he said, "I was just thinking about all the stories that used to circulate about you and your gang when you was in your heyday. How you was the Robin Hood of Texas. Hell, it hasn't been that long since some old boy who knew I knew you told me about the time you and your bunch came by their farm and left off a couple of hundred dollars that saved the day. Said if I ever saw you I was to tell you how grateful he was. If I've heard that story once I've heard it a hundred times. I was just wondering if something like that might not be in your mind. I mean, hell, you don't need the money, not with that casino."

I put my head back and laughed. "Yeah, I've heard some of them stories, and they are all the biggest bunch of hooey ever put out by the mouth of man. In the first place we were moving too fast to know who was poor and who wasn't. And so far as most of that bunch that rode with me was concerned, money was for two things—women and whiskey. Les and I used to cache some of ours when we'd make a good haul, but I don't recall ever playing Robin Hood." I shook my head. "Naw, it ain't about giving money to the poor. Lauren is doing a right good job of that as it is. I think I'm supporting about a hundred families across the border. Wouldn't surprise me if one of *them* didn't own a Cadillac motorcar, the way she hands it out."

He got up and walked over and looked at some photographs on the wall, pictures of his bred-up line of cattle. "What I don't get, Wilson, is where in hell you are going to find enough men to go in with you on this. I'm sure there are plenty of crazy folks on the border, but even they ought to be able to see how long these odds are."

I thought about it for a moment, staying so still that he finally turned from the wall to look at me. Speaking slowly, I said, "If I do it, it will be a single-hand job. Won't nobody else be involved."

That kind of brought the conversation to a stop. Justa sat back down at the opposite desk and stared at me. He finally said, "I didn't hear you right, did I? I mean, I think anybody that would try and loot that gold is crazy, but I almost thought I heard you say you were going to do it alone."

I nodded slowly. "That is, *if* I do it. I ain't made up my mind about that yet."

"Well, yeah," he said, "I know if *I* was going to take on that chore I sure wouldn't want to share the glory with nobody else. I'd just march up to that bunch of soldiers and say, 'I'm Wilson Young. Give me your gold and be damn quick about it. And no back talk, either. Savvy?' "

"Go ahead and laugh, Justa. I don't blame you. But I'll tell you that when I first got the idea I knew that it had to be done in such a way that no blood would be shed, including mine. Now, I don't know what that way is and I may not be able to think of it in time, but that is the way it has to be. I don't intend for a shot to be fired."

"I'll tell you the way and you won't have to give it no further thought. There ain't no way, Will! And you know it. Not a shot fired. Oh, my great-aunt Agnes. I never heard of such. I am here to tell you, young man, that the federal government is damn touchy about that gold and they ain't going to give it up easily. I think some of them bullet wounds you must have taken during your career are starting to catch up with you. Sounds to me like the doctors missed a slug and it has finally worked its way up to your brain. Either that or you have taken one drink too many."

"I could get fifty men," I said stubbornly. "I could maybe get a hundred. There's plenty of that kind on both sides of the river would roll the dice for that kind of payday. But it would be a slaughter. God only knows how many innocent bystanders would get shot down." I shook my head. "No, no, I ain't having no part of such. If I can't do it alone and without any gunplay I ain't going to do it at all."

He looked at me a minute, idly playing with a cigarillo. "Let me ask you this. You don't need the money, right? Let's say you somehow figured out a way to steal that gold. What in hell would you do with it? That's a hell of a lot of gold bullion."

I shrugged. My thinking hadn't gone that far. Absently I said, "Give it to Lauren somehow so she could use it for her good works and her charities and what not."

Justa laughed. "Heaven's gold," he said. "I wonder how the Almighty would take to that? You reckon He would approve you giving Him a helping hand in such a fashion?"

"That's a little out of my department," I said.

"But then you'd have to tell Lauren where you got it. And she wouldn't touch it with a cattle prod."

"I'd tell her I won it in a poker game."

"A *quarter* of a *million* dollars?"

"I've told her I'm a real good poker player. She believes me. In fact, she believes damn near everything I tell her. Makes lying too easy. Takes all the fun out of it."

We didn't talk much about anything after that, and after a drink or two more, we turned in and went to bed. I didn't sleep right off. Instead I lay there thinking about Lauren and what a stunt like what was in my mind could do to her. Then and there I resolved that if I couldn't find an absolutely foolproof method I'd give up the idea.

Maybe it really was nothing more than the yearning of a man fast becoming old to turn the calendar back one more time.

Justa himself drove me in the next morning in a buggy. To make the one o'clock train we'd had to leave right before lunch, but Nora had a sack lunch put up for me to make a meal on the train. Justa added a bottle of first-rate whiskey and I was all set. I took my leave of Nora with a kiss on the cheek, a promise to give her love to Lauren, a vow that we'd all get together again real soon. After that I loaded in with Justa and we set out. For a while we talked of old times together, him pointing out where such and such a fight had taken place when rustlers had struck or when some fool had tried to drive cattle loaded with Mexican tick fever through his range.

But finally Justa had to get around to what had brought me to him in the first place. For myself I was willing to give the whole subject a rest. About a mile out of Blessing, Justa said, "Now you claim that you are wanting to rob that gold out of a feeling of duty and to see justice done. Does that cover it? You think the federal government is playing bully boy by trying to get us hicks down here in the hinterlands to loosen up and spend that paper money like it was real. Is that it?"

"The government can always print more paper money," I said. "But they have a hard time laying their hands on gold. Yeah, they are trying to create an element of trust without telling folks the real reason, namely that they need money to finance a war. And most folks down here ain't getting paid five dollars a day like the workers in Henry Ford's plants are."

He was persistent. "But you do claim that you've got some principled reasons for what you want to do. You ain't acting out of some silly notion."

I frowned. "Of course not. Hell, Justa, ain't you been listening at all?"

He gave the buggy horse a little slap with the rein to hurry him along and gave me a big smile. "In other words," he said, "you want to steal that gold for the same reasons Willis went over to France to fight the Germans."

"Justa Williams," I sputtered, "you are twisting my words. You know that ain't the way of it! Damn your eyes!"

All he did was laugh.

He saw me onto the train. I found a seat next to the passenger platform and put the window up so we could have a last word. I thanked him for all his hospitality and said I wished that he and Nora would come for a visit.

"We'll make it as quick as we can." Then he smiled, big. "We'll be right close in about a month. I figure to have business in San Antonio. Hear there's going to be some kind of big show."

"Go to hell," I said.

Just then the cars jolted forward and began to move. Justa walked along the platform, keeping up with the train. "You know what I think? I think you are giving thought to this because you are Wilson Young and you can't help yourself. I think you'll be Wilson Young as long as you can stand upright. I think all this other talk is you trying to convince yourself otherwise."

But Justa had reached the end of the platform and the train had left him behind. He was too far except to yell something and I didn't want to do that. I gave him a final wave and pulled my head in and shut the window.

CHAPTER
5

I WAS mighty glad to be home and to be with Lauren, which, to me, was the same thing. I'd gotten to where I didn't like to go off and leave her even for short visits like I had just made. If somebody had told me, twenty-five years previous, that I could feel that way about a woman, I'd have told them they had the wrong man. Other than Les Richter and then Warner and Justa and, to a certain degree, Chulo, I had never really been close to anyone. And these had all been men with whom I shared a common bond or a common goal. We had depended on one another, in one way or another, and our friendship had been founded on that.

But women had been more for fun and play. I loved women in that way. I loved their bodies, I loved their conversation on occasion, I loved being around them. But to actually form an attachment that would make me miss them? No, that could never be for such as myself. By nature partly, but more by the circumstances of my early youth, I was a loner. There were a few people I trusted and was loyal to, but I was only faithful to myself. I knew it was a selfish life and one that was lacking in some ingredients I saw in the lives of others, but there wasn't a damn thing I could do about it. If you were my friend I would go to hell for you and bring back a still-smoking coal, but when the night came and the shutters were drawn and it was time to be with the one you were closest to, I was with myself.

At least that had been the way I'd been before Lauren. No, I had continued that way for quite some time after our paths crossed and then joined. Lauren was the kind of person you wanted time to study. There was so damn much to her that she deserved and needed close examination. On the surface she was worth whatever price was being asked, even without a tryout. But then later, maybe years later, you discovered that the handsomest pocket watch you'd ever bought wasn't just gold on the outside, but was filled with jeweled works and a quality of craftsmanship so that it would always be exactly true to the time. About then I started learning about that word I'd heard so often, love, and began to feel the first flush of the emotion. As the time had passed and the watch had kept clicking off that trueness, the love had just grown and grown until I was as conscious of it as I was of a horse underneath me or the weight of a revolver at my side.

I got home a little after five, just in time for supper. I had wired Lauren from Victoria when I was sure my train would be on time so as to be sure and get my name in the pot. She had hugged me and kissed me like I'd been gone a month and I'd gone through my usual carrying on like it was way too much and why did women have to get so emotional. Hell, I'd just been off on a little business trip. But if she was that hard up I'd try to accommodate her just as quick as we could get upstairs.

Of course, it had never fooled Lauren. She knew me too well. Sometimes it worried me how well she did know me. I'd come in

the door feeling guilty for what I'd told Justa and what I was thinking of doing. I'd about half hid my face until I could get my feet
under me for fear she'd see it and go to grilling me, which was a
process she was amazingly good at.

Now we were eating fried chicken and mashed potatoes and
gravy with some sliced tomatoes and iced tea to drink. We were
eating in the dining room. With only the two of us I always wondered why we didn't take all our meals at the breakfast table instead
of going to the bother of setting up in the dining room. But Lauren
had given me to understand that ladies and gentlemen did not take
all their meals in the kitchen like pig farmers. Especially not *Virginia* ladies of good family.

I was busying myself with a piece of white meat when the proper
Virginia lady said, "Wilson, that is boneless breast of chicken. Mrs.
Bridesdale has filleted it. You are supposed to eat it with your knife
and fork."

Without looking up I said, "Lady, I have always used my hands
and mouth on breasts, chicken or not. How'd you like it if I took
a knife and fork to that fine set you've got?"

She said, in that dry, droll voice she used when she was making
fun of me, "Oh, my heavens! How lewd. How shocked I am. Hor-
rors! Is that all you ever think about?"

I gave her a sinister look. "Listen, woman, I been away for quite
some time. Soon as this house settles down I plan to give you several shocks. All in the same place."

She went, "Tch, tch, tch. Now, Wilson, I have warned you about
promising what you can't deliver."

Some lady, my wife—though, indeed, she and her sister were
from one of those fine old Virginia families that went way back to
Thomas Jefferson and Robert E. Lee and that whole bunch. At one
time the several families that had made up the batch had been
more than just a little prosperous. But the Civil War and its after-
math, as in so many similar stories, had shrunk their land and cut

their crops and stock. At one time I had teased both Laura and Lauren that about the only commodity their families had left to market was all the daughters. And in a way it was true, although none of them, as far as I knew, had much trouble making very successful marriages. You got that whole clutch of young women together, cousins and sisters and what not, and you had a sight that would tighten the jeans of any full-blooded American boy. Laura and Lauren had often teased me and Warner back by claiming they were the disgrace of the family since all they could bag were a couple of Texans, and one of them was a dishonest horse trader and the other a bank robber. That pair of sisters could play rough when they set their mind to it.

Lauren said, "Well, you haven't said how things went in Blessing. Did you get one?"

I was now eating with a knife and fork, though I didn't think the chicken tasted as good that way. "No, Justa already had the only one available. Her name is Nora."

"Very funny," she said. "I think you should have married a schoolteacher. Tell me again how Blessing came to get its name. I have forgotten."

I took a drink of iced tea. "About thirty-some years ago all the cattlemen in the area around the Half-Moon Ranch were petitioning the railroad to run them a spur line down into the area so they could ship their cattle and not have to make such long trail drives. Finally the railroad come to its senses and run a railhead down to a central location. Of course the town sprang up around it. When they went to name the place somebody remembered that Justa's daddy had said, 'What a blessing' when they finally got the last rail laid. So they took that for a name."

"It's good you weren't there."

I looked up. "Why?"

"Because you'd have said, 'What the hell took you so long?' I don't think that would have been a very nice name for a town."

I changed the subject. "What have you been up to since I been gone? You are mighty full of vinegar and ginger for a Christian lady who supposedly has been going around doing good works among the poor and needy."

She gave me a smile. "Just counting my blessings at having my husband home. Tell me, weren't you a little anxious at the train station here in Del Rio?"

I looked at her blankly. "What? What are you talking about?"

"That you were standing in Del Rio, but you were bound for Blessing. That must have worried you."

I wrinkled my brow. "Why?"

"Well, you can't see Blessing from Del Rio. And you've always said you didn't believe in what you couldn't see." She gave me an innocent look. "Are you telling me that you set out on a journey on nothing but faith that Blessing would be there?"

I could smell a trap, one of her religious traps. Only she said she was a Christian, which might or might not be religious. But whatever name she wanted to put to it I knew where she was headed. I said stubbornly, "I've looked at a map. Blessing is on it. So is Del Rio. And then there is the railroad timetable."

She gave me her damned innocent look. "Oh, so you have faith in maps. Well, my goodness, we have several maps around the house. And they are absolutely without error."

I knew she was talking about Bibles, but she wasn't going to catch me that easy. A man don't really feel comfortable talking about the spiritual when he's trying to work up the courage to tell his wife he's thinking about robbing a bank. I said, "I been there before. I knew it hadn't been moved."

"Now, Wilson," she said gently, "you didn't *know* Blessing hadn't been moved. You had faith it hadn't. Isn't that so?"

I sighed and put down my knife and fork. "All right, make your point. You've got me hemmed up and I can't see no clear space to bust out."

She gave me one of her sweetest smiles. "Honey, I'm not trying to hem you up. I'm only amazed how easily you put your faith in some things and not in others. Faith is very simple in Christianity. It is the assurance of things hoped for, the conviction of things not seen. Now, were you convinced, or convicted, when you stood on the station platform at the depot that Blessing would be there? You couldn't see it, but you went ahead. And you went ahead with assurance, didn't you?"

I made a face. "Lord's sake, Lauren, not now. I was thinking about us going up to bed."

She took a sip of iced tea. "Talking about faith is not going to keep us from going upstairs. Don't you have faith that I would want to?"

I frowned. "Now, damnit, Lauren, you got to cut this out. You are constantly bullyragging me about this spiritual business and I have told you I don't want no part of it. I thought we was supposed to have religious freedom in this country. Hell, I ain't even got any in my own house. My own dining table, even."

She said mildly, "Why would you think I was bullyragging you? We have discussions on other matters where we disagree and you don't get upset. Maybe you are bullyragging yourself. Maybe something inside you is nagging at you. Could that be it, Wilson?"

"No, no, and *no!*" I threw my napkin on the table. "I ain't hungry anymore. But I'll keep you company." I was very near sulking, which I didn't want to do because it would certainly interfere with how I wanted the evening to end.

She reached over and put her hand on mine. "Will, I'm not nagging you. You do what your own soul tells you to do. But you are very dear to me and I want you to have the same feeling of freedom that I do. If you did you wouldn't get so wrapped up in daily cares."

I patted her hand with my free one. "I know, Lauren. But I think it's best to leave my soul alone. I think I dropped it some time back in a getaway from a bank job and never went back to find it. Likely some road bum is wearing it to patch up his jeans. I reckon it had about shrunk to that size by then."

She leaned over and kissed me in the corner of the mouth. "Now, I haven't heard all about Justa and Nora. What was Nora wearing and what did she say was the latest fashion in that part of the country?"

It was hard to believe, but I welcomed the change of subject to women's fashions. But in hopes of heading off the topic I said, "I thought we had a peach cobbler for dessert."

She raised her eyebrows and gave me a mocking look. "Peach cobbler? I thought you wanted something else for dessert?"

I stared at her. "Lauren Young! Accuse *me* of being lewd! You ought to have heard yourself. Now I'm the one that is shocked."

She gave me a sweet smile. "If we had electricity in the house so I could have an electric refrigerator like the hotel in San Antonio, you might get shocked more often. I bet Nora has one, doesn't she?"

I looked away and said, "What about that peach cobbler? I'd almost rather you'd Bible thump at me than talk about that damn electricity."

She got up to go to the kitchen. "Anybody ever tell you you were behind the times?"

"You mean an old stick-in-the-mud?"

She paused at the kitchen door. "I already know that Nora has a telephone. And Justa being the kind of husband he is, I'd almost bet he's had electricity put in. And them way out in the country and us in town where it is all around us. Does Nora have an electric refrigerator?"

"No," I said. "Nobody does. Only restaurants and such. She's still got the same old icebox. Gets ice out of town twice a week."

"I think I'll just write her and see."

"Now, hold up there, woman. You calling your husband a liar?"

But she was already through the kitchen door.

I sat there, thinking. From the general direction of the conversation I didn't reckon it to be the ideal time to ask her opinion about me robbing another bank. But I did think a little more spade work might not be out of order. So, when she came back through the door carrying the cobbler, I let her sit down and get us both served before I said anything. She was pouring cream on mine and handing it over to me when I said, "I don't think I'm being behind the times when I say that all these so-called modern conveniences are doing a harm to the working men of this country. Justa Williams talked about some farm machinery that could do the work of ten men. Well, what are those ten men supposed to do? How they supposed to feed their families? If you can turn on a switch and have electric lights, what is supposed to happen to all those folks who have been making gaslights and kerosene lanterns and what not? You think that lightning rod salesman was progress? Hell and damnation, Lauren, open your eyes. The North is manufacturing the goods and making money and the South is going broke trying to buy them! We ain't got no damn industry down here. Or haven't you noticed that?"

She tried to interrupt but I wouldn't let her.

"You want to talk about God, all right, let's talk about God," I said. "God breathed the breath of life into every living creature on the face of this earth. Standard Oil didn't do it and neither did the General Electric Power Company or the McCormick reaper folks. Henry Ford has got to pour gasoline in his damn buggies to get them to run and they quit when they run out of that gasoline. But the breath of life that God gave us goes right on until he figures we been around long enough. I believe in muscle power. This country was built on muscle power. Man muscle, oxen muscle, mule muscle, horse muscle. And that's a machine that runs on a fuel supply that ain't ever going to run out, the breath of life as give us by God Almighty!"

She looked at me. "You through?"

"For the moment. Though sometimes I wonder who it is that believes the most in God around here."

"Will, I do not disagree with anything you say," she said. "I only wish you would quit working yourself up about it. Of course I don't understand about economics and money and all of that like you do. But I understand you, and you worry me. Will, you can't just close your mind to what is happening. The world is changing and there's nothing you can do about it. I know you'd like to go back twenty-five years when it was your world and you were young and carefree and everyone admired you and all the pretty girls chased you. But that time is past. The world is different. You are different. But there can be as much happiness in this time of your life as any other if you will only make an effort at acceptance."

I glared at her. I was getting the "act your age" talk that I had been trying to avoid. It had not been what I'd been talking about. My age didn't have a damn thing to do with it and I still felt I could get all the pretty young girls I wanted, if I so desired. In fact I almost said that to her. Instead I shoved my bowl away. I said, "This is the worst damn peach cobbler Mrs. Bridesdale has ever made. What'd she use, sour grapes?"

Her eyes suddenly snapped. "*I* made that cobbler!"

I stood up. "Then I reckon we better get the jobs straightened out around here. Mrs. Bridesdale is being paid to cook. If she ain't going to do that then I reckon she better get upstairs and sleep with me. She's got to earn her money somehow." I walked straight out of the room and down the hall and into my office and slammed the door.

ONE MORNING a couple of days after what Lauren had come to refer to as the "peach cobbler rebellion," I was down in my office in the saloon when one of my bartenders came in and said there was a soldier wanted to see me.

I was surprised. "A soldier?"

"Yes, sir. A sergeant." He made a motion down his arm. "One of them as has all the stripes on his sleeve."

"What does he want to see me about?"

The bartender looked uncomfortable. "Aaah . . . I don't really know."

He knew, all right; he just didn't want to say. I said, "All right. You can send him in, but give me a few minutes. I don't want this sort of thing to turn into a habit. Next thing this office will begin to look like a train station with people coming and going. You understand?"

"Yes, sir."

"I mean, I own this damn place, I don't work here. Which makes me ask, by the way, why ain't he seeing J.J.? He's the damn manager."

The bartender looked embarrassed. "He done seen him. Mr. Jones told the sergeant it was your orders and you was the only one could change them."

"What orders?"

"About serving soldiers."

I frowned. "And this soldier insists on seeing me? Does he reckon he's going to get me to change my mind?"

"I don't know, Mr. Young. I don't know what is in the man's mind. I just said I'd see if you'd talk with him, and you said you would."

I grimaced. "So I did. I guess that means I'll have to. But he better not come in here getting me in a bad mood. I'm in enough trouble at home as it is. He comes in here and gets me in a bad mood and I take it home with me and catch hell, I won't be the only one gets it. Am I making myself plain?"

He looked nervous. "Yes, sir. Maybe I better tell him no."

I reared my head back. "Didn't I just say I'd see him? You want me going back on my word?"

"Yes, sir. I mean, no, sir. Uh, I mean, I don't want him gettin'
you in a ugly mood and you taking it home."

"We'll have to take the chance. Send him in."

Actually, I wasn't in any trouble at home, in spite of the "peach
cobbler rebellion." I had sat in my little office at the house, drinking and sulking and feeling sorry for myself until I judged it was
late enough that Lauren would have gone to bed and most likely
was asleep. I had made such a fool of myself that I had no wish to
face her so soon after the incident because I didn't know exactly
what to say. I'd gotten angry and I had to defend that anger as right-
eous, at least for a little time, or else admit that I was a bigger fool
than I'd acted and spoken. It was a little after eleven when I finished my last cigarillo and drink. I got up, turned the lamp out on
my desk, and then went out and started climbing the stairs. I could
see a little glow on the landing, but Lauren always left a light burning until we were both in bed.

Our bedroom door was slightly ajar. I pushed it open and
jumped slightly, not sure what I was seeing. There was a figure
wearing an ugly woolen nightgown lying on top of the covers with
her head on a pillow. She had on a poke bonnet to hide her hair,
and her face was covered with a horrendous mud pack. On her
gown front the figure was wearing a large piece of letter-sized paper
with the legend, MRS. BRIDESDALE. I started to laugh and then caught
myself and took a step toward the bed. I said, "Why, Mrs. Bridesdale, I have never seen you looking lovelier."

Then Lauren sat up and laughed and everything was all right.
Of course there was the business of her getting that mud pack
washed off and getting out of that awful gown, but after that, matters went better than a man could have hoped for. What she'd
done had humbled me and made me that much more conscious of
how lucky I was. It ain't every wife who will go get a shoehorn to
help her fool husband get his foot out of his mouth.

About then the door opened and a tall, burly man dressed in

khaki came marching into my office. He had more stripes on his sleeve than I could count at a quick look and was walking ramrod stiff, squaring his corners until he came to rest before my desk. In a kind of bark he said, "First Sergeant Rollie McMartin takin' the pleasure of your acquaintance, Cap'n Young, sir!"

He had a stiff-brimmed, round-crowned hat under his arm, being careful not to squash the brim. It was, I knew, what they called a campaign hat, one of those with little acorn-shaped leather decorations coming off the hatband. But what I noticed most was that, while he appeared to be talking to me, he was looking straight over my head at the wall behind me. I turned around to see what had captured his attention. "Sergeant McMartin, is there something on that wall has taken your fancy?" I asked.

"No, sir, Cap'n, sir!"

"Then what are you staring at it for?"

"Sir, it is not permitted to look at an officer whilst a member of the rank is standin' at attention, sir!"

I had to laugh slightly. The man had something of an Irish accent, but I had the feeling he was also pulling my leg. I said, "Sergeant McMartin, I'm not an officer. You don't have to stand at attention. And why do you keep calling me captain? I'm not a captain."

He suddenly relaxed by spreading his feet apart and clamping one arm behind his back, the other still holding his hat. He said, "Beggin' your pardon, sir, I was just after conferrin' the honorary rank on you. An' it not near high enough, sir. You should be a colonel because that is what you be after lookin' like."

I was amused. "Sergeant, is this what I've heard referred to as blarney? Are you feeding me a dose of that?"

His big, creased face took on a look of amazement. "Blarney, your honor? Me? Me as has been a serving member of the United States Army for over twenty-six years? Begging your honor's pardon, but the thought of such shenanigans would be beneath the dignity of a soldier of my rank and standing."

I chuckled. He said it all with such sincerity I could almost have believed him. Even though he was carrying a few excess pounds he still looked like a man you would not want to cross lightly. I guessed his age at about ten less than mine, though it was hard to tell from the wear and tear his face had suffered from the weather and other elements. His nose had clearly been broken more than once and there was the trace of a scar along the underside of his left jaw. I said, "Well, Sergeant, what can I do for you?"

"Ah, Your Honor, and now that is the question, isn't it? And a man like yourself, important and busy as Your Honor is, would be for getting right to it. Yes, sir, you would have had a fine career in the army and no mistake. Ah, what an officer you would have made, sir."

"You're not going to tell me what you want?"

He took his arm out from behind his back and took a swipe at his mouth with his sleeve. "Well, Your Honor, I'm sure it must be some sort of mistake. And them do get made, even in the best of organizations. But it seems there's a rumor afloat that you won't be serving soldiers in your fine emporium."

I nodded. "It's not a rumor, Sergeant. I assume you are from Camp Verde. I had heard it had been reactivated. I gave my manager orders that soldiers were not allowed in. That answer your question?"

He had taken a faltering step backward at my words, shock, real or imaginary, all over his big, hammy face. He put a big hand up to his brow and blinked rapidly. "Sure and it is not what I'm hearing! To not make the nation's finest welcome! Your Honor, sir, I'm that surprised I stand without a word coming to my mouth."

"I bet it's been a long time since that happened."

"Sir, a first sergeant can never be at loss for words. It's his duty to them as is under him who, as a group, are not much smarter than the mules they drive. But the words of Your Honor have knocked me over as if I'd been smashed with a wagon tongue."

"I take it you want to know the reasons."

He shook himself. "Aye, I would that, sir. It has come as such a bolt from the blue I'm still trying to get the feel of the ground beneath my feet."

I was curious about the man. It had occurred to me that I'd been thinking of robbing a shipment of gold guarded by soldiers and I didn't know a thing about the military. I decided I might learn something from Sergeant McMartin. I said, "But first tell me why you want to come in my place." I waved my hand toward the street. "This is the border. There's no shortage of whiskey. There's a dozen places up and down the street will give you a drink at a reasonable price. The whiskey might be a little new, but it will have the same effect."

"Aye, and that is true, Cap'n. But I've asked a dozen men on that same street and they've all said that the place to get a square drink for a square price is your fine establishment. And I say that without fear of bein' accused of layin' on the blarney."

I laughed and shook my head.

"But there's another reason, Your Honor, that is more to the question," he went on. "You see, Your Honor, when a soldier gets in a little brannigan in town he's first going to get punished by the townsfolk. As is right and just. I'm not complainin'. But then he's got to go back to his post and face his commanding officer and that, Your Honor, is a rub of the green, if you take my meaning."

"Bad, huh?"

"Sir, if it be one thing the army does not care for, it is to have their soldiers get in bad in the town. Makes a ferocious commotion all around." He stopped and wiped his mouth with his sleeve again. "It is said that no shenanigans are allowed in your fine establishment, Cap'n. It's said a man is out the door before he can get into trouble."

I nodded. "That is true. We sell whiskey, not trouble. I got three men out here on salary whose job it is to see that everyone has a good time and lets his neighbor have a good time. They know their job."

"Aye, Cap'n, and that be my very point. I'm a drinkin' man. I'll admit to it."

I thought the remark was a little unnecessary since I could see the veins in his nose from where I was sitting. I said, "So you want a place you can get a fair drink for a fair price and not end up in trouble. Is that about it, Sergeant McMartin?"

"Aye, Your Honor, that would be meat of the nut. Yes, sir."

"Sergeant, how much does a soldier earn?" I asked.

He blinked. "A soldier? What kind o' soldier? They comes in all outfits and sizes and ranks. What would be the rank you are talking of, sir?"

Hell, I didn't know anything about ranks. "What's the lowest?" I asked.

"That would be your private, sir. Nothing much lower than a private. Maybe a goat."

"All right, what does a private earn?"

"Fourteen dollars a month and all the swill he can eat and what little sleep I let them have."

"That's your answer. I have customers who easily spend that much in a night. I can't have my saloon cluttered up with men finding out they can't afford to be here." I didn't want to tell him I blamed the army for what was happening in the country. At least partly.

He looked shocked. "Oh, my sweet heaven, Your Honor! I never meant for no *privates* to be crossing the threshold of your fine establishment! Lord save us. I'd throw them out myselves. Sir, all the privates will be in training. They are just starting to arrive. They be raw recruits. I am part of the advance guard getting the old camp shaped up and I'll be in charge of the training of these wee boyos we've got to turn into soldiers." He shook himself again as if to rid himself of a bad thought. "Privates? No, sir!"

"All right, privates are out. What's next?"

"Corporals. But they couldn't afford this place either, no reflection on your prices, sir. But we wouldn't be after having such slumgullion as corporals and buck sergeants frequenting such a fine establishment."

I leaned back in my chair. "Who does that leave us with then, Sergeant? Who are you trying to get in?"

He gave me a big innocent look. "Why, top sergeants and the first sergeant himself, being myself, and the officers."

"Who? Officers?"

"What's an officer? Is that the question, Cap'n?"

"Yes."

He thought a moment. "Well, sir, they is all kinds. The lowest form of the breed is a second lieutenant, but they hardly count. Then you've got your first lieutenant and then—"

I put up a hand. "Sergeant, this is going to take more time than I thought. Get that chair and pull it up next to my desk." I pulled open a drawer and took out a bottle of twenty-year-old whiskey that was so special it didn't even have a label on it. If I was going to pump the sergeant it appeared I'd better prime the pump. I put the whiskey on my desk and then fetched two glasses and set them beside the bottle. I said, "You will take a drink, won't you?"

He rolled his eyes. "Oh, I knowed you was a darlin' man the instant I clapped eyes on you."

I let him get his chair pulled up and then I poured us each a full tumbler and shoved his over to him. He picked up the glass of amber liquid with reverence in his eyes. I watched him take the first little sip and saw his eyes take on a sort of awe.

"Aye," he said weakly, "I think I may weep."

"Now then, Sergeant McMartin," I said, "in view of a horde of soldiers about to descend on us, I'm going to appoint you my personal military adviser. Start telling me about how the army works and who the bosses are. Just all of it."

He hunched forward, hovering over his glass of select whiskey like a biddy hen over a chick. "Your Honor, if it's about the army you're wantin' to know, then Rollie McMartin is your man. Man and boy, I've served the country and never had to back up to the pay table to collect my pay."

I sat back and listened to the sergeant and poured him whiskey to keep him going. Not that he needed much prompting. Still, whether I was learning anything useful or not, it was humorous to hear his flowery language accented by his slight Irish brogue. The only time he left off talking about the army and his own career was to look at the glass in his hand and swear such nectar had never passed his lips before. I had been wrong about his age. He had joined the army when he was sixteen and with twenty-six years in was forty-two. I guessed that hard living and hard responsibility had aged his face. Or maybe it was his taste for whiskey.

I had not started out to quiz him with any particular idea in mind. I had just thought that it might be useful for me to understand something about the army and soldiers if I was planning on sticking up twenty-one of them and relieving them of a quarter of a million in gold. But as the sergeant talked, the small kernel of an idea began to form. It had no shape or thrust, but it was a vague thought that would not entirely go away.

I came clear on one fact. There were officers and then those in the ranks. But of those in the ranks the most exalted was the first sergeant, or top sergeant, as McMartin sometimes referred to himself. He said, with a certain delicacy, "You see, Your Honor, these officers dreams up these ideas an' then it is up to the noncoms—that is a noncommissioned officer, beggin' your pardon, sir—to see that the actual plan works. Most times it takes a good-sized boot to get the job done, and I reckon the Lord blessed me in that department. We've got near a thousand raw recruits comin' in first of the week and by the time they leave most of 'em will have their butt—pardon me, Your Honor—kicked clean up between their shoulder blades. But that's the way you make a soldier, sir. You got to break him down 'fore you can build him up."

It startled me, the number of troops that were coming to Camp Verde. I said as much. Sergeant McMartin shrugged. "Ah, sir, we're a small part of the Trainin' Command, that bein' what we are called. The big camps like Fort Bliss in El Paso and Fort Polk in Louisiana and Fort Davis out west, they'll be getting a hundred times the men. We're to train teamsters, but first we have to teach them how to soldier."

"Why such rough country?"

He finished his drink, looking longingly in the empty bottom, and said, "Ah, sir, you'll not be thinking that battles is fought on a village green, now, would you? You trains 'em hard in hard country."

I looked at him a long moment, thinking. Here was a man who could very easily have an opinion about what was going to happen. "Sergeant, is there going to be a war? I know there's already a war, but are we going to get in it?"

HE LOOKED at his empty glass again. I took the hint and reached over and poured it full. Relief flooded his face. "Ah, Your Honor, you're a darlin' man and no mistake." Then he knocked off half that smooth whiskey in a gulp before he set the glass down and wiped his mouth with his sleeve. He thought a second. "Are we after getting into that European war. Weeell, if the officers were here they would not answer you and would not let me answer you." He looked away. "Of course, I'd hope not for the sake of the green lads, though war is the only way for an old soldier such as myself to get a promotion. But us in the war? Well, Cap'n, I'll leave it to your good sense. We've got three months to train two hundred thousand men because another two hundred thousand will be coming in right behind them. And Black Jack Pershing is down in Mexico practicing with his trucks and his automobiles and his aeroplanes in rough country. Either we are going to war or we are going to have a large force of young men who ain't trained for much else. Maybe to rob banks." He took a delicate sip of his drink. "Not that I could be sayin', you understand, Your Honor. Among the ranks I'm the top kick, but officers make the statements for publication, beggin' your pardon, Your Honor."

I let him talk on while the idea I was playing with continued to grow. Finally I said, "Sergeant, if there was a, say, twenty-one–man detachment guarding something, supplies say, or ammunition . . . "

"Detail, sir," he said.

"What?"

" 'Twould be a detail you'd have guarding or escorting your provender, whatever it might be. A detachment is a force you sever from your main body of menand send off on detached duty."

I was getting quite an education in military lingo and, if the idea that was forming continued to grow, I would need it. I said, "All right, a detail. Who would command something like that? Would it be a sergeant? Or an officer?"

"Beggin' your pardon, Your Honor, but twenty-one men is near a platoon. You'd be after needing a platoon leader and that would have to be an officer. A lieutenant."

I was learning. "First or second?"

"Ahh," he said, "now that would depend on how important your provender was. If it was the colonel's whiskey it might even be a captain. If it was mule feed it would be a second looie. Second lieutenant."

I narrowed my eyes. "Say it was the payroll."

He glanced up at me. "Beggin' your pardon, Your Honor, but we don't call it that. It's the P and A. Pay and allowances. The paymaster is usually a captain. But it's a clerk's job, Your Honor. The officer ain't really a proper officer in that he knows how to count. In civvy life like he'd be a bank teller."

"What about the soldiers with him?"

He shrugged. "Same thing, sir. Not proper soldiers. Only proper job for a soldier is with a rifle in his hands and an enemy in front of him. Nobody is going to be fool enough to rob a pay shipment. They'd have the whole of the United States after them. Naw, Your Honor, they may carry rifles, but they be clerks. Soft and lazy. I'd like a crack at a few of them. I'd turn them into proper soldiers soon enough."

But I was bothered by the numbers that were going to be at Camp Verde only some seven miles north of town. "Sergeant, am I to understand that there will be something like a thousand soldiers flooding into this town?"

He gave me a little smile. "Lord bless you, sir, no. We've got a thousand recruits coming in for training but the only part of this country they'll see is the parade ground and the forced marches over the rough country and what other such little pleasures as the permanent party can devise for them."

"What is the permanent party?"

"Sir, that would be your camp commander, a lieutenant colonel, and his officers, and then the noncoms such as myself and them under me. Then there is the cooks and the medical staff and the Quartermaster Corps. All told there is no more than a hundred of us, if that. No, sir, you needn't fret yourself about the recruits coming into town. All they'll be looking for at the end of the day is a bed."

I eyed him a moment. "Sergeant, there is something that bothers me. You say you want to come into my saloon for a fair drink at a fair price and because you can't get into trouble here. Those aren't good enough reasons. What's the real one?" I leaned forward on my desk so as to bring us closer together.

He ducked his head down, and for a moment I thought this big, rough-looking man wasn't going to answer me. Finally he looked up. "Your Honor, my family come to this country when I was but a bairn. Two years old, maybe. My old dad went down in the coal mines in West Virginia. He always told me, 'Son, to be quality, you've got to get near it so some will rub off.' With no education to speak of, the army was my only hope. Of course, there was no chance for me to be an officer, but I done my best to be around the swells as much as I could. Your establishment is quality. It would be a blessing of my life if I was allowed to come in here and drink with them as is from whole cloth." He held up his glass. "Your Honor, do you know when I last had whiskey that tasted like this? *Never* would be your answer. Ain't had nothing like it since I was weaned from mother's milk."

I was still contemplating him. "You asked some questions around town. Do you know who I am?"

He was a second in answering. I think he knew what I meant by the question but he wasn't sure what the right answer would be. Finally he said cautiously, "Seems as if I heard, one place or another, that Your Honor was considered the sort of man you did not get careless with." Then he hastily added, "I mean that in the fairest sense of the word, Cap'n. I'm sure when you came out here this frontier was a place fit only for a man as could handle himself. Aye, all the remarks I heard referring to yourself was said with the finest praise for your skill with the sidearm. Most said yourself was a man would walk away from a fight."

I wanted to laugh. He was being so careful. I said, "I also robbed banks, Sergeant. Did you hear that?"

He bobbed his head energetically. "Aye, that I did. And 'tis said you done a fine, brisk business at it. Many's the time I'd have done the same, broke and all, if I'd had the nerve."

Now I had to laugh. Then I shook my head. "Sergeant, I might well have need to talk some other matters over with you. Would you like to make some money?"

A sadness came over his face. "Aye, Cap'n, that's the second time I've had such a question put directly to me. The last time I said no and joined the army. I'll not be making that mistake again. What can I be doing for you?"

"I don't know yet," I said. "Mostly talk, I'd think. But you'd be paid well. How do I get in touch with you?"

He tilted his head and brought his palm up and blew an imaginary bit of fluff off it. "Just whisper the name of Rollie McMartin on a northbound breeze and I'll be at your side before you can turn around."

"What about your duties at the camp?"

He smiled. "Ah, Cap'n, that's about the only reward an old soldier gets. I'm the first sergeant. I'm the one makes out the passes. The only difficulty is when the officers are getting up to something. I'm obliged to be there to untangle the mess."

I nodded. "Well, for the time being, Sergeant, will you call that bartender who brought you in here? His name is Bob."

He was instantly on his feet and at the door before I could blink. For a big man he moved uncommonly fast.

Bob came in with the sergeant hanging back. I said, "Bob, until further notice the sergeant is allowed in. And his drinks are on the house." Then I pointed my finger at Sergeant McMartin. "That applies to you and you alone, Sergeant. Don't be bringing any of your buddies in here."

He looked like he was about to weep. "The saints preserve us, sir. Sure and I never thought I'd see the day when Rollie McMartin would be the guest of an elegant establishment like this." He gazed ceilingward. "It's my mother's dream come true."

I stared at him. "Your mother dreamed you'd get free drinks in a saloon?"

He gave a little laugh. "Ah, bless you, Your Honor. My mother dreamed I'd someday hobnob with the swells and the quality. And now it has come true."

I could only shake my head. It was amazing to me what little it took to make some people happy. "Well, you go along now, Sergeant, and I'll be getting in touch with you."

He gave me a snappy salute and marched out. Bob looked at me questioningly. Free drinks in my saloon was a long way from being a habit.

I walked home just before lunch, deep in thought. I had set myself quite a task—that is, if I intended on actually going through with the robbery. The remark I had made to Justa about playing a lone hand had not been careless or insincere. If I actually engaged myself to steal that gold I was not going to involve anyone else. One fool on a job like that was enough. But the most compelling reason it had to be done single-handedly was that I wanted to be sure I could control any shooting. A single spark in that crowded space could cause a bloodbath, and I damn sure didn't want that to be my legacy and, most likely, my eulogy.

The thought that had popped randomly into my head as I'd been talking with Sergeant McMartin was continuing to grow and grow. It had great possibilities, but it also had a number of drawbacks, chiefly my ignorance of the military and their methods and customs.

Lauren noticed my pensive mood at lunch. "What bank are you robbing now?" she asked.

I reckon I jumped about a foot and almost dropped my fork. We were having breaded veal cutlets and french-fried potatoes and I had been sort of pushing the food around with my fork. "Bank!" I said. "What bank? What bank are you talking about?"

I must have looked guilty as hell because her half-smile turned to a frown. "Wilson, what have you been up to? You look like a cat scheming to get at the canary."

I shook my head violently. "Not me. I was thinking about horse racing. Thinking about writing Warner about that mare I've got that will be coming in season, seeing about shipping her up to him to breed to one of his studs."

She gave me a careful looking over. "That is quite a lot of explanation for someone so innocent."

"Damnit!" I said. "You—"

"Don't swear in the house, dear."

"I was cussing. You— What was I going to say? Oh, yeah. You got more damn ways to get me turned around and confused than any ten people I've ever known. No wonder I act guilty. The way you are always ready to pounce, I damn well feel guilty ninety-nine percent of the time."

"I want to ask you something."

My heart tightened up like a green persimmon. I felt like she was looking in my soul. Warily I said, "What?"

"It's personal and it's really none of my business."

I was still wary. "What? Don't keep me hanging. You got no idea of what I'm imagining right now."

She bit at her lower lip in a way she had. Laura had told me she'd done it ever since she was a little girl. Finally she said, "Will . . ." She cleared her throat. "Will, did you— Oh, this is not a very Christian thing to ask."

"Ask, damnit! Ask! What?" By now I was certain Nora Williams had somehow contacted her or I'd talked in my sleep or something.

"All right, I will, then." She looked me square in the eye. "Will, did you know very many women before you met me?"

I stared at her, dumbfounded. In twenty-one years of married life she'd never before asked me about my previous love life, if it could be called that. I blinked and looked away. The question looked and felt like a lit stick of dynamite to me. I said, stalling, "Now why in hell would you suddenly ask a question like that at this time?"

"I have my reasons. It's a simple enough question. Straightforward."

"It's about as straightforward as a shotgun blast and about as simple as a rabbit trail. I can't for the life of me understand why, out of the blue, you'd up and ask me such a thing."

She touched her napkin to her mouth, her jaw set. "All right, I'll give you an explanation. For the last ten days or two weeks you have been acting very strange. No. I shouldn't say that. You have been acting differently than you normally do. But ever since you got back from San Antonio you've gone around like a man who is missing a piece of the puzzle. You've been distracted. Your mind wanders. Your eyes even wander. I have thought and thought what could be taking up so much of your mind and I can't think of anything within the ordinary. I know your business is good because you say it is and because I see the books from time to time. You have insisted that your lawyer, Mr. Bixby, keep me abreast of matters. Our lives appear to be running smoothly. You haven't drunk any more than usual; you don't seem worried about your racehorses." She gave me a frank look. "That left me only one area to be concerned about."

I tell you I was afraid she could hear my heart beating from where she was sitting, I was that scared. I didn't know how she knew about my plans for the gold, especially since I wasn't sure of them myself, but it was plain she knew. The only question was how I was going to settle her down before one hell of a row got started. I reckoned she'd asked me about the number of women I'd known before her by way of saying I'd better get ready to go hunt some of them up if I intended what she thought I intended. I decided to put a bold front on it. If she was going to get an admission out of me it wasn't going to be done by sleight of hand, though that was one of her ways. She'd have made a hell of a boxer. She'd give you a feint in this direction and, when you rushed to cover that flank, too late you'd realize you'd left your front wide open. That was what all this business about previous women was about.

I said flatly, "So you think I've been acting strange, different, and you've got it narrowed down to one area. And just what would that be?"

She put her hands on the table, one near mine. Still a little hesitantly, she said, "Dear, please don't take this the wrong way. I've talked to some of the other ladies and they say it is perfectly natural in a man."

I stared at her. What in the hell was she talking about? She'd been talking to other ladies about robbing gold bullion? And the other ladies said it was perfectly natural? Hell, she had me so confused I didn't know if my lunch was on the table or on the ceiling. I said, "Would you try a little harder to explain what in hell you are getting at? Damnit!"

"Don't swear in the house, dear."

"I was cussing. What are you talking about?"

"I know you've been a worldly man, Wilson. I knew that before I married you and I accepted it. The past was the past." She hesitated for a second and then went on. "And I also know that you are a man of principle and character, that you are loyal and faithful and true to your code." She paused again and then blurted, "So I never, not even for a second, thought of you, well, you know, stepping out, as they say."

All I could do was stare at her. My heart rate was slowing slightly, but I was still at sixes and sevens.

"We've been married twenty-one years," she said, "and you've reached an age. The other ladies say a man gets restless about that time. That he, oh, wants to prove he's still cock of the walk or something like that."

A dim light was beginning to dawn. I said, "Are you fixing to tell me I've been distracted because I'm going to be fifty-eight and I'm afraid I ain't as attractive to the girls as I once was?"

She looked embarrassed and fiddled with her napkin. "Weeell, something like that. You've always been such a virile man I could see how you might . . . might . . . oh, say, give it one more fling."

"Just for the hell of it?"

She shrugged. "I guess you could put it that way."

I was so relieved she hadn't found me out that I could have sighed. But I didn't. Here was a brand-new game and one that looked like it might be a lot of fun. "I see. Well, let me ask you this: Have you brought the subject up by way of giving me your permission? Because if you have, I think you're being damn fair about the whole matter."

She looked slightly shocked. "Am I right? Is that it? Has it gone that far?"

I lounged back in my chair and said comfortably, "Oh, much farther than you'd think. I got to tell you the whole affair—excuse that word—has had me worried sick. All this sneaking around. And now the way you're taking it."

Her eyes got little sparks in them. "I guess I'm a little slow, Wilson Young. The trip to San Antonio. What'd you do there? Then you have to go see Justa Williams on business. What business? The only thing you told me about the trip was that Nora was getting a commercial electric refrigerator. And you always talk over your business deals with me. Always." She folded her arms under her bosom. "Except I guess this was one piece of business you couldn't very well discuss with your wife!"

"Hold on, now. What is this? A minute ago you were being all nice and understanding. Said the ladies you'd talked to said it was perfectly natural. Now you are getting het up. You have got me in a storm that is fixing to turn into a bad stretch of weather the way you're acting. I thought you were going to be all mature and understanding."

"I *am* being understanding. And mature. Though I doubt you know the meaning of the word. Has she got a name?"

I gave her an innocent look. "Who?"

"Who!" She glared at me. She really was getting heated up. "Who, hell!"

"Don't swear in the house, dear."

"Don't try and be cute, Wilson. It ill becomes you. I asked you if this floozy had a name."

"Floozy? Why does she automatically have to be a floozy?"

"Because you are a married man," she said stiffly. "And nobody but a floozy would fool around with such."

"There you go, judging somebody. What has happened to your Christianity? I thought you wasn't supposed to judge folks."

She gave me a cool look. "Let's leave my faith out of it. I believe we are talking about some woman you are trying to relive your youth with."

I started laughing. I couldn't help myself. In twenty-one years, I reckon I'd seen Lauren lose her composure maybe half a dozen times. Oh, she had a temper, no mistake, but then she just got angry. Now she was angry and flustered and trying not to show either one and doing a damn bad job of it.

She said stiffly, "This may strike you as funny, but I can assure you I am not amused in the least. I thought you, of all men, would be different, Wilson. I am very disappointed to finally find out that I'm married to just an ordinary man."

That stung a little and I damn near flashed back at her. But I said, "Well, Lauren, ordinary or not, a man is a lot like a horse. They will graze where the grass is greenest. If they crop it all down in one part of a pasture they'll move on to the next patch. Maybe it's ordinary but it sure is natural."

Her eyes clouded over a little and I saw I'd gone too far. I'd hurt her, and that was the last thing I wanted. "I see," she said. "So now I'm barren pasture, is that it? You've moved on to greener grass. I guess younger grass."

I could see that I had let the misunderstanding go too far, mainly, I reckoned, out of relief that she wasn't after me about what I had feared she was on to, but also because the subject was such an odd one for me and Lauren to be discussing. She didn't cry very often, but I could see she was getting close to it. She was also shrinking into herself in a way that looked an awful lot like hurt and disappointment. I reached across the corner of the table and took her hand that was lying on the tablecloth. She didn't respond. Gently I said, "Lauren, this is all just silliness. There ain't no other woman in my life and never has been since you accepted me. I'd shoot my best horse before I'd cheat on you. Don't you know that?"

She looked at me uncertainly, awkwardly, like a horse caught in the middle of a gait change. With the slightest tremble in her voice she said, "Are you saying there's not someone else?"

I had been right; there was a small well of tears in her eyes. I squeezed her hand. "Of course there's nobody else. Are you crazy? Woman, I got the best. What in hell would I want to be fooling around and run the risk of losing you for? *I* ain't crazy, at least not that crazy."

Her voice was still a little tremulous. "But other ladies say that their husbands get a roving eye when they get up to, when they reach an age that . . . that . . . Oh, I don't understand it."

"I don't know about other husbands. I only know about this one. And I ain't worried about my age since I turned sixteen. It's you that keeps bringing it up, you and Justa Williams. Hell, I don't feel like I got anything to prove because I've passed the midpoint. You got hold of one crazy idea, Lauren. And I am surprised at you."

Her eyes were searching my face. "Have I been imagining that you've been distracted and thoughtful? Withdrawn, like you get when you've got something important on your mind?"

The question naturally made me uncomfortable as hell. I didn't at that moment want to lie to her, but I sure as hell wasn't ready to get into that particular subject. Choosing my words, I said, "No, no, you haven't been wrong. I have had something important on my mind. And it doesn't have anything to do with my age, either."

"Well, what is it?"

I cleared my throat and looked away. "Lauren, right now it is not well thought out. It has still got some gaps and holes to plug. Fact of the matter is, I ain't even got the frame of the idea built yet. So, if you don't mind being patient for a time, I'd as soon not get into it right now."

Her face had cleared and the teary look had been replaced with a gimlet eye. "Is this something I am not going to like, Wilson?"

I gave her as innocent a look as I was capable of at that moment. "Now, how in hell am I supposed to answer that?"

"I think we understand each other well enough on that score. For instance, when you tried to sneak the purchase of those Mexican dancing girls by me."

"Oh, hell," I said in disgust, "that was a cabaret act. You make it sound like I was going into the slave trade. I was going to underwrite this show act that was going to play down in South America. I would have probably made a wad on the transaction, too. Buy dancing girls! My sakes alive!"

"All right. Fair enough. But do you remember when you and a couple of your drunken friends were going to open a bank?"

I gave her a look. "*That* was fifteen years ago. Was I to start running in the fool things you've done going that far back, I might find a few myself."

She rolled her eyes. "It might have been fifteen years ago, though it seems like it was yesterday. You all came rolling in here pied to the eyeballs and talking big and acting big. Going to start a bank for the little man. Take over one of the empty stores downtown and do some good for the town, for the little man, for the poor, for the widow, for the orphan. Did I leave anyone out?"

I grimaced. "For someone who was willing to throw me into the arms of another woman not five minutes ago you have sure got critical."

She ignored that. "I can see you three now—primarily you, though, since you were the only one that had any money. I was very sorry to spoil your fun by telling you that you needed a charter from either the state or the federal government to open a bank. Wilson, I was really surprised at you, a bank robber, not knowing that."

I picked at my lunch. "I didn't hang around banks in those days. Pretty much in and out in a hurry." It was making me uncomfortable, her talking about bank robbery.

"I wish you would tell me what's on your mind."

I took a bite of tomato. "I'm not ready to tell you."

"Is it something you are going to be ashamed of?"

I gave her a look. "I never done anything in my life I was ashamed of. I damn sure ain't never *planned* anything in advance I was going to be ashamed of. Man that does that is a damn fool. Man that does that don't think much of himself."

"Then why won't you tell me?"

I put my fork down. "Because it ain't all thought out yet, Lauren. Like I just now told you. Besides, I haven't made up my mind if I'm going to do it. There is a considerable amount of detail to this proposition and I ain't looked into it deep enough yet."

"I'm not going to like it, am I?"

I gave a sigh. "Hell, Lauren, I don't know. It might well raise some money for your charities."

She perked up. "Really? How?"

I shook my head. "I said *might*. This whole matter is a long shot."

That diamond-hard look came back in her eye. "Is it dangerous?"

I got a toothpick out of my shirt pocket and began rolling it around in my mouth. "Far as I know it can be dangerous getting up in the morning. It can be dangerous crossing the street. Eating something out of a can. Didn't I read in the paper where somebody died from a can of tomatoes?"

She grimaced. "That was from botulism. That's one chance in a million."

"That's my point. Before I can tell you if it is dangerous or not, I got to know what you think is dangerous. Right now I think eating canned tomatoes is dangerous. You don't. You think carrying a gun is dangerous. I don't."

She said sternly, "Wilson, you are trying to get around me. Don't think you are fooling me one little bit. You are trying to change the subject."

I gave her an innocent look. "Is that dangerous?"

But try to make light of the moment as I would, I knew the cat was out of the bag. Lauren now knew something was up and she would scheme and wheel and deal and wheedle and squirm until she got it out of me. I didn't know if women got into as much trouble as cats did with their curiosity but I knew they were no less energetic. I knew I was going to have to tell her eventually; even if I decided against the plan I would have to tell her what had been on my mind. But if I did decide to go through with it I was going to have to pick my moment and my setting very, very carefully, because I knew she wasn't going to like it one little bit.

I was also getting worried about the time element. The gold display did not stay at each bank for a set time. They seemed to vary it according to the size of the place and the kind of interest they were getting. The best I could figure, I had somewhere around three weeks to make my decision and make my plan and have all the factors in order. It wasn't a hell of a lot of time, especially for such a tall order of business.

To sort of slide out of the whole discussion before Lauren could get to brooding further about something she considered her business, I said, "Let's go back here a minute to what kicked off this little jamboree."

She put her napkin on the table and picked up her glass of iced tea. With it poised in the air she said, "Oh? And what would that be?"

I lounged back in my chair. "Well, it would seem to me that if a wife was starting to wonder about her husband maybe stepping around, she must have had some little feelings that maybe she wasn't doing her job as well as she might."

She wrinkled her brow. "What job? Doing what job? Or not doing what job as well as I might?"

I lifted my eyes, indicating the upstairs. "You know what job. Don't come the innocent on me."

She blushed ever so slightly. "I'm sure I do not know what you are talking about." She took a quick drink of iced tea to cover her fluster.

I leaned toward her. "Fucking, Lauren, if you want me to be plain-spoke about it."

Now she really did blush. Her mouth fell open and she said sharply, "Wilson Young, what kind of a way is that to talk!"

"You say it," I reminded her calmly.

She was still blushing. "Yes, but that's . . . that's . . . "

"That's what? You ain't denying you utter the word from time to time, are you?"

She was still blushing. "No, but that's, that's—"

"In the bedroom?"

She gave me an exasperated look. "You know what I mean very well, Wilson Young. You are just being mean, drawing this out."

"Well, when do you say it?"

She slammed her glass down. "At the appropriate time! There, are you satisfied? You are the meanest man in the world, Wilson Young."

I was enjoying myself immensely. It was not often that I could get my very cool and composed lady of a wife off in a hurricane. I said, "You mean you say 'fuck' when we are fucking. Is that it?"

She got up. "I am not going to stay here and be hectored like this for a moment more. You can just get your own dessert."

I said to her back, "I'd like some pudding. If I go up to the bedroom will you serve it to me?"

She was marching regally out of the room, but she said over her shoulder in a stiff voice, "You'll be lucky if I ever let you *in* the bedroom again."

I called after her, "Now, it is just that kind of attitude and behavior that drives men into the arms of other women! Don't say you ain't been warned."

She just kept going, her head up, her carriage erect, unwilling to be sullied by such as me. Well, at least it would be a spell before she got to wondering again about what I had on my mind. I tell you, she was one tough lady. You had to stay on your toes around her.

CHAPTER

7

LATER ON that afternoon I was in my saloon, sitting out front for a change, enjoying my own hospitality. Naturally, though, I had a bottle of my own special stock sitting on the table. It was a slow time of day, about three o'clock. Most of the afternoon drinkers had already had their pumps primed and were probably at home, resting up, getting ready to beat hell out of demon rum that night. The evening crowd would start coming in a little after six, so for the time being it was just me and a few die-hards trying to convince their stomachs they hadn't had enough. I was sitting against the far wall from the bar and about halfway down the length of the saloon. I no longer felt the need to sit with my back against a wall; it was just a hard habit to break.

I was giving the place a good looking over, checking for wear and tear and seeing where I might give the joint a little more tone. The saloon was fashioned after a first-class New Orleans bar and saloon rather than the ordinary Texas joint. For instance, there wasn't any sawdust on the floor. It would have looked a little out of place on top of the carpeting. On the walls we had some good, tasteful paintings, including the one we had behind the bar that was painted on a mirror. The reason I knew the paintings were tasteful was that Lauren had picked them out and she'd told me so. The painting behind the bar was of an attractive young lady reclining on a velvet divan and covering herself at strategic points with the aid of a filmy scarf. The mirror was eight feet long, so the young lady in the picture could be said to be life-sized. Lauren thought it was scandalous but I'd heard many a toast drunk to the lady and many a boast made as to what the speaker would do to her if she'd only come to life.

As far as I knew, mine was the only saloon short of Dallas or Houston that featured upholstered chairs and ornate tables. Of course, there was no poker-playing. If somebody wanted to gamble they could go right next door to my casino.

The front door was two big double doors with an oval glass panel in each. That was so the drunks coming in could see the drunks going out and they wouldn't collide with each other and harm my business. As I looked at the doors I was surprised to see Sergeant McMartin come in. I didn't know if he'd seen me or not, but he paused to study the room, as any prudent man would, and ended up with his eyes on me. I raised my glass to him and he came marching over, removing his campaign hat as he did.

I said, "Well, hello, Sergeant. Back so soon?"

He nodded vigorously. "Yes, sir. I am a man has a hard time getting enough of a good thing. Would I be disturbing Your Honor?"

"No, no. Just having a quiet drink." I motioned with my head. "Sit down and have one with me." As he pulled out a chair I signaled to my bartender to bring over another glass.

When we both had a drink and he'd sipped at his, rolling his eyes appreciatively, I said, "Well, Sergeant, working for the army must be a pretty easy job if you can take off of an afternoon and head for a drink and a little shade."

He gave me a wink. "Ah, Your Honor, that only comes with being a first sergeant. Like I told you, I'm the one makes out the passes. And I'm the one makes out the duty roster. Outside of the commanding officer, Colonel White, I got the run of the place. Course, some officers try and lord it over me, time to time, but they soon learn."

Frowning slightly, I said, "You know, you got me all akimbo with this sergeant and first sergeant business. How many ranks are there?"

He smiled. "I'll be explaining it if you like, Cap'n. You see I have six stripes on my sleeve, three down and three up, the bottom three being called rockers. Now, if that was all there was I'd be a master sergeant. But that little diamond in the middle, between the stripes, that makes me a first sergeant."

"What's down from there?"

"All right. After master, you got your staff, that's five stripes, then your tech, that's four. Then your buck, which is three. After that comes the corporal with two."

"And one is a private, right?"

He shook his head. "No, Cap'n, that would be your private first-class. A plain private is a slick sleeve. No stripes at all. Lowest thing on the face of the earth. And we got a thousand of them pouring in out at the camp." He gave me a keen look. "Begging Your Honor's pardon, but would you just be a gentleman who likes to know about everything or are you asking after this army business for a reason?"

I shook my head slowly. "No, no special reason."

"Because if there be something special you was wanting or wanting to know, Rollie McMartin is your man."

I was about to shake my head but I noticed he'd taken a silver dollar out of his pocket and was walking it across the back of his fingers. It was an old cardplayer's practice, a way to keep the fingers supple. A thought struck me. "Tell me, Sergeant, how do you get paid in the army?"

"Oh, in cash, Your Honor. The men wouldn't be caring very much for a bank check."

"What kind of cash? Do you get paid in hard currency or specie, paper money?"

He chuckled. "Aye, it's clear Your Honor hasn't had much to do with soldiering. No, it's the gold and silver we draws come payday. A soldier walks into a bar and drops money on the bartop, the bartender wants to hear it ring. Paper money don't make enough noise to suit him. Of course, it ain't that way all about. But your camps way out of the way, the civilian folk don't take too kindly to money that crinkles. They're afraid of it. Don't believe it's the real thing. No, you want the stuff in your pocket that jingles so they know you got it and is prompt with the serving of you."

I sat back in my chair and looked up at the ceiling, remembering. "I think I once had something to do with an army payroll," I said. "In my career as a bank robber the biggest haul we ever made was in a little bank in El Paso. Took forty thousand out of there, mostly in gold and silver. We like to have foundered our horses carting it away."

The sergeant nodded. "Aye, sir. Fort Bliss. I reckon you took the cash was all set for the paymaster's table."

"I ought to be ashamed of myself, but I was a pretty wild kid. Hell of a thing to do to a bunch of men in the army. Take their pay out of their hands."

Sergeant McMartin shrugged. "Oh, I wouldn't be giving that no thought, Your Honor. Likely the paymaster went around to another bank or banks with a government chit and drawed what he needed."

"It's just funny thinking back on those days. Been twenty-five or thirty years since the governor pardoned me and I went out of business. But it still seems like yesterday." I picked up my glass and took a sip. "Hardly a thing for a respectable citizen to be telling to one of the army's heroes."

"Ah, Cap'n, it's a rare treat to hear such a story. I reckon you'd be the first bank robber I ever run into. I reckon you know they tell some very interesting stories about you and your ways."

I shrugged. "Folks got nothing better to talk about. I'm lucky I'm not sitting in a prison cell. It's nothing to be proud of."

The sergeant squinched up his face. "Well, now, sir, I don't be knowing that I agree with the whole of that. Back in Ireland in the earlier days we had highwaymen and they was romantic figures. Yes, sir. Romantic figures. Many a lass would swoon at the mention of Black Billy, the prince of the road. When he held up a coach he used to rob all the men and kiss all the ladies. Strikes me, sir, you was doing the same mischief, only you didn't take the luck of the draw but went to where you knew they kept the real stuff."

I smiled a little. Something he had said had reminded me of Les. Les had tried that highway routine on me, trying to make it seem as if we weren't doing any wrong. "I had a friend—" I stopped.

"Yes, sir? You was saying?"

"Oh, nothing much. We were wild kids, me and my partner. Not one of us twenty-one and we'd already robbed twenty or twenty-five banks. I remember one time he let out a big shout and said how it was too bad what we were doing was illegal because it was so damn much fun." I stopped and looked down at my drink. Of course, that had been in the early days. After a while it hadn't been so much fun, but there didn't seem to be any way to stop.

One night me and Les was sitting up at a cold camp, about one jump ahead of a chase party and taking what nourishment we could from the moonlight. The rest of the bunch were trying to snatch a little sleep. Les had said, in that slow way of his, "Will, we ain't robbing Yankees and carpetbaggers and scalawags anymore. We're just robbing."

And he was right. Ten years had passed and Reconstruction had been over for a couple of years. I'd said, "I know, Les. But what the hell do we do? How does a man get off the owlhoot trail once he's got both feet on it?"

"I don't know," he'd said. For a lighthearted man he could sound dead serious sometimes. "I flat don't know. But if we don't figure out a way it's going to end bad. I got that feeling."

I shook my head hard, trying to shake the memory.

Sergeant McMartin said, "Something wrong, Cap'n?"

I looked up and smiled slightly. "No, guess I was rattling my brain around trying to get it up and moving."

He looked around the saloon. "A gent that's got an establishment this fine sure ain't short in the thinking department. I tell you, Your Honor, this is a real treat, real plush. Last time I was in such a place was in Chicago at the Palmer House. I could have stayed in their bar the rest of my hitch in the army." He leaned forward. "By the by, Your Honor, I'm after hearing you got a son already in the fighting. They say he's an aviator. They say he's in France."

I said matter-of-factly, "He's a damn fool is what he is. It's not his fight."

"Maybe he just fancies a scuffle, Your Honor. Lot of young men like that."

"Then he's more the damn fool." I looked at the sergeant. "Fighting for the sake of fighting makes about as much sense as hitting yourself in the head with a hammer."

Sergeant McMartin said softly, "Unless you be a politician or a general. Then you get the fun of it and none of the hardship and blood."

"You in favor of us going to war in Europe, Sergeant?"

He shook his head slowly. "No, Cap'n, I ain't. But maybe not for the reason you'd be thinking. I've gone as high as I can go in the enlisted ranks. And I ain't got no hankering to be an officer, so I wouldn't be after having a battlefield commission. It's been offered and refused. But if I was, say, a couple of stripes short then I'd maybe be hoping we'd get in it. War means promotion to a soldier, sir. It's a harsh thing to say, but that's the reason of it. Man can stay the same grade for years and years in peacetime, but a nice war will jump him up in a hurry."

I had to laugh. "And hell, here I was feeling embarrassed about having been a bank robber. I'm just a pint-sized villain."

The sergeant smiled. "That you are, sir, when it comes to crime on the grand scale. For that you want your presidents and your senators and your kings and potentates and what not. And of course your generals and your colonels and such. Aye, I can tell you there is many a major and colonel and brigadier general who is saying his prayers every night hoping we'll get in this brannigan so they can get some new brass."

"What about the men who own the factories, the big ones up north?"

The sergeant chuckled deep in his chest. "Aye, them. That lot is lighting so many candles it's a wonder you can see the sun for the blaze."

"I almost joined the army one time," I said casually.

McMartin looked surprised. "You, sir? Beggin' your pardon, but you seem too much of an independent turn to be takin' the orders of your inferiors."

In desperation, Les had once said, "Listen, Will, I can't take this much longer. We could turn mean, like Todd. So far we ain't killed nobody carelessly or without just cause, but we are changing. I can't abide that, Will."

I'd said, "Then tell me a way out?"

He'd chewed at his lip. "I've thought on this. Let's make our way to New Orleans and take ship for someplace else, like South America. We got money."

I'd nodded slowly. "Yeah, we got some money, but we ain't got enough to live the rest of our lives and that's what we'd have to do if we went down to one of those countries south of Mexico. Les, we ain't got no trade. We don't know nothing except robbing and stealing. How long before we'd have to go to doing that down there in that South America? Hell, we've never robbed a bank in Mexico because we always wanted to keep that place safe to flee to. Well, the same can be said for Mexico. We could cross the river and go down into the interior and there wouldn't be no law looking for us, but the money wouldn't last. Then what would we do? You know damn good and well what we'd have to do. Then they'd be after us on both sides of the river."

He'd looked unhappy. "All right, I know one place where we can hide where we'll get fed and lodged and even paid a little. Let's head out west, Arizona or New Mexico, and join the cavalry."

I had just laughed. "Oh, yeah, I got a big tintype of me and you all dressed up in a blue uniform and marching around and being told when to get up and when to go to bed and when to take a piss. Yeah, that would last about as long as it took for the sun to get up."

I said to the sergeant, "Well, no, not really. A friend of mine had the idea we could have hid out in the horse cavalry until things cooled down for us a bit. We never really give it much serious thought."

But Les had. He'd brought it up several times. I'd always advanced the same argument, that we wouldn't be able to abide it. He got killed not too long after that and I'd gone on alone, picking up gunmen as I found them. It had never been the same, though, and I had been glad when the governor had extended me the chance of a pardon.

I got a little box of cigarillos out of my shirt pocket and offered one to the sergeant. He shook his head. While I was lighting mine, I asked him if he'd ever been in a war.

"Aye," he said, "a rub of the green. That's the Irish way of saying a little good luck rubbed off on me."

I raised my eyebrows. "Good luck? War?"

He nodded. " 'Tis what I been sayin', Your Honor. War is the soldier's business as cattle are to the rancher. No cattle, no business. No war, no business for the soldier." He took a sip of his drink.

"Aye, 'tis a hard thing to be sayin', but I'll tell you the way of it. I shipped to Cuba with my outfit in July of '98. For near ten years I'd moved up from buck private, a slick sleever, to finally make PFC, private first class—if there be such a thing—with no more promotions in sight. Ten years and one stripe. Then I'm in on that bit of fighting in Cuba and I come out of it a lance corporal. Six months and another stripe. And by the way, Your Honor, for your own information that wasn't much of a war. The only troops that got bad hurt was that bunch following that rare idiot Roosevelt. They talk about the charge up San Juan Hill. Was never no charge up that hill on the horses. Too steep. His boys went up fighting on foot and took near thirty percent casualties. Was more lost in that bit of flummery than was lost in the rest of the fracas. Course, his boys weren't proper soldiers, not properly trained soldiers. They was out for a bit of a lark." He looked grim. "I reckon the man that gets killed on a lark is just as dead as any going about business."

I reached over and filled both our glasses. He was looking thoughtful.

"Aye," he said slowly, "there was a war for the politicans and businessmen. Never was a reason for that war." He looked up. "But it got me on my way."

"What was the other war?"

A smile tugged at his mouth. "Well, they weren't calling it a war. Said it was an insurrection. Your Honor will be remembering that we got the Philippine Islands from the Spanish after we whipped them down in Cuba. Turns out the Filipinos didn't want us holding the reins, so they up and insurrected." He shook his head. "It may not have been a war, but it was about the bloodiest three years I ever saw. Made that little dance in Cuba seem like a tea party." He sighed. "I come out of that with a couple of medals and a piece of iron in my hip and four stripes. One stripe in ten years of peace and three in about three years of war. Can you be seeing my point, Your Honor?"

"Oh, yes." I nodded. "And I can't gainsay you it. You are a professional soldier. War, as you say, is your business."

"It got a little warm over there in the Philippines to be calling it business. 'Twas more like a bloody bar fight. You'll be knowing about the Colt forty-five semiautomatic, will you not, Cap'n?"

"I've heard of it."

"Then you'll have heard about the Moros. Savages they were. Not like our red Indians, but regular wild men. You couldn't stop them. Pass a copper-clad Springfield cartridge right through them and they kept coming. Officers and noncoms had thirty-eights for sidearms and you could no more stop one of those natives with a little pop gun like that than stop a freight train with a bale of hay. So they come up with the forty-five semiautomatic. Has Your Honor ever used the weapon?"

"I've fired one. Ain't too long on accuracy."

He smiled. "Aye, sometimes you had better aim throwing it at the little buggers. No, you waited until he was right on top of you and then put that half a pound of lead right through him. Stopped them wild charges they was so fond of."

We both fell silent for a moment. McMartin, I figured, was remembering the wiry little unstoppable savages he'd grown fond of and I was thinking about the half-formed plan for the gold bullion that kept trying to take shape in my mind but still remained so hazy. The problem continued to be that I flat didn't know enough about the army and its ways to bluff my way through the scheme I'd come up with. But it was the only way I could think of to do the matter bloodlessly and with some expectation of coming out alive and out of prison. I couldn't imagine where the idea had come from. It had sort of popped into my head one day after I'd come back from seeing Justa and had hung around, half growed and not getting any bigger. I glanced at the man across the table from me. He had in his head all the knowledge I needed, but I didn't know of any way to get at it without putting him wise, and I didn't think that would be too healthy. He appeared to respect me, but I didn't know if that was for the free drinks or my record as a bank robber. He looked as if he'd been in and out of a few scrapes himself, and not necessarily in his uniform, either. I decided I would try a little sally to see what turned up. In the army I understood they called it sending out scouts.

"Tell me," I said, "you ever been married, Sergeant?"

He tilted his head and got a bemused look on his face. "Well, now, there be two schools of thought on that matter, hers and mine. At one time several years past I was part of an honor guard in the nation's capital. Some big to-do about Independence Day. If Your Honor will accept it I don't mind priding myself on being able to turn out as spruce as anyone as ever wore khakis. Boots shining, brass you can blind an eye with, uniform fitting as snug as a glove and pressed to the crease. Them's the kind as gets picked for the honor guard duty. And it's good duty. You march the parade and stand at attention for a few hours and you've got yourself several days' leave. And Washington is a good leave town because of all the high mucky-mucks the place is thick with. Draws all the pretty young ladies what is looking to make a connection, if you take my meaning, sir. But there's always more than enough to go around. Finally, a few gets desperate and works their way down to the sergeants. And some pretty choice bits, I might add. So, to make a long story short, which is against my Irish, I wakes up one morning after about a three-day drunk to find a young lady in my bed what has got the claim in her mouth to be my wife and the paper to prove it."

"You didn't remember marrying her?"

He shook his head sadly. "No, sir, I didn't. And more's the pity. I'd like to have been in at the celebration if I was going to be the honoree at the wake. Fact, sir, and the devil take me if it ain't true,

I had no memory of the young lady at all. Mind you, I was not after complaining about the goods. They was quality. I just wasn't after owning them."

"So what'd you do?"

He shrugged and took a healthy pull at his glass. "Slung my barracks bag over my shoulder and bid her better luck next time." He looked down. "Unfortunately, that wasn't the end of it, sir."

"No?"

He shook his head. "She took her case to the army and the judge advocate's office deemed she had proof of marriage, witnesses and all, and consummation."

I raised my head. "She had proof of *that?*"

He chuckled. "Aw, no, sir, bless you, sir. But she had enough that the army declared she was my wife and eligible for spousal allotment. At least that's what they call it." A note of bitterness crept into his voice. "I got another name for it, Your Honor. I won't be giving tongue to it out of respect for my surroundings."

I smiled. "You're the one getting fucked now."

He gave me a quick look and nodded gratefully. "Well spoken, sir. Well spoken."

"Have you tried to get a divorce?"

He grimaced. "From the first day she started taking fifty-five dollars and forty cents a month out of my pay. But getting a divorce in the army ain't the same as in civvy life. In the first place you got to file where she can get to the court. Well, that means where she is. And how you going to get time to go there and stay there long enough to make the thing happen? But the worst part was that I'd gotten married without my commanding officer's permission. Did me no good to argue I didn't ask his permission because I hadn't expected to get married. The army is a great one for letting you lie in the bed you've made."

I was astonished. "You have to get your commander's permission to get married? Like you were some kid?"

"Aye, that's the way of it. In some ways it makes sense. Soldiers, because of the life, mix in with a bad lot of women who are after that allotment. The young ones are especially sitting ducks, home-sick and can't meet a proper girl. No, no, 'twas my own fault. Actually, by the book, 'tis a court-martial offense and I could have lost a stripe or two and pay and allowances. But the old man took a gen-tle hand and I got out with a letter of reprimand in my permanent record." He paused. "And *her,* of course." He glanced over at me. "Can Your Honor be imagining what it's like to be paying out al-most half my pay to a woman I can't even remember having the taste of? But there's affidavits from witnesses and the judge who married us and the court clerk what registered the affair." He shook his head. "Your Honor, I was so sorely tested by the matter I come near swearing off the whiskey."

"How long this been going on?"

"Near four years."

"Where is she?"

"Baltimore. At least that's where my fifty-five dollars and forty cents goes every month."

"Have you tried buying her off?"

He nodded. "Aye, she'll give me a divorce, for a price."

"How much?"

"I got a little over three years to go to make my thirty years and retire. She figured it out that her allotment for that time would be a shade over twenty-two hundred dollars. She said she'd let me out for fifteen hundred, cash. But it had to be quick."

"Why don't you do it?"

He gave me a look. "Begging the cap'n's pardon, but where would I be after getting fifteen hundred dollars? She takes forty-two percent of my pay. The rest is little enough to get through the month. If you jerked me up and shook me by the heels a couple of dollars might roll out of my pockets, but not much more. And the hell of it is, Your Honor, when I retire on half-pay she'll continue to get part of that! Can you imagine such a stone around a man's neck!"

I said slowly, "How'd you like to earn that fifteen hundred? Quick?"

He looked at me uncertainly. "Aye, you wouldn't be offering a glass of water to a drowning man, would you, Your Honor?"

I took a long, slow look at him, thinking hard. If I was ever going to come out with it the time was perfect. But I couldn't quite make myself. I hedged. "I ain't talking charity here, Sergeant. I'd want something for my money. But I don't know if I can trust you or not."

He said feverishly, "Cap'n, if you knew how bad I wanted to be rid of that bitch! Anything! You can trust me with anything." He stopped. "Well, you'll be understanding anything short of murder. But if it is in my power, well, I've got a fine set of hinges on my conscience that swings the gate back and forth. 'Tis one of the reasons we Irish make such good Catholics. Confession is a wonderful thing, Your Honor. And mighty handy."

I looked away from the sergeant. "One thing I need to know . . . I have this detachment being led by an officer, a captain, say."

"Sir, it'd be a detail. Not a detachment. Remember we been through this before."

I nodded quickly. "Yeah, right. All right, a detail. And I come up and I'm a higher-ranking officer than the captain . . . Is that the right way to put it?"

McMartin nodded. "Yes, sir."

"Can I just up and give him an order and have him turn the detail over to me?"

McMartin pursed his lips. "Well, yes, sir, you could. If you was both of the same command, of the same outfit, and you were his direct superior."

"But what if I wasn't? Say I was a major that he'd never seen before and I walked up and told this captain that I'd be taking over?"

The sergeant shook his head. "You couldn't just do that, Your

Honor. It ain't chain o' command. You are a major, but you might
be in artillery and the captain in the infantry. The only way you
could do such a switch, take command like that, in the field, so to
speak, is if you were a field grade officer. Then it is all different."

"What's a field grade officer?"

"Full colonel and up."

"Up? What's up?"

McMartin smiled. "That would be your generals, sir. Beginning
with one star, which is a brigadier. Your Honor, beggin' your pardon, but you keep coming to this. If you'd up and tell me what it
be that you're after, why, Rollie McMartin is your man."

I looked at him. Finally I said, "Sergeant, I'm talking about something illegal as hell. If I told you, it might be like lighting the fuse
of a stick of dynamite that is right under my ass. With all respect
and no offense meant, I don't know you that well."

"No offense taken, Your Honor." He looked me square in the eye.
"But you'll find a way to trust me. And you won't be sorry, either."

"You need that money pretty bad, right, Sergeant?"

He shrugged. "Aye, I'd like to get the bitch off my back, but I'd
also like to help your nibs. If it don't harm my mates or me, then I
don't give a damn what it is. You say it is illegal. That is only so if
you get caught. Would that not be the law, Your Honor?"

I smiled. "You wouldn't be involved, Sergeant. You'd never be
near the scene."

He held up his hands. "Then what is the holdup? How could I
do you harm?"

"You used the right word," I said. "Holdup. But you could do
me harm because you'd know in advance and you could turn me
in."

His face got a little stiff. "Pardon, sir, umbrage taken."

"If that means the same thing as offense, none was meant."

"Then none taken. But it's a hard charge to have leveled at a
man—that he might run squealing like Missus Murphy's pig."

I chuckled, though without much humor. "It wasn't meant that way, Sergeant. And the only way you could understand why I would have to be careful of you or any other soldier would be if I told you what was in my mind. And I'm not willing to do that right now."

He lifted his hands and let them drop. "I'm aflame with curiosity, Your Honor, but I can understand you keeping a closed mouth. Likely it's been the habit of a lifetime."

"Likely," I said.

We passed a moment in silence and then the sergeant said, "Must be passing strange, sir, for an old horseman such as yourself to have a lad soaring around up amongst the clouds in one of those flying machines."

I shrugged. "I can see him doing that a lot easier than running around in one of them damn rattletrap automobiles. I hate the very sight of them. I kind of see the flying machine like a horse on a prairie, free to go where it wants to. But the damn automobile has got to follow roads, like a train, except there ain't many roads and them there is ain't worth a damn. They were built for good strong mule teams or oxen, not flimsy little flivvers."

"It would be your son, Cap'n, got you in a swivet about the war. Would that be a fair statement, Your Honor?"

I looked at him. "What makes you think I'm in a swivet about the war? What makes you think I give a damn one way or the other?"

He made a half shrug. " 'Twas just a remark, Your Honor. I was of the mind that you talked about it a bit and I hadn't noticed other civilians paying it much mind. Except them as was itching to get in the army to get a square meal."

It was getting late and I was due home. I said, "What are you talking about? What men looking to get a square meal?"

He chuckled. "Well, you spoke once of joining the army. Here until about three or four months ago you couldn't have. They wouldn't be after having you. Door was closed. But then *bang!* Down come orders to sign up recruits. That's where that bunch of blockheads I got to make soldiers and mule skinners out of come from. Out of the back alleys and the soup kitchens."

I looked at him in some amazement. "That many men out of work?"

He nodded. "Aye. I hear we have let in over sixty thousand recruits and just getting started. Don't have the officers and noncoms to train more or I think there would be more. O' course you don't see the out-of-work in a place like this. You see them around the cities. The poor have a better chance for a handout there."

"I don't understand. What is the army going to do with so many men it doesn't need?"

A little smile flickered across his face. "Why, find work for 'em, Your Honor."

"What kind of work?"

"Why, soldier's work, sir. War."

"You think we are going to war? You wouldn't say before."

"Beggin' your pardon, Your Honor, that ain't for the likes of me to be sayin'. I only know what I see. That's a rare piece of yard goods, that coat you are wearing, sir. Done by the hand of a first-rate tailor."

"Why are we talking about my coat all of a sudden, Sergeant?"

"But even as fine as the tailoring is," he said, "it still don't quite conceal Your Honor's shoulder holster."

I stared at him. "What's your point, Sergeant?"

"The government is wearing a fine coat itself. But it can't quite conceal its intentions, now can it, sir? Not to a quick eye. Our president says no war. But then I look at all the new recruits."

"And what about conscription?"

He laughed. "The Lord bless you, sir, it will never come to conscription. There'll be more than plenty to join up on their own. Course, if we go to war there will be a great chunk of new jobs and won't be as many poor. Might just have to use that conscription."

I stood up and looked at my watch. "Sergeant, I've got to go. Due at home." I pointed at the half-full bottle. "Just help yourself to all of that you want."

His face lit up. "Aye, if I were a mite more genteel man I'd be after saying that no, I can't take your private stock. But that's nectar and I'm Irish and weak."

"Indulge yourself, Sergeant."

As I started around the table and toward the door he said, "By the by, Your Honor, might I be after asking why you still carry the weapon? You aren't after robbing any more banks?"

I looked around at him and shrugged. "Holdover from other days. Old habit."

"Aye," he said. "Old habits die hard."

He was giving me such a frank look I thought for an instant he could see right into my mind. But I shrugged and gave him a little wave. "Reckon so."

He snapped off a half-salute as I turned for the door. I thought he would turn back to the whiskey, but I could feel him watching me until I had pushed my way through the big glass doors and stepped out onto the boardwalk.

By the time I got home I was as full as a milk pitcher and my brain was whirling every which way. It seemed to me that I had about decided. I was going to rob the gold and I was going to do it solo and I was going to dupe them out of it. But I couldn't figure the sergeant—rather, I couldn't figure whether to trust him or not. It was clear he bore no great love for the army, or at least some parts of it. He'd the same as said he didn't much like taking orders from officers he didn't think knew as much as he did. That, of course, could have just been the Irish in him. He had a cynical attitude toward the great monuments of our civilization, but then so did I. Hell, I'd flouted every law and broken every Commandment there was. He needed money and seemed willing to go to great lengths to get it, but that part I didn't much care for.

I was going to have to make up my mind about the man. I maybe could do it without him, but I could do it so much better and easier and safer with him. As I went up the front steps I could only shake my head. Matters such as were churning around in my brain were better thought on after a good supper.

THE TRAIN had, unaccountably, stopped well short of the border. I had planned to stop it just at the river and then load the gold into the ox-carts I'd have waiting. But here it was, creaked to a halt an unknown distance from where I wanted to be. It was just coming evening and a soft breeze was blowing. I jumped down from the boxcar and walked up the line, stepping carefully over the gravel and rocks of the roadbed, to see what had caused the delay. I could hear the engine huffing and chuffing ahead and I was starting to get more than a little angry. Here I was with a hell of a load of gold to take care of and some damn engineer had decided to stop right in the middle of some big-ass prairie.

I noticed the grass. It seemed taller than when I'd gotten out of the boxcar. Hell, it was lush, nearly knee high, and appeared to be growing. There was nowhere in that border country that you found grass like that. Mostly what I should have been seeing was stunted mesquite and grease-wood and cedar brakes and brambles. But this was prime pasture. It made me suspicious and I stopped and put my hand on the butt of my revolver. I stepped away from the train roadbed, moving a few yards into the grass. I could hear the wind sighing and see the grass ripple. I looked back over my shoulder. Somehow the train had moved quite a distance away. It had moved sideways, like I'd walked off from it a half mile or so. But I knew I hadn't. Something was bad wrong. I slowly drew my revolver and held it at the ready. Somebody was after my gold, but they were going to pay hell getting it. The gold was mine. I'd taken it fair and square and I was going to get it into Mexico if I had to kill every son-ofabitch that got in my way.

All of a quick I became aware of distinct movement in the grass up to my left and ahead. I went into a crouch and swung my revolver up, pulling the hammer back to a cock.

And then they showed themselves. It was soldiers, a whole bunch of them. They suddenly rose up out of the grass and went running, running stooped over, to take up positions. A couple of them were carrying a machine gun. They ran with it and then stopped and set it up on its tripod and swung it around, pointing it at me. The other soldiers were carrying rifles and they'd spread out in a line facing me, going down to one knee, leveling their rifles in my direction. I could hear the bolts being clicked back as they slung shells into the firing chambers.

It looked like a fight. I yelled out, "I'm Wilson Young! I don't want to hurt none of y'all! Now just go on about your business and leave me to mine."

Then two things happened. The rifles and the machine gun started firing. I could see the orange flame spitting from their muzzles. But even with all that going on I was more astonished to see Les Richter suddenly appear beside me, revolver in hand. I was about to ask him what the hell he was doing there when, all of a sudden, I could see his cousin Todd, and Chulo and Kid Blanco and a half-dozen others I had ridden with over the years. I wanted to yell at them, to tell them to get away, that this was my fight. I especially wanted Les to get away, get clear of the danger, get out of something he wasn't suited for. I yelled, "Les, I done told you you ain't suited for this line of work! You are a hair too slow! You think too much! You don't react! That's what got you killed in Nuevo Laredo when I wasn't there to protect you. Now run! Get out of here!"

But I guess the guns were making so much noise that he couldn't hear me. They had been firing for quite some time, but it was only after I had yelled at Les that the bullets began to arrive. I didn't know what had taken them so long.

It was awful to see. Bullets were just bursting right through Les. He was being hit again and again, and each bullet seemed to drive him farther and farther back. He wouldn't go down, just kept on taking those hits that powdered his shirt and knocked off little bits of cloth. I could see the others were catching the same and not faring much better.

"Damn it!" I yelled at the soldiers. "Stop it!" I ran at them, firing my revolver. I shot six times, aiming carefully, but I couldn't seem to hit anyone. Finally the hammer clicked on an empty cylinder. I turned to go back to see about Les.

I WOKE up sweating. I sat bolt upright in bed and put my hands to my face. They came away damp. I glanced over at Lauren. She was sleeping quietly, lying on her side. It was too dark in the room to see the clock so I got up and went quietly across the floor to the big side window. The sky was dark, the moon down. I guessed it to be somewhere around four in the morning by the look of the night. I shuddered and felt a shiver run up my spine. I wanted it to be morning, to be light. I wanted to go down and have breakfast with Lauren in a sunlit room. The dream had been too real, and I knew the part of it that had bothered me the most. It had been Les getting shot. Getting shot over and over. There had been no blood to be seen and I knew the reason for that, too. I had not been there when he was actually shot that day or night so long ago. We had split up. The bank robbery in Uvalde had been his last. He was finally coming off the owlhoot trail. But we'd been chased and we'd had to run for Mexico. Only he and I had made it. He'd gone on to Nuevo Laredo, with me telling him that was too close to the border, and I'd headed on deeper into Mexico. Of course, he was killed by deputies who had illegally crossed the border.

But the fact remained that I hadn't made him quit soon enough. He had quit after one bank robbery too many. And it had done for him.

I wanted a drink. I wanted a drink as bad as I had ever wanted one in my life. I knew there was a bottle in the bathroom and I went in there and fumbled around until I found it and then took a long pull straight from the mouth of the bottle. I didn't feel guilty about Les, or at fault, but I did feel like I could have looked after him better. I couldn't have made him quit robbing banks any sooner than he'd decided. But I knew in my heart of hearts that I hadn't tried as hard as I could have. The truth of the matter was, I wanted him with me. He was the most dependable man I had ever known and I'd have been a damn fool not to have wanted him siding me. Even though I knew he had no business being there.

I went back to bed but didn't go to sleep for a while. I lay there thinking about the dream, thinking about the soldiers and their rifles and the machine gun. A revolver wasn't much good against such firepower. I wondered if the dream was about me and being out there in the middle of the plaza. I wondered if the bullets I'd seen ripping through Les and the others were a foretelling of what was to be for me.

To hell with it. There were about fourteen thousand ways to die and only one way to live. And that one way was to simply go on with it. What was going to happen would happen. But I sure as hell wasn't going to mention this dream to anybody.

THE NEXT morning I was sitting in the breakfast room reading the San Antonio paper. It came overnight on the train and, even a day late, it was better than the local rag unless you wanted to know how many tons of freight had gone over the bridge or who was at what party or whether or not church attendance was up. Breakfast had been over a good half hour, but I was in no hurry, especially after that dream I had.

I was drinking coffee with a little whiskey in it when I heard a knock on the front door. Mrs. Bridesdale was generally busy out back and never answered the door so I was about to get up and tend to it when I heard Lauren coming down the stairs and then going down the front hall. I heard her open the door and a short murmur of voices and then the door closed. The next thing I knew she was in the breakfast room, white-faced and shaking. She had an envelope in her hand that I recognized as a telegraph wire. It was unopened. She came toward me, holding out the envelope. "Oh, Wilson, it's a telegram." I could see tears in her eyes. "You open it," she said. "I'm too scared. I just know it's about Willis."

I got up as quick as I could and took the flimsy envelope. I said, "Come on, honey, ain't no use buying trouble until it goes on sale. Might be from your sister."

She brushed at her eyes. "Telegrams are always bad news. Who else would send us a telegram except the government about Willis? Oh, open it, Will! Hurry up!"

I had been trying to keep it light to reassure her, but I was a little worried myself. When you didn't get telegrams as an ordinary matter and you had a son in a war in France, a flimsy piece of paper could be frightening. I ripped it open and gave it a quick look. It was from Justa Williams. It said:

WILL TELEPHONE YOU AT THE DEL RIO CENTRAL EXCHANGE AT 4 PM STOP

HAVE INTERESTING NEWS SHOULD INTEREST YOU STOP YOU MAY BE

RIGHT STOP

I read it a couple of times while Lauren stared at me with worried eyes. I said, "It ain't about Willis. But I'm damned if I know what it's about." I handed it to her.

She read it and then looked up at me. "What's this all about? What interesting news that should interest you?"

I sat back down at the breakfast table and picked up my cup. "Well, I don't know. You was the one told me I never went to see Justa, that I was out stepping. Must be something to do with that."

She sat down across from me. "Oh, stop it, Will. How long are you going to beat on that old horse? And what does he mean here when he says you might have been right?"

"Might *be* right. Not *might have been* right. I reckon that has to do with them two girls we was choosing between. He claimed the blond knew more tricks and I said I already had a blond and they didn't know anything. I said the black-haired one had the most spirit and could jump and kick at the same time."

She gave me a look that would have fried eggs. "I don't want to hear any more about that." She shook the telegram at me. "Now what does all this mean? And why is he going to telephone you?"

I put my coffee down and looked at her. I said truthfully, "I haven't the foggiest idea."

She fixed me with what I called her inside-outside look. Whenever she thought I was up to something she'd take her eyes and turn me inside out like you would an old feed sack and then give the exposed contents a good, thorough looking over. She studied me for what I reckoned was a good half a minute, though it seemed longer. Finally she got a disgusted look on her face like a roper when he misses with his first loop. "Well," she said, "there's more here than meets the eye, but you are covering up pretty well."

I put my hand on my chest. *"I'm* covering up? What the hell am I supposed to be covering up?"

"I don't know. Why would Justa call you on the telephone? Have you ever even talked on the telephone before?"

I gave her a look. "Listen, lady, I didn't just swim across the river. I been to two thunderstorms and a double-ring wedding. What do you mean asking me if I ever talked on the telephone? Hell yes, I've talked on the telephone. I ain't no hick. Just because I don't approve of something don't mean I'm ignorant of it."

She was still giving me that eye you could have mounted in a ring. "I bet you don't even know where the central exchange is. I'll have to go with you."

"I don't reckon that is going to be necessary. I been getting around and able to walk without assistance for quite some time."

She was still frowning at me. "Wilson, you are up to something. I would bet my bottom dollar on it. And it must be something pretty awful if you won't even tell your own wife."

"My own wife worries too much. There are some things it is best for her not to know."

"Ha!" She fixed me with that gimlet eye. I felt like a bug on the end of a pin. "I'm only amazed after what you've said about modern conveniences that you'd lower yourself to touch one of the nasty things. Next you'll be riding around in automobiles. What is Justa telephoning you about?"

I got up. Obviously telling her I didn't know wasn't going to be good enough. "I would imagine what he and I talked about when I was up there. They got this new device you can buy, kind of like a cork only a little more effective. When your wife won't shut up you can ram this in her mouth and she can't say a word. Likely Justa has found the place where they can be bought and he is calling to let me know."

There was a bowl of fruit on the table and she picked up an orange and heaved it at me. I didn't even have to duck. She never could throw worth a lick. I went out of the room and headed for my office. I'd been thinking about Sergeant McMartin when the telegram came and I wanted to finish doing that.

CHAPTER

8

THE CENTRAL exchange office was in a little building next to one of the banks, facing the river. The place had one
time housed a pretty good saddle shop where you could find a good
selection of bits or girths or, if you were of a mind, a custom-made
saddle. I stepped up onto the boardwalk and stopped. Where the
saddle maker's announcement had been in the plate glass window,
it now announced itself as the exchange for the telephone company.
A little notice with an arrow pointing toward the doorknob said,
PLEASE WALK IN.

I stood there thinking. By my watch it was ten minutes to four.
I could not for the life of me imagine what Justa was calling me
about, but I sure as hell hoped it would be something I could tell
Lauren. I knew the minute I got back she was going to be all over
me like grease on a goose. I had better have something to tell her
and it had better be something she'd believe.

I wasn't hesitating because I was scared of talking on the telephone. I'd done it several times before when Lauren and I had been in San Antonio and Dallas and places like that. Of course, it hadn't been what you might call an official call, more like a kind of demonstration at the hotels we'd been staying at. But this was my first town-to-town talk. I wondered what it would be like and if we'd be able to hear each other and make out what was being said. I reached down and turned the knob and opened the door and stepped inside. The place didn't look like much. In fact, it was the next thing to being empty. There was a counter that ran nearly clean across the front, the same kind of counter you might sell yard goods or jeans across except this one was nearly empty except for some papers and what not. But over at the back wall were four ladies, all wearing white blouses and blue skirts with little watches hanging on ribbons pinned to their blouses, busy in front of some kind of apparatus. They were all seated in little chairs, each facing a kind of board with a bunch of holes in it, along with a bunch of wires with little points on them like the head of a gun cartridge. As I watched they were busy pulling a wire out of one hole and sticking it in another and then reaching down and getting another one and plugging that one in and then disconnecting another one and so on and so on. Each woman had something strapped around her head and neck that ended in a little conelike gadget in front of her mouth. I could hear the ladies saying different things. "Hello, central! Your number, please. Connecting." And "I'm sorry, that number doesn't answer," or, "Go ahead, I have your party."

Lauren had told me we might be the only people in town that didn't have a telephone, but I hadn't believed her. Now, as busy as this place looked, I near about could.

There was a lady walking back and forth behind the four ladies. I reckoned she was some kind of straw boss. She took notice of me and came up to the counter. "Yes, sir, may I help you?"

I told her who I was and what I was there for. The words sounded kind of silly in my own mouth. "I'm supposed to get a telephone call from a Mr. Justa Williams at four o'clock. He sent me a telegram."

She reached up and tilted the little watch lying on her ample left bosom. "Well, it is five of. I expect we'd better get you in here and get you ready."

Sounded like I was going to a party—get me ready. She indicated I should pass through a little swinging gate at the end of the counter. That put me in the same area with the women who were giving the wires and the holes a good workout. The lady said, "I expect you might as well go on in the booth."

She went over to the side wall and opened a little door. Where I'd thought there was a closet or a connecting door was a little cubicle with a chair in it and a telephone mounted on the wall. She ushered me in. It wasn't no bigger than four feet by four feet. You couldn't have swung your hat around your head. But I sat down in the chair and she asked me if I'd ever had a long-distance telephone call before. Naturally I didn't want to appear like no greenhorn, so I said, "Well, that depends on what you mean by long distance. We was in a hotel in San Antonio and my wife telephoned to a theater. I didn't step it off but I'd reckon it was a pretty good distance."

She said, giving me a sweet smile, "No, no, Mr. Young, I meant over a long, long distance. Miles."

"Oh, you mean town-to-town. Well, no, I don't guess I ever actually done that."

"All right." She leaned over me. She was a nice enough looking woman, though a little plump for my taste. But she was wearing nice lilac water. She patted the telephone, which was a wooden box with a black cone coming out of it and a thing on the end of a wire that was hanging on the side. She patted the cone and said, "Now, when the call comes you talk into this. It is called the mouthpiece."

She picked up the black thing hanging by the side. "This is the earphone. You put that to your ear and listen. Do you want to try it? Get the feel of it?"

I shook my head. "Naw. I reckon I got it. Looks the same as a number of other ones I've used."

She said, "It should be coming through any minute now. The operator outside will take the call and plug it in for here. You'll hear the ring quite distinctly."

She was in her forties and, I reckoned, had to work to support herself. Likely she'd lost her husband when she'd rolled over on him some night in bed. I was glad to see she had work, but I wished mightily she'd get the hell out of the booth and let me concentrate.

I said, "Lady, I nearly went to work in the telephone business, so I got this down."

Just then the bell on the instrument in front of me rang and we both jumped. She said, "That's it. That's it! Remember, talk into the mouthpiece and put the receiver to your ear."

I made a little wave at her and she backed through the door. Just before she closed it she said, "You don't have to yell. Remember to talk in a normal voice."

I picked up the ear thing about the same time she closed the door and put my mouth down next to the mouthpiece, scrunching down to get close. It suddenly occurred to me I didn't know what to say. Lauren had told me there was something you said when you answered the phone but I couldn't remember what it was. I could hear some buzzing and crackling sounds coming out of the ear instrument. I said hesitantly, "Howdy, this is Wilson Young."

A woman's voice said, "Go ahead, Blessing, we have your party on the line."

Then I heard a little more crackling noise and then a man's voice. "Will? Justa Williams."

Well, he could have been standing right next to me it was that clear. I said, "I know who it is, you idiot. You sent me a telegram."

"Listen," he said, "we better talk fast as this line out of here comes and goes. They tell me it has to do with the traffic in and out of San Antonio, whatever that means."

"Then start talking. What's this all about?"

There was a crackle, and then he said, "It's about what Norris has been saying. He's been down here. At the ranch. Will, do you know what the stock market is? And I don't mean cattle."

Raising my voice in spite of what the lady had told me, I said, "Listen, cowboy, I been having a fat lady treat me like I was Ned in the first primer about this damn telephone. I don't need you to start. Hell yes, I know what the stock market is. In New York City. Hell, I got a broker in San Antonio buys and sells stocks for me all the time." It was almost true. Lauren and I bought and sold stocks, but she handled the details. "Is that what this telephone call is about?"

His voice was distinct. "It was the queerest thing, Will. Norris said damn near the same thing you did, only he said it so I could understand it. I never thought I'd see the day you and Norris agreed."

"Me neither. What'd he say?"

He started to talk but I couldn't understand him. I raised my voice in spite of orders. "You sound like you fell down a well!"

Then there came a great crackling roar. I held on to the receiver, holding it tight against my ear. Finally the noise subsided and his voice came through clear as a bell. He'd apparently gone right on talking. "—so it's Norris's belief that all the money is getting concentrated in too few hands and that we are headed for trouble in the economy."

"Start over," I said. "Damnit, didn't you hear me tell you you sounded like you'd— Never mind. Start over."

He paused. Then he said, "Hell, I don't know where I was. Mainly, Norris says that folks are spending too much money, money they ain't got. He said wages are being sucked up by capital. I take that to mean that the wage earner is buying all the gadgets you were talking about. Norris says it can't keep on. He said if there wasn't a free circulation of money that hard times were coming. He's getting us out of the stock market and into government bonds. Did you hear what I said about the war? I mean what Norris said about the war."

"No. What war?"

"The Europe war, what do you think?"

"What'd he say about it?"

"He said the only thing that could stop us being in a depression within a year was if we got in the war. He said there was nothing like a war to perk up the economy. Hell, ain't you impressed with yourself, Will?"

I was silent for a moment. I didn't know what to say. All I felt was a great swell of dread run through me. It was as if the decision about the gold had been made for me and I was out of choices. I said, "Well, I'm not sure if that's exactly what I said. I don't know anything about depressions. The only depression you run into in the bank robbing business is one about six foot deep."

"He said it different but it was pretty much what you said. He even brought up that part about machines putting people out of work. Remember? You said that. I was talking about a cotton gin could do the work of ten men and you said what were they going to do for work to feed their families? Well, Norris said all that kind of stuff was fine, but we've been going too fast. He said you can't take all the buying public's money or there won't be no buying public and then you'll have to figure out a way to feed them."

"He said a war would help?"

"He said it was the only surefire solution."

I said grimly, "Then tell him not to worry. Tell him he can depend on a war. Within the year."

"How you know that?"

"Never mind. Listen, we got to think of something for me to tell Lauren why you telephoned."

"Tell her what we've been talking about. Hell, she ought to be proud of you."

"You damn fool, I can't tell her about that. Have you forgotten the reason I told you all that stuff? Trying to make you understand why I thought I ought to do something? Have you forgotten?"

There was a silence and I thought the damn thing had quit working. "Justa?" I said.

"Yeah, I'm here." His voice sounded worried. "You ain't still thinking about that, are you? Will, it's crazy!"

"Let's don't talk about it now," I said hastily. I didn't know how these damn gadgets worked. As far as I knew everyone that owned a telephone might be listening. "Forget about that. Don't worry your pretty head. Listen, I'll think of something to tell Lauren. I'll tell her you called to tell me to get out of the stock market or something like that."

"Will, you are worrying the hell out of me. I wish you'd get that idea out of your head."

"Forget about it. Listen, how do you stop doing this? Talking on this gadget? Do you wave or tip your hat or what?"

He laughed, but he didn't sound happy. "You say good-bye. But I'm going to write you a letter and you better damn well read it."

"Good-bye, Justa. *Hasta la vista.*"

He said grimly, "I'm liable to be *hasta*ing your *vista* before you know it."

"Good-bye."

"So long, Will. Take it real easy."

I set the earpiece down on top of the wooden box and stood up. The plump lady was there to open the door for me. She brushed past me into the booth and hung the earpiece back up and then came bustling after me. She said, "Why you did fine, just fine!"

"Much obliged," I said.

I went through the little swinging gate and through the door to the outside. For a moment I stopped and stared around. Everything looked different. I even felt different. I felt scared, something I hadn't experienced in a long time.

As I walked over to my saloon to have a drink in my office I turned over in my mind a lot of things, not the least of which was this sudden dread I was feeling. I wasn't sure I could put my finger on it. The feeling seemed to be composed of a lot of different matters, some of them so entangled they would not bear sorting out. I didn't know how much of it was fear of dying, of being killed in that adventure. I had been in a lot of tight scrapes in my time and I could not remember any similar feelings. In my youth I simply had never thought anybody or anything could kill me. As I'd grown older, though still young enough to be wild and daring, the thought of death had never spent much time in my mind. I'd always thought it was something that happened to other men, not me. Even Les's death had not shocked me or given me new insights. Les had been careless. I'd cared for him as a brother, but he had allowed another man to get the advantage on him. That was something I tried never to let happen. And, I suppose, through the years I hadn't set any great store by my life. I didn't seem to have much to lose. I had some money, but other than that and a few friends, my luggage was pretty light.

But then had come Lauren and my life had changed. Oh, not right off, not the first year or two, or even three. But little by little I had put down roots that I had never counted on. The ritual of being a husband and then a father, not to mention an upstanding citizen, had come to be very precious to me. The years that had passed had only served to strengthen that feeling and give it an illusory sense of permanence.

And then there was the matter of practice. I could not remember when I had last used a gun against another human being or tried to take something that wasn't mine. It had been a long time, especially for the stealing. I had continued to be a fair gun hand after my pardon, though I seldom had to prove it.

Now I was considering robbing the United States government of a quarter of a million dollars in gold bullion. I sat at my desk and poured myself a drink and fairly trembled inside at the thought. That was some new degree of audacity for me.

Then there was Lauren. What the hell was I going to tell Lauren? *Was* I going to tell Lauren? What the hell was I going to do?

It was no good telling myself I still hadn't decided to do the job because I knew I had. If I'd been waiting for some sort of sign as a go-ahead, the telephone call from Justa Williams had settled the matter. A man couldn't go around preaching a lot of important-sounding palaver unless he was ready to back it up when the conditions he'd predicted came true. And having Norris agree with me was proof enough. Him and Sergeant McMartin. McMartin had as good as told me there was going to be war, and it didn't take a river-boat gambler to set odds on the matter.

I turned Sergeant McMartin over in my mind, Sergeant Rollie McMartin. That he was an intelligent man I had no doubt. He might even have been educated. I didn't know if he'd become so through formal schooling or simply on his own by reading. I reckoned him to be a courageous man. By his own story he'd risen in rank in time of battle, and I didn't reckon you got promoted by simply being there and standing around.

On another side you could hear the contempt in his voice for the officers who were superior to him in rank but who he didn't think knew as much. I calculated him to be an opportunistic man, but then who wasn't? The blarney and the "Your Honor" and the other smooth operating didn't bother me. He was a man who'd started out poor and wanted to get ahead. Hell, I could understand that. I just hadn't bothered with the blarney but had gone straight to robbing banks.

The main question was, could I trust him? I was now perfectly certain in my mind that the safest way to rob the gold was to dress up as an officer and order it given to me. But I didn't think I could pull it off without the direct help of Sergeant McMartin. The next question was how best to be sure I could trust him. Buy him off? With money or with the hope of future reward for seeing me safely through the matter? If I were to take him on as a friend and sponsor him I could introduce him to that world of quality and gilt he seemed to want so badly. It struck me that the man wanted respect more than he wanted money. But how was I to say, "Rollie, you help me and I'll make quality out of you, teach you how to be genteel. Or at least I'll turn you over to my wife and let her teach you."

But there was one little stumbling point to all of it. How did you say to a man, "Look here, I know you are a sergeant in the U.S. Army, but I want you to teach me how to be a high-ranking officer so I can steal a quarter of a million in gold. Just a small thing. Take your time and give it some thought." It wasn't a remark you up and said to somebody on a regular basis.

I sat there staring into my empty whiskey glass. Just as the man had said, there were no answers in the bottom of a glass of whiskey. And there was no way I could make a decision to trust Sergeant McMartin or not based on anything more than a coin flip. I hadn't known the man that long. And even if I had I doubted I would ever have known him well enough to know for certain I could put my faith in his loyalty. Hell, after a lifetime I didn't know more than three or four people I could say that about. I put the bottle of whiskey away in my desk drawer and got up. Maybe I'd think of some way to ease into the subject with him.

Walking home, my thoughts turned to Lauren. If something happened to me she would be well provided for financially, but I knew she depended on me as her partner and kind of as the boss. I made all the decisions, at least the major ones. I'd be cutting her adrift with a lot of good years left to fend for herself. She was an extremely attractive woman—and that wasn't just her husband talking—who would have money. She'd have every slick talker in six counties on her scent. So, did I, for my own reasons, have the right to take chances with her future? It was a nice question and one I had no intention of trying to answer at that moment.

SHE TOOK longer at supper to bring up the telephone call than I would have thought possible. For a change we were having a bottle of wine with our meal, a nice French wine that went very well with the steaks and baked potatoes Mrs. Bridesdale had fixed. I tell you, that angular Irishwoman hurt your eyes to look at with her pinched-up face and gawky limbs, but she could cook a treat. Lauren said she was an excellent housekeeper and I suppose she was; I never paid much attention to that sort of thing. As for Mr. Bridesdale, I so seldom saw him I couldn't have described the man under oath. He always seemed to be hurrying away to some chore every time I saw him. Lauren said he was good about fixing stuff and that he was an excellent gardener. I only wondered what he did when it came time to go to bed. I bet he slept in a pitch black room.

Lauren said, "By the way, you never told me what Justa had to say."

"Haven't had the chance. No more than get home and get a drink than you are hustling me into supper. What I'll never understand is why a body has to eat a meal at such a fixed moment. You'd think the walls of this house would come tumbling down if we didn't sit down for supper at the exact second of six o'clock."

She favored me with a cool look. "Are you evading, Wilson? Your behavior and your errands grow more and more suspicious. If you think I'm going to be drawn into a discussion about what time we eat *dinner* and forget about Justa's call, you are sadly mistaken."

I gave her a blank look. "How you do carry on. That thought

never entered my mind for a second. I was only explaining why I hadn't told you about the call. It was because I didn't have time. And there you go again, accusing me of mischief and devious behavior when no such thing was on my mind. I swear, you can make a body feel guilty with one look. Hell, Lauren, it ain't right."

"This is not working, Wilson. All you are doing is increasing my curiosity."

I sat up straighter in my chair and gave her what I considered a stoic look. "All right," I said, "I have been evading. And with good reason. That telephone call was embarrassing for me. I had to talk to a man about some business that my wife handles and I had to do it in such a way that he wouldn't know that he was talking to the wrong party. I had to lie and I had to shy and duck my head because it would ordinarily be man's business, and that was why Justa was calling me."

She looked perplexed. She put her napkin on the table and swiveled around a little to face me better. "I am going to be very interested to hear what kind of business this was that you didn't handle and found embarrassing because you were not in charge of it."

I let her wait a second and then said, with a little bitterness in my voice, "The damn stock market. Not cows and horses, but that thing up on Wall Street in New York City that you write that broker about."

She looked blank for a second. "The stock market? You haven't got the slightest interest in the stock market. Or the bond market. Or securities of any kind. You once told me your idea of security was extra ammunition or something like that."

"Yes," I said, "but that don't necessarily mean I want the whole world to know that my wife does the trading in this house."

"Why would Justa call you about the stock market? Why would he even think you knew about the stock market?"

I pushed my chair back and looked outraged. "Well, we were

talking about the way the country was going, how things were faring for folks in the South. And the North, for that matter. That took us around to the market."

She gave me a disbelieving look. "You don't know anything about the stock market. Why, I'll bet you don't even know one stock we own."

"You'd lose your bet," I said warmly. "We got that, that damn Standard stock. The one makes gasoline for them tin lizzies. Ain't that right?"

She shrugged. "Well, you remember that one because you nearly had a fit when you found out I'd bought it."

I snapped my fingers. "Oh, yes, there's that Morgan stock."

"Morgan Fidelity and Trust. You thought it was about Morgan horses."

"I did not! I thought it was funny, us owning stock in a bank. Considering what I've been. And I remember one other. That threshing stock. The ones make the reaper."

"McCormick." She shook her head. "I'm very much surprised. Don't try and name any more, Will, you might hurt yourself."

"We making any money?"

She nodded. "Yes. About eight percent."

I laughed. "Eight percent? I mark my whiskey up a hundred and twenty percent and I'm one of the fairest."

"I'm sure you do, but this is different. I still don't know why Justa would be calling you about the market. He wasn't actually asking you for advice, was he?"

"No, he was calling to warn me. While I was up there I was giving him my views on what was happening in the country."

She rolled her eyes. "Oh, your gadget speech. Or the lightning rod speech. Too many things for people to waste their money on."

I lifted my head. "All right, Miss Smug, let me tell you what Norris had to say to Justa when he was just down at the ranch. The words were different but they all came out the same, to the same conclusion."

Leaving out any reference to the gold bullion and what Norris had said about war, because of Willis and her worries about him, I told her what Justa had passed along. "Norris is unloading his stocks and going into some kind of bonds, city bonds or something like that."

"Municipal bonds."

"Yeah, that. Whatever it is. Anyway, he was calling to let me know that Norris agreed with me and that he thought I ought to get out of the market. He thinks a big slowdown is coming. There was another word for it."

"Depression?"

"Yeah."

She looked off into the distance. "So Norris thinks too much money is leaving the wage earner and going to capital."

"And too many jobs are being lost." I pointed at her. "Like that damn McCormick reaper. Replacing twenty men. Where they going to get jobs? Norris said only a war could—" I stopped quickly.

She looked at me. "What?"

"Nothing," I said. "Just something about the European war might create some jobs if it keeps up much longer." I was a smooth liar when I had to be.

She reached over and patted my hand. "I am very impressed, Will. *Norris* agreed with you? On economics? I really am impressed."

I said stiffly, "I ain't just another handsome bank robber, you know."

"Ex-bank robber, dear. Would you like some dessert? I think Mrs. Bridesdale made a cake."

I pushed my chair back. "I don't reckon. I been eating a little too well here lately. Many girls as are after me, I got to stay trim and fit so as to be able to outrun them."

She gave me a bland look. "Why would you want to do that? You never have before."

I got up. "Go on making fun. But what you better do is go in my office and write that broker and sell us out."

She frowned. "I'm not quite ready to do that yet. I will write him and ask what he thinks."

I gave her a look and said sarcastically, "Why not go to the telephone central and call him? And don't act like you never have. I seen the bill one time. They sent it to my office at the saloon by mistake."

She colored and put her hand to her mouth. "Oh, my. Oh, dear. Now I guess I'm going to get lectured."

"What? After the nice way you finished calling me a man who could only count revolver cartridges? I wouldn't think of saying a word to you. I'm going in the sitting room and read the paper. Bring me some whiskey and a glass before you get settled doing anything else."

I had finished the paper and was on my second drink when she came into the room and settled on the overstuffed sofa like she always did. She had gotten out of her day clothes and put on a lounging robe. It was a silk one with all kinds of flowers on it that I had bought on a trip to Dallas. She looked good in lively clothes. Some women could do that; most were better off sticking to colors that didn't call attention to themselves. She had a pensive look on her face, with a little frown worrying her forehead between her eyes. I asked her if something was the matter.

She looked away. "Will . . . do you think the war is going to go on much longer?"

Of course I wasn't going to tell her how I felt about that or what I knew. I said, "Don't get me started on that damn war."

She shivered a little. "I worry about Willis all the time. Oh, God, I wish he wasn't over there."

I said grimly, "I didn't see any bunch of men carrying shotguns show up at the door."

"Oh, I know no one made him go. He's an idealist. He thought he was doing right."

I snorted. "He wouldn't know an idealist if one slipped up behind him and hit him in the ass with a bass drum. Things were a little too slow around here for him, so he felt like he had to go seek out the action. Only thing he forgot was they ain't playing for fun over there and he ain't had no damn training in taking care of himself."

She gave me a hard look. "Had you? When you set in robbing banks had you been trained? Where do you go to get trained to be a bank robber?"

"There is a considerable difference between what I started out doing and jumping in feet first right in the middle of a war that is already up to full speed. I knew the country and I knew the language and nobody had to teach me how to ride a horse. He don't know the country, he don't speak the language, and he is going to have to be taught to fly an aeroplane and an aeroplane that is going to get shot at. Plus I had it a whole bunch harder than Willis, growing up. I didn't set out to rob banks because I was an idealist and wanted to right some wrongs. I set out to rob banks because they had the money. Now, if you can't see that difference I don't know any other way to explain it to you."

She put one hand up to her face. I could see the pain in her expression. After a moment she said, "I suppose you're right. Maybe if I had supported you more in your opposition, he wouldn't have gone."

I got up from my easy chair and crossed over and sat down beside her and put my arm around her and pulled her head over on my shoulder. "Now, don't start blaming yourself. You were opposed. You put up every argument you could think of. But he's a strong-willed boy. You thought I was being too harsh in my attitude and you tried to soften it. It would have helped if you hadn't, but I still think he would have gone."

Her head moved on my shoulder and she let out a little sigh. "He's so much like you, Will, that sometimes it scares me. I know he gets his daring from you. I just hope he inherited that same sense of survival you've got. I hope he knows how to protect himself."

I was very surprised. It was supposed to be my well-kept secret that I was a daredevil fool who, like a fool fucking or fighting, went at it without fear or forethought. And here she was revealing that I always calculated the odds and always had an escape route planned and always sought the advantage. It was almost embarrassing that she knew me so well.

And then I thought about stealing the gold bullion and wondered how I was going to find a position of advantage to do that. And finding an escape route with five thousand people watching might be a little hard, never mind the odds between me and the guard detail. That was easy to figure: twenty-one to one. Against.

She was still shivering a little. I pulled her closer and said, "Come on, honey. Hell, he's my son. He's dumb as a plank and stubborn as your whole family, but he's got *some* savvy. I've watched him with people. He's good. He studies folks before he rushes in. I know he ain't never fired a gun in anger at anyone, but that ain't all that important. The actual shooting part isn't anything. You've got to have it in your mind, and I think he has. I think he knows how to defend himself. He's like me, he calculates the situation before he commits. Hell, I wouldn't reckon that fighting in those little aeroplanes was much different than a pistol duel. Figure out where your opponent is weak and then attack him there."

I didn't believe or mean a word of it. I thought he was a headstrong little whelp that needed to be taught a good lesson. He went off to war and I reckoned he hadn't had ten fistfights in his life, let alone faced a gun or worse. But you don't say those things to a worried mother. You tell her what she wants to hear.

She raised her head off my shoulder. I thought I heard a slight sniffle, but I wasn't sure. We'd had this selfsame discussion about two dozen times and sometimes she cried and sometimes she didn't. She said, "I wish you hadn't been so hard on him. You practically told him if he went, there wasn't much point in his coming home. That was harsh, Will, harsh."

"Lauren, I had to take my best shot," I said patiently. "Wasn't nothing going to work on him by half measures. He had the bit in his teeth and was running away. I had to club him with a fence post just to get his attention. I didn't mean it. You know I didn't mean it."

"Then why don't you write him and tell him so? Let him know you don't feel so hard against him."

I took my arm out from around her and leaned over, propping my elbows on my knees. "It ain't that easy, Lauren. The boy has got to know he doesn't defy his father and then get off scot-free." I looked around at her. She wasn't crying. "Hell, do you think I liked sending my only son off like that? Especially considering where he was going? You think I ain't heartsick? You think I don't worry every minute of every day?"

She reached up and touched my cheek. "I know you do, honey. But why do you have to be so hard all the time? You could soften up toward Willis."

I looked back down at the floor. "It wouldn't do him any good. At least right now he's got something to be angry about, and maybe that anger will get him through the first of this thing until he can get a little experience and learn his weapons and learn his enemy."

"Write him, Will."

"Damnit, no!" I stood up and walked a few paces away. "Against my wishes—hell no, against my *orders!*—he defied his father. He had a future right here. He had a chance to get a good education, a chance to be a damn respectable citizen. He'd have had money to burn. And what the hell does he do? He hitches up his britches and reckons he'll go on over to Europe and whip all the bullies and tyrants and anybody else that is trying to stop the world from being safe for democracy. And what reason does he give? That a bunch of his pals up there at that damn university felt the same way and they were going. Have you heard about any of them being over there in any of those letters he's written? I reckon not!" I was angry all over again and pacing up and down. "And all his professors and teachers and what not had opinions on the subject. Said it would take America's industrial might to defeat the Huns and the Turks and whoever else is in the damn thing. I don't reckon there's any professors over there either." I pointed my finger at Lauren. "But your son has taken it upon himself to go off on the damn foolishest errand I have ever heard of. Never heard the sound of a bullet whistling through the air right by his ear but he up and jumps into a war with both feet!" I threw my hands in the air. "What'd you want me to do? Send him off with my blessings? Hell, that would make me as big a goddamn fool as he is!"

"Will, don't use the Lord's name in vain. Especially now."

"That wasn't the Lord. That was one of them false gods. One of them Greek or Roman ones." I went and sat back down on the couch and put my arm back around her. "Maybe I can get him back. Or maybe in a safe job. I been thinking of a way to get the government's attention."

She turned to me, hope in her face. "Have you, Will, have you? Oh, that would be so wonderful."

"But before it gets completely lost in the shuffle I'd like to bring up a point."

"What's that, dear?"

"I wonder if there has ever been a husband who had a wife who believed him about anything without getting an outside opinion."

"What ever are you talking about?"

"I'm talking about what is happening to the financial condition of the country. When I was saying it you just rolled your eyes and acted like I was off eating locoweed. But then, *then* Norris agreed with me and all of a sudden it is chapter and verse. I want you to explain to me how that is?"

She colored slightly. "Why, Will, I listen to you on any number of matters. But the economy? I know you understand the whiskey economy and the gambling economy and"—her voice got grim—"the whorehouse economy. But it never occurred to me for one second that you knew anything about the actual day-to-day running of the country from a financial standpoint."

I nodded slowly. "Oh, I don't think that's quite all of it. I can't think of any other examples right now, but as best I remember, it generally takes another opinion in agreement with mine to make you take my word."

"You are just overly sensitive." She leaned over and kissed me on the cheek.

Lauren went to bed after about another hour, but I sat up late thinking and drinking. Mostly I thought about Willis and wondered how he was doing and was there some way we might make it up, with him still realizing who the daddy was. His going off like that had hurt me so bad—Lauren didn't have half an idea how much. I had wanted for him all the things I'd never had as a young man coming up. I hadn't wanted to take his dash or his daring but I'd wanted him to be able to go anywhere, anytime, with his head held high and the money in his pocket and the education in his head to command respect. Going off as he had done had thrown all those plans on the trash heap.

I got up to get myself another drink, and as I was pouring it out, it suddenly struck me what a hypocrite I was being. I had disowned my son for going off to get into a war when he was angry at his own country for not lending a helping hand. I had called him a fool and worse for mixing into an affair that was none of his business. And yet here I was about to commit a robbery, if it could be called that, to thumb my nose at that selfsame government that Willis had been angry at. Hell, it was none of my affair if the powers that be wanted to let the country go to hell on roller skates. It had nothing to do with me. Yet I was about to stick my thumb into a very hot pie and it was a gut cinch I wasn't going to pull out a plum.

The similarity of what I was planning to what Willis had done were so striking as to seriously disturb me.

I sat for another hour, thinking, not that it did much good. What I couldn't seem to figure out was how I'd gotten myself into such a mess—and it was a mess—without half trying. I hadn't actually done anything yet, but I knew I would. When I told Lauren my plans—and I knew that night I was going to have to tell her—I could only hope that she wouldn't notice and bring to my attention the coincidence in what the son had already done and the father was about to do. Finally I went on up to bed with a heavy heart. One of the greatest benefits of my marriage to Lauren had been to have another shoulder to put to the wheel of trouble. Unfortunately, this wasn't a situation where she could help. I felt mighty lonely as I lay in the dark, listening to her light breathing. Hell, robbing banks was a young man's trade requiring young man's nerves. Only old fools tried it after their day was over.

THE NEXT day I spent out at my thoroughbred ranch on the Texas side. It was where we actually put the animals that had come of age through their training. I had a trainer, Charlie Stanton, who had come up under Warner Grayson. Sometimes I thought that Charlie might just be the equal of Warner, but I made it a habit not to go around saying so.

I took lunch out at the ranch with Charlie and his assistants and then got back home around three in the afternoon. I was looking forward to a good bath and a drink or two before dinnertime, to use Lauren's term for supper. I had my boots off and was enjoying a little brandy for a change when Lauren came back to the parlor where I was sitting and said there was a man outside who wanted to see me. I asked her to send him in, unless he was some kind of salesman.

"No, he's not a salesman, I don't think," she said. "He's a soldier. Very stiff and proper but he says he fears to come in because of the condition of his boots. Says he's afraid he'll track up my floors. Wilson, his boots are cleaner than my floors. At least they are shinier. I think he wants you to come out. Is this some more of your mystery?"

I sat up and started pulling on my boots. "Did he have stripes on his sleeves?"

She pulled a face. "I don't know what that means, but yes, there were markings on his upper sleeves. Now, what are you trying to hide from me?"

I got up and gave her a sarcastic look. "The saloon business, my love. That is more than likely a sergeant who is trying to get me to allow soldiers to come in the bar. They could mean trouble and they can't afford the place. We are trying to reach a compromise."

"Oh," she said, looking disappointed. She'd already lost interest. She was dying to catch me at something and I'd given her a reasonable explanation.

But as I hurried toward the front door I could not imagine what errand would have brought Sergeant McMartin to my house. He seemed too much of a man in tune with the social niceties to call 'round uninvited.

I opened the wooden door and pushed back the screen door and stepped out on the porch. It was a fine, sunshiny day, but the porch gave some shade. Sergeant McMartin was standing back by the railing, as far from the front door as he could get and still be on the porch. As usual he was starched and ironed and shined to the gloss of a new dime. I reckoned as first sergeant he had to set an example.

I said, "Well, Sergeant, I have to say I'm surprised to see you. What brings you by on such a nice day?"

He touched his hat brim in a kind of salute and said, "I'm sure Your Honor will be after pardoning me for the great liberty I'm taking by calling at your residence, sir. But they told me down at the saloon that you weren't to be expected in today and I thought you wouldn't take it amiss if I came by with some information I think you'd be after fancying to know."

"Well, there's no use standing out here in the sun, Sergeant. We can go in the house."

He coughed discreetly into his cupped hand. "Excusing your pardon, Cap'n, but this may be the kind of information you wouldn't be wanting all the members of your household to be hearing."

"We can go in my office," I said.

He touched his hat brim again in a respectful gesture. "Beggin' the cap'n's pardon, but out here in the open is after my way of thinking the safest."

I frowned. "Sergeant, I don't know what kind of information you've got but there's nothing you can say that I wouldn't want my wife to hear."

He got a little twinkle in his eye. "Well, sir, I'm after thinking this might best be kept between you and myself, if Your Honor takes my meaning."

I was getting a little irritated. "Sergeant, if this is about that money I said you might earn to buy your wife off, I—"

He cut me off by shaking his head violently and putting up his hands. "Oh, no, sir! No, sir! Your Honor, I was caught in a weak moment. With quality like yourself I wouldn't be after having a red cent pass between us. It would be my pleasure to assist your good self in any way I can. And you have my word on that as an Irishman and a noncommissioned officer. And my word is valuable to me, sir."

I stared at him for a moment. He was as hard to get hold of as mercury. "All right, Sergeant, what have you got to tell me?"

He reached in his back pocket and took out a folded piece of paper. He took a moment to unfold it carefully and straighten it out smooth. "Sir, this is a regimental general bulletin that circulates amongst the camps and posts in this district. It is not a secret document, it's after more like being a newsletter. It keeps us up on what is happening at the different army installations in our area. There is an item that I think you will find very interesting."

"And what would that be?"

He turned slightly so that I could see the paper. It looked official enough. There were a number of paragraphs, each obviously pertaining to a different subject. He put his thumb on one two-thirds down the page. "It's this one, sir. This one about the progress of that gold display that the Treasury Department is sending around. According to the way I read the schedule, it appears that they will be bringing that gold into San Antonio on the twenty-fifth of this month. That only leaves us seventeen days, not counting today, to start getting you ready to impersonate a high-ranking army officer so that you can take that gold away from them."

I stared at him blankly for a second. If ever a man had caught me off guard he'd just done the best job of it. My mouth went dry. "Whatever in the hell are you talking about, Sergeant?"

For answer he looked at me, a small smile flickering around his mouth.

"Where would you get such an idea?" I said. "I'm an *ex*-bank robber, Sergeant."

"Yes, sir. I understand. But there's little enough time for it, sir. We'd better start making plans."

I almost stuttered I was so off balance. "Wha— Where in hell did you come up with such a harebrained idea?"

"Why, you told me, sir."

"Like hell I did."

We stood there staring at each other.

CHAPTER

"I ASKED you where in hell you got such a loco idea?"

"Like I said, sir, you told me. Oh, not in all them many words, not them exact words. But you asked a bushel basket of questions. You asked about rank, you asked about a detail—only you called it a detachment—you asked if one officer could up and take over the detail from another. You asked what kind of men would be guarding what kind of shipment." A smile flickered over his mouth again. "Cap'n, I am bound to tell you that not that many folks are interested in the army, especially not gentlemen of your standing. And I might add, sir, that you treated me uncommonly good. Now, you may have been after doing it out of the kindness of your good heart, but then you went to implying there might be a way for me to make some substantial money. Your Honor, fifteen hundred dollars is most likely pocket change to you, but it is a treasury to such as I."

I said stiffly, "That's all you got to go on?"

He frowned slightly and looked away. "Well, it was more like a feeling I had, Your Honor. At first I thought you were interested because of your lad over in France. But then you straightened me out on that score. And you showed a great interest in the likeliness of war. Begging your pardon, sir, but you showed a power of interest that seemed unnatural, just two men over a drink. And I knew about that gold shipment. Ain't much goes on in my district I don't know about." He switched back around and looked at me. "And you will allow, sir, that you've had a bit of experience at taking gold from other folks."

I slumped my shoulders and looked down at the porch. "This is a hell of a mess."

"Aw, sir!" he said. "No cause to be looking down in the mouth." His voice got cheerful. "Here, I've gone and saved you all the worry and bother about guessing how to ask me to help you without putting me in the know. It couldn't have been done, sir. You're going to need a uniform and the proper insignia and brass. But most of all you was after knowing how to talk and act like an officer. Sir, you can't do it without me, and I'm eager for the chance."

I gave him a tight look. "You're crazy as a bissy bug."

He cocked his head. "I can see that Your Honor is still having a hard time deciding to trust me. Let me make you a proposition. I've no doubts that you can lay your hands on a couple of hard boys. I offer myself up as hostage."

"What are you talking about?"

"A way to convince you that you can be after trusting me. Rollie McMartin ain't ever gone back on a deal in his life and he ain't starting now, sir."

"What do you mean by hostage?"

He shrugged. "I've got some leave time coming. I get you all trained and polished up and then your two hard boys take me back into Mexico somewhere. If something goes wrong and it looks like I betrayed you, why, then, well . . . " He spread his arms. "I reckon I don't come out of Mexico."

"You'd do that?"

He nodded. "In the blink of an eye, sir. I know I ain't going to betray you and I trust you because you are quality. Sticks out all over you. And I know you ain't got no reason to trust a rough stick of wood like me."

I gave him a grim look. "Put the soft soap up, Sergeant. It ain't the time for it. You're about as rough a stick of wood as a pool cue. But we got one question ain't been asked an' answered. Why would you want to do it? I admit I can't do it without you. I admit I've been searching for a way to approach you. I admit you nearly knocked me off the porch just now when you out and said what you did. But the question still remains, why would you want to be involved in such an illegal effort?"

He gave me a bland look. "Why, to help you, Your Honor."

"Cut out the blarney, Sergeant. We are down to the nut cutting."

He smiled faintly. "Why, for the same reason a man would want to own a whorehouse—fun and profit."

"What profit? You said you didn't want to see a red cent pass between us."

"Aye, Cap'n, that I don't. But I don't reckon you'd be after keeping all that gold to yourself."

That brought a smile to my face. He'd shocked the hell out of me, and now I was about to do the same to him. "Sergeant, I have absolutely no intention of keeping that gold."

He looked at me as if he'd misheard. "What is that you say, Your Honor?"

"I'm not going to keep the gold, Sergeant. It's not really a robbery. I'm going to take it, yes, but then I'll find some way to get it back to the bank or the army or the Treasury or whoever it belongs to."

He stared at me for a good long interval, then cleared his throat. "Beggin' Your Honor's pardon, but that ain't the way of the thing, you understand. If a man goes to the trouble and risk of stealing a quarter of a million dollars, why, some of it is supposed to rub off on him."

I shook my head. "You will find this hard to believe, Sergeant, but I'm not doing this for the money the gold represents. It's not a robbery. It is my way of expressing an opinion."

"And a fine one it is, sir. Opinion, that is. But it would be just as good an opinion with a handy little sack of them small gold bars."

I shook my head. "No, Sergeant. And if that is the only reason you want to help me, then I don't reckon we can do any business."

He shook his head as if trying to clear it. I could see he was having a hard time taking in what I was saying. I reckoned he'd lain awake in his bunk at night and figured out what a good job it would be to have part of a quarter-of-a-million-dollar gold robbery. Now I was telling him something completely different to what he'd based his thinking on. I reckoned it was a little difficult for him to turn his mind completely around and understand it. He opened his mouth and then shut it and appeared to think for a moment. Finally he said, "Ah, beggin' Your Honor's pardon, but yourself wouldn't be having a little joke at the expense of an old soldier, now, would you?"

I shook my head. "Get it straight in your mind, Sergeant. I'm not a robber no more. I'm not going to keep this gold. I doubt I'll have it in my possession over an hour."

He nodded slowly, his eyes still clouded over with surprise. "Would Your Honor be minding if I ask after why you are doing this, this business of taking gold you are after giving back?"

I shrugged. "I doubt you'd understand. In fact I'm not even sure myself why I'm doing it."

"Is it about the lad? Would be a fine noble gesture to be doing to those who held back when he rushed forward like the stalwart young man he is."

I gritted my teeth. "No, it is not about my son. Look. I'll try and give you an explanation. I'm thumbing my nose at the goddamn government because they are trying to make fools out of the people of this country and I happen to be one of those people and I don't like some idiot thinking he can make a fool out of me. They are flashing that gold around like they are saying there is plenty more so go ahead and spend, spend that paper currency. We can print more of that. We can print enough to finance a war, which is what they are up to. But if I take their gold it's going to be a little embarrassing. They got to dig up more gold and it ain't easy to find. I'm calling the goddamn government a bunch of sharps, a bunch of three-card-monte sharps. Turn the card over and if it's the ace of spades you win. See this gold? We got a lot of it, no use you holding on to yours. Remember how I asked you how they paid the soldiers and you said in gold and silver? Well, there are plenty of folks like that bartender you spoke of who want to hear a noise when the money hits the mahogany."

For a moment he lost his military bearing as he slouched and reached up and scratched the back of his head. "Your Honor, I never looked at it like that, but it does make a power of sense. I was after wondering why they was showing that gold around down in the way-back places. Makes sense, it does, Your Honor, what you say."

"But now that you know there is to be no robbery, at least a robbery where the booty is kept, you'll want no part of the business."

He straightened up. "Cap'n, that be the first false words ever fell from your lips. That day in your saloon, out front, when I knew you was up to something and was pretty sure I knew what it was, I said Rollie McMartin is your man. That stands as spoken."

I looked at him a short minute. Hell, the cat was out of the bag and tearing all around the house. And, like we both knew, I couldn't do it without him. I said, "All right, Sergeant, I'm asking for your help. But only in the military matters. You are to have no hand in any part of the robbery or the getaway. I'm playing a lone hand. Do you understand me?"

"Aye, Your Honor, and 'tis a fine, noble thing you be doing."

I blinked at him. "What fine, noble thing?"

"Letting the bastids—excuse me, Your Honor—letting them in power know they can't grind down the little people with their glitter and their promises. Aye, Cap'n, you're a man after my own heart."

I almost burst out laughing. "Sergeant, do the Irish put a coat of bullshit on everything? I'm going to steal some gold. That's all. There's nothing fine or noble about it."

"Aye, and the very humility of yourself is touching me heart like a clutching hand. It's the grand ones who never see how grand they are."

Someone had once told me that if an Irishman described a rock to you you'd swear he was talking about cake. He'd said the country was so harsh and hard that they made up for it with the glory and the beauty of the way they talked. I said, "Think what you will, Sergeant. I've given up trying to figure out what you say or why you say it. But one thing is clear, I'm going to pay you for this job."

He put up a quick hand. "Oh, no sir, beggin' Your Honor's pardon. I wouldn't feel right. You making the grand gesture and me taking money." He shook his head. "No, sir. 'Twouldn't be right."

"Understand," I said, "you are to have no part in the actual robbery. I am going to pay you two thousand dollars to get me ready to pass myself off as a high-ranking officer."

His eyes got big at the sound of the two thousand. "Beggin' Your Honor's pardon, you spoke of fifteen hundred."

I was reaching for my billfold. "The extra five hundred is for sav-

ing me the trouble of figuring out a way to approach you." I opened
my wallet and took out five one-hundred-dollar bills. I seldom
went around with less than a thousand on me. Never knew when
I'd see a horse I wanted to buy or a poker game I wanted to get in.
I held out the five hundred. "There. Take that to seal our bargain."

He looked down at it, his face agonized. "Oh, Cap'n, what you
want to tempt a poor old Irish sergeant for. I never saw that kind
of money in one man's hand before in my life."

I knew he wouldn't reach for it, so I leaned forward and lifted
the flap of his shirt pocket and stuffed it inside. "There. The bargain is struck and we go on from here. You spoke of being able to
get leave? How much can you get?"

He was looking over his cheekbone at the wad of money in his
pocket. "All we need, Cap'n." He looked up at me. "That don't be
the time I'm worried about. I'm worried do we have time to turn
you out as a proper officer. Were it any other gent I've seen in these
parts I'd say it couldn't be done. But, begging your pardon, you've
got that bearing about you, sir. You look and act like a man used
to giving orders. I passed notice on that what little I saw you with
your employees at your emporium."

I said dryly, "I pay them well."

He nodded. "Yes, sir. But there is two kinds of men in this world
who give orders. There's them as gives an order and then watches
to see if it is getting carried out. The other gives the order and never
glances. He *knows* the order will be obeyed. You have that, sir, begging your pardon. In the military we call it command presence. So
we start with a power of head start for this job, though there will
be a world for you to learn."

"Sergeant, there is one thing you must understand. No one is to
be hurt by this rash action of mine, and that includes yourself. You
will spruce me up in secrecy and you will keep your mouth shut
and you will be nowhere near the site when the adventure com-
mences. Is that understood?"

"Aye," he said, "that part. I can see that. But you say no one is to be hurt. What about your good self?"

I shrugged. "If I do it right, if I do it like I've got it figured, I ought to get away scot-free."

"And afterwards? Won't they come looking for you? Beggin' your pardon, sir, but I've been stationed in Texas at least ten years and I've heard of you that whole time. You're not after being an invisible man."

"Nothing is without risk, Sergeant, but I think I've got that part covered. I won't tell you how at this moment."

He studied me for a long moment. With almost a touch of regret in his voice he said, "Cap'n, you're setting out to be a hero. Do you know the three things it takes to be a hero?"

I shook my head. "No. Why should I?"

"To be a hero there has to be an opportunity for heroism. Then the man has to bravely seize the opportunity. But the third is the most important. Would you be having any idea what that would be, sir?"

"Of course not, Sergeant. I've never been in the army."

"There has to be a witness, sir. It's no good performing an act of heroism if no one is there to testify to it. The hero can't come back and tell it on himself. Don't work that way."

I gave a short laugh. "Well, if it's witnesses that are needed I got the feeling I'll have them in the thousands."

He nodded. "Aye. And that is a worry to me, Cap'n. If you don't play your part exactly right some of them witnesses might become participants and you will be badly outnumbered, putting it lightly."

I leaned up against the porch railing and stared out at the sergeant's horse where he was tethered to the hitching post. The animal was standard government issue, mounted with a McClelland saddle and the ridiculous double rein and heavy, long-shanked bit. That arrangement didn't give the rider one dot more control over the animal and only served to irritate the horse. I figured the army insisted on such a rigging because they recruited so many plowboys who were used to the double reins on a plow horse. I said, "Let's go up to my office at the saloon, Sergeant, and start discussing the details. You ride on ahead. I'll step inside and tell my wife where I'm going and then join up with you."

He didn't move for a moment. "Are you after telling the missus about this, Your Honor?"

I gave him a level look. "Why? Have you got an opinion on that?"

He looked away. "She looks such a grand lady. 'Twould be a shame to worry her needlessly. You know how women are, always making more out of something than is there."

I gave him a smile. "You mean like a marriage you couldn't remember?"

He touched the brim of his campaign hat. "I'll just be for riding down to your emporium."

WE HAD reached agreement on several points. He would, unwillingly and not feeling right about it, nevertheless accept two thousand dollars for getting me suited for the role of a high-ranking army officer. He would work at this until the day of the robbery, then use what leave he had left, about two weeks, to go to Baltimore and buy a divorce from the woman who was draining his soldier's pay. He was to keep his mouth closed to everyone, drunk or sober, and was in no way to stick around and see how the robbery went.

He'd said, "Ah, them's harsh terms, Cap'n, harsh terms. You'd be taking the bairn out of the mother's arms at the moment of birth. Ah, well, if it's to be, let it be."

Now we sat in my office, him in a chair pulled close to my desk and me in my customary swivel chair behind the desk. We both had a glass of my private stock in hand. Looking at the amber liquid, he said, "Aye, Your Honor, I can't allow anything to happen to you. The thought of bein' cut off from this nectar for eternity is near more than I can bear."

"How do we begin?"

He hunched forward. "Cap'n, the time is short. Much too short. I blame myself the other day in this selfsame saloon for not broaching the matter, but I was shy of it."

"Why do you say the time is so short? How much can there be to learn in seventeen days?"

He grimaced. "Aye, it ain't only the learnin' Cap'n, it's also the matter of the uniform and the insignia and the brass and the proper boots and the Sam Browne belt. Aye, Cap'n, these things take their time, they do."

"Why can't I just go and buy a uniform? Or you buy it for me. They must sell them somewhere. Hell, we'll steal one if we have to."

He got a weary, frustrated look on his face. "Cap'n, you're not after understanding how these matters work. You will recollect, Your Honor, that I told you you'd have to be of field rank to up and take over a detail. That's a full colonel. Aye, and I reckon I'd better stop off callin' you Cap'n and get used to you hearing 'Colonel.' But what I'm saying, sir, is that gents of that rank are after having their uniforms made by a proper tailor. None of your government issue for them. You see, sir, officers get a clothing allowance and must buy their own uniforms. The little shavetails, lieutenants and so on, buy off the rack, but that wouldn't be fitting for a bird colonel. Why, you might as well carry a sign saying you was false."

I frowned. "Where am I supposed to get this done? Not around here."

"No, sir. We've got to go to San Antonio and, begging Your Honor's pardon, we've got to go as quick as I can get you a set of orders made, sir. I reckon I can be doing that tonight."

"A set of what?"

He got that worried look on his face again. "Orders, sir. You see, sir, in the army, every little change has got to be accompanied by a set of orders. We are after needing to get you a uniform made and a set of brass for a full colonel. Well, sir, you got to have orders to show for that. The tailor can't up and on his own make you an officer's uniform. You got to have the orders in your hand or else you got to go in there in uniform and you ain't got no uniform, begging the colonel's pardon. There, that sounded about right. Are you after feeling like a colonel, sir?"

"I'm after feeling like a damn fool," I said grimly. "Hell, Sergeant, I don't understand any of this. Orders. A set of orders. Is all the army that complicated?"

He shrugged. "Aye, sir, we have a saying. There's a right way, a wrong way, and the army way. You are allowed to complain but you are not allowed to do it different. Sir, if anyone could walk into a military store and buy a set of colonel's eagles and the other brass, why, everyone would be a colonel. No, I've got to get you a set of orders. I'll need one set promoting you from lieutenant colonel to full colonel. Then I'll need a set transferring you to the proper outfit for giving orders to the officer in head of that detail."

I stared at him. "Proper outfit? What are you talking about?"

He shook his head slowly. "Sir, you don't know a bean about the military, do you, Colonel, sir?"

"Will you quit calling me colonel? And, no, I don't know anything about the army. Why should I?"

"Sir, you need to get used to being addressed in that fashion. Now, proper outfit means you need to be in the same branch of the army as the ones with the gold. An officer of artillery, for instance, wouldn't go up to that detail and tell them to hand over the gold. They'd think he'd gone off."

"How many branches are there? I thought there was just the army. Period."

He shook his head. " 'Twas a lucky day I walked into your emporium. You was by way of committing suicide. How many branches?" He shrugged. "Infantry, Cavalry, Engineers, General Advocate's office, Records, Training Command, which is what I am in." He shrugged again. "A lot. But now, according to the bulletin, this job is being handled by the Quartermaster Corps. At least I'm after believing that the troops and transportation are being handled by them. But I will wager a copper coin that the officer or officers that are soldiering this detail are from Finance and Disbursement. I don't know which." He took a long stare at me and then shook his head. "Sir, you just don't look like Finance and Disbursement. You look like a cavalry officer, but you can't be that. Quartermasters it is going to have to be. It's not worthy of you, sir, being more like a storekeeper, but that's what it will have to be. The lads carrying the rifles will be Quartermaster and Stores and they will obey. It will make sense for you to be diverting the gold. Have you got a story in mind, sir?"

I smiled thinly. It was the only part I'd thought of and it also happened to be true. "I'm going to tell them to load the gold back aboard the train, that the area is not safe, that there have been reports of robbers in the area."

He threw his head back and let out a whoop and clapped his hands. "Bulls-eye, Colonel! Ah, you are one of nature's noblemen, sir. We'll make you Intelligence. That would be their proper job to scout out such goings-on." He thought a moment. "I'll make you the G-two—that's the intelligence officer, sir, on the general's staff of the Southwest District." He clapped his hands again. "And I'll learn you the name of the general and a few of the other officers on his staff, though those junior officers won't be after asking you any inquiring questions. If they do you'll be withering them with a look."

My head was reeling. "G what? Intelligence? I can't remember all this, Sergeant. Nobody can."

He fixed me with a look. "Ah, but you have to, Colonel."

"Quit calling me that."

"Get used to it, sir. If somebody says 'Colonel' and you are the only one there and you don't speak up, 'twould not be well."

"I guess so. If you say so."

"Oh, I do, sir. Can you be after leaving for San Antonio in the morning, Colonel?"

I thought a moment. There was Lauren. As bad as I dreaded it she would have to be told. But maybe it would be better to put it off until the last minute, get everything in order and then tell her. God only knew how much I dreaded it. I said, "Let's make the one o'clock train. True enough we won't be able to get it all done that day, but my wife knows I never take the morning train."

"Aye," he said. "Best not to upset the rhythm of matters just yet." He took a sip of his whiskey, which, uncharacteristically, he had not been attending to with his usual zeal. He gave me a long, thoughtful look. "So you are after just having the gold put back on the train. Begging your pardon, sir, but you ain't exactly robbed it."

"Sergeant, finally we are talking about a subject I know something about. The gold is too heavy to get it out of town by any other means than the way it came in. I'll simply direct the engineer of the train to head south and do so in a hurry."

"You'll be going up and telling the engineer yourself?"

"Of course. I intend on riding with the engineer heading south out of town."

The sergeant was shaking his head. "Won't do, sir."

"Why not?"

He shook his head some more. "Not proper, sir. If someone must ride in the sooty cab of the engine it would not be a high-ranking officer. He'd have one of the lads, a good dependable sergeant, under orders for the task."

I smacked the desk with the flat of my hand. "Damn it! This army business is too damn closed in. I've commandeered more than one train in my day and it was Wilson Young riding up there in the cab."

He shrugged. "Ah, yes, well, there you have it. It's foin for a bank robber, beggin' your pardon, sir. But not for a colonel. And why would you want to be up there?"

"Well, the way I got it figured so far is that I'm going to let the train run south for about twenty miles. No stations or switches along that stretch. About there I'll have the engineer stop the car and I'll tell the men to get out and take up guard positions. Then I'll get back on the train and tell the engineer to go ahead. Right then and there is where the robbery takes place. I have separated the gold from the soldiers."

He nodded. "That you have, sir. No one can gainsay you that. And then what is it to be?"

"About five miles further on there's a water tower at a place called Three Wells. Trains, if they need it, stop there to take on water. There's a little caretaker's shack and a small corral. I'll have two good horses there. I'll have the engineer stop and I'll get off. I'll tell him to go back and pick up the soldiers and take them back to San Antonio, that the danger has passed. After that I'll take my horses and strike for the border. Of course I'll change clothes first."

"You've a fine head, sir. Forgive me saying it, but you have planned this campaign in a military fashion."

I scowled at him. "You could have gone all day without saying that."

" 'Tis a compliment, sir. And from the time you get on that horse and take to flight I'm not a bit worried about you. It's the time in the plaza, the moving the men back on the train. Why let them get off the train at all? Why let them unload the gold?"

"Because I want it seen that the gold is there. In fact, I intend to stop them at the very door to the bank. Hell, it won't mean a damn thing unless I take it away from the very people they are trying to hoodwink. But there is a point we ain't discussed. You talk about making up these here orders for me. Ain't that kind of dangerous? Won't that be a trifle dicey?"

He laughed his Irish laugh. "Ah, bless you, Cap'n, no. My office is the orderly room, which is by way of being the headquarters of the headquarters."

"They make the orders up in the orderly room? I guess that makes sense."

"And himself here is in charge of the orderly room. Be a bit of nothing for me to turn out those orders."

"But doesn't someone have to sign them?"

He chuckled. "Aye, himself here. Course I won't be using my own John Henry, but the general commanding Southwest District."

"That could get you in trouble."

He shook his head. "Not for the slight use we'll be making of them in San Antonio. After they've served their purpose we destroys them and that's that. You'll want to be after leaving these details to me, Your Honor. You've got enough on your plate learning what you have to. By the way, since I don't think Your Honor will be wanting your own name on those orders, do you have any idea what name you might favor?"

I thought a moment and then smiled. "Les Richter. R-i-c-h-t-e-r."

"Have to be more formal, sir. Last name, first name, middle initial."

I shrugged. "All right. Richter, Leslie I."

"Be there a meaning?"

"For me only." I said it casually, but I looked away.

He coughed to cover the silence and took a quick drink from his glass. "Well, that's it, then. I'll be after making you a colonel of cavalry attached as intelligence officer to the general staff, Major General Wendell Peterson commanding. Aye, and a fine broth of a man he is." His face fell a little. "But it's sorry I am to tell you, Colonel, that the old horse cavalry is a fading glory. Now it's trucks and automobiles and motorcycles." He shuddered. "Fair makes an old trooper want to weep. Of course, now, being a cavalry officer you'll be wearing the boots and the cavalry pants. Colonel, it's sad to say, but I don't think there will be time to be having you a fine pair made, and there's a rare boot maker in San Antonio. I'm fearful they'll have to be ready to wear."

I said dryly, "The boots will be like the orders, Sergeant, just intended for the one occasion. I don't plan to make a habit out of them."

"You sure of your escape route, Colonel? Your retreat, or withdrawal?"

I nodded. "I'll be heading through the *brasada*. That means brush country in Mexican. They won't be catching me in any of their motorcars. And if they send an aeroplane over, all he'll see, if he sees me at all, will be a lone horseman. That's cow country. He'll see a lot of lone horsemen."

He said thoughtfully, "What might we be overlooking, sir?"

I shook my head. "I don't know."

"I have mentioned that the detail guarding the shipment will be a soft lot. So will the officers. But they might have one old hard sergeant along that will be hard to fool. If there is such he's the one you'll have to be on guard against."

"You say I shouldn't ride in the cab with the engineer. I suppose that means I'll have to ride with the soldiers. What am I supposed to say?"

He shrugged. "Nothing if you ain't a mind. Those junior officers will be scared to death of you. You sit off by yourself, Your Honor. They won't be after approaching you. By the way, do you know the makeup of the train?"

I shook my head. "No."

"Besides the engine and the tender and the caboose there are two cars. They keep two mules in the one car along with the caisson that they transport the gold on. A few soldiers stay in with that. The other car is a regular passenger car where the balance of the soldiers are. The train crew is an engineer, a fireman, and a conductor."

I nodded. "Much obliged for the information."

He stood up. " 'Tis best I be making my way back to camp. I'll be cutting the orders for you and arranging my leave. Is it your orders we should not recognize each other at the depot or on the train?"

"I think that would be advisable. Unless you want to lose your retirement and end up in a military jail."

He looked at me hard. "Speaking of jail, Your Honor . . . "

I shook my head. "It ain't going to happen."

"If you say so, sir." He turned toward the door and then stopped. "I'm after hoping your missus is an understanding lady. Was up to me I'd keep mum on the matter."

I smiled. "It ain't up to you, Sergeant."

He reached the door and took the knob in his hand. "Aye, there you'll be, on the road to Mexico with a train at your command and a load of gold on board. Many's the man couldn't resist the temptation."

"I told you, Sergeant, that I am not going to steal this gold."

He got an incredulous look on his face. "Then for the love of the saints will you tell me why you are going to all this trouble?"

I said evenly, though the question was starting to heat me up, "I have told you why I am doing it."

He stared at me. "Just for being after shoving a thumb up the bum of the high mucky-mucks, is it? Pardon my barracks-room language, Your Honor."

"No." I smiled slightly. "It's the best way I've heard it expressed."

"Aye." He suddenly came to attention and gave me a stiff salute, holding his rigid hand to the brim of his hat. "I must hold this, sir, until you return it."

"What do I do?"

"Just what I've done, only let your hand fall after you touch the air near your head. Very nonchalant."

I did as he instructed. "Is that all right?"

"We'll work on it, sir. Aye, you're a darlin' man, Your Honor. Sergeant McMartin requesting to be dismissed, sir!"

I laughed. "Dismissed, Sergeant. Go to the orderly room and write some orders. Just don't get caught, or my whole scheme is finished."

"Aye, sir!" He went out the door and I turned to the rest of my drink and the chore that lay ahead of me.

THE LORD help me, I could not keep it out of my mind. From Three Wells the railroad ran on to Hondo, about another ten miles. From there it switched. The southwestern track ran on toward Del Rio, with several small stops along the way. But the southeastern leg ran as straight as a schoolroom ruler to Laredo with no stops or switches the entire hundred or so miles to the border. There I'd be, as the sergeant had noted, with a train and a load of gold. I could bring my horses aboard at Three Wells, make up some story for the engineer, and then blaze a track for Laredo. I could have the train stopped short of the border, get the caisson and the caisson horses down, hitch them up, and then find a crossing and be in Mexico with a quarter of a million dollars in gold. It would be one hell of a way to crown a career. And not a shot fired. Just a bunch of soldiers standing out beside the tracks on a dusty prairie wondering what in the hell had happened.

THAT EVENING Lauren said, "Oh, Wilson, I do so hope you are not going to let the soldiers into your saloon. Some of them are just boys. They are too young to drink."

"They are also too young to pay my prices," I said.

She was doing needlepoint. She put it down for a moment. "Oh, that's right. There are plenty of other saloons and none of them are as nice as yours. Maybe you'd better let them come in yours so you can keep an eye on them."

I reckoned that was as naïve a remark as I had ever heard Lauren make. If you were in Del Rio you could get a drink if you had the price and it didn't matter how old you were or what day of the week it was or what time of day. And if you couldn't find one there all you had to do was walk across the border and somebody would probably give you one for nothing. "Lauren," I said, "it is too bad that you are not the mother or big sister to the world. If you were, there would never be such a thing as a bad boy, or a boy gone wrong, as my old aunt used to refer to me. That would mean there would be no fights, no thefts, no lies, no drunks, no gamblers, and no wars. Hell, if I'd met you soon enough I'd have never robbed that first bank. Think of that."

She picked up her needlepoint hoop. "If you enjoy making fun of your wife, Wilson, then go right ahead. But remember that it is a reflection on you. You chose me. What does that say about your sagacity?"

That was a word she used often but I had never found out what it meant. I was always going to go to the dictionary and look it up, but I somehow never got around to the task. And I damn sure wasn't going to ask her. I did what I usually did, tried to bluff it out. "Let's leave my sagacity out of this. I'm as careful and choosy as the next man. Maybe more so."

She laughed. "Oh, pshaw. You don't even know what the word means. It *doesn't* mean choosy. It means having a keen mind, being calculating."

"Well, I didn't rob banks for fifteen years and end up sitting here with the best-looking forty-year-old woman in the state by not having some of that sagacity."

"Oh, Wilson, I believe you could worm your way out of a drain spout."

I went back to my newspaper and she went back to her tatting. But a little later she lifted her head and said, in a worried voice, "Willis is so young. Do you suppose he's over in France drinking liquor in one of those . . . those . . . what do you call the places they drink in in France?"

"Whorehouses," I said without looking up.

She was scandalized. "Wilson Young! We are talking about our son!"

"Bistros, then," I said.

"What?"

"A bistro. That's what they call a French saloon."

She frowned. "And how would you know that? There's probably no such thing. You made it up."

I kept my nose in the newspaper. "I was once stepping out with a French countess and she took me around to a bistro and got me drunk and had her way with me."

She started laughing.

I looked up. "What is so funny?"

"The idea of you around some French countess, all dressed up in an elegant gown and jewels and you in your jeans and boots."

"At least I know what a bistro is. And that is where Willis is, probably, right now."

She looked up and into the distance. I could see the trouble in her face, but there wasn't anything I could do about it. I said, "He's probably all thumbs around those aeroplanes and will make such a mess of it they'll send him home."

She looked at me. "Do you think so?"

"I hope so," I said. "Anyway, I think that war has got to end soon. They've been sitting in their trenches staring at each other for over a year. So long as we stay out of it."

But she didn't want any of that talk. And neither did I, for that matter. She said, "That soldier that came to the door was certainly a polite man. Are you going to let him drink in your saloon?"

"Probably," I said.

"What was his name?"

"I didn't get it." I shut my paper and laid it on the table beside my chair. "It's getting late."

Later, as we were getting ready for bed, I told her that I was going to have to go to San Antonio the next day. "But it will only be an overnight trip, so I reckon all I need to take is my razor and toothbrush. I can get by with the same clothes."

She was sitting at her dressing table brushing her hair, making it shimmer. She turned half around. "You'll do no such thing, Wilson Young. You'll take a change of socks and a clean shirt. And underwear. I swear, Wilson, I never heard of a man not wearing underwear."

I was at the bureau. I turned around so I could see her face reflected in the mirror. "You just stepped out onto mighty thin ice, madam. How do you know how many men wear underwear and don't?"

She blushed. "Well, I had a brother. And there was my father."

"You saw them in their underwear?"

"There was the wash hung out to dry. There for all to see."

"Hmmm," I said. "That's a step toward safety, but not good enough."

"They sell men's underwear in stores. You see them advertised in the newspaper. Some men must wear them, even if you don't."

"Damn. I thought I had the blushing virgin cornered. Guess not." I turned back to hanging up my clothes.

We were about to get in bed when she said, "By the way . . . what are you going to San Antonio for?"

I climbed into bed. "I got to get fitted for an army colonel's uniform and get some cavalry boots and the necessary brass and insignia."

"Would you do me a favor? I need some Belgian lace and there's a little shop down near the Federal Bank. You remember it? You almost went there with me once. Can you take the time and pick me up some?"

I turned down the lamp on my side. "I'll try, honey, but that uniform business could take up all my time." I had no idea how I'd kept from flinching.

"All I ask is that you try."

We kissed and bade each other good night. Telling the absolute truth gave me quite a feeling of peace, but I found the coincidence of her naming that very bank as a landmark for her lace shop a little unnerving.

CHAPTER
10

THE TRAIN wasn't crowded, and by the time some folks got off in Hondo, the sergeant and I were able to share a seat under the pretext of sharing a drink. It was the sergeant's bottle and he made a face over drinking what he called "the ordinary" after my special old reserve, which, to him, was sublime.

"You see, Your Honor," he said, "whiskey, that rare whiskey you are after possessing, is like a virgin's reputation, to be savored and protected as long as possible." He held up his bottle of Bushmill's, which was passable Irish whiskey though I'd never developed a taste for it. "But this old whore. Aye, there's many a man has had her and is none the better for it. The insides of an Irishman's stomach is after being copper plated, and rare whiskey like yours polishes it for him and is the making of the man. But this stuff is for common folk who can expect nothing but suffering, which they are well used to."

Out the window we were leaving the last of the *brasada,* the brush country. It was strange to think that in not much more than two weeks I'd be fleeing through that rough country as I had not done for many a year. It sent a little thrill of fear and excitement through me.

I had looked at my orders. The sergeant had slipped them out of a little leather case he was carrying. They had certainly looked authentic. They were written on the letterhead of the Southwest District, Fourth Training Command, United States Army, and one of them detached Lieutenant Colonel Leslie I. Richter, cavalry instructor, from service with the Fourth Training Command and assigned him as acting G-2 to the Seventh Headquarters Group, Fort Sam Houston, San Antonio, Texas. The other promoted Lieutenant Colonel Richter to full colonel with all right of pay and emoluments accruing to that rank. They were typewritten and signed over the name of General Peterson.

I said, "Sergeant, I had no idea you could type. I hope you type-wrote these yourself."

He smiled. "Aye, sir. It was not a task I would have been entrusting to any of the clerks. Was near an all-night job, my big old fingers and them little keys. But I burned all my mistakes. Sir, we needs be talking about the kind of soldiers it will be making up this detail."

I listened while he talked about the differences between soldiers who worked in the Quartermaster Corps and those in cavalry or infantry or artillery. "And them officers—and I'm betting that there will be two of them—soft they'll be. More like civilians—no disrespect to you, sir, it's another kind of civilian I'm talking about. Soft and lazy and would rather work with a pencil than a rifle. Sir, you'll be wanting to show them the hard edge of yourself. Put the proper fear in them right off. After that you could give them any order and they'll jump to obey it. If you set them up proper, Your Honor, they'll never question another word you say. What Your Honor wants to be remembering is that they know others in the military don't consider them proper soldiers, and they be ashamed. But they likes that soft life in the Quartermasters and the Finance office. But they still be ashamed. Then along comes you, an elegant, daring, daunting-looking cavalry colonel. They will pee their pants, sir, forgiving my barracks mouth."

But I was still puzzled by something. "I don't really understand this officer stuff. You talk about them as completely different from what you call 'enlisted men.' "

Outside, the countryside was rolling and green as we neared San Antonio. It was one of the prettier parts of Texas with its clear streams and little limestone hills and rolling pastures of good grass. The sergeant said, "Aye, sir, but you'll have to be after understanding the tradition of the thing rather than the practicality. The commissioned officers is your nobles, you know, like the noblemen of old? Your knights and earls and barons and what not. The enlisted men are like the yeomen, the serfs and that lot."

"You telling me that the officers are like royalty?"

He chuckled. "A few thinks so, but, no, sir, it ain't that bad. An officer is commissioned by the Congress of the United States. Oh, I don't mean that every second lieutenant gets passed on by the Congress, but when you get up into your generals they get promoted by name by the Congress. No, it is simply said that they are officers and gentlemen by act of Congress. Enlisted men ain't allowed to be gentlemen."

"That's the silliest thing I ever heard. How do the ones who get to be officers get chosen?"

"Oh, there's many ways, sir, but it ain't all brains. Some I've known are still looking for theirs, searching around in cabinets and bureau drawers and saying, 'Now where did I leave my damn brains? I know I had them.' " He laughed.

"And you're a noncommissioned officer, but no gentleman?"

"Aye, there you have it, sir."

"Sounds silly."

"Aye, but it's the army way. You would have made a proper officer, sir. I'll be taking that back. For a little while you had better *be* a proper officer and no mistake."

We had another drink and then the sergeant said, "Sir, something's been bothering me. You'll be after walking up to that detail unattended. That ain't proper, sir. You should have your aide-de-camp or your first sergeant with you, sir. A regular colonel would."

I glanced sideways at him. He had the aisle seat. "What in hell are you getting at, Sergeant?"

He hesitated. "Well, sir, I was after thinkin' that might be a job I could do. And then, sir, don't you see, I'd be right there on the spot to see that you didn't go wrong. If I seen you needed an order given I could kind of prompt you, sir. 'Twould be a treat for me, sir. Tell my grandchildren about it."

I said harshly, "Sergeant, you better lay off the bottle. I think it's getting to your brain. I told you I'd play this hand solo. You want to end up in jail?"

He nodded. "I've thought on that, sir, and there ain't no chance. My story would be that you come along and commanded me to accompany you. Naturally, I ain't after refusing an order from a field grade officer. No, sir."

"That's as thin as an old maid's dreams. Nobody would believe that. By your own reckoning you've put up with hell to make your thirty years. Why would you want to risk that?"

He shrugged. "I was going for the thirty years because there was nothing better in the offing. I could retire tomorrow."

"You don't have to make thirty years to retire?"

"No, sir. A man can retire after twenty years' active duty, though his retirement pay wouldn't feed a dog and cat if they were a match for each other. But I got near twenty-seven. Wouldn't be a bad little sum to live on."

I studied him in profile. The sergeant was good company and a man I had liked instinctively from our first meeting. "Hell, why don't you retire, then? You are obviously about at the end of your tether for taking orders from officers."

"Not all of them, sir. They ain't all brainless. Just the wonders I'm pleased to serve under."

"You could come to work for me. Hell, I'd pay you twice what you make now."

His face lit up and he turned to me. "For a fact, sir? You wouldn't be after pulling old Rollie's leg? Having a bit of fun?"

I shook my head. "No. I can always use a good man I can trust. You could start off tending bar. Or I could put you in the casino to be sure all went smooth. You look like you got the muscle to handle such a job."

He looked into the distance. "Ah, that would be a dream come true. The only reason I was trying to stretch it to thirty year was so I'd have the money to open my own little saloon." He turned to me and said hastily, "Of course, nothing like what you've got, Your Honor. Just a little place." He grimaced. "Of course, that damn woman has been bleeding me so dry I'm after not saving any money as I had been."

"You work for me five years and I'll set you up in your own place."

His face was alight at the prospect. But then it fell. "Ah, sir, there's still this . . . " He let the sentence fall unspoken.

I smiled. "There's still a damn good chance I won't make it through this adventure. And then where will you be?" I clapped him on the shoulder. "C'mon, Sergeant, where's your faith, your belief? Do you always figure a thing will go wrong if it can?"

He laughed ruefully. "Aye, that's the Irish for you, sir. Always larkin' about with a mouthful of blarney and a heartful of woe betide. That's the truth of it, Your Honor, we go about singin' and talking like we're after having a tongue of quicksilver, but the truth be we're trying to hold off the black misery and the dark clouds. Don't ever look into the heart and soul of an Irishman, Your Honor. The sight would sadden you."

I laughed. "And here I've been thinking that you'd have made a pretty fair hand as a bank robber."

His face lit up. "Aw, Your Honor is having a lark with me." But he looked pleased. "My, what a prospect that would have been to have been a highwayman alongside the famous Wilson Young."

"But a bank robber has got to be an optimist," I said. "Got to believe what he's doing is going to work. He goes in with a hangdog look on his face, he's liable to be hung like a dog and get no gold, either."

"Aye," he said, nodding, "there's great truth in what you say, sir. No, no, don't take me as being in the black moods all the time. By nature I'm a man what sees the happy side of the coin."

"Even though you don't look a thing like him and you're older and he certainly wasn't Irish, you kind of remind me of someone."

"And who would that be, Your Honor?"

Through the window I could see the beginnings of little farms and ranches. It was a sign we were approaching San Antonio. I was sorry I had spoken of Les. I said, "Oh, not really anyone. Forget it."

But he was interested. "Was it a lad rode with you, sir? One that had a hand in the business of bank robbing?"

I grimaced. I really didn't want to talk about it, but it was me that had brought it up. Reluctantly I said, "Yeah. Yeah, we were together for quite a few years."

He said softly, "I can see in your face, sir, that he was a mate to you, as the Irish say. Close, was you?"

"Yes, we were close." I turned my head to look out the window, intending that the movement end the conversation.

The sergeant said, "I'll not mention it again, but I take it as a great compliment what you said. Could I perhaps know his name?"

"You already know it." I kept staring out the window.

He was silent for a moment. Then he said quietly, "Aye, sir, Leslie Richter. Colonel Leslie I. Richter."

That made me smile. "He'd turn over in his grave at the 'Colonel.' An officer and a gentleman." I stopped and thought a moment. "But that part would fit him. He was a gentle man. He was kind, he was honest, he was straight as a die when it came to sticking by a friend. Yes, he was a gentleman, more so than many I've heard referred to as such or who consider themselves such. I don't know about the officer part, though he could give orders and make them stick. Not that he liked it much." I looked back out the window.

McMartin said gently, "So putting his name on the commission is by way of having him with you on the adventure, as you call it."

I shrugged. "I don't know. He's been dead a long time."

"Aye, but not in your heart, Your Honor. They say that one never dies so long as he's alive in the heart of a good party."

I looked at him hard. "You really believe that?"

"Aye, I do, Your Honor. The good, gracious Lord told us to love one another. I'm after admitting that that is something of a chore with certain parties, but love is like the spirit, isn't it, Your Honor? And if the spirit lives on? Surely the good wise Lord had something in mind in bidding us love one another."

"Sergeant, you're making me uncomfortable."

"You're not wanting anyone to see that side of you, Your Honor." He smiled. "I vow to never look again."

I shook my head. "I don't believe this. Hell, I haven't even known you ten days and already I'm telling you details about myself and trusting you with my life on a fake robbery. Hell, Rollie! What is all this?"

He leaned back comfortably. " 'Tis no more than a colonel would be doing with his proper escort, his first sergeant."

I looked around at him. "That better not mean what I think it does, because that is one subject we ain't going to discuss. You ain't getting within ten miles of the robbery and you can fix your mind to that."

"Aye, sir," he said. But he had a little smile on his face that I didn't like.

SAN ANTONIO was a large center for the military. Fort Sam Houston was the biggest army post in the United States, and there was Kelly Field and several other smaller camps. There was, therefore, no shortage of military tailors, but the sergeant had the name of the best, and nothing but the one place would do. We got into town at about four o'clock and went directly to the establishment. There was little for me to do except to stand and glower and be measured. I made one unfortunate remark about not caring for gabardine, but before the tailor could look at me in amazement, the sergeant hastened in with a statement that "the colonel is just after having his little joke."

I didn't care at all for the "fitting," as it was called. The tailor took enough measurements to have been planning to set me in a plaster cast. But I played the part as given me by Sergeant McMartin. He'd said that I was to act bored, that I was to look stern, and that I was to occasionally find fault. I'd asked him what if I couldn't find anything to fault. He'd said, "Oh, but that don't matter, Your Honor. A high-ranking noble such as yourself would always be after finding fault. And if the tailor addresses you directly, sir, you are to act as if you didn't hear him and look to me for what he had to say."

"Do all officers act like that?"

"Oh, my faith, yes. Especially them as has attained as august a rank as yours, sir."

"Officers sound like a pain in the ass."

"Aye, sir, but wouldn't do for one such as I to be commenting."

I couldn't help but smile. "Rollie, do they know how slick you get around them?"

He gave me his innocent look. "Get around them, sir? Why, what after would you be talking about, Your Honor?"

Dress uniforms were obviously intended to be worn tight. Rollie said, "It's parade dress, sir. If it's snug, won't be a wrinkle showing."

"Parade? Do they go in parades?"

"Aw, you are after misunderstanding, sir. 'On parade' in the army is anytime an officer appears officially in public in dress uniform. I suppose there's a laugh in it, but you will be on parade when you interfere with the gold delivery. Which reminds me, sir, you'll need to be wearing campaign ribbons. We can't be after buying new ones. Don't have time to give them that worn look. I reckon you'll wear mine and any others I can find in the palm of my hand by a bit of luck."

"I don't know what campaign ribbons are, but then neither do I know much about anything else we're doing."

We bought the Sam Browne belt in the same shop as the boots. The Sam Browne was a broad belt worn outside the tunic. It had a strap that ran diagonally across the chest and down the back to connect with the back part of the belt. There were a couple of hooks for the holster for the .45-caliber automatic. The boots, I thought, were awful, but outside the store the sergeant assured me not to worry. "I'll have a recruit wear these in for you, sir. And the next time you see them they'll be polished so that people dare not look their way if the sun is bright."

There was a little trouble about the uniform. Sergeant McMartin informed the tailor that the article would have to be at Camp Verde within ten days. At the sergeant's direction, I had ordered two new uniforms because, as Rollie said, it would look odd for an officer coming in from the field to a staff job not to need at least two dress uniforms. He'd said, "Out in the field, sir, there's not many state occasions, but at headquarters there's dinners and receptions and all of that la-di-da. And you, being a staff officer, would be expected to attend. So the tailor might take it odd you asking for only the one."

Hell, I hadn't cared. They were cheap enough. A two-hundred-dollar bill would have covered the bunch of stuff.

But the tailor wrung his hands over the ten-day limit and swore he simply could not do it, that they were snowed under with orders. Rollie folded his hands in front of him and said, "Aye, very good, sir. And I'm sure it won't be hurting your business when the newest staff colonel on the general's staff shows up in his old field dress uniform. I know the colonel, being the kindhearted man he is, would never breathe a word about who let him down, but some of the enlisted men might talk, if you take my meaning, sir."

Of course, that changed everything. I reckoned I'd as soon not have Rollie blackmailing me. But once the issue was settled I plunked down an extra hundred-dollar bill and said, in my best command voice, "I'm a hard man, but I'm also just. Split that among your tailors."

Rollie remonstrated with me later for the gesture. "Aw, Colonel, you'll be ruining it for everyone else. Colonels don't make that kind of pay, sir."

"I've got a rich wife."

"No, sir, that would be Captain Georgie Patton. Fortunately he's down in Mexico with General Pershing playing ring-around-the-rosy with Pancho Villa. If he has his way, the day of the gasoline-burning cavalry is here."

I said, "Well, to hell with him, then. And all like him."

"Aye, sir, my sentiments exactly."

The last thing we did was buy the eagles, my insignia of rank, and the insignia of the cavalry, which was crossed sabers. Sergeant McMartin had been right. The man in the military store at Fort Sam Houston did look at my promotion papers before selling me the eagles. I had asked Rollie earlier if I wouldn't look odd dressed in civilian clothes, but he'd said, "Not at all, sir. You're between assignments. Temporary duty, we calls it. As such you can go about in mufti—that's civvy clothes, sir."

We had dinner at the Menenger Hotel, where I had gotten us a couple of rooms. It was an old, elegant cattleman's hotel that had become simply an elegant hotel. You still saw the big hats and the boots, but between them was most likely a silk shirt and an expensive business suit. I had thought that the sergeant might feel slightly out of place, but he acted like he stayed in such places every day. I said, "Rollie, I got to hand it to you, you act like you were born to the velvet."

He gave me a wink. "Aye, Colonel, and you can be after believing that it's them as wasn't can most take the joy of it."

Afterward we walked out into the night the few blocks to the Military Plaza. Without spoken suggestion we mounted the hard bricks of the big arena and strolled in the direction of the short street that led to the railroad depot, the spot from which the gold would start its journey to the bank. I was carrying another of my props, which Sergeant McMartin had insisted I get used to. It was called a swagger stick, though in reality it was nothing but a stiff riding crop. I'd asked him why it was called such. He'd said, "Aye, Colonel, because officers swagger. They carry the swagger stick because it helps with the job."

"All officers swagger?"

"Well, sir, them as has reached the rank to carry the stick. That's usually your major and above. Sometimes a captain will affect one, but it don't look right."

"No enlisted men carry one? Not even noncommissioned offiers such as yourself?"

He looked horrified in the moonlight. "Oh, no, sir! Enlisted men do not swagger. Why, I believe it is against army regulations. Might even be a court-martial offense. No, sir, enlisted men walk, they march, they creep along, they amble, the clumsier ones stumble along, but swagger? Lord bless you, no, sir. They ain't had the training, you see. But an officer—and I could be mistaken about this, sir—I believe the first thing they are taught is how to swagger."

"Not to command?"

He pursed his lips. "I'm not sure they teach them that, sir, in the officers' schools. They teach them to give orders, but not how to make sense of them."

Now we stood in the middle of the plaza. There were a few other people about, a couple on a bench, a few men walking aimlessly. But it was nowhere as crowded as it was going to be the day I stopped the gold and took charge.

Except for the noise from a saloon across the way and the quiet murmur of the other people on the plaza, it was as still as a church. The sergeant said, "Picturing it in your mind, are you, sir?"

"Sort of," I said. "I haven't got it all figured out yet, not down to the details. I'm thinking about where the best place to make the interception would be."

"I'm not after advising such a one as yourself, Colonel, but maybe somewhere in the plaza with all the big crowd watching. The soldiers and the junior officers will want to look smart for the crowd, and they should do an about-wheel with the caisson and march smartly back to the train. That is, sir," he added gently, "if you make it clear you want quick action and not a moment to lose with questions or other foolishness. I only thought of this a short time ago so I didn't mention it, but I'm going to draw up a set of orders directing you to see to the safe transit of the gold. Though I wouldn't be showing them unless it was the necessary thing to do, if you are after taking my meaning."

I gave him a small smile. "In other words, they will probably not bear close inspection."

He pursed his lips. "Let's just say, Your Honor, that such orders would be a little irregular. That is, unless you, being the intelligence officer that you are, had absolute proof of a robber gang lurking about to make off with the gold and kill half the civilians in the crowd."

"But I do, don't I?" I said.

He chuckled in his throat. "Aye, that you do. I'm after thinking that you know for certain about one individual with experience in robbing banks who has designs on the gold."

"Anybody that would actually try and steal this gold would have to be crazy."

"But you are the same as doing it, sir. If you was to run that train on to Mexico you'd get away with it."

I stared across the plaza. "Yeah," I said. "If I was to do that."

We were both silent. There was a huge, golden full moon hanging about halfway up the cloudless night sky. It looked near enough to touch. Sergeant McMartin said, "Tell me, sir, what are you feeling, standing here seeing it in your mind?"

I gave a slight, involuntary shiver and laughed softly. The laugh had a hollow sound in it. "To tell the truth, a little scared, a little apprehensive."

"Beggin' Your Honor's pardon, but you'd have to be dead not to feel that way."

"When I was a wild kid I didn't have much sense, but I also didn't have that much to lose. Now . . . " I shrugged. "I guess I'm older and I know bullets can hit me because they have. But it's not the bullets I'm afraid of. It could be very embarrassing."

He turned half around so that he was nearly facing me. "I'm wanting to be asking Your Honor something, but I don't know if I can get the words right."

Then I did laugh. "You, Sergeant? Hell, words are your stock-in-trade."

"Well, what I wanted to ask—it's clear you must have the sand and the grit for it or you wouldn't be standing here. I was wondering how you were just before the danger, just as it comes over you. Like in a battle. Some are calm and you think they are fine. Some act like they're half-drunk and then come through it like a top."

I thought a moment. "Yeah, I guess a bank robbery is like a battle. I'm a little fluttery right before it starts. But then it changes. Once the play begins it seems like everything slows down. I don't mean it actually does, but you can see more, you are more aware. You seem to have more time."

He said quietly, "Like you can almost see the bullet in its flight?"

I turned my head quickly toward him. "Yes. Like that. But how would you know about that? I've only mentioned that to one other soul and he ain't here."

He cocked his head. "Because, sir, that's the way it is for me in a battle. It's like the battle was being fought under water. You know how slow, slow, you move underwater. At least the rest of the chaps. You move fast and free and every move feels right. Is it anything like that for you, sir?"

I shrugged. "It's been a while, but, yes, that's about the size of it. You feel like you can see the bullets, coming and going." I shivered. "Let's get back to the hotel and get a drink and hit the sack. We got an early train in the morning."

But as we turned, my eyes lit on the building at the corner. "And there's the bank," I said.

"Aye, Your Honor, the very one that will not be putting on a heathen display of gold in close on to two weeks. Aye, we'd better get to bed and make that train. We've a power of work to do on you, begging your pardon, sir."

"You've got poor material to work with, Sergeant. The closest I ever got to the military, the cavalry, at least, was stealing a horse after mine was shot out from under me and I grabbed the nearest one at hand. Was in front of a saloon. I knew it was an army horse the minute I sprung onto that McClelland saddle. Do they make you ride those damn things as punishment?"

He laughed softly. "No, Your Honor. They buys them because they are cheap. They cost the army nineteen dollars the saddle.

You'll never see an officer using one. They have theirs made, custom like. They look a little like the McClelland, but they ain't."

"Well, I thought I was going to castrate myself on that one. Hell, I damn near stopped and surrendered. If it had only been myself I damn well might have."

We walked in silence for a block or so and then the sergeant said, "Aye, sir, you can't know what this means to me, being engaged in this fine, noble gesture by yourself, sir."

"Sergeant, don't make it out to be more than it is."

"Sure and there's no need. It's up to the little people. With the Lord's blessing you'll be after showing the government that they can't put the heel of their boot just wheresoever they choose."

"The Lord's blessing?" I said. "Sergeant, you better watch that kind of talk. I doubt that the Lord would much approve of what I'm doing."

"Oh, I don't be after thinking that way, sir. Didn't He chase the money changers out of the temple, laying about Him with a whip and turning over tables? Aye, them as thinks the good Lord Jesus was one to stand idly by when wrong was being done have got another think coming."

I felt very uneasy. "Sergeant, I fear you might be getting a little close to blasphemy there."

"Oh, no, sir. I know the right of a thing and I know your reasons. 'Tis heaven's gold you are after protecting from an evil use."

I stopped and turned to look at him, furrowing my brow. "Have you said that before?"

"No, sir, not that I recollect."

I shook my head. "Maybe I dreamed it, but it seems I've heard that before."

"Not from me, sir."

We went on back to the hotel.

Except for the uniform, which would be sent to Camp Verde in care of Sergeant McMartin, we were fetching the rest of the military gear back with us. The sergeant and I had made it up between us that we would make my ranch just across the river in Mexico our headquarters and training ground. Lauren didn't care for the place and never went there, and what few servants and workers I kept about the place were Mexican and not very concerned with matters that didn't involve them. Since the sergeant was on leave I suggested he stay there. I'd see that he had several good saddle horses to use, and I had a very good cook there, a fat little Mexican lady who was always fretting that I came so seldom she never got to cook for me. I figured the sergeant could give a good account of himself in the knife-and-fork department. There were several pretty young señoritas about the place and I thought to warn the sergeant that they were taken, but, then, he was a man of the world and I figured he could look out for himself. Aside from my training, our main worry was the uniform arriving in time for me to make use enough of it that it would wear natural. Already, with the uneasy education I was receiving from Sergeant McMartin, and the real training yet to begin, I was becoming more and more worried about my ability to pull the stunt off. When the idea had first popped into my mind it had seemed like the easiest solution possible and almost cut to order. I'd simply get me a uniform, pop up in front of the detail, and matters would take an easy course from there. How damn stupid I had been. If Rollie hadn't come along I'd have been shot or, worse, laughed at. This business of playacting as an army officer was a good deal more complicated than I had at first thought, and the more I learned the more I realized how much I didn't know. Hell, with a couple of weeks' practice I was going to step in and impersonate a man who might have been plying his trade for twenty-five years or more.

The train rattled along on our western route home. We'd already passed the switching point at Hondo and were only about some seventy-five miles from Del Rio. We had both been quiet for a time. Out of nowhere the sergeant said, "Maybe it be too early in the game to be after asking such questions, Colonel, but how are you rating your chances?"

I laughed uneasily. "You mean my chances of getting killed or jailed?"

"No, sir, bless you, Colonel. Knowing you to be a man not to do things by halves I meant to bring the matter off slick as a whistle and no one the wiser. You back home and no one suspecting and the government with egg on their face."

I grimaced. "I think I'd need a miracle at this point."

He looked a little surprised. "A miracle, is it, sir? Well, I'm after being glad that you're a man of faith."

I glanced around at him. "It was a figure of speech, Rollie. Why, do you believe in God?"

"Do I—" He turned toward me. "Do I believe in God? Do you believe in this train that is jerking us along at forty miles an hour?"

"Yes, but I can see this train."

He pulled his head back. "Oh, you're after wanting to see the sweet Lord before you'll give Him substance. Ah, there's the rub, Your Honor. It don't work that way. But so far as seeing, yes, I see God. Everywhere I look."

Such talk bothered me. As I said before, it always had ever since my prune-mouthed aunt had begun hitting me over the head with the subject. I expected such talk from Lauren, but the sergeant had caught me completely off guard. I wasn't sure but what he might not be larking, as he called it. I said, "You sound like my wife."

"Ah, your missus. And a wonderful lady she is. I could see the goodness glowing inside her at just a glance."

I picked up the bottle we had setting on the floor and had a pull. "All right. You're Catholic. As far as I'm concerned, what a man believes is his own affair."

His eyes twinkled. "Ah, Your Honor, beggin' your pardon, but I'm not of the Catholic persuasion."

"But you're Irish. I thought all Irish were Catholics."

"Aye, I don't know the truth or not of that, though I'd doubt it. But the fact is, Colonel, I'm only half Irish on my father's side."

I looked at him in astonishment. "Hell, you sound more Irish than anybody I ever heard. At first I thought you was some kind of overgrown leprechaun."

He laughed his throaty chuckle. "Well, I'll be telling you the truth of that, sir, shameful as it might sound. The Irish does well in the army, sir, at least in the enlisted ranks. And when I was a mere lad, first joined up, I was after noticing that a good many of the high-ranking noncoms and the top sergeants was Irish. 'Twould be a fair statement to say we give a leg up to our own, so I let what little brogue I had get broader, and I laid hands on a map of the Emerald Isle and committed it to memory and made up a passable story for my old dad, who never set a foot in the place. My mother was no more Irish than the cat. She was like the duke's children, a mixture of whatever was in reach." He chuckled. "I've been at the game so long, Your Honor, that I'm by way of half believing it myself. No, I'm no Catholic. It's the Baptist church what gets my patronage."

I looked at him and shook my head. "Why, you old fraud, Sergeant. If I ever happen across a meeting of the Sons of Erin I'm going to report you. Here you had me going about your religion."

He shook his head. "Oh, I'm not a religious man, sir. But of faith? Aye, that I am. There's no brogue to that."

"But you drink and you—hell, I don't know what all. And you're a soldier."

He held up a finger. "More the reason for the faith, sir. As for the drink and the rest . . . moderation, sir. The sweet Jesus himself said take a little wine for the stomach's sake."

"I never heard the mention of anything about Bushmill's and that other rotgut you drink."

He chuckled. "Aye, Colonel, someday you may understand."

"And you're hip deep in a gold robbery."

"Ah, 'tis not, begging Your Honor's pardon. 'Tis a grand and noble gesture you'll be making."

"That's what you think? That I'm making a gesture?"

"Aye, sir. And I think it's more for your lad's sake than you'll admit."

"Do you know what is going to be said about my 'grand and noble gesture'? It's going to be said that it was the act of a man growing old who wanted to see if he could go one more time. It's going to be called my last gamble. It's going to be said that I had to prove to myself I could still take other people's money. Won't be any talk about a grand and noble gesture."

"Aye, perhaps, sir, but we'll know the truth of the matter, as will the good Lord."

I just stared at him and shook my head. There didn't seem to be anything to say. In his mind, one such as I had suddenly become an instrument of faith. That, I figured, would give Lauren a good laugh. But the thought of Lauren took all the laugh out of me. The time was passing and she was going to have to be told. I shrank from the very idea, but there it was. There was no way around the project. And Lord only knew how she was going to take it. I knew she wouldn't quit me over the matter because she was the kind of woman who married for life. But I couldn't be sure that she wouldn't try to stop me in some way.

The sergeant said, "Sir, I will certainly hand you the bouquet on the business of buying lace. I don't believe I ever saw such a flurry in all my life. Your missus will be well pleased, I'd reckon."

I'd very nearly forgotten the lace. If we hadn't walked out on the plaza the night before I probably would have. But looking at the bank I'd noticed the little shop near it and remembered Lauren asking me to get her some Belgian lace. At least I had remembered lace; I had forgotten the Belgian part. The next morning, rushing to catch our train, I'd gotten them to open the little shop ahead of time and then I'd torn through it in a flurry. I didn't know a hell of a lot about lace so I bought Irish lace, Belgian lace, French lace, and English lace. I bought black lace, white lace, rose lace, yellow lace, pearl-gray lace; I bought lace until I nearly ran the legs off the little old ladies who were waiting on me. The sergeant had stood by quietly laughing to himself. It had come to quite a sum, much more than my military gear had cost, but I hadn't cared. A guilty conscience will open a wallet faster than good intentions.

Walking to the train, the sergeant had made just one comment. "You'll be well supplied with lace, sir."

"Did I buy too much?"

"Not if you are after making a circus tent out of it, sir."

As we neared Del Rio I said, "Rollie, what the hell do I do if the officer in charge of the detail just up and says he won't do what I tell him?"

"How are you meaning that, sir?"

"Well, what if he decides he doesn't have to follow my orders?"

"Decides? Decides?" He looked around at me. "You mean makes a decision, sir?"

"Yes."

He put his head back and guffawed. "Oh, junior officers ain't allowed decisions any more than they are brains or proper weapons."

"Weapons? Don't they carry sidearms?"

"Aye, sir. But that would be the forty-five semiautomatic yourself is familiar with. Lord bless you, sir, they're allowed to have them because they can't hit anything with the heavy little thing. I meant a proper weapon like a rifle. With one of those they are likely to do themselves or someone else an injury. No, sir, you need not concern your good self about the junior officer in charge of the detail challenging your order. If he does you should shoot him down on the spot."

Something was bothering me that had to be resolved. "Rollie, you have told me I might nearly get away with this little adventure because I look and act like an officer. But by your own account you hate officers. How can you be willing to help me?"

He laughed. "Bless you, sir, but I don't hate officers. I'm *afeared* of junior officers, and with good reason. But senior officers, especially the ones above the rank of major, have had time to get some common sense and come to the realization that they ain't descended in a direct line from Solomon."

"You're afraid of junior officers?"

He nodded solemnly. "Aye, Your Honor, and you would be, too, if they held the power of life or death over you. I look at every new second lieutenant and even first lieutenants and captains and shudder that I might have to follow their orders in battle. I will give you a for-instance. During the campaign in the Philippines me and a squad of men were pinned down by a well-placed machine gun. Well, along comes this second lieutenant, still wet from the afterbirth, and he orders me and my men to charge across this open meadow and destroy the machine gun emplacement." He looked around at me. "Sir, it was suicide. We was just inside a little line of trees and the machine gun was across this clearing some fifty or sixty yards distant and well dug in. The clearing was as bare of cover as a bald man's head. I had told my squad we would hold our position until some light field artillery could be brought up to knock out the machine gun. And then come this second lieutenant inviting me to commit suicide on his order. And he wanted it done, if you're after believing this, right now. His exact words, Your Honor."

"What the hell did you do?"

He grimaced. "Some very fast thinking, if the truth be told. It was a quandary. If we charged that machine gun, we were dead. If I disobeyed or refused to follow the lieutenant's order, that was cowardice in the face of the enemy, and that is treason and they stand you up against a post and shoot you for it. So as not to let the practice get in favor, you understand."

"What did you do?"

Now it was his turn to lean down and get the bottle and have a pull. I could see by the expression on his face that he was reliving the moment. "I stalled, Your Honor. I came as close to disobeying as it is possible to do without actually saying the word *no*. I checked every man's equipment, then checked my equipment. After that I decided every man should reload with fresh ammunition. I was about to have them sharpen their bayonets when the lieutenant ran out of patience. He had a little whistle around his neck on a cord and he said when he blew that whistle we'd better damn well charge or the lot of us was heading for a court-martial. Well, I looked at my lads and they was rolling their eyes about and looking proper scared, as what man with a lick of sense wouldn't. I asked the lieutenant if we couldn't skirt around the woods and get some cover, but he said we were holding up the movement of the whole line and he wasn't going to get in hot water over our cowardice." The sergeant rubbed his jaw for a moment, then shook his head. "Finally, when I seen there was no way out, I asked if he was going to lead. Why, you'd've thought I'd slapped him, which I badly wanted to do, the way he reacted. He said that he certainly was not going to lead any charge. He was on battalion staff and had been sent forward to scout up a report to take back to battalion and he could hardly do that if he was killed or wounded in some charge." The sergeant looked away. "Hell, he wasn't even a proper combat officer but a goddamn glorified clerk from headquarters."

"Did you have to obey him?"

"Of course, Your Honor. He was battalion staff and it was like the order had come from the battalion commander himself."

"Well, you're here, so you weren't killed. What happened?"

"He was standing, facing me, and about three of my lads, including a corporal, were drawing beads on his back. Now it *was* a quandary. Officers shot in the back on the battlefield ain't as rare as you might think. They was in retreat, don't you see. But it does raise a smell for a time and the other officers take a right hard view of it." He had another drink. Then he stared off into space.

"Rollie, what the hell did you do?"

He laughed softly. "I reckon it was the luck of the Irish, Your Honor. I didn't have to do naught. Just as I'm making up my mind whether to nod to the lads with the rifles or to motion them down, comes the sound of hoofbeats and the rattle of caissons and here comes the battery of artillery I'd sent for. Well, even the lieutenant could see there was no reason for a charge now, so he put his whistle down." He shook his head. "A near thing, sir."

"I see your point. A man with a little authority can be mighty dangerous in the wrong place."

"Aye, the army don't say you got to obey sensible orders. They say you got to obey *all* orders and never mind it is the mother's son of an idiot who is giving them. I tell you, sir, there's many a good man dead today because of an insensible order delivered by one who couldn't be trusted to hold the horses."

We parted at the depot, the sergeant to take my military gear and himself over to my ranch in a rented hack, me to walk home carrying my bundle of lace and the little satchel Lauren had made me pack. It was just a little past eleven in the morning and the air was still cool enough to breathe.

Lauren wasn't home when I got there. Mrs. Bridesdale came in, drying her hands on her apron, to tell me that Lauren was at a committee meeting but would be home in time for lunch and were pork chops to my liking?

I went into my office and sat down in my chair and got out my special whiskey and had a pull, trying to get the taste of the sergeant's Bushmill's out of my mouth. I had missed Lauren, as I always did, but I wasn't in any special hurry to see her. It had come down to that time when I couldn't crawfish no more. Before we went to bed that night I was going to have to tell her. Hell, I was going to be spending a lot of time at the Mexican ranch and that would make her more curious than she already was. The sergeant had made it clear that we couldn't work enough. He'd said, "If you ain't letter perfect, sir, in the business of being an officer, you ain't likely to get a second chance. We got to go over it and go over it and go over it. Takes six months to make a second lieutenant. You got to learn to be a full colonel in something like two weeks."

But that wasn't the real reason. Lauren had a right to know. If I got myself killed I at least wanted her to know that I'd thought I had a good reason for what I did.

"WELL, WHERE is it?" she said.

We were having Mrs. Bridesdale's breaded pork chops with mustard greens and garden peas, a little more vegetables than I cared for at one time. I glanced up at her, my mind a blank for a second. We were having lunch a little late on account of her meeting and she'd consented to eat in the breakfast room. "Where is what?"

"Wilson, don't be evasive. It does not become you."

"I don't know what the hell you are talking about."

"Honey, don't swear in the house."

"I was cussing. I still don't know what you are talking about. You tell me what 'it' is and I might can tell you where 'it' is."

"What do you bring back practically every time you go to San Antonio?"

"A case of the clap?"

She reached over and slapped the air in front of my face. "That's not funny," she said, but she smiled just a little in spite of herself. Lauren liked a little wit from time to time and she didn't care where it came from. "No. You know what I'm talking about. Warner ships them there and you go and pick out what you want. Maybe it's not an it. Maybe there is more than one."

"What in hell are you talking about?"

"I don't mind you spending the money, though I think our charities could put it to better use, but I have to admit you are generous enough."

I put down my fork and stared at her. "How did you go loco in one day? That's all the longer I was gone."

"A racehorse. That's all you ever come back from San Antonio with. You have bought another racehorse. Or maybe two, for all I know. But I do know you never tell me that's what you are going for, and you usually go up one day and come back the next. How many does this make? I bet you don't even know how many racehorses you've got, do you?"

"If I could get a word in here edgewise I'd like to say that I did not come back with a racehorse or any other kind of horse."

She shrugged. "All right. You bought one and they'll be delivering it later. That's the same thing."

I reached out and got hold of her hand. "Lauren, look here. Look here right at my mouth. Watch what I'm saying. I did not buy a racehorse in San Antonio or anywhere else. Do you understand?"

She frowned. "Did you trade for one?"

I made a sound in my throat, something like "arrrgh," and threw my napkin into the air. "Damnit, I didn't go to San Antonio for horse business. Can you get that straight? You been hitting that Lydia Pinkham's Tonic a little hard lately? That stuff is about half alcohol, you know."

She drew herself up. "I don't think I care to be classed with women who take Lydia Pinkham's or think they need to. I simply thought it was a safe bet that you'd bought another racehorse and I thought it would be a good opportunity to make you feel guilty and hit you up for another contribution to my charities. And of course you didn't remember my lace."

I glowered at her. Getting up, I said, "Lady, you are in for one hell of a surprise. I'm going to say this once more. A, I didn't bring home or contract or make any kind of trade for a racehorse, and B—well, I'll show you B." I walked around her and went down to my office and grabbed up the paper parcel. As I walked back down the hall to the breakfast room I managed to break the twine that was holding the package. The instant I got in the room I started throwing lace toward the ceiling. It looked like one of them fireworks shows. Lace was flying everywhere in every color. Lauren just sat there watching the display, her mouth hanging open. When the last piece had left my hand I leaned down and got in her face and kissed her before she could close her mouth. "Now," I said, "you still want to tell me I forgot your lace?"

She stared at the display, dumbfounded. One piece of organdy lace had landed on the table, dangerously close to the bowl of mustard greens. I moved it delicately to safety. Her eyes round, she said, "Are you an absolute lunatic?"

I sat down. "You sent me after lace, I come home with lace."

"That's enough lace to make a wedding gown and outfit the bridesmaids. Did you buy out the store? How much did you spend? I asked you for a little Belgian lace and you have cornered the market."

I knew the way to her heart. "Whatever the bill was, and it's in the package, I'll give you the equivalent for your good works."

She shook her head and got up and set about picking up the scattered finery. "Wilson Young, sometimes I think you are crazy." Then she made a swift move and kissed me on the corner of the mouth. "But you can also be mighty sweet and thoughtful. I'm not going to forget about your pledge for my charities. Oh, this is just lovely. Irish! Oh, wonderful. Wilson, did you know you can tell which county in Ireland the lace comes from by the way it's made? I think this is Coventry County. They do very exquisite work."

I reapplied myself to the pork chops. "My, my, think of that. Coventry County. I'll have to tell the men down at the saloon about that. They'll be so thrilled."

But making Lauren laugh and getting her in a giddy mood over some lace was one thing; telling her what had to be told was an-

other. I sat there, grimly watching her examine the lace, and con-
templated what was to come. I didn't have the vaguest idea how I
was going to begin. How did a body casually tell his wife he was
going to put his life and maybe their whole future in jeopardy for
an action the real reason for which he wasn't even sure? Well, there
wasn't going to be an easy way, and it seemed to me the sooner I
got it over with the better. I started to open my mouth to tell her
to sit down, that I wanted to talk to her. But she looked so girlish
and happy I couldn't do it. Maybe it would be better a little later
in the day. Maybe I could get a drink or two in her and the blow
wouldn't seem quite so sharp. Maybe tell her before supper, or
maybe after supper during that time when we sat around in the parlor having a peaceful time together, her doing a crossword puzzle
or sewing and me reading or just thinking. Sometimes we talked
and sometimes we were just content to be in each other's company.

But the decision to tell her came up a lot sooner than I had
planned. A little after lunch she was standing in the hall in front of
a mirror putting on a hat. I asked her where she was going. She was
in the process of sticking a long hatpin in place. She said, "I'm going
to run into town to the general mercantile. We're getting low on
staples, flour and sugar and coffee and such. Mr. Bridesdale is
hitching up the buggy for me right now. Oh, Wilson, I wish you
would stop being so silly and buy us a little automobile. You
wouldn't have to fool with it. I could learn to drive. Laura drives
theirs. If Warner is willing to have one I don't see why you have to
be so hardheaded."

Abruptly I said, "Take your hat off."

She turned from the mirror. "What? Doesn't it look good?"

"Take it off and let's go upstairs. We need to talk."

She cocked her head and looked at me. "Upstairs? To talk? Wilson, I'm going to the store."

Her remark about the automobile had made up my mind. I said,
"I meant upstairs to talk because it is upstairs and we can't be over-

heard. I don't want anyone hearing what I've got to say."

She took her hands down from her head. "You're serious. You've got something on your mind and it is not pleasant."

I nodded. "I reckon you could say that. I'll be in the bedroom. I'm going to stop in my office and get a bottle and a glass. Do you want one?"

"A drink? In the middle of the day?" She looked worried. "Wilson, you are scaring me."

I started off down the hall. "Then let's get at it."

I went up to our bedroom and took a seat in a big easy chair in the corner. I could see out through two windows. To the west I could see the back of our house, see the garden and the buggy house and stables and the small corral and vegetable garden. South I could see most of town including the upper story of my casino. At one time that part had been my cathouse, but, of course, Lauren had put me out of that business. Now it was used by several of my single dealers and bartenders for bachelor quarters. We even kept vacant a couple of rooms where we let some casino player sleep after an all-night gambling session or someone from the saloon who didn't want to show up at home in the condition he was in.

Lauren came in and closed the door behind her. She gave me a look, half curious, half worried. "If I'm not going to the store I might as well get out of these town clothes."

I sat there sipping at my drink and watched her. It didn't make it any easier to keep my mind on the serious business at hand watching her get undressed. When she changed her long slip for a camisole and bared her breasts the whole project damn near went out of my mind. But then she put on a silk wrapper and covered all her charms up and my mind got back to the business at hand. I couldn't say which I was more afraid of: the actual adventure or telling Lauren. There was a little settee catty-corner to my chair that allowed her to curl up in one corner with her legs under her but still be facing me. She said, "Well?"

It sounded like the bell of doom. I cleared my throat. In one way or another I had been searching for a way to broach the subject for the better part of a week, but there just wasn't an easy way. I stared at the floor.

Lauren said, "Will, if this is going to be bad news I wish you'd get to it."

I nodded but didn't look up. "All right." I cleared my throat. "You know how I've been talking for some time about how I think the government is running the country into the ground, bankrupting the little fellow by getting him to spend himself into debt, trying to get him to use paper currency because they can always print more?"

"Yes. I've heard you. I don't know that I ever said I agreed with you."

I glanced up at her. "We ain't talking about how you think. I'm telling you how I've been thinking."

"What I think doesn't count?"

"That ain't the point. I'm about to tell you about something I've decided. It's got to be based on what I've been thinking."

"All right. I can see that. But hurry up. You're scaring me to death."

"You agreed with it when I told you about Norris telling Justa the same thing. Which, by the way, irritated the hell out of me."

"All right, all right. Fine. I agree with you. But what has that got to do with you, with us?"

I leaned back in my chair, crossed one leg over the other, and took a moment to refill my glass of whiskey. "I think the government is doing all this to get the country set up to enter the war."

She stared at me blankly. "That's not what the president is saying. Didn't he run on the peace platform?"

"It has been my observation that what politicians say and what they do ain't necessarily the same thing."

"I still want to know what it has got to do with us?"

"You can't put hundreds of thousands of men out of work and

keep on getting elected. You can't sacrifice the poor to the rich or vice versa and get elected. You got to do something to keep them all happy."

"Are you going to run for office?"

I gave her a grim look. Hell, if I was scared there wasn't any reason she shouldn't be too. "This ain't the time for jokes, Lauren."

"Then what is it all about?"

I studied her. She looked composed, but I could tell she was a little jumpy. "You know they are parading this display of gold around the country," I said, "showing off the government's assets, running a sandy, pulling a con. It's due in San Antonio in about two weeks."

She got a wary look on her face. "As I read in the papers it is guarded by a large group of soldiers."

"A twenty-one-man detail is all."

"That's all? You call twenty-one soldiers with rifles a detail?"

"Do you want to hear this or not?"

"I'm listening."

I took a sip of my whiskey. "It is my intention to interfere with their little show in San Antonio."

She stared at me, quiet for a second. "What do you mean, 'interfere' with it?"

"I'm going to steal the gold."

Again she was silent. Then she unfolded her legs and got off the settee and walked over and took the glass of whiskey out of my hand. As she walked back to the settee she said, "You were right, I did want a drink. I just didn't know it."

I let her get settled back down. I'd said the part I had dreaded. Now it was a question of defending my position.

She took a healthy swallow of the whiskey and didn't shudder in the least. Her hand was steady, but I heard a little quaver in her voice. "I don't suppose there is the slightest chance that you are somehow making an elaborate joke."

I looked back at her steadily. It wasn't a question as needed answering.

She waited a moment, to bring herself under control, I reckoned. Then she said, "You have never been a stupid man, Wilson, quite the contrary. And you're not one who does foolish or reckless things. Even at your wildest you said you planned every move. You said that was what kept you alive more than your prowess with a revolver. Isn't that true?"

I nodded.

"Then would you mind telling me why you are thinking of doing this stupid, insane act? You don't have a chance. Are you trying to be a martyr? You've never been that before."

"I don't know about that."

"What, being a martyr?"

"No, about not having a chance. I think I got a pretty good one to pull this off."

She took another drink. Now her hand was trembling ever so slightly. "You do realize that this could ruin us? Our home, our marriage. Your life."

I got a cheroot out of my pocket and lit it. The moment I did Lauren got up and fetched me over an ashtray. It was so like her. Her world was crashing in around her ears but she was still going to respect the manners of the house. She was a very stylish lady. I said, "Not necessarily."

She sat back down on the settee and looked at me. "What can I say or do to talk you out of this insanity?"

I shook my head slowly. "Nothing. I want you to understand and I'd like your agreement, but I know I ain't going to get it."

She stared at me. "Wilson, I read the papers also. There will be a crowd to see that gold arrive. There might be thousands of people. And the soldiers. You call them a small detail, but I think twenty-one soldiers are more than that! Do you have any idea what kind of slaughter and bloodshed there is going to be in a crowd like that? Innocent bystanders?"

I drew on my cheroot. I was strangely calm. Maybe it just felt good to finally get it all off my chest. "If it goes right, there won't be a shot fired."

She rolled her eyes. "Oh, Wilson! Come on! I know you are the resourceful and daring Wilson Young, bank robber extraordinaire, but you think they are just going to hand you that gold?" She paused and took another sip of whiskey, made a face, and then set the glass back on the floor. "Honey, are we really having this talk? Am I dreaming this? It is crazy. Wilson, you told me you haven't robbed a bank since 1888! Why would you want to take such a risk now?"

I rolled the cheroot around in my mouth. "You didn't listen to my reasons?"

She waved a hand. "Oh, that. I don't believe you're doing it for that. When did you start playing Robin Hood? Wilson, I am starting to get damn angry. Sometimes I think you have never grown up. This is insanity!"

"I guess," I said slowly, "that you can't see through to my real reason."

"And what would that be?" Her voice was taking on an edge.

"You said you read the papers. Then you ought to know that that war in Europe is just about spent, just about over. Both sides are worn out. They are like a couple of barroom brawlers who have fought 'til they can't fight no more. They are both sitting on the saloon floor, staring at each other, their chests heaving, too tired to make a fist. Well, that is the way it is in Europe. They are sitting in their trenches staring at each other across what they call no-man's-land and they are worn out. They are out of ammunition, the barrels of their artillery are worn smooth, England is bled white for fighting men, the French army has mutinied, and the Germans ain't got no more stomach for the mess. Another couple of months and they will both quit."

"So?"

I got up and faced out the south window, looking toward town. "But if Woodrow Wilson and his industrialist friends drag us into that war it will last another couple of years. It will take that long to get our factories back up to production making war goods and get everybody to work. Wars, I'm finding out, are mostly about money." I turned around to look at her. "We go into this war and that will add two years to the chances of our son getting killed or seriously hurt. I may not stop it by exposing to the people what the government is up to, but I can damn sure give them a scare." I leaned down and put out my cheroot.

She was staring at me hard. After a moment she said softly, "Is that really the reason, Will? Is it really about Willis?"

I turned back to the window. "I know what *you* think is the reason. Go ahead and say it, Lauren. Don't hold back on my account."

CHAPTER
11

⌒─────⌒ I ALMOST didn't recognize Sergeant McMartin the next morning. He was got up in a rich blue suit, complete with matching vest and a necktie tied in a four-in-hand knot. But the crowning glory was the black bowler he wore cocked just off the straight and narrow over one ear. He was standing on the board-walk in front of my saloon waiting as I came walking toward him. "Rollie?" I said, a little uncertainly.

He gave me a little salute. "Aye, Your Honor. And how would you be doing this fine morning?"

I came up to him, trying not to laugh. "You preaching some-where?"

He smiled. "Ah, Your Honor, you don't know what a pleasure it is to get out of khaki and get a bit of color about your person. One of the girls out at your ranch pressed this up for me along with a shirt, and I couldn't resist the walk down civvy street in proper clothes."

"How about the plug hat?"

He reached up and gave it a little thump with a thick finger. "Aye, it's a dandy derby, ain't it, Your Honor?"

I said, "Let's get in off the street before somebody shoots it off your head."

"Ah, they wouldn't be after doing that."

"We got some characters around here are after doing anything. Let's go in my office and get a drink."

We got settled in with the door closed and I got out a bottle and poured us out a drink. It was about ten of the morning, too late for coffee and too early for buttermilk, as a friend of mine used to say. He'd always added, "Guess we'll have to force this whiskey down."

We had a toast and a little swallow and then the sergeant hunched forward and gave me a looking over. "Aye, Colonel, I see a bit of strain in your face. Your eyes got a kind of look that don't bedeck a happy thought behind them, as it were."

I grimaced. "I reckon you can guess what has caused it. Though I didn't know it showed."

He said gently, "I take it you told the missus."

"Yeah. Started in about midafternoon yesterday."

"Aye." He made a little clucking sound to show he knew I'd been through a chore. "I'm after thinking you've not left her the happiest of women."

"That's a pretty good guess."

"Did it resolve?"

I shrugged. Hell, I didn't know myself. "I guess you'd have to ask her that. I don't know whether she accepted it or we got so tired we went to bed. She didn't say anything this morning. But she was awful quiet."

"I'm sorry for your trouble, Colonel. The task you've set yourself is enough of a burden. It's after being too bad that you've got more added to your load."

I snorted. "Hell, Rollie, you didn't think she was going to agree with me, did you?"

"But couldn't she see that it was for the lad that you're after taking on the chore?"

I gave him a look. "I tried that line of country, but I don't think she believed it any more than I did. She didn't say it, but I believe she thinks what everyone else will think, that it is Wilson Young showing his spots. Once a bank robber, always a bank robber. Another governor's pardon wasted. Still wild, still an outlaw. Getting on in years, you know, had to try it one more time just to see if he still could. And on and on like that." I shook my head. "It won't matter what I say, people will think what they want."

"But, sir, didn't you tell her you wasn't exactly going to steal the gold?"

"Wouldn't matter, Rollie. All she can see is me in front of thousands of folks with a drawn pistol in my hand fixing to get myself shot to pieces or arrested. I told her about every way there was to tell her that I would never pull a gun. In fact, I was thinking of not having one with me. She didn't believe that."

He looked troubled. "Ah, 'tis a shame, Your Honor, and no mistake. Can I be after asking how it was left?"

I shook my head. "With her quoting Scripture at me."

"Ah, your missus would be a God-fearing lady, then?"

I frowned. I'd heard the expression but never really understood it. "I think she's more of a God-loving person. Or God grateful or worshiping. I suppose if you believe as she does you'd be a little fearful. I don't know."

" 'Tisn't the same for you, sir?"

"I ain't handy with that kind of talk, Sergeant. What say we steer clear of it? I ain't a disbeliever; I just ain't so sure as some folks."

"And what was the Scripture, Colonel?"

It was all making me uneasy. I didn't much care to go over the discussion of the night before, if it could be called that, and I didn't care to get into the spiritual part. I said, "Oh, it was something about a blind man at a gate and Jesus and his disciples passed by and one of them wondered if the man had been blind since birth on account of his sins or the sins of his folks."

The sergeant nodded. "Aye, that would be in the Gospel of John. And His disciples, not understanding, asked that question and the good, sweet Christ answered them and said the man was put there, blind, so that the works of God might be displayed in him. He was there for the glory of the Lord." He stopped and frowned. "I wonder why she might be after using that one on you."

"She only trotted it up toward the last," I said tiredly. "Kind of like a parting shot. Didn't seem like her heart was much in it."

The sergeant looked thoughtful. "Maybe she's after thinking you'll be a good example to someone."

I shrugged. "That's kind of the way she said it. She said, 'Maybe you'll be like the blind man at the gate. Maybe there's a reason for this.' But the only thing I can figure out of that is that I'm going to be an example of what happens to them as takes the government's gold. That don't sound too promising."

"No, no, no." He shook his head. "No, your missus is a lady of faith and faith is all for the good. She say anything else?"

I looked at him. "Anything else? Hell, you might as well ask me what she didn't say."

"No, I mean along the lines of the Scriptures."

"Yeah. She used the one she uses on me a lot. I've damn near got that one by heart. Let me see . . . " I thought a moment. "Now, faith is the assurance of things hoped for . . . the, uh, something, convictions. Yes, convictions. The convictions of things not seen."

The sergeant smiled gently. "Ah, it's the purity of faith, that one. Hebrews it be. But it goes on. My memory ain't what it was, but it's 'By faith we understand that the worlds were prepared by the word of God, so that what is seen was not made out of things which are visible.' Don't you see, Your Honor? It's blind trust."

"No, I don't see. What is all this about things being made out of what was not visible? That don't make no sense."

"In the beginning there was the Word."

"What's that supposed to mean?"

"Nothing to those who are blind." He nodded his head. "Aye, Your Honor, I begin to see the line along which she is attacking."

"Well, I'm glad one of us does." I was about halfway irritated with his attitude. "For a drinking, carousing soldier, you seem damn conversant with the Bible."

He gave me a small smile. "The appearance of piety ain't necessarily the guarantee of the real thing, Colonel."

"I wish to hell you would quit calling me that."

He shook his head. "You've got to get used to it, Colonel. I wish you could begin to think like a colonel."

I gave him a disgusted look. "How am I supposed to think like a colonel if I don't know what a colonel thinks like? Did you bring me a horse?"

"Aye, Colonel. All saddled and ready out front."

I finished my drink and got up. "Well, let's get at it. I don't know why you got on them glad rags, but if they are your working clothes it's all right with me."

It was about five miles to my ranch. The sergeant had ridden one horse and led me a mount, a smart little quarterhorse I'd been using for at least ten years. He was getting along in years now, but he still liked to do his bit.

As we clattered across the International Bridge, entering Mexico, I noticed that the sergeant was riding half a length behind me. I thought it had something to do with passing through Mexican customs, but they simply waved us on across, as they always did. As we passed through the little town of Villa Acuña and started out the road to the ranch I saw that the sergeant still maintained his position with the head of his horse just behind my saddle. I said, "Rollie, what the hell are you doing back there? This road is wide enough for us to ride up together."

"Beggin' the colonel's pardon," he said, "but all members of the colonel's staff, be they junior officers or his attending noncommissioned officer, maintain a decent interval to the rear. It's a sign of respect, sir."

"The hell with that. We're not on parade now."

He did not ride up alongside me. Instead he said, "That's bully, sir, that you would know we are not on parade, but you must not turn your head backwards when you speak to me or any other aide. You speak straight ahead, begging Your Honor's pardon, in a command voice. It is the job of myself to hear the colonel's words."

I said in disgust, "The army is more full of nonsense than any outfit I ever dealt with."

"Aye, sir, but it all has a purpose."

"What purpose? Damnit, get up here!"

"Thanking you kindly, Colonel, but familiarity is destructive to the chain of command. You ease once, you might ease at the wrong time and then woe betide the troops and the command. You see, sir, you can't have an army without discipline. And you got to maintain it in peace or you won't have it in war. An army without discipline is just a mob, and mobs don't win wars."

I was getting damn tired of talking to the empty road ahead. "How is this supposed to contribute to discipline?"

" 'Tis a sign of respect, sir. The army has a great big chest full of traditions that are intended to make for respect. And respect, sir, is what causes discipline."

"Do you believe that horseshit?"

"Let me be after asking you, Colonel, did the men in your gang respect you?"

I shrugged. "Hell, I don't know. The subject never came up."

"Did they follow your orders?"

"Hell yes. I was the leader."

"Did you take care of them?"

"Best I could."

With some satisfaction he said, "Do you still want me to answer the question, Colonel?"

The turnoff to my ranch was coming up. "I reckon not," I answered. "Hell, you was willing to charge that machine gun emplacement on the word of an officer you had no respect for. Explain that."

"I didn't respect the man, sir, but I respected the rank. It was higher than mine. I was duty-bound to either follow it or turn into a mob by letting my men shoot him in the back."

"You never have told me what you would have done if that artillery hadn't arrived when it did."

"Aye, sir, and I reckon I'll never be after telling you."

We pulled up in front of my hacienda and one of my young vaqueros came running to take our horses and see to their care. The sergeant and I strolled on into the ranch house. It wasn't much next to my other two places. It wasn't but six rooms, and the place was half adobe brick and half stucco with a red tile roof. It had a nice cool porch that extended out in front where you could sit of an evening and drink a cool beer or a fruit drink and feel at peace. I had a special connection with the place because it was the first piece of permanent property I'd owned. I'd bought it while I was still robbing banks and had used it as a hideout. It was not luxurious, but there was a familiarity and solidness to the place that I liked. Before we could sit down, the sergeant and I were brought a glass of cool, mixed fruit juice by one of the pretty young girls that worked around the place. I knew any moment that Señorita Rosita Garza-Garza, my fat lady cook, would be out to give me a hug and chastise me for waiting so long to visit.

Me and Rollie got settled with our drinks and I found out why he was wearing his blue suit. He had taken the occasion of meeting me in town to go on out to Camp Verde and make sure my boots were being broken in right. He said he'd worn the suit to show the boys a bit of high-tone flash, but, since he'd requested leave to go to Baltimore to get his divorce, he wanted his commander to think he was dressed for traveling. I said, with some relief, "I'm glad to hear that. I was scared you was going to go around like that the whole two weeks we're practicing."

He hunched forward in his chair. "You say your missus didn't take it strongly that you were doing this for the lad?"

"Hell, Rollie, it's no good telling you about this. It's between my wife and myself. I even went so far as to tell her that if we get in this war it could add two years to the chances of the boy getting killed. I told her them European countries were about to quit, that they were worn out, but that if we got in, the damn war would go for at least another couple of years."

He said quietly, "You weren't lying, Colonel. I could be after taking her out to Camp Verde and showing her the thousand new faces. And 'tis but the tip of the horn of plenty. We're only after training a thousand mule skinners. Reckon on the numbers being trained in the infantry camps and the artillery."

"Hell, Rollie," I said, "that would only make a liar out of me. How am I supposed to try and prevent a war with this grand gesture of mine, as you call it, if war has all but been declared? I read where Colonel House, the president's adviser, is back from England. I bet he could put a bug in her ear. But here I am saying to her that I'm doing it for the boy, to try and stop us going to war, to wake the American people up, and it's already been decided."

He swallowed the last of his juice. "Don't be being too hard on yourself, Colonel. Congress hasn't voted to declare war yet. And it's that what it takes to make it all tidy and official. You want to expose the money side of the scheme, the war to help the factories and the big industry. Sure and it's a sham the government is putting on the little folk. Even a lummox like myself here can see that. It is no small thing you aspire to, Colonel."

I cocked my head at him. "Rollie, you are about as far from being a lummox as a jackrabbit is from a racehorse. Tell me, where did you get all that education? You keep surprising me the way your mind works. Did you go far in school?"

He laughed out loud. "Lord bless you, sir, I've the barest of formal education. Three grades and then 'twas time to earn a bit of money to bring home. If you won't be after laughing at me, sir, I'll tell you from where came what little education I claim."

"I'm not going to laugh."

"A soldier's life, especially when you're after being stationed in some hellhole of a place in the big middle of nowhere, is a lonely life. I'd met up with a schoolteacher in my early days of soldiering and she taught me about books. Gave me lists of books. Sent me books. I read, Colonel." He blushed slightly at this confession. "Used to get me quite a bit of ribbing, but now, of course, the boys would rib me at their peril. They'd find themselves on guard duty for a month. I know it don't seem like a very manly thing to do, sir, but yes, I read."

I looked at him curiously. "What? What do you read?"

He shrugged. "Anything I can get my hands on."

"Dime novels? Penny thrillers?"

He nodded. "Aye, them too. But I've read all of Twain and Dickens and some of them Russki writers and Henry James and your thinkers like Thoreau and Charles Lamb and that lot."

I was amazed. "I'm about knocked off my pins. Maybe you're the one ought to be the colonel."

He shook his head quickly. "No, sir, you are the one with the bearing and the presence and the command voice. We only have to work on those few details." He stood up. "And I reckon we had better get started. I believe you have been after diverting me with my own tongue, sir. I think we had better be starting with the salute."

I had never really thought much about a military salute, but in the next several hours I learned a good deal more about saluting than I thought there was on the subject. I found out there were all kinds of salutes, from the snappy type rendered by a smartly turned-out noncom such as Sergeant McMartin, to the bored touch of the hat brim with the swagger stick by such people as the colonel I was aping. I found out that a salute could be used as a form of punishment. When a soldier inferior in rank to the officer he was saluting threw up a salute, he had to hold it until the officer returned it. If an old, crusty colonel such as myself so desired, he could force the junior officer to stand there with his hand and arm in the air as long as he chose. And I learned that enlisted men did not salute other enlisted men. The salute was exclusively reserved for officers. And officers like myself, who had been saluted hundreds of thousands of times, were bored with the whole routine and returned a salute with a careless gesture that said, "All right, now let's get down to business."

The sergeant said, "Of course, sir, if you was saluting an officer ranking yourself, which would be a general, you'd want to give the impression of respect by coming to attention just a trifle and making a little bit of an effort to snap one off. But then you won't be seeing no generals, so it is only important that you learn how to return a salute."

Finally, after about two hours, I was disgusted and flung the damn swagger stick away from me. "Damnit, Rollie, this is just too much. I don't believe it is that damn important. Hell, the whole business ain't going to take more than fifteen minutes at the outside. Who the hell is going to notice?"

He shook his head. "Colonel, 'tis the little things could make it all go awry. Sir, let's be after saying you're fifty years old. That would mean you'd been in the army at least twenty-seven or twenty-eight years, after you'd graduated from the West Point Academy or maybe VMI. Sir, them years stick out so plain that even a doughboy with a year's service could tell if you was a proper officer."

"I don't believe it."

"Sir, you could march a hundred thousand men past me and if only two of them men had seen as much as four years of army duty I could pick them out."

We were out in the cool under the front porch roof. As I dropped into a cane chair I said, "Then we are done for and I'll have to do it another way. I can't get all this down so it feels natural in the time we got. I don't think I could do it if we had ninety years. Hell, I ain't the soldier type!"

But after some talk and a drink of whiskey we proceeded. Rollie thought I should practice with the swagger stick and its multiple uses, but he decided we would work on one practical application: using it to gain attention when I walked into the bank to tell the manager that the gold would be delayed until I was certain there was no danger about. Apparently, what senior officers did when they wanted to get folks' attention was to give the top of their cavalry boot a smart rap with their riding crop. The sergeant said, "You see, sir, you're way above going in and saying 'You people listen to me,' or some such like that. No, sir. You marches in, stands there 'til a little notice is taken, and then you cracks your swagger stick against your boot. Makes a nice sharp sound. Then, when you got their attention, I says, 'Attention to the colonel!' "

I gave him a look. "Except you ain't going to be there."

He nodded. "Aye. I was thinkin' of the matter in its proper form. Well, sir, you cracks your boot and then you say, 'Attention to orders!' "

"Orders?" I frowned at him. "Hell, I'm going to be talking to a bunch of people in a bank. They ain't soldiers."

He chuckled. "Ah, bless you, sir. You be a colonel, and a hard one at the least. You give orders to everyone. Lord, sir, if you had children you'd make the bairns line up for inspection before break-fast. You can't help yourself, sir. It's in you, don't you see, Your Honor. Now, let's give it a try."

The only problem was that a cavalry boot reaches all the way to the knee and I was wearing short-topped walking boots. My first attempt gave me a stinging slap on the side of my calf. "Damnit!" I yelled, hopping around and rubbing my leg. "What are you trying to do, Rollie, get me to kill myself?"

He was all concern. "Ah, Colonel, I'm a bleedin' idiot. I should have thought. I reckon we will be after laying that aside for a bit. I'll be fetching your boots in a couple of days. They should be good and broke in by then. I reckon maybe we can move on to some other uses a senior officer makes of his swagger stick."

"Why the hell can't you call it a quirt or a riding crop, which is what it really is?"

He gave me a sorrowful look. "Ah, sir, you've got to get these little details in your head. 'Twouldn't do to slip at the wrong instant." He snapped his fingers suddenly. "Ah, there is one detail I wish we could lay our hands on. Might be worth my time to make a trip to Fort Sam Houston and hunt for one."

"What?"

"A ring from the academy. You have one of those on, sir, and I promise you the junior officer in charge of that detail will knock himself out saluting you."

"The academy?"

"Aye, West Point. Them as graduates from there is on a one-way express train to the top. It's the military academy, sir. Ah, but 'twould look splendid on your finger, sir."

We took a rest and tried mixing a little whiskey in with the fruit juice. It wasn't all that bad. The sergeant asked how it had been left with Lauren. I said, shrugging, "It's up in the air. She is trying to figure out where to hit me next. For her, the argument is a long way from being over."

"Does she know how you're planning the adventure?"

"Of course. By the way, she wants to see you."

A look somewhere between uncertainty and fear came over his face. "Beggin' your pardon, Colonel, but are you after saying your *wife* wants to see me?"

"Yeah. At least that's what she said."

He cleared his throat. "I take it, then, that you've mentioned me, Colonel?"

"I had to tell her how I intended to pull off the robbery. Hell, she thought I was going to go in there with drawn pistols and a handkerchief over my face. Silly woman don't know the first thing about bank robbing. When I told her there wouldn't be a shot fired she went to pressing me about it. Naturally, I had to tell her about impersonating an army officer."

He said a little timidly, "You didn't, ah, by any chance suggest it might have been my idea, now, did you, sir?"

I shook my head. "No, but I told her if it hadn't been for you I wouldn't have a chance. I told her I was just dumb enough to think all I had to do was get a uniform somewhere and march in and everyone would fall down. I told her I was learning from you how involved it was."

"Aaah," he said, not looking particularly happy. "Ah, yes, Your Honor. And now she wants to see me, does your darlin' wife. Aye, I can see how she would."

I gave him a look. "What the hell is the matter with you, Rollie? You look scared. Hell, she don't bite."

He looked away. "Colonel, you wouldn't be after understanding. Ladies of her class can put the fear in me faster than a Gatling gun. Your dear wife is going to view me as a source of encouragement to you. She is going to consider if I'd stop helping you that you'd give up on the plan."

"You don't know that."

His eyes came back to my face. "Can you be after thinking of any other reason she'd want to hold conversation with a rough old soldier such as myself?"

He had a point, but I wasn't going to take it. "Look, it don't matter what she says to you. I am going on with this adventure one way or another. All I need is that uniform. I think I know enough now to pull it off."

He looked sad. "Ah, Colonel, sir, what you don't know is the bulk of it."

"I bet I could get by."

"Sir, you'd be betting your life on it."

"Just get me the uniform and you can walk away. You won't ever have to face my wife. And I got to agree that that can be an unsettling experience."

He said gently, "Colonel, sir, where do you put the eagles on the uniform? Where does your cavalry insignia go? What kind of angle do you set your campaign hat at? That would depend on what cavalry outfit you was with. What's the name of your outfit now? Who is your commanding officer? Where were you commissioned at? What are you going to reply if the junior officer commanding asks if the men can trail arms on the return to the train?" He stopped and looked at me.

I didn't say anything.

"Well? Will you be answering me, sir?"

"Don't be a smart ass, Rollie. Hell, I had to tell her about you. In fact, I think it kind of reassured her, kind of pepped her up a little. Made her think I wasn't going off half-cocked and get myself killed."

"And now, sir, she knows there is a soldier, a first sergeant, who is going to be after helping you steal gold from an army detail."

"Listen, I guarantee you she don't give a damn about that. Rollie, she is used to people getting talked into things by me. I the same as told her I put enough whiskey in you you'd have agreed to anything."

"Ah, thank you, sir. Now I'm to be presented to a lady as a drunken traitor."

I had to laugh. "Rollie, you are making too much out of this. When shall I tell her you'll be coming?"

He gave me a wry look. "I reckon, sir, at her convenience. But, sir, make it for teatime. That will surprise her a trifle. Teatime, sir."

"How'd you know she had a teatime?"

He gave me a wise look. "All real ladies have tea."

We knocked off practicing for the day and set in to discussing strategy, the actual way I was going to go at the job. It had gotten to be past noon and my fat cook broiled us a couple of steaks and made a big salad with salsa on it.

While we were eating I wanted to discuss the actual words I was going to say to the officer in charge of the detail, but Rollie said it was too soon. "You've got to go to thinking like a colonel before you can talk like one, sir."

I wished the notion had never struck me. I reckoned I could still call it off somehow, but it had become like a runaway train, gathering momentum of its own.

I rode the saddle horse Rollie had fetched for me back home. Lauren was going to notice that I had left walking but had come home horseback and she was going to want to know why. I was going to lie. I was going to tell her I'd got tired of not having a mount around the Del Rio house and I'd sent over to Mexico for one. I was going to lie because I didn't want to tell her I was at the Mexican ranch practicing how to act like a colonel. I didn't want or plan to tell her anything further about the damn gold robbery. At least I didn't intend to volunteer anything. If the subject came up I was going to do my best to turn it aside or evade it or cut it short. I was near about as sick of the subject as I had ever been of any consideration.

*　　*　　*

NOT A whole bunch happened in the next week. I managed to spend a few hours every day across the river going over what the sergeant called the "military courtesies," though they didn't have a thing to do with courtesy. They were about style and conduct and various procedures and protocols. I was damned if I could figure out when the army ever had time to get around to fighting a war, they were so caught up in the appearance of matters and who was allowed to say what and when. We had all my equipment except my uniform, and each day I would put on the boots and the Sam Browne belt and walk around with the campaign hat on my head and the swagger stick under my arm. The sergeant said I had to get comfortable and feel at home with them. Well, I was going to do that about as quick as I was going to feel at home looking and acting like a damn fool. We had attached the military holster to the Sam Browne belt and I was carrying the sergeant's Colt .45 semiautomatic weapon to get used to the weight. The thing was heavier than I was used to. The military holster had a flap that covered the handle of the weapon, which seemed like less than a bright way to go around carrying a gun. But the sergeant said it was so that second lieutenants wouldn't lose the weapon when they forgot which way was up. The flap had a little grommet latch to secure it so it might take you three or four minutes to get the gun out in case you needed it. Again Sergeant McMartin said that the feature was intended to aid second lieutenants and keep them from actually firing a weapon and doing harm to themselves or others. He said the latch had been tested on a batch of new second lieutenants and the quickest any of them had been able to open the flap and actually get at the gun had been a little over three hours. The sergeant said the army considered that a sufficient safety margin.

The sergeant, I was beginning to believe, was not a great admirer of junior officers.

But of all the gear I had to practice with, the silliest I found was the spurs. It seemed that anytime a cavalry officer wore his boots they must be worn with spurs, whether he intended to mount a horse or not. But they weren't what I called real spurs. They didn't have rowels, just blunt shanks sticking out from the U that went around your heel. And they didn't have any straps to hold them in place. The U was an exact fit to slide over the heel of your boot and each spur had a little set screw you turned to tighten it so it wouldn't work loose. They weren't like any spurs I'd ever seen and, except for appearance's sake, seemed about as useful as tits on a boar hog. The sergeant had nodded wisely and said, "Aye, sir, and you've grasped the point exactly, Colonel. Of course they wouldn't help you control a horse. If the army had horses that you needed real roweled spurs to catch hold of and control, why, the officers wouldn't be able to ride them anyway. So they get horses you don't need spurs to ride, but they still want to wear spurs. So they came up with these little blunt gewgaws which are gold plated and look good on the officer's boots but ain't likely to irritate the horse should the officer be so clumsy as to strike the animal with the business end."

But it was the business end of the sergeant that was starting to slightly irritate me. He was forever going on about how I had to practice being a proper officer or I'd give the whole game away. Hell, I'd been robbing banks when he was learning how to steal sugar. I'd directed and ordered men about when one small slip or one foot put wrong could have got us all killed. I wasn't going to tell him to his face, not considering the affection I felt for the man, but he was not much short of being a nervous Nellie. I knew I'd be ready when the time came but he didn't seem to share my self-confidence. I couldn't explain to him that a man who successfully robs banks over a period of years has got to have one commodity in quantity and that commodity ain't a fast horse or a fast gun but a cool head and a wagonload of belief in himself. And there just ain't no way to explain that to another fellow, especially one that ain't ever been in the game or followed the owlhoot trail.

During a spell when I was taking a rest under the porch, enjoying the shade, and the sergeant was standing out in the sun on what he chose to call the parade ground, ragging me to get back to work and practice at being a proper officer, I decided we'd better get a few matters straight. It wasn't enough that he was giving me the eye and letting me know he thought I was slacking off; he was doing it in a damn tie and vest in the hot sun. This was the man supposed to be teaching me and he didn't have sense enough to know how to dress for the country or to get to shade when he had the chance.

I got up, shifting the awkward-feeling holster around on the Sam Browne belt, and started toward the sergeant tapping the swagger stick in my left hand. He was standing there with his legs apart and his fists on his hips. I got up to him and said, "Sergeant, you are a squadron of cavalry."

He said, "Huh?"

I wheeled around and got up in his face. Coldly I said, "What did you say, Sergeant? Did you say, 'huh?' Is that what you said?"

He took his fists off his hips and kind of straightened up. "Why, sir," he said, "I ain't for being sure."

I got square in his face, making a rat-a-tat-tat on my boot with the riding crop, making my eyes hard and flat. "You don't know? You don't know, Sergeant?" I let my voice rise at the end of each sentence. "You don't know whether you said 'huh?' A drooling fool says, 'huh!' A falling-down drunk says, 'huh!' Am I to understand that a sergeant, a first sergeant, also says 'huh'? To a colonel? Is that what I'm to understand, sergeant!"

He was looking bewildered. I was enjoying myself immensely. He said, a little haltingly, "I, well, I, uh, I don't know, sir. I mean—"

"You don't know, Sergeant? What don't you know?"

"I—"

"Come to attention when you address me, Sergeant!"

He looked startled, but his instincts took over and he popped up stiff as a ramrod. I was about to give him an order when I caught him cutting his eyes over to me.

I was on him like foam on beer. "Sergeant, you are at attention! Did you move your eyes? Did you?"

"I—"

I jumped him. "YOU ARE NOT TO MOVE AT ATTENTION, SERGEANT! WHERE DID YOU TAKE YOUR TRAINING, SERGEANT? IN THE NAVY?"

He froze, staring straight ahead, not even blinking.

I took two steps back. "First two squads, mount at the command. Mount!"

That left him looking confused, as I had intended. He even broke from the position of attention long enough to give me a flickering look and say, "What, sir? Mount?"

I was in his face in two strides. "Sergeant, what am I?"

"Sir?"

"Don't give me any of your Irish blarney. What am I, Sergeant?"

He was helpless. He staggered around in his brain trying to figure out what I was after. "Why, why, I don't be after knowing, sir."

I jammed my face in his, blasting him back with sound and fury. "I AM A COLONEL! I AM A COLONEL OF CAVALRY! AND WHAT DO COLONELS OF CAVALRY COMMAND, SERGEANT? I WILL TELL YOU SINCE YOU ARE TOO DUMB TO KNOW. COLONELS OF CAVALRY COMMAND CAVALRY! YOU SAY YOU DON'T SEE A HORSE TO MOUNT? YOU BETTER DAMN WELL FIND A HORSE TO MOUNT. THERE HAD BETTER BE A HORSE RIGHT BESIDE YOU, SERGEANT, BECAUSE I AM A COLONEL OF CAVALRY. IS THERE A HORSE RIGHT BESIDE YOU, SERGEANT?"

He swallowed but maintained his position of attention. He said, a little unsteadily, "Yes, sir."

I stepped back. As if I were indeed speaking to a squadron of cavalry I shouted, "MOUNT!"

After the sergeant had gone through an awkward and silly pretense of getting on a horse I gave my next order. "First squad! Column of twos! Leeeft wheel!"

I proceeded to march the good sergeant all around that baking front yard amid the dust and the scraggly grass and the sun. Once, while we were discussing the cavalry, he had gone over a routine of standard marching commands. They had stuck in my mind and I proceeded to reel them off. "Left oblique! Right turn! Right flank! Right oblique! At the trot! Line abreast, wheel!"

After about ten minutes of that I abruptly left the sergeant in mid-maneuver and turned around and walked back to the porch and took my chair in the shade. My drink was still cool. It took him about two minutes, mainly because I'd left him marching in a direction away from the ranch house, but he finally noticed that I was no longer in command. He turned around and stared at me for a long moment. Finally he came walking toward the porch, loosening his tie and collar. I could see he'd worked up a pretty good sweat. He came up to the porch and leaned against one of the support posts. As he was taking off his tie, he said, "Ah, Colonel, that was darlin'. I'd have never knowed you had it in you, sir. Sure and that was a foin display."

I took a sip of my fruit drink sweetened with whiskey. "You liked that, did you?"

"Aye. 'Twas a performance worthy of a proper parade ground officer." He unbuttoned his vest and took it off. I could see with no little satisfaction that his shirt was good and soaked. "Just the one thing, sir, I be after wondering about."

"And what might that be, Sergeant?"

"Will you be able to put on such a foin performance with the thousands of people present?"

"Sergeant, you probably don't know this, but when you rob a bank you generally tend to draw a crowd. And most of that crowd is shooting at you."

He rolled up his sleeves and then took off his silly plug hat and fanned himself. He was quiet for a moment and then he said, not slowing up on the fanning, "It was the hat, wasn't it, sir?"

I nodded.

"And the vest and the tie?"

I nodded again. "Man ought to have better sense than to stand out in the sun dressed like that."

I thought I had carried the day, but he fixed me with as close to a gimlet eye as I'd ever seen him employ. "But it did be after getting you to come out and practice, beggin' your pardon, sir."

"Are you saying you connived me, Sergeant?"

He nodded. "Aye, sir. I connived you."

I said grimly, "Don't laugh yet. You've still got my wife to go visit."

THERE WAS a sort of uneasy truce going on at home. On occasion Lauren would make some mention of the frolic that was to come, but it was usually just a glancing blow and not the preamble to a serious discussion. On my part I evaded and ducked and kept down low and talked about the most cheerful things. Still, I had to be careful on that subject. At one point, trying to offer up some tribute, I made mention of us perhaps sailing over to France on one of those great oceangoing liners and perhaps getting a chance to see Willis. She looked at me coolly and said, "I don't believe there is time before, Wilson. Or had you thought of it as your escape after San Antonio, assuming you're not dead?"

It was tricky going around the house. If I'd had any sense I'd've told her the night before. But, then, if I'd had any sense I'd've never come up with the idea in the first place.

Three days after the summons, the sergeant dressed up in his best dress uniform and went to call on Lauren at four that afternoon. My presence was not wanted and I had waited for him down at my saloon. I was sitting at a table out front when he came in. I said, "Well, you seem to have survived. I told you she didn't bite. Well, I mean she don't bite anybody but me."

"Ah, Colonel," he said, "you are a blessed man. I have met some fine ladies in my time, but she is nigh royalty. As genuine as any queen ever was."

I took a hard look at him. It was clear she had done a job on his Irish romantic side. For a second it scared me. I was fearful she might have talked him out of helping me, hoping I'd see the folly of going it alone. I said, "What did you talk about?"

He shook his head. "Ah, sir, beggin' the colonel's pardon, but I can't be for telling you that."

I stared at him. "You can't be what? Say, who the hell you think you work for?"

He shook his head. "I'm sorry, sir, but I made a vow to a lady and Rollie McMartin will not break such a vow. And I was sober this time, too."

"How much money she offer you, Sergeant?"

His eyes went suddenly hard. "I beg your pardon, sir?"

"Never mind," I said. "Never mind. No offense intended."

He relaxed slightly. "None taken, sir."

"You got to tell me what was said, Rollie."

"I can't, sir. It's a vow I can't be for going back on."

My heart was sinking. "She talked you into not helping me any more."

He went stiff again. "Sir, I made a vow to you also."

I sighed. "No offense meant."

"None taken, sir. Though you are getting fair close."

"Rollie, you got to give me some idea of what got said. I've got to protect myself. She may have gotten information out of you that she can blindside me with. You don't know her. That woman is something to reckon with at times."

He looked at me steadily. "I gave my word, sir."

I came at him from every angle I could think of. Finally I said grimly, "Sergeant, she hasn't got near as much money as I have."

His eyes shifted away from mine. "Sir, would you be after forcing me to take umbrage?"

"I ain't questioning your honor, Rollie, but my wife can set her teeth and move a freight train when she's of a mind. She don't want me doing this, I can assure you of that. And she'd do anything to stop me."

He sighed. "I will go so far as to put your mind at rest about one matter, sir. She did not offer me money and she did not ask me to hinder you. I might add, sir, begging your pardon, that she was too much of a lady to even think of offering me money."

I had to laugh. "Well, that is a backhanded slap if I ever got one. Do I understand you want me to withdraw my offer of money?"

"I didn't say that, sir. You're no lady."

The touchy moment had passed, but I was still being eaten up inside to know what they had talked about. After a little time had passed I said, "You actually had tea? Real tea?"

"Yes, sir."

"Out of a cup?"

"Yes, sir. It was a high tea."

"A what?"

"A high tea."

"What's a high tea?"

"We had cake and pastries."

I thought a moment. "I suppose if there's a high tea there must be a low tea. Is that right?"

"Yes, sir. At a low tea you have bread and jam. Or butter."

"So she trotted out the first-class treatment for you, is that right?"

"I would expect, sir, that a lady of your wife's gentility would always serve high tea. No matter who the company."

"How long did you stay?"

"About an hour, sir."

"What'd you talk about?"

He glanced over at me. "We talked about tea, sir."

As it turned out I was looking for attack from the wrong quarter. About a week after I had told Lauren my plans I walked into my house at about two o'clock one afternoon and found Warner Grayson and his wife—my wife's sister, Laura—sitting in the parlor. I didn't need one of them mind readers to tell me what they were doing there. Laura already had her fighting face on.

CHAPTER
12

Before I could say a word Laura said, "Wilson Young, have you lost your goddamn mind?"

I started to make some kind of joke about not swearing in the house, but somehow the climate in the room didn't seem right for a joke. Warner was sitting beside her on the big overstuffed sofa looking uncomfortable. Warner was not and never had been much of a one for mixing in other folks' business.

I said, "Well, thank you, Laura, I'm doing fine. How about yourself?"

She got up and marched over and put her face up toward mine. "You ought to be ashamed of yourself. You are scaring the hell out of my sister and scaring me and scaring Warner."

I glanced over at Warner. He was studying the pattern on the rug. I came back to Laura. "Age cannot wither, nor time dim the beauty of your wrath, Laura. It is a rare thing to behold. I just hope you never get mad at me."

She stamped her foot. "You know damn good and well I'm mad at you, Wilson Young. You were crazy the first time I ever saw you and you haven't changed a bit."

"Oh, yeah," I said. "I guess it was me was going to breed Andalusian stallions worth two thousand dollars apiece to saddle horses and come up with the ideal cattle horse. Wasn't that what she was up to, Warner?"

He made a little hmmphing sound and looked away. He showed all the signs of a man who wished he was somewhere else.

Laura was still in front of me. Even though she was older than Lauren by several years I had to admit that she carried them well. She was still a beauty, though her looks had taken on a hard edge. She was slimmer than Lauren, but she was still ample where ample was called for. She said, "You're not going to get around me that way. Maybe I didn't know enough about the horse-breeding business, but I got sense enough to know you can't steal gold off the United States government. Hell, Will, you were always crazy, but you weren't dumb. This is plain dumb."

I wondered where Lauren was when I needed her. I also needed a drink. I signaled to Warner and made a drinking motion. He nodded and got up. I said to Laura, "Would you please excuse me? I won't be long. About five or six drinks and I ought to be able to stand another two minutes of this."

Warner followed me into my office and we sat down and got a bottle between us. He didn't look much different than the last time I'd seen him, which would have been about two years past. He still had that serious, youthful look on his face. He was still slim and still looked, in spite of the gray in his hair, like he could work horses all day long. When our glasses were filled I asked him how it had happened.

He shrugged. "Laura got a telegram about a week ago and she wired back, and then another telegram came and then they talked on the telephone somehow." He shrugged again. "Next thing I know we are on the train heading for here. I told her that we didn't have no business interfering, but you know Laura."

"I know Lauren," I said grimly.

He sighed. "I would reckon it is about the same. From what I have observed they can both work a man, they just use different methods. I reckon the plan here is to hit you from both sides at once."

I looked at him over the rim of my glass. "What do you think of it?"

He looked away. "I never knowed you to do a thing without having a damn good reason. I ain't heard your reasons."

"It was about six weeks ago I wanted to talk to either you or Justa. I went to Justa because he was closer. He couldn't argue with my reasons, but he still didn't think I ought to try it."

"They'll be here tomorrow."

I drew my head back. "The hell you say!"

He nodded. "Lauren said the midday train."

I swore softly. "I'm a sonofabitch. Who else is coming? Or maybe it would be easier to ask who ain't coming?"

He shrugged. "Your wife ain't resolved to this, Will. That is one thing I can tell you for sure."

I set my face. "Resolving herself to it and not getting in the way are two different matters. This is my business and I think I got good and sufficient reasons."

Warner took a drink of whiskey. "Hell, Will, them two fillies is out of the same bloodline. I could have told you you were going to have a fight on your hands."

"Where the hell is Lauren? Upstairs crying?"

He smiled slightly. "I wouldn't reckon. No, we had an overnight layover in Houston and Laura went shopping. She found a gown suited her fine so she bought one for Lauren, them being the same coloring. She's upstairs trying it on."

"How much do you know?"

He shrugged. "Oh, some of it. Lauren told it in such a rush and a jumble that I couldn't exactly get the straight of it. Somehow you figure to keep us out of the war by robbing that quarter of a million in bullion the government is flashing around." He shook his head. "Seems like a powerful load to put on just the one robbery." He shook his head again. "No, I'd have to say I ain't quite got the slant of it yet."

I poured us out another drink. "What nobody seems to understand is that it is only me that has to know why I'm doing it."

Warner got a cigarillo out of his pocket and lit it. "I told Laura it was none of our concern and to stay the hell out of it. But you ought to know how much good that did. You are married to the other half of the set."

"Oh, I ain't blaming you, Warner. Hell, I ain't even blaming Laura. Or Lauren, for that matter. They both think what they are doing is for the right. But, goddamnit, I don't want anybody, and women especially, telling me what to do! She is convinced I am trying one grandstand play before it's too late. One last gamble. One last bank."

Warner looked at the coal on the end of his cigarillo. "Well, ain't you?"

I gave him a sour look and finished my drink and stood up. "We better go back and join the ladies. I'm going to have to listen to them in relays, so I might as well get started."

Warner started out the office door. "Don't look for no help from me. You was the one started this mess. I'm going to get down so deep behind a log they won't find me until spring. You'll remember you got down on Willis because he went off to fight somebody else's fight. Well, you damn sure ain't going to be able to accuse me of that."

I reached out and squeezed his shoulder. "I appreciate that, Warner. I've always known how much I could depend on you. Man couldn't want a better friend in a tight place, especially if he was being attacked by two female wildcats. Yeah, you'll do."

"You want to get your ass shot off, you go ahead and get it shot off. But you ain't getting me in the middle of them two women. I got to live with that skinny one and that is chore enough for any one man."

We walked back into the parlor. Now Lauren was there, dressed in a light blue, filmy gown with a low-cut front that looked mighty good on her. Without preamble I said, "I hear Justa and Nora are coming tomorrow."

Lauren nodded. "Yes. They are very anxious to see you."

I looked at her grimly. "You have been pretty busy, haven't you? I reckon I ought to have known something was up, as quiet as you have been about the matter this last week."

She looked back at me steadily. "You're doing what you think is right. Well, don't deny me the same privilege."

"Do you know if Nora plays poker?" I asked.

She looked puzzled and I heard Warner laugh softly behind me. Lauren said, "What?"

"I was wondering if Nora played poker. I know that you do and so do Laura and Warner and Justa. And, naturally, I play. I think a six-handed game is better than five, don't you? Hell, we could invite your friend, the sergeant."

Warner laughed again and then I heard the sound of a slap and he stopped abruptly. Lauren glanced past me to where they were sitting on the couch. Then she came back to me. "Wilson, what in hell are you talking about?"

"Passing the time," I said. "And poker is a good way to do that.

We are going to need something to do because I know what we *ain't*
going to do, and that is discuss my affairs."

That seemed to quiet matters down for a while. We passed a rea-
sonably pleasant time until supper. I halfway had the notion that
Lauren was biding her time, waiting for her full force to gather when
Justa and Nora came in. I didn't expect much from Nora, about the
same as Warner, but Justa would fall right in with Laura and my
wife and I'd be fighting with my back to the wall. I calculated that
Lauren wouldn't do much leading; she'd probably reserved that role
for her sister.

And, sure enough, supper wasn't half over before Laura cracked
a shot over my head. I had hoped we could get through the meal
without disturbance because Mrs. Bridesdale had made chicken and
dumplings and I knew there was a blackberry cobbler to follow and
I didn't want anything upsetting that.

Laura said, "Wilson Young, have you got any idea how old you
are? You're two years older than Warner, and if he was to come up
with an idea as crazy as this one I'd have him put in one of those
insane asylums. Hell, you're fifty-eight damn years old."

In a way it tickled me. Earlier in the week the sergeant had said,
"And one other fine thing in our favor, sir, is that you are the right
age to be a colonel at fifty."

I'd said, "What does my age have to do with it?"

He'd said, "Well, you see, sir, if you were, say, up close to sixty,
like fifty-eight or so, what with the ribbons you'll be after wearing,
by rights you should have a star."

"What?"

"Ah, Colonel, that's a one-star general. A brigadier general, so
called because he's usually head of a brigade. Of course, the weather
out here will age a man beyond his years, but you look exactly
proper to be a full colonel. You see, sir, 'twouldn't be the job of a
brigadier to be intercepting a detail like that. But if you was to come
up looking older and only being a colonel, why, the junior officers

would wonder if maybe you hadn't been passed over for promotion. It could cut into the respect they show you. But we are fixed up very nicely."

Trying to keep a straight face, I had said, "You think I look fifty?"

He had been quick to cover any possibility of offense. "Oh, no, sir. Like I said, this country will age a man. I'd reckon you to be a couple of years under that age, the way you are set up and all."

It had tickled my vanity. Someday I'd set the sergeant straight, but not right away. I said to Laura, "Was I you I wouldn't be flinging ages around. Fact of the matter is, I was taken for under fifty just the other day."

"Did you put a quarter in his tin cup?"

"Ha, ha. He ain't blind, Laura. But I doubt if he could tell the difference between you and a hellcat."

She leaned across the table toward Warner. "Are you going to let him talk to your wife like that?"

Warner was elbow deep in a plate of dumplings. Without looking up he said, "That's Wilson Young, the bank robber. Very dangerous man. You want somebody to fight him, fight him yourself. I'm scared."

Lauren had done an excellent job of avoiding my eye from the moment I had walked into the house and she had come downstairs. She was sitting at the other end of the table from me. The leaf had been put in so it was stretched out for more people. Loudly I said, "Did you hear that, Lauren? Warner just told his wife to fight her own battles. Reckon there is a little lesson in that for you?"

She bristled far more than I had expected. I had thought she would be ashamed, at least a little, for sending for outside help. Her response was anything but remorseful. She put her fork down and glared the length of the table at me. "Wilson Young, if you think I'm going to stand by while you take this family down the road to rack and ruin you have got another think coming. I'll play every card in my hand and some that aren't, but you are not going through with this. You are not going to throw your life away for some fool notion, and God alone knows what it is because I don't and I doubt that you do!"

I stared at her for a long moment. Laura and Warner were silent, occupying themselves with their food, trying to act as if they hadn't heard. Quietly I said, "Well, have you quite relieved yourself of that burden? I'm sure our guests were thrilled to hear you talk to your husband that way. You got anything to add, any more hurtful words?"

She stared back for a moment and then her face began to squeeze up, and she jumped up from the table and hurried out of the room. Laura got up almost instantly and within a moment I could hear their feet on the stairs, going up to the second floor.

Warner looked over at me. "You handled that mighty well, Will. Hell, I thought you was a man always picked the place and time for his fight. At least that's what you preached to me."

I had been wrong and I knew it, but I wasn't about to give it admission. I said defiantly, "She drew first blood."

He laughed without humor. "And also made you look like a damn fool. A man that makes his wife cry in front of her sister and brother-in-law? No, I reckon you come off a bad second on that one."

Nothing much else got said for the balance of the evening. Lauren came downstairs, along with her sister, and they sat back down at the table like nothing had happened. Lauren was wearing a white dress with a yellow collar that went exceedingly well with her color. Laura had on light green, which suited her as well. Neither Warner nor I commented on how nicely turned out they were. I didn't say anything because I didn't feel like the time was exactly right and Warner didn't because he probably hadn't even noticed what his wife was wearing. He could tell you the markings and color of every horse he'd ever traded, sold, or bought in the last ten years, but I would have bet he couldn't describe what either one of the women was wearing if I was suddenly to command him to shut his eyes.

After dinner we went back in the parlor and Warner and I had whiskey while the ladies took a small glass of brandy. I didn't know what we talked about and I reckoned nobody else did, either. It was one of them strained kind of times when there are a million things people want to say but can't, so they end up saying next to nothing.

About ten Laura and Warner went up to bed and, a few minutes later, Lauren followed them. She turned around at the door and looked at me. "Are you coming soon?"

She looked so sad I felt like crying. "Soon as I finish this drink and this cheroot. I'll probably beat you to bed."

I watched her until she turned out of sight, admiring her figure. Of course I knew there was no point in having any thoughts about making love. And it had nothing to do with the disagreement that lay between us. Laura wouldn't make love with people in the house, especially if the people were kinfolk. I had never been able to figure that one out. There were five or six walls between our bedroom and the far guest room where Laura and Warner were sleeping, and they couldn't have heard us even if we'd both had cowbells on. The curious thing was that Lauren had no such reservations about hotel rooms. On more than one occasion I had pointed out to her that we had just made love with people in the next room and the walls paper thin. I asked her how she squared that with her attitude about people in the house. She'd said she didn't have to square it, that was just the way she was. Warner had told me that Laura was the same way. He said they'd gone up to visit her folks in Virginia and he'd finally had to take her out in the middle of the night to the barn if he wanted to get any. He'd said, "Can you imagine that? House as big as a hotel and we end up on a blanket on a pile of hay. Damnedest thing I ever ran into."

This had been before I had met and married Lauren, and I'd told him I'd've done without before I would have put up with such foolishness. Some years later a similar subject had come up and he'd given me the eye and said, "You still hold with that now that you got Lauren, that you'd do without before you'd go to the barn?"

It had made me blush, and I don't blush. Maybe three or four times in my life. What had made me blush was that we'd been visiting an aunt and uncle of hers and staying with them, and me, knowing her ways by then, had carefully arranged to rent a hotel room for just one purpose. I hadn't answered Warner's sally, but I reckoned my blush had been answer enough.

When I got upstairs Lauren was in the bathroom and I sat down on the side of the bed and took off my boots and socks and then my shirt. She came in about then, in her nightgown and robe, and sat down at her dressing table without saying anything. I said, "Lauren, I'm sorry I raised your hackles tonight, especially in front of Laura and Warner. I guess if the situation was reversed I'd be doing everything I could think of, too. It kind of took me off guard is all. I hope you won't hold it against me."

"No, Will, I won't hold it against you." Her voice sounded tired. "I guess all our nerves are a little on edge. I appreciate you understanding that I've got to do everything I can to stop you."

"Does that include what you said to Sergeant McMartin?"

"How do you know what I said to the sergeant?"

"I don't. He said he made you a vow not to tell me what y'all talked about. I just hope it ain't anything that is going to interfere with my plans." I looked around.

"Sergeant McMartin is the one bright spot in this whole mess." She leaned toward the mirror, daubing cold cream on her face. "He is a real gentleman. You can thank your lucky stars for his help. No, Will, I wouldn't do anything to interfere with the robbery if you go through with it. But I will try, right up to the last minute, to make you change your mind."

I shucked off my pants and climbed into the bed. It was a pretty warm night so I didn't bother to get under the sheet. I said, "I wish you could see my point of view on this, Lauren. I can't ask you to think like me, but I think you ought to quit trying to get me to quit being me. I wouldn't be planning this little frolic if I didn't think I had good and sufficient reasons."

"Willis, huh? Going to shorten the war, are you, Will?"

I thought carefully before I spoke. I felt that Rollie might have already told her about the war preparations under way. "There comes a time, Lauren, when a man can't just sit around and gnash his teeth. He's got to do something about what is bothering him."

"You are talking moonshine, Wilson, and you know it."

I rolled over on my side where I could see her. She was busy wiping the cream off her face. "I know what you're thinking," I said. "But if I had wanted to rob a bank to see if I could still do it at my age, why in hell have I waited so long?"

She looked around at me and shook her head. "Don't gold-plate it, Will. Robbing a bank, any bank, wouldn't have been enough. Not enough of a challenge for the great Wilson Young. Ah, but robbing the government of a quarter of a million dollars in gold bullion with soldiers guarding it—now that would be something. That would really be going out in a blaze of glory."

I rolled onto my back and stared up at the ceiling. "I'm sorry you had to drag our friends into this. Your sister I could understand, but what in hell did you have to call Justa and Nora for? Hell, Justa already knows about this. That was the reason I went to Blessing, to talk to him about this. I needed someone to talk to."

"And it couldn't have been me?"

That almost made me laugh. "Yeah, I could see you giving it deliberate thought. Hell, you got upset because you thought I was going to see another woman."

"Now I almost wish you had."

"I still wish you hadn't drug Justa and Nora into this. They'll be here tomorrow and I won't have a damn thing to say to either one of them."

She was brushing her hair. "As it happens I didn't call Justa, or Nora. All I did was wire Laura that I needed help. She arranged to telephone me like Justa did with you. Then she insisted on coming and bringing Warner with her. I didn't know that Justa and Nora were coming until Laura and Warner got here. She thought that you'd be too much for Warner and that Justa would be a help." She put her brush down. "I think she said something about we needed all the level-headed people around you we could get."

"Well, Justa has already had his run at me. Of course, at that time I hadn't made my mind up. I was still thinking about it."

"And now you have it definitely made up?"

"I would say so."

"Nothing anyone can say is going to change your mind?"

"I don't see how. It appears to me that you've put some people to considerable trouble for nothing."

"Oh, I wouldn't say that."

"Why not?"

"We can always use the time to plan the funeral."

"Now, that is a hell of a remark for a man's wife to make. Hell, Lauren, give me a little credit."

She turned toward me. "I cannot believe what we are talking about. Do you realize we are sitting here actually talking about you robbing a gold shipment, a United States Treasury gold shipment? Protected by the army? If anyone had ever told me this could happen to me I'd have said they were crazy. Are you crazy?"

"I don't think so. But I will admit that I'm a little amazed at this whole business myself."

"Are you made out of ice? Wilson, don't you realize you could get killed? Oh, I know, you have this wonderful plan and not a shot will be fired, but plans don't always go the way they're supposed to. Aren't you at least nervous?"

I said frankly, "I'm scared to death. If you want the truth I am fairly well frightened at the whole idea. My mouth goes dry sometimes when I think about it."

She picked up the brush and slammed it down on her dressing table. It made a loud crack. "Then why in the hell are you doing it? And don't give me any of that watermelon talk about stopping the war."

I stared past her for a second and then shook my head. "I don't know. And that's the honest truth. I *do* know that I have never cared to be fooled or made a fool of or pushed around or flimflammed. And that's what I feel like the federal government is trying to do. Maybe it goes back to the days when the Yankee federal government took my daddy's land and killed him in the process. I don't know. All I know is that I am angry."

She slung the brush across the room. "Are you fighting the Civil War all over again?"

I shook my head. "No. I'm pretty sure it's not that. All I know is that I can't stand by and watch without doing something." I paused. "You know how much I love you and you must know that I hate making you unhappy like this, Lauren, but I got to do it."

She got up and started toward me, taking off her robe and her gown as she did. "Then I guess we'd better fuck as much as we can in what little time we've got left."

She couldn't have startled me more if she'd walked downtown naked. I stared at her. In a constricted voice I said, "But what about Laura and Warner? I thought you didn't—"

She got on the bed. "They are way down the hall. What do you care, anyway?"

I reached for her. "I don't really. Guess I was just being silly."

JUSTA WILLIAMS said, "Will, it strikes me that your method of settling your quarrel with the government is like the fellow who couldn't think of any other way to get out of the rain except to jump in the lake. You are not going to get dry and you are adding the chance of drowning to your other calamities."

We were out at my horse ranch west of town. On the pretext of looking at my racehorses and seeing Charlie Stanton, me and Warner and Justa had ridden out in the buggy. The women and Warner had all, in different ways, had their run at me. Now it was Justa's turn and I figured he was considered their best hope, because he'd been saved for last. He was a good choice, too. Justa was logical and he was well spoken and everyone knew I respected him. Of course, I respected Warner no less, it was just that Warner was not so inclined to speak up. Besides, I had the sneaking suspicion that he half agreed with what I was about to do.

I said to Justa, "That is a good point, my friend. But I don't think I'm getting in over my head. Besides, I can swim."

Justa took a draw on his cigar and blew out a cloud of blue smoke. "Not if the current is going to be as swift as I think it is. Will, it's all been explained to me about you impersonating an army officer and slicking them out of that gold. But I got to tell you, I'd sooner believe a pig in a ball gown than I would you in an army officer's uniform."

"Will you come with me to my ranch over in Mexico tomorrow? I'll show you. I'll show you and Warner. Maybe I can convince you and him enough so you'll come back and quiet those women down."

We were sitting out on the big front porch of the Spanish-style ranch house. We could see the barns and see Warner and Charlie going from one horse to the other, inspecting them. They looked like a couple of surgeons hovering over a body they were fixing to invade with their scalpels. It made me smile. I had never seen two men who cared more or knew more about horses than those two. I knew horses like a man who uses them. They knew horses like a mother knows her baby.

Justa flipped his half-smoked cigar out in the yard. "Hell, Will, I ain't here to tell you your business. I've known you for a good many years as a man who gives a lot of thought to a matter before he plunges in. I don't know what your reasons are for this action, but I've got no doubt they are important to you. They may not be important to me or the rest of us, even Lauren, but that don't matter. It's what counts with you. And I want to tell you that it wasn't my idea to come down here and jaw at you. Laura and Warner got me on the telephone. I say Laura and Warner, but you know as well as I do it was mostly Laura. She said we had to try for Lauren's sake. I told her that once you'd made your mind up you might as well try and milk a steer as change it. But she thought we ought to all come down anyway." He laughed. "I guess to say good-bye."

"Aw," I said, "you ain't got no idea how uplifting that is."

He looked around at me. "How you calculate your chances, Will?"

I shrugged. "I'm balancing on the head of a pin. It could fall in any direction. Clearly I'm doing something I've never done before. If something goes wrong I'm going to have to do some mighty fast thinking on my feet. This sergeant I've got hired seems to know it all by the book. But it ain't going to be his ass standing out there bare in the middle of that plaza. Something we ain't allowed for comes up, I'm not going to be able to turn around and say, 'What do we do now, Sergeant?' "

"Can't you get him to go with you?"

"Oh, he's more than willing. Wants to, in fact. He's an Irishman and he don't like the army. He thinks this is one hell of a joke to play on them."

"You trust him, then?"

I nodded. "Yeah. Yeah, I do. I'm paying him, but I think he'd do it for nothing." I looked over and smiled. "He went to tea with Lauren."

"Tea? An Irishman?"

"Yeah, high tea. That's when they have cake. If y'all will go over with me in the morning you'll meet him. He's got my uniform and I'm supposed to start getting used to it."

"And you ain't going to steal that gold?"

I shook my head. "It's gonna go just like I told you." I said it, but now I wasn't completely sure I meant it. It would be so easy to get that train headed south and just keep going. Wouldn't be any trouble with Mexico. The Mexican government was already mad as hell at the invasion of their country by Pershing and his troops. They'd probably give me a medal. They'd also probably take most of the gold away from me.

Justa lit a fresh cigar. "You're going to be recognized, Will. I know you ain't as famous as the president, but there's going to be somebody in that crowd will know your face, uniform or not."

"I'm working on that," I said. "I'm counting on the surprise and the confusion to distract people. And I got another thought I'm fiddling with."

He sighed. "Well, I wish you wouldn't do it. But I say that for my sake. I don't think this world would be near as much fun without you around to liven it up."

I didn't answer him. Warner and Charlie Stanton were walking toward us. We had not talked in front of Charlie and did not intend to. I studied them as they neared. They didn't favor in the least, but yet they somehow looked alike. Charlie was a good deal skinnier than Warner and was sandy-haired and fair-complected where Warner was dark. But there was still something between them that made you think they were related. I reckoned that maybe they were both descended from the same stallion. The way they knew horses, you had to figure there was a little horse somewhere in their background.

"What are y'all doing?" Warner asked.

Justa stood up. "Getting ready to go back to town. If you're finished."

Warner said to me, "Your horses are looking fine, Will. But then you don't need me to tell you that. Charlie and I agree that that mile-and-a-half horse you got is getting a little long in the tooth. I figure I better go to looking around for a replacement. There's going to be some good meets next year with some good purses on the longer races."

It sent a pang through my heart to hear him talking about next spring. Hell, I didn't feel like I could look much farther forward than the next five days.

As we rode back to town in the buggy Justa said, "You got to understand, Will, me and Warner have got to appear to be trying to talk you out of this, at least around the women. So don't get your back up if we act like we're sticking our noses in where they don't belong. We both wish you wouldn't try this stunt, but it's your business and we ain't going to be seriously trying to talk you out of it."

I thought to myself that I wished they would make a real try. I wished they'd tell me how I could get out of the mess I'd gotten myself into and still have a little honor left. Hell, they didn't know how easy it would have been to get me to change my mind.

But I said, "Wait until you see me in that uniform. You might want to join up."

They both snickered. Warner said, "I got me a big picture of you in a soldier boy's uniform."

"Now, Warner," Justa said, "don't you forget to salute, you hear? Like this." And he stuck one particular finger up in the air.

I said, "I'm going to tell your wives what you've been saying."

That sobered them up in a hurry.

CHAPTER

13

I said to the sergeant, "The last time anybody helped me get dressed was over twenty-one years ago, and that gentleman sitting out on the front porch, Mr. Warner Grayson, was helping me get into a boiled shirt and some kind of royal getup so I could get married to the sister of his wife."

Rollie was busy pinning the campaign ribbons on my chest. "It's called a tie and tails, Colonel."

"What is?"

"That best bib and tucker you wore for your marriage to Mrs. Young."

By now the sergeant was pinning my cavalry insignia on my lapels. We had just spent a long five minutes tying the dark brown tie in a four-in-hand knot. I said, "And I think that occasion may have been the last time I wore a tie, also."

"You'll need to practice, sir."

"Well, I will. But I'll tell you, if I had to get up every morning and put this rig on I'd throw in my hand. This coat is tight as hell."

"Tunic, sir. A military jacket is called a tunic. You've got to be after remembering these little details. They would be the very ones would trip you up." He stepped back to look me over for a moment. "Almost done, sir."

The tunic was of a dark gabardine and went on over a lightweight khaki-colored shirt. It was a summer dress uniform. The trousers, which Rollie had informed me were called jodhpurs, were of a much lighter tan than the tunic and flared at the hips, narrowed down to the knees, and then clung to the legs all the way to the ankle. Of course that part was covered by the boots, which came to the knees.

Rollie said, "You have some fine gentlemen for friends, sir. I have heard of your Mr. Warner Grayson. Back when I was in the cavalry he was called in to try and start a breeding program that would improve our mounts. Was at Fort Riley, in Kansas. I think he gave up in disgust because the army would not buy the quality of stock he could do anything with. I think he was heard to advise the commanding general he ought to try breeding mules. Did the gentleman never mention his army adventure to you? We were told he was the best."

"No, but that's Warner for you," I said. "He trained a horse that won the Kentucky Derby one year but since his name wasn't mentioned in the paper I never found out about it until two years later and it wasn't from him."

Now the sergeant was pinning my eagles on the shoulder flaps that were called epaulets. I said, "Rollie, what in hell do they have these here epaulets on a uniform for? They are just wasted material. They there to have something to run that leather strap from this Sam Browne belt under?"

"Ah, bless you no, sir. They have a purpose."

"And what would that be?"

His attention was on carefully running the pin of the eagles through the material of the epaulet flap. "Well, you see, sir, it was back during the Civil War that they found they was wanted. They had a whole raftful of new officers who were especially fumble-fingered. When they were pinning their insignia of rank on their shoulders so many of them stuck themselves that, as a result, more of the lads died from blood poisoning than was ever killed by the Confederates."

I pulled my head back so I could see his face. "You got a hell of a sense of humor, Rollie. But what I'd do is I'd put the insignia and the ribbons on the coat before I put it on."

"Tunic, sir. And I wish you wouldn't be after saying remarks like that. You get in that habit and they'll find out you are too smart to be an officer." He stepped back to admire his work. "Now put the campaign hat on, sir, just as it feels natural to you."

I put the hat on like every hat I'd ever worn, set square and even. The sergeant nodded. "Does you proud, sir. It's natural like. The way your hat sets proclaims you are a straight-ahead man and no nonsense allowed."

"All that from a hat, huh?"

"Now just the spurs left, sir. I'll be doing them for you this time, but after, you'll have to learn all this by heart."

"Oh, hell, let's leave off the spurs, Rollie," I said. Warner and Justa were sitting out in front waiting for me to make my grand entrance and I could guess what they'd say about the silly-looking spurs.

"Ah, sir, we've got to be thorough."

In a moment he had the brass-colored spurs set on the heels of my highly polished boots. He stepped back a few paces and looked me over with a critical eye. "Now snap the swagger stick under your arm, Colonel, and hold it nonchalant."

I did as he directed, though I felt a great fool.

Finally he smiled. "You look a proper toff, Colonel. If I hadn't

put you together myself I'd swear you were an old campaigner.
You've got your proper ribbons, including the ones from the Indian
campaigns I borrowed. An old cavalryman such as yourself would
not have missed out on the end of that fighting. The uniform fits
you a treat. Your—"

"Does this damn coa—tunic have to be so damn tight? What the
hell is the point of that, Sergeant?"

"Ah, sir, that's for your military bearing. All the world's officers
aren't blessed with it such as yourself. And you'll not be repeating
this, sir, to the other officers, but some has a bit of belly to hold in.
Of course, not yourself, sir. Now you'll be turning around so we
can be after having a look at the whole of you, Colonel. Sir, 'tis a
treat to be looking at you. Ah, it's a fine sight."

I faced back around. "Are you complimenting me, Sergeant, or
yourself?"

He had the good grace to blush slightly. "Ah, sir, I'll just be after
saying I couldn't have done it without you."

"That's damn modest of you, Rollie."

"Now I think we ought to be after having a little practice. I'm
going—"

"But Mr. Williams and Mr. Grayson are waiting out on the porch.
You wanted to spring me on them full-feathered."

"Aye, sir, but I want to see you swagger a bit. 'Tis important we
get you used to the wearing of the uniform and moving in it in the
proper manner."

"And what's the proper manner?"

"You're after being the cock o' the walk, sir. You're after looking
at the rank and file but you ain't actually seeing them, if you take
my meaning, Colonel, sir."

"A snob."

He shook his head. "Oh, much more than a snob, Your Honor.
Divine right would be closer to the way senior officers view their
power."

"What am I supposed to do?"

"I'm going to be after standing here at attention, sir. I know I'm in civvies, but pretend I'm in uniform and pretend there are twenty more like me. You walk up and down in front of us, staring at us, and be after tapping your swagger stick in the palm of your hand. You don't want to look pleased, sir, because you ain't ever pleased. As smart as we look we could always look smarter. Now give that a try, sir, and I'll be calling the men to attention."

I felt a little silly but I nevertheless followed the sergeant's instructions and strolled back and forth, as best the confines of the room would allow, before an imaginary squad of soldiers. I tried to look haughty, tapping the end of my swagger stick in the palm of my hand in such a way as to show my displeasure.

"Capital, sir!" the sergeant said. "Capital. You've got the knack for it, sir, and that's a fact."

"Should I have spoken to any of the soldiers? Told them to button a button or get a shine?"

He rolled his eyes and looked pained. "Ah, sir, you'd sooner roll around on the ground as speak to a common soldier. No, sir. No, sir. You *never* speak directly to one of the rank and file."

I looked frustrated and felt it. "Then how am I going to order the men to carry the gold back to the train if I don't speak to them?"

I thought he would faint. "Sir, was you looking to be unmasked on the spot you couldn't find a better way. You speaks to the highest-ranking officer present and gives him your wishes and then he tells the next officer who tells the ranking noncom who then gives the order to the detail. Ah, Colonel, don't be after frightening me like that. We're not after starting to work on that yet, sir. We won't begin drill on the actual situation until a couple of days before time. What's important now is that you look and talk and feel like a colonel."

"How is my talk?"

He nodded his head indecisively. "It's fair, Colonel, sir. But we are going to make it considerable better. The problem is you look so mean and tough, meaning no disrespect, that it is going to be a job of work to get you a command voice to match it."

"I look mean and tough?"

"Sir, you look like you brought Geronimo and Sitting Bull in single-handedly. Was I a junior officer and I saw you coming I'd be after making myself so small I could hide in a teacup. But we'd better go on parade before your friends. They might be getting impatient."

"No, they got a bottle of whiskey," I said. "But let's get on with it. I feel silly enough as it is."

"Will you be wanting to wear the eye patch now, sir?"

I shook my head. "No, they'll have enough to josh me about as it is."

He looked disapproving. "Ah, sir, you must not allow that to happen. They are your friends and they know you are not a colonel, but you must be after acting like one. This is serious business, Colonel."

I gave him an astonished look. "You're telling *me* that? Who the hell you think it is going to be standing out there in front of the army and half of San Antonio?"

He nodded. "That had a nice tone to it, sir. But it should be a little rougher."

I gave him a grimace. "Rollie, you are a rogue. Lead on."

I followed him into the front room and then out the door to the front porch, where Warner and Justa were sitting in cane-bottomed chairs. I was a little embarrassed. Even though I was going about a deadly business I couldn't help but feel like a kid playing dress-up. I ambled through the door and out onto the porch, slouching a little. I reckoned I was trying to make it not seem so serious. Rollie had walked on past the porch and turned to watch me. Justa and Warner had swiveled in their chairs to look back as I came out the door.

Distress was all over the sergeant's face. He said, "Ah, Colonel, darlin', where's your bearing? You're after slumping. You be walking like a washerwoman."

Justa snickered and Warner was about to when the sergeant turned on them. He said, a little coolly, "I'd remind you gentlemen that Mr. Young is not dressing up for a costume party but for a deadly bit of business."

They both got serious in a hurry. The sergeant didn't have a bad command voice himself. Warner got up and came over and stood in front of me and looked me over. After a moment he said, "Will, you probably don't know it, but I've had a little to do with the army. Got commissioned to set them up a breeding program."

"Yeah, with mules."

His eyes narrowed. "How'd you know that?"

I nodded. "Sergeant McMartin was there. He told me."

Warner turned his head, nodded at Rollie, and then came back to me. "Tell you the truth, Will, you look pretty much at home in that getup. I was around a lot of them high-up officers and I got to tell you, you don't look bad."

Justa had stood up and was looking me over. "I got to agree, Will. I mean, you understand I'd buy you out of this idea if I thought it was for sale, but you'd pass muster, I think that's what they say."

The sergeant said, "Yes, sir! Them exact words."

Of course Justa couldn't let it lie at that. "At least in a bad light. You still look like what you are, a bank robber."

Then the sergeant asked me to parade up and down and practice my stuff as a colonel. I refused. But he was firm. "Your Honor," he said, "if you're feeling awkward acting the part in front of two friends you trust enough to let them know what you're about, then how will you be in front of a crowd of strangers?"

Justa said quietly, "He's got a point, Will. If you are dead set on doing this fool thing you had better get it as right as you can. I don't look good in a black suit."

"We're not going to laugh," Warner said. "I don't find a damn thing about this business very funny. You've hired a man here to tell you how to do it. I don't know about you but when I hire a man for a job I generally let him do it, especially when he knows a hell of a lot more about it."

I sighed and gave in. For the next fifteen minutes I marched or swaggered or moved with measured tread up and down in front of the three of them. I carried my swagger stick in all the positions I had been directed. I used it to rap on my boot to command attention, making a rat-a-tat-tat to show I was not pleased. I returned Sergeant McMartin's salute in every way he had taught me. I returned his salute as if he were a captain, a second lieutenant, a sergeant, and a man in the ranks. At one point he bade me call the troops to attention. I was about to do it when I suddenly remembered. I gave him a cool look. "Attention to orders, Sergeant. Call the detail to attention."

Rollie was pleased as punch. "Capital, Colonel! Ah, you're a darlin' man. I never thought you'd pick that up so quick."

When I was done even Warner and Justa looked impressed. Warner declared himself convinced, but Justa was not so sure. "We're civilians," he said. "We don't know that much. But it's going to be real soldiers you'll be putting this act on for. They might not be so easily convinced."

Sergeant McMartin said, "Aye, sir, and that's going to the hard truth of the matter. I preach at His Honor here but he won't listen."

I said, "Hell, Rollie, I do every damn thing you tell me."

He gave me a sorrowful look. "I've asked you to be for taking your uniform home and wearing it around the house so as to be getting the better taste of it."

"I've told you we've got a housekeeper, and her husband is the handyman around the place. What you reckon they'd think?"

"A proper colonel would scheme out a way. Do they come upstairs in your house?"

"All right, all right," I said. "I'll take it home with me. Ought to give my wife a nice fright."

Justa said, "Now we are getting down to the truth of the matter. Ain't the housekeeper at all. We been there two days and I ain't laid eyes on her except when she serves the table, and I sure as hell ain't seen the handyman."

Rollie shook his head. "And me trusting your every word, sir. Ah, fair hurts my heart, it does."

I glared at Justa. "Thank you very much."

Riding back in the buggy, Justa let us get almost to the International Bridge before he said to Warner sternly, "Here, now, quit that slumpin'. You be walking like a washerwoman, Colonel, darlin'."

I was driving and Warner was between us so I had to lean forward to give Justa another look. "We'll be at the river in a minute and I know for a fact you can't swim. Want to make any other cracks?"

But as we were rattling over the bridge Warner said, "I don't know what you're paying that sergeant, Will, but whatever it is I'd double it. Right now, by my way of thinking, he's the most important thing in your life."

"I'd add a big amen to that, brother," Justa said. "Without him teaching you the ropes of this army business you'd be a dead man. I thought you was crazy before but now I'm kind of coming around. Don't get me wrong—I think you're a damn fool for doing this, but then you've always been a damn fool. Why change now? If you've got to do it, and apparently you think you do, then after what I seen this afternoon I'm about halfway convinced you got a chance. Not much of a chance, but at least a slim one."

Warner said, in that serious way of his, "You looked pretty good, Will, you really did. But I'm like Justa. I'd still be willing to buy you out of this idea if it was for sale."

I waited until we had quit the bridge and were rolling through town before I said, "I'll tell you both something in confidence. But

I damn sure don't want it getting back to Lauren, and if you tell your wives it will."

Justa said easily, "You are right now wishing to hell you had never got yourself involved in this mess."

Warner turned toward me. "That right, Will?"

I nodded slowly. "I wish the idea was for sale myself. I'd buy me out if it broke me."

"Then call it off," Warner said urgently. "Don't do it. Hell, Will, not that many people know."

I shook my head. "I can't."

"But why not? Why the hell not?"

"Because he's Wilson Young," Justa said. He leaned forward so he could see me. "You been nailed in that box for a long time, ain't you, partner?"

I nodded slowly. "I reckon."

Warner wouldn't let go. "Give it up, Will. Hell, what you are planning is damn dangerous. This is no cinch you're betting here."

"Save your breath, Warner," Justa said. "See, it don't matter who else knows. He knows. And that's all that counts. He also knows he needs a miracle to bring this off and he don't believe in miracles. Ain't that about the size of it, Will?"

I nodded slowly. "I'm afraid that is the truth."

Warner started cussing in a low voice that gradually rose. He cussed me, he cussed the government, he cussed people in general, he cussed men for being so damn proud, he cussed pride, he cussed guns, bullets, and the holes they made, he cussed women for being so damned desirable men did damn fool things for them, he cussed children who didn't listen to their fathers. Before he was through he had cussed hard enough to raise dust on the street.

"That was a pretty good run, Warner," Justa said. "I didn't know you had it in you."

Warner turned to me. "I want to thank you for making my life hell. Now go and get yourself killed and what I been going through won't be nothing to what I'll catch."

I frowned. "How did you buy a hand in this game?"

He gave me an outraged look. "Because I introduced you to Lauren. Because we were friends before y'all were married. Everything you do that makes Lauren unhappy gets blamed on me! I may not live though this little stunt."

We all laughed at that, which was just as well as I was turning in to the path to my carriage house. Mr. Bridesdale spotted us and came hurrying over to take charge of the horses and the carriage. As we got down I said, "Hell, let's go in my office and pretend we're talking business and get about half drunk."

Justa said, "Hell, let's get all the way drunk."

"You get drunk," I snorted. "I'm surrounded by hostile women and I've got to have some of my wits about me."

Right before we went into the house Warner stopped me and stepped around so we were face-to-face. With real urgency he said, "Will, I ain't said much so far because it's your business, but I feel I got to remind you of something. You ain't that nineteen-year-old outlaw that come riding into my horse yard that day one step ahead of a posse. You ain't a bank robber no more. You ain't a gunman no more. You got a wife and son, you got a family. You got a good business. Leave this kind of foolishness to someone else."

I put my hand on his shoulder in about as near to an affectionate gesture as I ever made to a friend and said simply, "I can't, Warner."

"Save your breath, Warner," Justa said, a little edge in his voice. "Let the damn fool kill himself. He's not robbing a bank. Hell, that's small potatoes for him now. He's saving the goddamn country, didn't you know that?"

*   *   *

WE HAD a pretty sociable dinner that night. They had all done their duty to Lauren by declaring me crazy and wrong and dead set on destruction and selfish and thoughtless of not only my wife but my friends and all the widows and orphans who depended on me. Lauren was quiet, but she seemed to be enjoying herself. Mrs. Bridesdale had baked a sugar-cured ham and we were having that along with yams and redeye gravy and butter beans and fresh-baked bread. They were leaving in the morning and I knew that was bringing Lauren down a little. All her support was leaving her, but that really wasn't it. As long as they were there that awful day that would see me off to San Antonio could be put off. With them gone there'd just be the two of us and I'd be there as a constant reminder of what was shortly to come.

They would be taking the early train. Mr. Bridesdale was all primed to hitch up the big carriage and drive them to the depot. Lauren said to me, "Will, if you weren't such an old stick-in-the-mud, you'd have bought one of those big Cadillac touring automobiles like Justa has and they could be taken to the depot in style instead of in that old carriage."

I looked at her carefully. "Who'd you say had a Cadillac automobile?"

"Justa. And Nora. Though she says she's scared to drive it."

I fixed my eyes on Justa, who had suddenly gotten busy buttering a piece of bread. "Who told you Justa had a Cadillac automobile?"

"Why, Nora. What difference does it make?"

Justa was still giving that bread hell with his butter knife. I said, "Old friend, how long you had that Cadillac automobile?"

He still wouldn't look up. "Oh, I don't know," he said. "A little spell."

Nora said, "Why, nearly a year. Remember, you were the first to buy one."

"So you had that Cadillac automobile while I was there talking about Cadillac automobiles?"

He glanced up and smiled slightly and shrugged. "Might have."

"And never said a word to me."

"Well, you seemed so down on so much I didn't see any point in upsetting you any further." He took a bite of bread and looked at me, chewing.

I just shook my head. "I hope it bucks you off and then backs over your sorry ass. Some friend."

But all in all we had a good time. Me and Justa and Warner had started dinner about half lit from the whiskey we'd drunk. But the women weren't long in playing a little catch-up on the wine being served with the food. And then, with coffee, we had some fine cognac, and only Nora didn't take a hand in that.

Lauren wasn't going to be the only one sorry to see them go. I was flattered that they'd thought enough of me to come so far to save me from myself. But then, when they left, I'd be in the same situation as Lauren, just waiting for that day. And it was coming terribly fast.

It appeared we were going to end a pleasant meal and retire to the parlor until Justa Williams spoke up. I figured he done it out of mischief because of my attitude toward his Cadillac automobile. "Me and Warner saw the colonel here in full regalia this afternoon," he said. "Quite a sight. Will, why don't you get your rig and put it on for the ladies? Ought to get quite a reaction."

I looked quickly at Lauren. There was pain in her eyes. She said, "You don't mean you have it in the house? What if Mrs. Bridesdale finds it?"

I said, "It's hidden, sweetheart." I shot Justa a look that should have sunburned him. "The sergeant thinks I should get used to wearing it. But he meant in private." I gave Justa the second barrel and he kind of ducked his head. He knew good and well he'd misspoke.

Awkwardly he said, "I'm right sorry, Will. I thought Lauren had general knowledge of what was going on. I need to keep my mouth shut."

Lauren shook her head. "I would have found out tomorrow. And after all . . . " She shrugged. "What difference does it make? I'll see it sooner or later. He's not going to change his mind, you know."

That little bump in the conversation kind of lowered the level of gaiety. We finished up our brandy and coffee and set out to the parlor. I was trailing the bunch when Laura dropped back and said she wanted a word with me in private. "I'm not going to enjoy this, am I?" I said.

"I don't know," she said. "I suppose it depends on how honest you are with yourself."

We went out the front door and sat down in the porch swing. We rocked back and forth a few times before she said, "You have the right to hurt yourself, Wilson, but you don't have the right to hurt Lauren."

I turned my head so she could see me clearly in the moonlight. I said, "When Warner took up with you I could have told him it would be about as comfortable as living in a barbed-wire cage with a bad-tempered bobcat. But I didn't. I minded my own business. I could have also told him that reasoning with you would be about as productive as carrying water in a bucket without a bottom. But I didn't. I could have told him that you were selfish, spoiled, and would make every effort to turn him into a steer. But I didn't. The man was my friend and I respected his judgment and his wishes."

She stared back at me when I'd finished. After a moment she said, "So you are telling me I should do the same."

"Nothing gets by you, Laura. You're quick as a whip."

"All right. We're agreed. You're hurting my sister and I don't much like you for it."

"You never did much like me. You didn't want Lauren to marry me in the first place."

She shook her head. "That's not true, and you can ask Lauren. I thought you would make a good match and I told her so. But I also told her to expect to have her hands full since I'd known you several years before her. You are wrong if you think I have ever disliked you. You called me selfish and spoiled. I take that as a compliment coming from the king of that species. I always thought you had a little more self-confidence than was wanting in just ordinary day-to-day living."

"That's why I ain't never been willing to live an ordinary day-to-day life. You got much more you want to say?"

She shook her head. "No. But don't think you can fool me with your high and mighty talk about a gesture and getting back at the government and helping Willis and all that other bullshit you've been shoveling out. You are doing this for your own damned reasons." She got up from the swing and started for the front door. "Whatever they are. You're the only one who knows or will ever know. But for Lauren's sake I wish you good luck." She looked back and flashed me a smile. "You and I are too much alike to ever really get along." She opened the door and disappeared.

I sat there for a moment more, then shook my head and smiled. They were a rare pair, those two sisters. After a few more minutes I got up and joined the rest of the party. I felt like I needed to ease up beside Justa and let him know I hadn't been upset by his remark. The situation I was in, a man couldn't afford to go to losing friends.

CHAPTER
14

WE SAW them off the next morning, waving good-bye from the front porch until they were just a cloud of dust in the distance. Lauren said, "Well, that's that."

"It was a good visit," I said, hoping to keep her spirits up.

"Yes," she said. "For all the good it did."

Before I could make reply she went into the house, leaving me alone on the porch. I stared out at the harsh landscape. That was one thing you could say about the border country—it didn't play favorites. It was as ugly to the eye of the beggar as the banker. Yet, oddly, coming from beautiful country like Virginia, Lauren had never once complained about where I chose to live or to change my mind. She even seemed to like it and had learned to speak Spanish faster than I'd've thought possible. In fact, if anything, she spoke it much better than I. I was one of those arrogant gringos who insisted I be understood in whatever language I cared to use.

I stood there thinking. There were four days and some few hours left. The papers, especially the San Antonio papers, were full of the news of the coming of the gold. Hell, you'd have thought it was being brought down for distribution among the poor and needy.

The papers were now able to furnish a hungry public with details. The gold train was expected the next Saturday morning at approximately ten o'clock and the gold would be off-loaded within the following half hour or so. It was expected to arrive at the bank sometime before noon and would go on display, if all went as scheduled, at about one o'clock. The public would be obliged to view the great glittering display through the bank's plate glass windows on Saturday and Sunday. Only on Monday would the gawkers be allowed to actually enter the bank and get within ten feet of their gold, which would be displayed on green velvet. It was clearly pointed out that the gold would be guarded around the clock by riflemen of the 23rd Quartermaster Corps. An officer, a Captain Griffin Bell, was in charge of the detail. His second-in-command was a Lieutenant Wood. There was a picture of Captain Bell, staring straight into the camera. I took him for a man in his early forties. He had a fat face and was wearing rimless glasses. I could see the insignia on his shirt collar wings, but I didn't recognize it. I was sure Rollie would have a line on the subject. I caught myself thinking he looked a little old to be only a captain, and that made me smile. I was starting to think like a soldier. Some of Rollie's intense teaching was starting to rub off.

Captain Bell was quoted as saying that the public was certainly in for a "treat" seeing all that much gold. He said their reception at other small cities had been overwhelming and that the public had seemed much gratified and awestruck at the sight of the "mighty mountain of money." He said that he and his men were happy to be able to give the public a view of the gold reserves held by the country even if it was just a small sampling, and that he thought people were as reassured by the sight as if they had been able to walk into Fort Knox.

I didn't know if the good captain was going to turn out to be as smug as he sounded in the newspaper, but just reading his comments made me want to get him by the neck and jerk him off the ground and give him a good shaking.

The article closed by saying the gold would leave San Antonio sometime between the bank's closing on Thursday afternoon and early Friday morning. The populace was advised that strict order would be maintained along the route of the gold's delivery from the train to the bank, and those wishing a good view of the proceedings were urged to come early for a good vantage point. Reading the article made me angry all over again. The reporter's tone and especially that of Captain Bell made it seem as if the government was doing a special favor for the people of the area, who were damn fortunate to get a chance to see so much money in one pile. Who the hell's money did they think it was, anyway? That wasn't the Barnum and Bailey Circus they were bringing to town, it was gold that belonged to every man jack who would be lining the streets to see how the government was taking care of his property. At one place in the article Captain Bell said—superiorly, I thought—that it was a "chance not to be missed because never again will any man or woman of the town be able to see so much money in one lump sum."

Well, of course it was the only chance they would have to see that much money in one lump sum, or any number of lump sums. But what good was it going to do them? All they could do was look. Looking at a beer wouldn't make you any less thirsty, looking at a beautiful woman wouldn't make you any less lustful, and looking at a good horse wouldn't make your feet hurt less from walking. And yet the idiots were going to line up on the streets around the plaza to watch the gold being transferred from the train station to the bank. And they wouldn't even see any gold. Likely it would be in strongboxes secured with big locks. Could be anything inside the boxes for all the crowd knew. They'd be watching the caisson passing and saying, "Oh, look, there goes a quarter of a million dollars in gold bullion." For all they knew it might be forty dollars' worth of beets or two hundred dollars' worth of gold-colored lead. And then they were going to run over and stand in front of the bank and mill around until the big shades were let up and they could press their greedy little noses against the glass and see all that gold.

Except it wasn't going to get that far. Not if I had my way.

I went back into the house. Lauren was nowhere in sight so I went into my office and got myself a morning whiskey and sat down in my chair. Laura had surprised me by something she had said before they'd left. She'd got me off to one side and said, "Will, I want you to understand that I meant it when I said good luck. And I don't mean only for Lauren's sake. I've been too hard on you. It was Warner pointed it out to me last night. You were wild when Lauren married you, just like Warner was horse crazy when I married him. Both of us went into the arrangement with our eyes wide open. It's just that what you are planning to try isn't something you expect your husband to pull on you." Then she'd looked at me. "That is, I guess, unless you're married to Wilson Young. I've only got through telling this same thing to Lauren. For nearly every man this is not ordinary or expected behavior. But, hell, you never have settled down. Now that I think about it, I'm surprised that I'm even surprised. But at least it gave me a chance to drag Warner out of the horse barn and come see my sister."

"How did Lauren react to what you said?" I'd asked.

She'd shrugged. "She can understand it up here." She'd pointed to her head. "But it still hurts here." She'd pointed to her heart. Then she'd touched my shoulder. "But I think she's accepted it. She doesn't like it, naturally, but I don't think she's going to fight you on it anymore."

I appreciated what Laura had done and said. Me and her kind of rubbed sparks off each other, but she was an uncommonly honest and good woman. Warner was nearly as lucky as I was.

After lunch I took the little valise I kept my uniform in and rode across the river to the Mexican ranch. I'd had a solitary lunch of meat loaf and mashed potatoes with buttermilk and spring onions. Lauren had to attend some function so she'd eaten ahead of time and gone sailing out the door pinning her hat in place. Mrs. Bridesdale had commented that the "dear lady" never ate enough to keep a bird alive and now she was eating even less. I hadn't sought to enlighten Mrs. Bridesdale on what was bothering Lauren.

I took the newspaper with me, and Sergeant McMartin took one look at the picture of Captain Bell and said, "Aye, sir, a blasted Finance officer. And likely the second in command is, too. They'll have a sergeant in charge of the Quartermaster boys. One blaze of your eyes and they'll melt into the bricks of the plaza."

"Rollie, I ain't all that sure about that," I said. "I've known some of these little officious types, bankers and accountants and what not, and you give them a little power and they can swell up like a pouter pigeon."

He nodded. "Aye, that's true, sir. But right now we had better get to work and start preparing you for the first part of our little play."

We had decided that it was vital that the bank be neutralized, that they not expect the gold, that they stay out of the proceedings between me and the officers and the detail. To do that I was going to have to put on a hell of an act for the bank manager. I was going to have to be at my swagger-sticking, boot-popping best.

Rollie said, "Sir, you've got to make him certain that he is standing in the presence of the might and majesty of the whole United States Army in the person of yourself and that if he so much as blinks an eye or is after clearing his throat, Black Jack Pershing will roll a battery of artillery up the street and blow his pitiful bank to smithereens."

"Hell, Rollie, I was never that threatening when I was robbing banks for real with a loaded revolver."

"Aye, sir, but it was then when you wasn't funnin' and you knew it and they would be after knowin' it. Now the conditions be a bit different. And civilians ain't used to listening to the soldiery. You need to keep him out of your business for at least ten or fifteen minutes. Remember, there is danger about and you are there to protect that gold and keep the robbers from succeeding. He's got to believe you about the danger."

I half smiled. "I don't think I ought to have much trouble convincing him there is a robber around. I'll be standing right there in front of him."

But though we agreed that the business at the bank had to go right we could not agree on the army regulation-issue Colt .45 semiautomatic pistol he wanted me to carry. My own revolver would not fit in the stiff holster that was shaped to fit the heavy automatic. I was in favor of not carrying any gun at all. I said, "Damnit, Rollie, I'm not going to fire it, I don't care what it comes down to. So why in hell have it on me? It's heavy as hell."

"Aye, sir," he said. "And that's the point. The uniform don't hang right on you without the weight of the gun in the holster."

Of course, we were practicing in full garb and he marched me back to the bedroom where there was a bureau mirror that showed the top half of me. "Now, sir, be after looking here." He pointed out that, without the weight of the revolver, the Sam Browne belt did not hang right, and that made the tunic not fit exactly right. "You see, sir? The purpose of that diagonal strap is to take some of the weight of the automatic. If it ain't in there it all goes cockeyed."

He was right and I had to agree. I took the .45-caliber gun he'd brought and slid it in the holster. "Can't I wear it without the clip?" I asked. "I don't need the clip, do I?"

He cocked his head. "The weight, sir, the weight. The clip and the bullets weigh a good deal."

"Where the hell did you get this damn gun? Is it yours?"

He gave me a startled look. "Mine, sir? With the serial number registered to my own name? And it floating around at the site of a robbery? Do you think me daft, sir?"

"Then where did you get it?"

He looked nonchalant. "Ah, sir, us old noncoms takes care of each other. That weapon couldn't be traced to nobody. It disappeared years ago out in New Mexico."

"Rollie, you're a damn thief." I pulled out the weapon and pulled back the slide to throw a shell into the chamber. It was a little stiff but could be managed without much strain. I let the hammer down to half-cock, which was the safety position, and then thrust it back in the holster and buttoned the flap over the top. The new leather fairly shone and on the outside of the holter the initials *U.S.* were clearly imprinted. I said, "This is one hell of an awkward rig. It looks like something the government would dream up."

"Aye, Colonel," he said, "it's always been a source of great comfort to us soldiers to know our weapons was made by the lowest bidder."

I had to laugh. "You mean the money that passed across the top of the table?"

"Aye," he said, nodding.

So the days ticked along. The sergeant and I practiced in the morning and the early afternoon, going over and over material that had long since become familiar but couldn't be polished enough. In the evenings Lauren and I took supper together and talked and made love after we went to bed. We never talked on the subject at hand but on inconsequential matters like her charities or committee work or how my businesses were going. She was quieter than I'd ever known her, but as Laura had predicted, she made no direct attacks on my plans. To those who didn't know her well enough she seemed untroubled, but I'd catch her off guard at times and see the worry and strain in her face. It hurt me to be hurting her, but I didn't know what to do about it. A man can't always order his life in such a way that he can have all he wants. Sometimes there's a price.

On Thursday I sent my best vaquero from the Mexican ranch with two very dependable saddle horses. He was to take them by train to Three Wells and then keep them there in the unused corrals until the morning of the coming Saturday. After that he was to make his way back to the ranch. I had bought the ticket for him and arranged for the stock car and the stop at Three Wells. All he had to do was get off and take care of the horses so they'd be there waiting for me when I arrived sometime around noon. There was a train that came through at 7:00 A.M. on Saturday and I had made arrangements for it to stop at the water station to pick up my vaquero. He was a good, dependable man and I knew that the horses would be waiting for me in good shape and ready for the hard, two-day ride back to the border. I had given him fifty dollars as a gift. It hadn't been necessary, but it had made him happy as hell.

Rosita, my fat cook at the ranch, had put me up a supply of jerked beef and some cheese and saltines and canned tomatoes and canned peaches. It was enough food for the trip. I also had two five-gallon canvas water sacks that the vaquero would fill at the watering tank. I doubted I'd need them, or the food for that matter, but you never knew. I had also included a change of clothes as I intended to get rid of the uniform and boots and hat just as quick as I was through with them. The vaquero had rigged a little pack saddle for the extra gear, though it was mostly packed into two sets of saddlebags. Neither horse was going to be a pack animal. I intended to ride both of them hard, switching off as one tired. I figured to travel, if the horses would stand it, about eighteen hours a day. I wanted to be home as quick as possible. In fact, I wanted it to look like I'd never left, even though I knew that probably wasn't possible.

With alarming precision the details of my plan were falling into place. Each day another piece of the background work was done and the time came closer and closer to when it was going to be my turn to be the main actor in the little play I was staging. A moment would come when all the behind-the-scenes planning was accomplished and it was time for me to step naked onto a stage in front of an audience. A month before it had seemed so easy to get angry about what the government was doing and how they needed to be shown. Now I wasn't so sure.

On Thursday night the talk I had been half expecting and dreading came. It was right after supper and Lauren and I had gone into the parlor. The day before, a letter had come from Willis. I had seen it on the hall table as I'd gone out. There'd been a sealed note in it for me. It had begun, *"Dad,"* a name I could never get used to. My father had been Father. It had said:

I didn't write this to Mom because I don't want her to worry about me being in the fighting. This morning I had my first taste of aerial combat. I was up on a lone dawn patrol. It was my first solitary sortie but it was a quiet sector over the Somme so they like for us new ones to get the feel of it. I jumped a Rumpler. That's a German two-seater. The seat behind the pilot is used by a machine gunner. He can hit you if you come from behind or from either side. The pilot has a machine gun that shoots straight ahead. I thought about what you'd always said about trying to work yourself some kind of advantage. I decided his weakest spot was his belly so I dropped below him and then climbed up and gave him a burst. He tried everything he could to get away from me but his clumsy aeroplane was no match for my nimble little Nieuport. I kept climbing up and giving him a burst in the belly until he finally went down. You said I was fighting somebody

*else's fight. Well, that fight was mine and he'd have killed me if I hadn't
killed him. I hope you don't still think I would be over here if I didn't
believe in what I was doing.*

I had handed the note to Lauren with the single comment, "Your
son has discovered self-righteousness."

She read the note, her eyes narrowing. Finally she had laid it
aside. Looking straight at me, she said, "Sounds like he's found out
how to do what he likes and then justify it later."

"You ain't going to say anything about him coming by it honestly?"

She'd shaken her head. "Why? Would that bring him home?"

"Or stop me from my own foolishness?"

She hadn't replied, but I knew it was only a delay. As we went
into the parlor she said, "Will, I want to talk to you and I don't want
you to get upset or angry. I've got a few things to say and I don't
want an argument." I knew what was coming.

But then she didn't bring up the letter or Willis or anything to
do with false justification, which was what I had been expecting.
Instead she'd sat down and said, "Honey, I know you are going to
go through with this. It scares the hell out of me. I think there's a
chance you could get yourself killed. If you are going to go into that
kind of danger then I've got no choice but to make one more attempt to talk to you about your . . . your spiritual life."

She caught me so off guard that, for a long second, I couldn't
reply. We hadn't had this conversation in a long, long time and I
thought the whole issue was closed, that she'd figured out I might
someday find what she claimed she had but that I'd have to do it
on my own. But now here she was getting right up close about it.
And hell, I was leaving the next day and I knew I was making her
unhappy. It seemed like the least I could do was let her have one
more good go at me. But it wasn't that easy. I groaned and reared
back in my chair and looked up at the ceiling and said, "Aw, Lau-

ren, you ain't going to start that tonight, are you? Hell, I got a lot
on my mind."

She looked uncertain, but her voice was firm. "Sweetheart, I'd
be less than your wife, less than a Christian if I didn't try one more
time. Especially right now."

I sighed. "Honey, this ain't right. If I was God and I was sitting
up there listening to me undergo a sudden conversion I'd have to
figure, if I was Him, that I was listening to a guy trying to hedge his
bets. Don't you see, Lauren, this is exactly the wrong time. Hell, as
scared as I am—" I stopped when I saw the look on her face.
Quickly I said, "As scared as I am of making a fool of myself. What
I mean is, I don't think this is the appropriate time."

She was looking at me steadily. No more than five or six feet separated us. She said, "I know what you meant, Will. You should be
scared. And not of making a fool of yourself. What I can't understand is why you won't even give yourself a chance to believe.
You've had your mind made up from the first. You're not a closed-
minded man, sweetheart, and this is not like you. God is not going
to think you're a hypocrite. You can be accused of a lot of things,
but being a hypocrite is not one of them."

I was still squirming. "Honey, listen, that religious stuff is all right
for you. You grew up with it. It came natural. I didn't. I came up
hard and rough and I didn't believe in anything I couldn't see or
lay my hand on. You get in a tight place, there ain't no time for pray-
ing. I ain't running down your faith, you understand. I just can't
seem to get a handle on it."

"You say you believe in only what you can see or what you can
touch. Do you believe in the Pacific Ocean?"

I fumbled a cigarillo out of my pocket and lit it. I was wishing
I'd thought to bring in a drink with me. "I know if I were to travel
west long enough and far enough I'd eventually run into the Pacific Ocean."

"But you don't believe that if you practiced faith long enough you'd run into God?"

She was hemming me up good. "Aw, hell, Lauren," I said, "that kind of stuff is fine for you. You're a woman and women take naturally to that church stuff."

"It's Christianity, Will, and the church has nothing to do with it. I'm talking about your soul now. I'm talking about faith as the assurance of things hoped for, the certainty of things not seen."

I looked down at the floor. "I've heard you say that before."

She got up and came over and knelt beside my chair. "I'm the wrong one to be talking to you about this, Will. We're too close. But somewhere, somehow, there is someone who can reach you."

"Some preacher?"

"No, I'm not talking about a preacher. No one can save you but yourself, Will. If Christ wants you it will happen. I guess I'll have to comfort myself with that thought."

I got her under the arm and lifted her up and sat her in my lap. She curled back against my shoulder. I said, "Honey, I'd do anything to make you happy. I don't know why I resist this business of yours, but it don't seem right for me. I can't conceive of this God you believe in so strongly. I'm glad you do because I can see what comfort you take from it, but you are asking me to believe that He made the whole ranch, from the stars right down to the smallest insect. That's a whole big load to handle."

"Have you got a better explanation?"

I shook my head. "No, I guess I don't."

She got up out of my lap. "People have been arguing about the existence of God since time began. No one can *prove* that God exists, except in here." She touched her heart. "But no one can prove He doesn't. All I can do is pray. It may be that you were never intended, but I will still pray."

I got up and took her in my arms. "You're good enough for both of us. I figure to piggyback my way into heaven on you. I'm going to get a drink. Do you want one?"

She looked at me and half smiled and shook her head. "Oh, Will. You are something. Why did I ever fall in love with a man like you?"

"I know the answer to that one. What I don't know is if you want a drink or not."

"Oh, why not. But just a glass of wine."

I started out of the parlor but her voice stopped me before I could get to the door. I looked back. "What? Rather have brandy?"

"No, that's not it. I thought you ought to know that I am going to San Antonio with you."

I snorted. "Like hell you are. I ain't going to no quilting bee."

"Nevertheless, I am going to be there."

I gave her a good hard look. "Lauren, don't start talking nonsense. You and I both know that wouldn't be the place for you. I'm going for a purpose. You don't have one."

"If my husband is going to put himself in danger I am going to be there."

I started for the door again. "I don't want to hear any more about this. Do you understand?"

Her voice followed me. "You won't. Hear any more about it."

ON FRIDAY there were three trains that ran from Del Rio to San Antonio. There was an early morning train and then the one that came about one o'clock. But besides those two there was a train, an American train, that ran from Monterrey, Mexico, stopped at Del Rio, and then went on to San Antonio. It was a curious arrangement, but I supposed it was a convenience for trade between the two big cities. It came through Del Rio at ten at night. For a time I dithered about taking that train. It would put me into San Antonio at a little after two in the morning, and the attraction was that I'd be spending less time in the city and would therefore be that much less likely to be recognized. But in the end I decided to take the one o'clock train. I was going to need a good night's rest because, once the so-called robbery was completed, I would have two days of hard riding ahead of me. Also, there were some necessities I required and I preferred to buy them in San Antonio rather than Del Rio. I didn't want anyone to be able to come forward later and say that, yes, they had sold me such supplies.

Friday morning came, just as I knew the next morning was to come, and I got up early, slipped out of the house before breakfast, saddled the horse I had been keeping, and rode across to see the sergeant for the last time before the business. I had drawn several thousand dollars out of the bank and wanted to give him fifteen hundred, the balance he had coming on our deal. Also, I wanted to go over all the last-minute details and see if I had forgotten anything.

Riding over, I was troubled. I had, unaccountably, dreamed about Les Richter the night before. I had awakened with the dream as fresh in my mind as if it had just happened. We had met in the hallway of some old hotel, some hotel from our past. It seemed Mexican, but then again it didn't. Just one of those old run-down kinds of places that our kind stayed at, a place to get a bath and a night's sleep in a bed and then on down the road toward the next bank.

In the dream it was like we had met coming from different directions. We were facing each other. He looked as young as the last time I had seen him, but there was a weariness in his face. He didn't speak. I kept asking him where he'd been and what he'd been doing, but he never opened his mouth. Finally he gave his head a quick little shake and walked on past me. I turned to watch his back as he went down the hall, but he never looked back.

It had been a disturbing dream, a dream that had left me feeling uneasy and kind of down. I could take no meaning from it. There didn't seem to be any meaning unless it was some kind of sign I was fixing to see him in a place where they didn't do much talking. But I didn't care for that interpretation. Didn't care for it at all.

The sergeant surprised me by saying it was too early in the morning for him to drink. That didn't stop me from adding a good wallop to my coffee. He was drinking some of that fruit juice that Rosita made. As far as I was concerned, a little of that went a long ways. It was closing on for eight of the morning and I didn't want to absent myself too long from Lauren. I knew she'd be wondering where I was, slipping out as I had. But there wasn't much left for me and the sergeant to talk about. If I didn't have it right by then I wasn't ever going to get it straight. We sat out on the front porch, mostly just gazing off into the distance and making small talk about nothing. I had already given him his money, which he'd taken without argument. That had surprised me, though I wasn't sure why. I said, "I expect you'll be taking off pretty quick and getting yourself that divorce."

"Aye, sir, that I'll be. And a relief and blessing it will be. Of course, if I'm to be going to work for you she'll not be after getting my army pay so easily."

I smiled. "Is that your way of saying you think I'll pull through this business?"

"Ah, Your Honor, I've never had nothing but the longest of faith in you. You're a gentleman, Colonel, and ain't many as can be called that without a flaw in the saying of it."

I sipped at my coffee and looked ruefully out over my pastureland. "I reckon my wife would agree with that, but she'd be a great deal happier if she could call me a Christian instead."

"She speak at you, did she?"

I shrugged. "You can't much blame her, considering the circumstances." I told him what she'd said and how I'd reacted.

He was silent for a moment and then he smiled slowly. "Aye, Colonel, faith be an odd business. Once you've got it you wonder how you ever got along without it. But until it has took you—and when it takes you it takes the whole of you—it seems like so much useless baggage."

I gave him a quick look. "Don't tell me you're in that camp?"

He gave me a wink. "Me and Mrs. Young agree on a considerable number of matters. But you've already been beckoned to and I won't add to your confusion. But like your good lady said, 'tis not you who decides, 'tis the Lord Christ Jesus. When He comes He'll take you the same as He took Saul on the road to Damascus. And if there was ever a sinner who would not be convinced, it was old Saul. Or so he thought. But I'm after filling your cup a little full, Colonel. Are you after having any last questions? Have you seen to every last knot and lashing? Is your cargo secure?"

I shrugged. "Near as I know, Rollie. But likely I'll forget the very thing I need."

"Only don't forget you are a colonel. At least for that little while." He squinted and gave me a close look. "Though I'm after sayin' you don't look much like one at this time."

I wasn't wearing my usual linen coat. Instead I had on just an old western-cut shirt, blue and white checked, a pair of jeans, and an old pair of boots. "No, I'm saving the look of the colonel for the right time."

"And I see you're not wearing your revolver in your shoulder holster."

I shrugged. "I'm not taking it, so I put the whole rig away. Besides, it's a little hard to hide without a coat."

"You'll not be forgetting the forty-five?"

I shook my head. "No, First Sergeant."

"It will show, Your Honor, if you don't have it in the holster."

"It's already packed. It's in the valise with the uniform and the boots and the Sam Browne belt and everything else. I'm taking the campaign hat in a cardboard box. I'll go in looking like a saddle tramp and come out a colonel."

"Aye," he said, "and you'll be every inch of him."

I swallowed the last of my coffee and stood up. "I better be getting on home. Likely Mrs. Young will have some things she's forgot to say." I put out my hand and he took it and we shook. "I am much obliged to you, Rollie. If I hadn't run into you I'd have made a hell of a mess out of this impersonation business."

He smiled. "Aye, Colonel, that you would. But you remember your lessons and you'll do foin. I'm glad I could have a part."

I stepped away from the porch, toward where my horse was tied. "One thing I might ask you, Rollie. If you are still here Saturday, I wonder if you might not stop in and reassure Mrs. Young. I know it's asking a lot, but y'all seemed to have hit it off."

"Aye, I'll be doing that, Colonel. Well, I wish you the best of luck. And I'll be looking forward to that job."

"Oh, that's a ways off, ain't it, Rollie?"

He smiled. "A body never knows, do they, Colonel?"

I left, riding for the bridge. I was a little irritated by the casualness of his good-bye. He acted like we parted under such circumstances every day. Well, he was, after all, a paid employee and I shouldn't have figured on him caring how I came out, one way or the other. Still, I thought he could have pumped me up a bit more.

We had an early lunch, Lauren and I. I had expected to find her subdued and worried, but she acted about normal. Mrs. Bridesdale had made breaded veal cutlets, which were one of my favorites, along with brown gravy and black-eyed peas and sliced tomatoes. I figured I'd better tuck away a good feed while I had the chance. As the meal was winding down I thought I would say something that would make Lauren feel better. I said, "You know, honey, I've been thinking about it. Maybe I'll start going to church when I get back from San Antonio."

Without looking up she said, "Wouldn't that be like you wearing a blindfold to a burlesque show?"

That nettled me. "Hell, Lauren, I thought you'd be glad. Seems like you been after me to go to church since before we were married."

"There's only one good reason to go to church, Will." She looked at me and said dryly, "And that reason isn't to please your wife. Or try and placate her when you feel you're doing something that is making her unhappy."

I was trying to act contrite. I didn't want a scene right before I left. "Is that why you said church didn't count? You kind of surprised me with that."

She gave me a sad little smile. "Oh, Will, how you do try. And I love you for it. But you don't want a lesson this morning. You just want me to feel like you'll stand for one. A church does count, but not without belief. Without belief it's just a building."

"Well, hell, Lauren, you make the damn business so hard. You're a good person and it comes natural to you. For me it would be something I'd have to work at, and I never got around to it. That damn Sergeant McMartin said something funny this morning. He said once you had faith you couldn't see how you'd ever made your way before, when you were without it. But until you got it you wouldn't give nothing for it. That's a hell of a thing to say. How can something be worthless one second and so valuable the next?"

She looked amused. "That's the mystery, sweetheart. And it's one you'll never solve until you don't need to. That's when you begin to believe."

"Well," I said uneasily, "maybe that'll happen someday." I got out my watch and looked at it. The time was going on half past noon. I had Mr. Bridesdale set to pick me up at the front door at ten minutes to one. I planned to catch the train just as it was starting to pull out of the station. I didn't even plan to buy my ticket from the passenger agent, who would know me, but to wait and get it from the conductor on the train. Lauren already knew that I was not a big hand for good-byes, that I liked to make them short and sweet.

I said, "Getting on for that time. I reckon I better be thinking about leaving."

She looked a little surprised. "You're not going like that?"

"You mean these old clothes? Yeah, I thought I would."

"Will, you've always been careful of your appearance."

I smiled faintly. "I'm taking a change with me. Except I don't plan to wear that particular set of clothes until the right moment."

She pulled a face. "Your uniform. You and Willis, both in uniform."

It almost made me angry, but I caught myself in time. "Yes, and we both got about the same amount of business in one."

She said innocently, "Isn't it illegal for you to be wearing that uniform?"

"Yes," I said, "and you can bet that worries me. Easily the worst thing I have ever done." I stood up. There wasn't much more to be said. I'd long ago gotten my affairs in order in case anything ever happened to me. My lawyer had full instructions and signed orders, as did the bank. Everything went to Lauren except for a hundred thousand acres of worthless land I'd left to Willis after he decided to go fight in a war that was none of his business. It had been a mean gesture, but now there was no time to rectify it. Not that it mattered. Lauren would see that he was well taken care of.

"Well," I said, "I reckon I better get started. I'm glad you gave up that foolish idea about going with me."

She stood up and came close and put the palms of her soft hands on my chest. "Oh, I'll be there."

I smiled. "Yes, I know. In spirit."

She smiled. "If you want to call it that."

"Well, as the sergeant would say, I'd better be for after kissing you good-bye, my love."

It was a brief kiss. I was determined to make it seem like nothing more than a quick business trip to San Antonio and then home in a few days. Pulling back, I said, "Well, you look out for matters here and I'll be back before you know it."

" 'Bye, sweetheart. Be very, very careful."

I flashed her a confident smile I didn't feel. "You know me, I'm always careful." I turned my back on her and walked down the hall to my office and collected my valise that contained the uniform and all the paraphernalia that went with it, including the loaded .45. The campaign hat was in a cardboard box to protect its stiff brim. I collected it and glanced back as I stepped out into the hall. Lauren was nowhere in sight, which was the way I liked it. We'd said our good-byes and now it was time to go.

THERE WERE several rooming houses within a four- or five-block walk from the Military Plaza. I selected one and rented myself a room for the night for two dollars. It was a place that served meals and the landlady said I could have breakfast for a dollar more if I was of a mind. I didn't plan on joining in with the rest of the boarders for the morning meal. Folks at a boarding table have a way of asking too many questions, like you're all part of the family. I wasn't in much of a question-answering mood. The landlady showed me upstairs to my little room and pointed out where the bathroom was. I thanked her and then waited until she'd left before I hid my valise and box in the corner and then let myself out of the room and down the stairs and out the front door. I walked toward the business section of town. I was looking for an apothecary and a dry-goods store. I found the dry-goods store first and went in and bought a cheap gray slicker. After that I found the drugstore and went in and bought some gauze bandages and adhesive tape and a sling like you use for a broken arm. When I was all done with that I went into a saloon for a drink or two. I had a bottle of my good whiskey in the valise, but I wasn't ready yet to go back to that small room. The time had crept along and the sun had gone so that it was about seven o'clock when I hunted up a resturant that looked like it would have good food but wouldn't be too grand for my old clothes.

I made a leisurely meal and then took myself, still lugging my purchases, down to the Military Plaza for one last look around. The Federal Reserve Bank was just at the corner, the southwest corner, as far from the train stop as you could get. I looked at it. It was a big building with big plate-glass windows in front. Tomorrow a crowd was going to be expecting to look through those windows and see something. If things went right there wouldn't be anything to see. Finally I turned my steps toward the rooming house.

I got in bed and lay for a long time trying to think of any item that had been overlooked. Nothing came to mind. I was very conscious, maybe more so than at any other time in my life, of how empty the other side of the bed felt. But I knew I could not let my mind linger on such thoughts. I'd robbed a lot of banks in my time, but never had I attempted such as I was going to try in the morning. If I hadn't been Wilson Young I might have given in to the frights.

I was up early the next morning and out the door in my old clothes. The house was bustling, but it was the boarders sitting down to breakfast. None of them saw me as I slipped out the front door and went hunting for a café. I found a good little place and had steak and eggs and toast and coffee. I figured it might be a long time until my next meal.

I wandered around until about eight o'clock and then went back to the boardinghouse. I had been careful to stay away from the Military Plaza, but I got the impression there was an especially large number of people in town.

Without much trouble I slipped into the boardinghouse and up to my room. It was about half past eight and the place was quiet. I figured them as was going someplace had already left and them as wasn't were settled down in their rooms. I slipped down the hall, found the bathroom, and locked myself in. I stripped off my clothes, took a quick bath, and then shaved very carefully. I didn't want any nicks on my face. The sergeant said that a colonel would have something called an orderly who shaved him and cleaned his uniforms and kept his boots shined. My uniform and shirt had been sponged and ironed by Rosita just before I'd tucked it away until it made its grand appearance.

It was nine-fifteen by the time I got back in my room, and I had that feeling of time slipping away too fast. I dressed with deliberate haste, first pulling on the long socks and then getting carefully into the jodhpur breeches. After that I put on the shirt and then stood in front of the bureau mirror to tie the tie, the dark brown woolen tie that the sergeant handled so dexterously.

I couldn't tie the damn thing. I couldn't make the knot come even and look neat. I tried it half a dozen times, closing my eyes and making the motions by memory. It still wouldn't come right and I was beginning to sweat. I was very near to panic. No colonel would be walking around on the street with a disarrayed knot in his tie.

I tried it every way I could think of; it still wouldn't fall into place. Finally I turned around and imagined the way the sergeant had stood behind me the first time and showed me in the mirror how to make the knot.

It came right. Maybe it wasn't the most evenly knotted tie, but it would pass muster. I knew I wasn't going to disturb my best effort so far, not with time becoming dangerously dear.

I pulled on the boots and then shrugged into the tunic and buttoned it. The insignia and emblems of rank and campaign ribbons had already been put on by the sergeant. The colonel part of the disguise was complete except for the hat. Now I had to work on myself. I put the black eye patch that was held in place by an elastic loop over my left eye. Then I took the gauze bandages and the adhesive tape and bandaged the left side of my face from the lower part of my chin all the way up to my sideburns. It gave the effect of a man who had suffered a pretty severe facial wound that included his eye. It was not an especially neat job, but it would pass. Lastly I slung the sling over my neck and put my left forearm in it, resting it as if I'd lost the use of it, at least temporarily. The sergeant had been very enthusiastic when I'd told him how I'd planned to disguise myself. "Aye, Colonel," he'd said, "that be grand! Grand! You'll look like the old cavalry colonel who's been forced by injuries to go on staff. And you a fighting man. Confined to a desk. Ah, Your Honor, you're a darlin' man. No wonder they never caught you."

The sling didn't do much as a disguise but I thought it would be something that people who saw me would remember. I wanted the sheriff looking for a one-armed man with a damaged face, a face no one was quite sure about.

I put the loaded .45 in the holster and turned the grommet to close the flap. Then I set the campaign hat squarely on my head. I looked in the mirror. I thought it looked a hell of a lot like me and wasn't likely to fool anyone. But it was too late to worry about that. The die was cast. I packed my old clothes in the valise. I had already transferred my valuables to the pockets of the uniform. Finally I slipped on the gray slicker and buttoned it up so no one could see the uniform except for the boots. It was done. It was time to go.

I took the campaign hat off and held it by my side as I opened the door and slipped out into the hall. Then I was down the stairs and out the front onto the street as quick as could be. I walked toward the west for a couple of blocks, looking for a likely spot, even though the Military Plaza was back to the east. Finally I saw an alley strewn with debris and trash. I pitched the valise as far as I could down its dark length and then quickly took off the slicker and threw it away. After that I put the campaign hat on, snapped my swagger stick under my right arm, and began walking toward the gold. It was just ten o'clock. Sergeant McMartin had said I would draw no attention as uniforms were a common sight on the streets of San Antonio. That may have been so, but right then I felt uncommonly lonely.

I CAME upon the bank by the side street that led
to the southwestern point of the plaza. Of course the bank wasn't
ordinarily open on Saturdays and really wasn't open for business,
only for the reception of the gold. I was walking carefully, being
certain to maintain a military bearing. I was a little nervous, but not
as much as I'd expected. It was important to do well in the bank.
Both the sergeant and I had decided that the bank absolutely had
to be kept out of the matter. So long as it was colonel to captain we
felt there would be little resistance. At one time it had been my
thought to intercept the gold at the train and never let them unload it, but Rollie had argued to the opposite. He'd said, "Sir, it'll
be a whole hullabaloo at the train. They'll be unloading and their
officers will be after running about and seeing to matters and you'll
have to seek them out. Don't you see, sir, you want *them* to come
to *you*. And if you meet them on the plaza they'll be on parade. All

drawn up nice in formation with their officers in proper position and the soldiers all trying to look good because of the crowd. And you'll be standing there in the bright sun looking every bit like a colonel. Impatient. Don't want no nonsense. Slapping your boot with your swagger stick. And the crowd will be buzzin', wondering what the big doings is all about. No, sir, you don't want to be back there in the dark around the train, not in all that commotion. You want the commanding officer's *full* attention. Don't you see, sir?"

And, of course, I did. But I was so used to holding folks up with as little attention as possible that I kept forgetting that what I was doing was legal, or at least was intended to appear so.

The sergeant had said, "And you'll be after standing there in that sunshine in the plaza. All that crowd around you. And that bank clerk with the captain's bars on his shoulder is after having to march straight up to you. And what does he see? A full-blown colonel. And not any colonel, mind you, but an old warrior with blood in his eye looking meaner than Mexican whiskey. Aye, sir, that's the place to nab him. Off balance he'll be. And you'll not give him time to catch his breath. Orders will be issued and them little fat toddlers will be after listening."

After much discussion we had calculated that the ideal spot to intercept the detail would be about a third of the way across the plaza. That would put them out where the crowd could see them and make for a short march back to the train. It would also be a good ways from the bank in case any of their officials wanted to take a hand in the proceedings. We had not discussed what I should do if Captain Bell refused my order or demanded authorization. The sergeant had faked up a set of orders giving me emergency authority over the gold shipment, but they were pretty weak and not much to be relied on. The sergeant had had to use order forms that were clearly from Training Command, and even a weakling like the Finance officer would know they would have to come from the staff of the Southwest District. Rollie had said, "Don't show them, Colonel, unless it comes to it. And then do it carelessly and very, very briefly. You'd be better off bluffing the captain with your pistol."

I turned the corner and was immediately into the bright sunshine. The side of the bank building had been shielding me from it as I'd walked along. Now I was just in front of the west corner of the bank. I could clearly see the plaza except for the line to the south. That view was obstructed by some building overhangs and the way the street fell back. There were not as many people as I had expected. Oh, there were several thousand, but they didn't look like so many spread over so much area. The Military Plaza itself was absolutely deserted. The people were all regulated back across the street on the sidewalks in front of the stores. I peered across the plaza to the train station to see if the train was in and the soldiers had started unloading, but the street that led from the plaza to the tracks was lined with three- and four-story buildings that shaded it enough that I couldn't see anything. You can't see from light into dark.

I wished, though, that I had some idea of where the gold detail was. The timing was going to require a nice bit of calculation and pace. But I had to get the bank manager out of the way first. I turned and looked in through the nearest plate-glass window. I could see a good deal of activity going on inside. There looked to be about half a dozen people racing around either being busy or trying to look busy. I stepped to the door and put my hand on the knob. Rollie and I had calculated it would be locked. If it was, I was simply going to rap on the glass until I got someone to open it. But the door was open. I turned the knob and pushed it back and stepped inside. It was all marble, or so it seemed. Marble floor, marble tellers' counter with wrought-iron cages. It was quite a big bank lobby. I walked a few paces forward until I was in the center of business. Off to my left several young ladies and a young man were busy constructing a big display table that had several risers on it like bleachers in a grandstand. They were covering it with green velvet. I figured that was where the gold was going to be displayed. I'd read in the newspaper that the bars were six inches by three inches wide and an inch thick. They were said to weigh not quite two pounds each. They had given the number of bars but I had forgotten the number. It was considerable.

I wasn't drawing any attention. It was time to use the trick the sergeant had taught me. I got my riding crop by the handle and brought it down, snapper end first, against my stiff, polished boot. It made a hell of a crack in that marble-lined vault. All the hustle and bustle immediately came to a standstill and all the men and women turned to stare at me. Going for the command voice the sergeant said I possessed, I barked, "Your attention!"

A little man in a vest and sleeve garters and wearing rimless glasses came bustling out from behind the tellers' cages toward me. He said, "My dear sir, we are closed today."

I ignored him and looked around. "I am Colonel Richter. I want to see the bank manager right now."

The little man said, "I'm Mr. Carstairs, the head teller. Perhaps I can help you?"

I looked at him coldly. "No, you cannot help me, Mr. Carstairs. I want to see the manager. Immediately." I glared at him. "Is that clear?"

He swallowed. I could see I was making the little man nervous. He tried to slick back what little hair he had and said, "I'm sorry, sir, but Mr. Gilbert is not here right now."

"Not here?"

"No, no, sir."

I slapped my boot again and this time I meant it. The crack was even louder than before. Likely Gilbert was over at the train. That was the last thing I needed, a Federal Reserve Bank manager mixing into my business. I said, "Damn!" and cracked my boot again.

"When is he going to be back?"

A man in his early thirties or so came forward from the display. "Sir, I'm Mr. Sanders, the cashier," he said. "Can I help?"

I gave him a hard look. "Did you not hear me tell this man I wanted to see the manager? Where in hell is he?"

Mr. Sanders said, "I'm not quite certain, sir. We've had quite a few arrangements to make. The gold, you see. I think he's with the mayor."

This was a happenstance we hadn't counted on. I tapped the end of my crop rapidly against my leg and asked Mr. Sanders, "No idea when he's to return?"

"No, sir."

"Damn! This is army business. I can't be discussing this with rank and file. Who is next in command?"

Mr. Sanders, who was a pleasant-looking young man, said, "I am, sir. In addition to being cashier I'm also the assistant manager."

I stared at him, my mind working. There was a clock on the wall and I could see it was already twenty-five minutes past ten. For all I knew the soldiers and the caisson carrying the gold could be halfway across the plaza. "I am not prepared to wait," I growled. "I've got business elsewhere, damnit!" The bandage helped keep my face stiff and that made my voice come out stiff. Sergeant McMartin would be pleased. "You say the damn man's name is Gilbert?"

The assistant manager looked like he wasn't used to hearing his boss referred to as "the damn man," but he nodded politely and said, "Yes, sir."

For a moment I paced back and forth, slapping my stick idly against my thigh. I must have looked a sight with a scowl and a white bandage on my face and my left arm in a black sling. I figured if Rollie could see me now he'd no longer take me for fifty years old. I walked over to the door and stared out. Naturally I couldn't see anything. But I could not risk waiting any longer. The plan was for me to take up a position on the southwestern corner of the plaza and then watch for the detail to emerge from the connecting street. As soon as they mounted the plaza I would start toward them, calculating that my faster pace would cover twice the distance they would. Still facing out, I motioned with my stick. "Sanders! Come over here."

In a moment the man was at my shoulder. I didn't look around at him. I said, "This information was to have been for the manager's ears only. But he's not here, so I'll have to tell you. And you'd better get it straight."

"Yes, sir."

"I am Colonel Richter of Staff Intelligence. Do you understand that?"

"Yes, sir." He didn't sound sure.

"Staff Intelligence to the Southwest District, General Peterson commanding. Now, do you understand that?" I was biting each word off like it was a bad taste in my mouth.

"Why, yes, sir, I reckon," he said.

The eye patch was not working out as well as I'd expected. Maybe it was doing a fine job as a disguise, but I'd always had good vision out of the corners of my eyes, and the young man was on my left. I finally had to turn half around to see him. I said, "I don't have time to wait for the manager. What I'm going to tell you would be considered a military secret. Do you know what that means?"

He looked more uncertain. "Why, why, yes, I reckon so, sir."

I turned a little more so I could fix him hard with my right eye. "It means we'll stand you up against a wall and shoot you if you let it out of your mouth except to the manager. Understood?"

"Why, uh, yes, sir."

"The gold will not be arriving as planned. We have information that robbers are about in force and a try might be made for the gold. I'm going to move the bullion out of town for a period until we can determine how serious the threat is."

He looked horrified. "Robbers! I—"

In a low, gritty voice I said, "Keep your goddamn voice down! Now. I don't know how long the delay will be, but you are charged with informing Mr. Gilbert and no one else. Understood?"

He was nodding rapidly. "Yes, yes, yes, sir. But if there be robbers about, how come the sheriff didn't—"

I stared him into silence. "Is that the sheriff's gold? Is that the sheriff guarding it?"

"No, sir, but—"

I took hold of the door knob and opened the door. "You are to inform Mr. Gilbert pronto. And no one else, savvy?"

"Sir?"

I shook my head slowly. "Don't you damn civilians know anything? Tell him as soon as possible. And tell him to stay the hell out of the way."

With that I walked through the door and out into the sidewalk. Toward the corner I could see a man with a badge. A deputy. I expected to see a lot of them around during the next hour.

But right then I was considerably worried about having wasted too much time in the bank. I was anxious to get to the plaza and see where the gold detail was. The farther they had come, the farther I would have to march them back and the greater the possibility my deception would be discovered. I left the sidewalk and walked diagonally across the street toward the corner of the redbricked plaza. As I did I caught sight of a very familiar figure approaching me at an angle. He was wearing a dress khaki uniform without tunic and had a lot of stripes on his sleeve. It was Sergeant McMartin. As I looked at him his right hand came up in a snappy salute. My heart sank. He had betrayed me after all. Now he was going to expose me in front of several thousand people to whom I'd once been a sort of hero. But as he approached he hissed through gritted teeth, "Return my salute, Colonel! Please."

Without thinking about it I touched the brim of my campaign hat with the haft of my swagger stick. His hand snapped down and we both stepped up onto the plaza at just about the same time, though he was to my right and a pace behind. I said, also through gritted teeth, "What in hell are you doing here? Are you crazy? Get the hell out of here."

"I can't do that, Colonel. You would have never been after believing me, but you'd have looked as naked as a jaybird out here without a noncom or junior officer in attendance. Full colonels don't go about by themselves, sir, beggin' your pardon."

We were about ten yards up on the plaza, heading toward the northeast corner, where I was searching for some sign of the gold detail. Without turning my head I said, "Get the hell up here so I don't have to talk over my shoulder."

"Ah, I can't be doing that, Colonel. One pace behind and to the right. Too many soldiers in that audience would spot it immediately. And by the way, Colonel, hadn't we better be after halting 'til we get some sight of the caisson?"

I stopped immediately. Without turning I said, "Where in hell do you come away with pulling a stunt like this, Rollie? I told you I was playing a lone hand. Are you wearing a sidearm?"

"Aye, sir. There be robbers about."

"Is it loaded?"

"Aye, sir. There be robbers about. Ain't that what you was after telling them in the bank?"

"The manager wasn't there."

"You didn't speak with the manager, Colonel?"

"I told you he wasn't there. I spoke to his assistant. I couldn't wait for him because I didn't know when that detail would be coming into view."

"If you'll look close, sir, I believe you'll see them just coming out of the end of the street leading from the train. They've caught the sun now."

I squinted toward the far end of the plaza. It was about four hundred and fifty yards away, but I could just make out the movement of the gold detail. "It's too soon to start toward them."

"Aye, Colonel," he said. I heard amusement in his voice. "It would seem, begging the colonel's pardon, that the doctor barely pulled you through."

"Go to hell, Rollie."

" 'Tis a nice job, Colonel, and no mistake. As badly wounded as you are, sir, 'tis a miracle you are here at all."

I could hear the faint sound of clapping and cheering as the gold train came into view of the crowd. I said, "Sergeant, I want you to get the hell out of here. Do you understand me?"

"Aye, but I can't be doing that, sir. I gave my vow and I can't be after breaking it."

"What vow? To whom?"

"To Mrs. Young, sir, your wife. When I was done explaining how silly you would look without me along as your aide she asked me to be by your side, and I made her the promise. That was why I couldn't tell you what we talked about, Colonel."

"You're a villain, Rollie," I said sourly. "Using a man's own wife on him."

"Besides, by your own orders, I had to be here."

I glanced half around but couldn't really see him even though it was my good side. "What the hell are you talking about?"

"The colonel will recall he instructed me to be with Mrs. Young on Saturday morning. Well, Your Honor, this is Saturday morning."

I turned and glared at him. "Where? And when?"

He nodded toward a spot across the street. "To the colonel's right and about fifty yards ahead. We come in on that late train. After you were long gone."

I looked. Somehow, vaguely, I had already seen her. There had been a woman in a pale green frock who had attracted my eye as I had stepped up onto the plaza. But I had been so distracted by the sergeant that I had not taken a second look. But, sure enough, and exactly where the woman had been, there stood Lauren in a pale green dress, her golden hair unburdened by a hat. There was no mistaking her. Then I got another shock. Standing next to her was Warner Grayson, and just to his right was Laura. Justa Williams finished out the line. I did not see Nora, but I assumed she was somewhere about. I swore softly under my breath. "Anybody else here I don't know about? Did my son make it in from France?"

"Don't be after blaming the lady for caring about you, sir. She can't help that."

"This could go bad in a hurry. I did not want her to see it."

"It will be all right, Colonel, darlin'. If you'll keep your wits about you. We had better start toward them, sir. The advance guard is on the plaza and the mules are after pulling the caisson up behind them. Remember to step out with your left foot, sir."

We started across the hot bricks under the cloudless sky. I was very conscious of the crowd that ringed the plaza on all sides. They were quiet except for a little ripple of applause as the gold detail came in line with their vision. I could not, for the life of me, understand people watching, much less applauding, a detail of twenty-one soldiers and two officers leading two mules pulling a little cart that the army insisted on calling a caisson. You'd have thought they were fetching the gold to be divided up amongst the onlookers. Out of the right side of my mouth I said, "Rollie, you are going to get yourself court-martialed or worse."

"Aye," he said cheerfully. "It's a crying shame I didn't think to bandage my face all up. Sure and I would not have recognized you if you hadn't been carrying your swagger stick all wrong, Colonel. You're after wanting it under your arm now, not in your hand. You hold it in your hand only when you are doing something with it."

I hastily stuck the crop under my arm.

"You'd better step out a bit, Colonel. We don't want them getting too far from the train."

I quickened my pace, able now to clearly see the detail heading on a direct line to us. I could not pick out any of the khaki-clad figures but I could see the mules and the caisson surrounded on all sides by soldiers. I assumed they were carrying rifles. I was uncomfortably aware that Lauren and my friends were no more than fifty yards to my right. Even as I was concentrating on the approaching detail my mind played with just what circumstances had arranged them to be in San Antonio on the big day. I had no doubt it was some of Lauren's work, or Laura's. And I had no doubt it had been arranged while they were at my house. I doubted that Warner and Laura had even gone home, it being much farther than Justa's ranch. I was willing to bet my saloon against a lame horse that they'd all gone back to Justa's and whiled away the four days there before coming to San Antonio to either rescue me or bail me out of jail. It made me mad as hell.

Behind me, the sergeant said, "We got to do it different now that I'm with you, sir. It ain't proper for you to march all the way to him. In a second I want you to sing out something to the effect of me to go on ahead and fetch their commanding officer. Tell me to go at the double."

"What's that?"

"Never mind, sir, just rip it out. Command voice and all. Compliments to their commanding office and that kind of blarney and he's to report to you."

"Now?"

"Quick, sir."

I flung my right arm out with my swagger stick extended and made a forward sweeping motion with it. In my best command voice I said, "Sergeant!"

"Sir!"

"At the double. Advance to that detail and halt it. My compliments to the commanding officer. I will see him here. Put his troops on the ready."

"Aye, sir!" As he passed me he whispered, "Very good, sir, especially about putting his troops on guard."

At the double was a trot. The sergeant, I noticed for the first time, was wearing cavalry boots. He looked fairly clumsy lumbering along, but he was covering the ground. I came to a complete halt and stood erect, my supposed good arm behind my back, fingering my swagger stick and looking impatient.

It seemed forever, especially in front of a crowd that was growing more and more curious. I had no worry about the sheriff or any of his men. This was an army operation and they had probably been warned not to interfere. It was, as I had told Mr. Sanders, the army's gold train.

Finally I saw the sergeant slow to a walk and come up to the lead figure. He saluted and then I could see him standing at attention, talking. I saw the officer look over his shoulder in my direction. For answer I snapped my swagger stick against my boot. It didn't make near as loud a sound out in the plaza as it had in the bank. But it all seemed to get straightened out, because the sergeant did an about-face and started toward me at a quick march. The other two men had to hurry to keep up. As they neared I could see they were short and running to plumpness. In another fifty yards I could see that their khaki shirts were blossoming with sweat. I guessed them to be Captain Bell and his second in command, Lieutenant Wood. I didn't want to deal with two officers. I resolved to get rid of Wood.

As they approached I paced back and forth, chattering my swagger stick against my thigh. I was not having to put on the impatience. I was very anxious to get that gold turned around and on the train and out of San Antonio before something could go bad wrong.

As they neared, I was pleased to note that the sergeant looked crisp and starched while the two officers were showing signs of being out of breath. As they came up I turned to face them. Sergent McMartin drew up at attention and popped a hand to his hat brim in a perfect salute. I noticed that he was suddenly wearing cavalry insignia. I was going to have to ask him later when he'd gotten transferred out of Training Command. Loudly he said, "Beggin' the colonel's pardon, Captain Bell and Lieutenant Wood reporting as ordered, sir!"

They both started up with a salute, but before they could complete it I said, "Wrong! Lieutenant Wood, get back to those troops! And they had better be in skirmish array!" I looked at Rollie. "Sergeant, did you not tell the captain to put his troops on guard?"

He was staring straight ahead, rigid. "Aye, sir."

I gave Lieutenant Wood the best I could do out of one eye. He wilted a little. "Lieutenant Wood, you obviously invited yourself along. Now invite yourself back to those troops and go on full readiness. DO I MAKE MYSELF CLEAR?"

He had to swallow before he could speak. "Yes, sir."

"THEN AT THE DOUBLE!"

He did a clumsy about-face and started trotting back toward the gold detail. He ran like a girl. Now I swung my gaze to the other officer. "Captain Bell?"

"Yes, sir!"

He put up a salute but it was so sloppy and unmilitary that I let him hold his chubby little hand against the brim of his hat for a long few seconds. I could see him trembling. I could also see Rollie trying to keep a straight face. Finally I returned the captain's salute by casually touching my stick to my hat brim.

"Did the sergeant inform you who I am?" I asked.

He was doing his best to stand at attention and keep his eyes focused, but they kept wandering to my face. "Yes, sir."

In a hard voice I said, "Captain, you are at attention. I don't know what they teach you boys in Finance, but you better damn well find out how to stay at attention in front of me. Do you understand I am Staff Intelligence Officer, Southwest District?"

"Yes, sir." His eyes had snapped back to the front. A little bead of sweat was hanging off his pug nose and his glasses didn't seem to be set quite right.

I stepped a stride closer to him so that my face was no more than a couple of feet from his. "Captain Bell, I have reason to believe that there are hostile bandits in the area who have designs on the Treasury Department's gold. Accordingly, I am going to see it to safety. I want you to return to your command immediately and prepare it to return to the train. My sergeant will be along to—"

His eyes shifted. "You mean we are not to take it to the bank?"

My voice would have frozen running water. "Did I give you permission to ask a question, Captain?"

He swallowed. "Uh, no, sir. I—"

"You nothing. You will immediately return to your detail and start it back toward the train. Do you understand that?"

His eyes flickered again and his little pink tongue came out and licked at his lips. "Well, uh, yes, sir, I understand, but—"

Leaning down even closer to his face, I hissed, "Captain, I have demoted officers in the field for *hesitation*. I don't know what I'd do if one of them had ever actually questioned one of my orders. Am I making myself clear?"

He swallowed again. "Yes, sir."

"Captain, your uniform is a disgrace. I hope, for your sake, that your troopers are more representative of what a soldier should look like."

"Yes, sir."

Out of the corner of my right eye I could see that the sergeant was still having trouble keeping a straight face. I said, "Now do you understand what you are to do?"

"Yes, sir. I am to return to the detail and turn back for the train. What then, sir?"

"Then my sergeant will be along to organize the loading of the train and the positioning of your troops."

"Your sergeant? But, sir—" His voice had a whine in it.

"Understand me well, Captain Bell. You and your men are nothing but clerks and accountants. I doubt that any of your men knows how to load a rifle, much less fire it. My sergeant is a fighting man. Do you understand me?"

"Yes, sir." But he didn't look certain.

I said, "When I join you we will take the train south out of town where I have a detachment of cavalry waiting to provide proper escort. We will not come back into town until the threat has passed. Do you understand that?"

His face was troubled. I thought it had to do with the disposition of the gold and I was ready to meet his objections with cold hard orders. But that wasn't it at all. Glancing at Sergeant Mc-Martin, he said, "Sir, are we supposed to take orders from a sergeant?"

I stared at him as if he were a bug. "Even as badly as you need someone to give you orders I can't expect commissioned officers to be subject to commands from a noncom, no matter how able he is. All I ask, Captain, is that you and your lieutenant stay out of the way while the sergeant organizes matters. Is that clear?"

"Yes, sir." He swallowed. I could see his lip tremble. "You understand, sir, that I am responsible for the safety of the gold?"

"That also means you are responsible for the *loss* of the gold, Captain," I grated. "How will you have it? There's little enough time as is. There's a gang of robbers around that bank set to attack you when you disorganize to take the gold in by hand. Will you lose the gold and be responsible for all the soldiers under your command who will most likely be killed by armed desperadoes? And what about the innocent citizens who will be killed? Are you responsible for them? Speak up, man. Speak up, you sniveling clerk! Don't tell me about responsibility! Will you also be responsible for disobeying a direct order I gave you? Well?"

"But it's never happened before, Colonel." There was anguish in his voice. He was in deep water and didn't know how to swim.

I said, "You've been in Texas before, have you? You've been in San Antonio before, have you, which is the same as being in Mexico if you count the *bandidos?* Well, have you?"

"No, no, sir." It was almost a whisper.

"You've got three seconds to make a military salute, about-face, and double time to your troops," I barked. "After that I'm going straight to staff headquarters and put in court-martial papers for disobedience in the face of the enemy. Would you say this is in the face of the enemy, Sergeant?"

Sergent McMartin quivered to attention. "Aye, Colonel. Aye, I would."

But the captain was already making an attempt at a limp salute. I returned it sourly and then watched as he turned and waddled back across the plaza. I was aware of the murmur of the crowd. I looked at the sergeant. "Well?" I said in a low voice.

He rolled his eyes and gave me a wink. By now the captain was out of earshot. Rollie said, "Ah, 'twas grand, Colonel darlin'. I think he pissed his pants. I said, didn't I, that you was a natural officer. But hell, we should have made you a general. The saint's truth, Colonel, you had me scared. I thought you was going to be after shooting the fat little bugger. 'Tis glad I am that I'm not under your command. Shall I start for the train? You should come slowly, Colonel, on account of your wounds. Colonel?"

But something had caught my eye. A man was crossing the street diagonally from behind me and to the left. He was a tall slim man wearing a dress uniform exactly like mine except that he had a star on his epaulet. He was a general. But it was not that so much as took my eye as the way he walked and the glimpse I could get of his face. "Les?" I said tentatively. "Les Richter?" He was still ten yards away, but the nearer he came the more certain I was that it was Les. I felt paralyzed, unable to move, barely able to speak. My limbs felt as if they weighed a ton.

From a far distance I heard the sergeant say, "Colonel? Colonel? You all right?"

I made no sign to him. The figure had come close enough that I could see it was Les. He walked in that same easy way he had, with that carefree look. His face seemed as young as the last time I'd seen him, thirty-four, thirty-five years before, but there was a weariness there I'd never seen. As he stepped up on the plaza I said, "My God, Les, it is really you. How come you ain't dead?"

He still hadn't spoken a word. I heard the sergeant ask uncertainly, "Colonel, should I carry on? Take over the gold shipment?"

I didn't look his way, just sort of gave him a salute. "Yes, Sergeant, carry on."

He said, "Sir, you ain't exactly looking right. You've gone kind of white in the face. I better get you some help."

I was still staring at Les. He had come to a stop a few yards from me. His face was grave and there was pain in his eyes. I was aware that the sergeant was making some sort of beckoning motion. I said, "Sergeant, I told you to carry on. Now be quick about it."

"Yes, sir." His voice sounded like it was coming from a long ways off.

I SAID to the best friend I'd ever had, "Les, say something. What in hell are you doing here? Hell, I seen you dead. And what are you doing in that general's uniform?"

He gave me that slow, crooked grin of his. "I figured I had to outrank you before you'd listen to me."

"Listen to you about what?" I could not believe what I was seeing. It was all I could do to keep from pitching over on my face.

"Will," he said, "you don't want to be doing this. Neither one of us wanted to do it in the old days. It was against our nature, but we done it anyway. Well, it's time to stop."

"But I ain't going to rob this gold. It's just a stunt."

He stared at me with those gray eyes of his. "Will, this is not the kind of gold that counts. And you already know that. You're just fighting your head. This is wrong, Will. Give it up and go the way you know is right. You've always been a fair man, an honest man.

Now I want you to be more than that. You can be a rich man, Will, but not with this kind of gold. You've got eyes and ears. I want you to see and hear. I won't be able to help you again."

Then he suddenly stepped past me. I stood there in stunned silence for half a second and then turned to look after him. There was nobody there. I started to call his name but there were suddenly hands on my arms. I looked quickly left and right. It was Warner Grayson and Justa Williams. They were leading me across the street. My mind was whirling. "Did you see him?" I said. "Did you see Les? Justa, you never met him, but, Warner, you knew him a little. Wasn't that him? I know I didn't dream this."

Justa answered firmly, "Walk, Will. Walk. The crowd thinks your wounds have overcome you. I don't know what has happened, but we got to get you out of here and in a hell of a big hurry."

We had crossed the street by then and the crowd was falling back respectfully as we headed toward a side street. I caught a glimpse of Lauren hurrying toward me and was about to ask if she'd seen Les Richter when Warner waved her away. He said, "We need him out of here, Lauren."

They almost marched me. Halfway down the side street Justa said to Warner, "If you reckon you can handle him I'm going to run on ahead and get the automobile started."

I didn't know what the hell he was talking about. I didn't know what was happening. I only knew that I had seen Les Richter for a moment and then he had disappeared. I said again to Warner, who was holding me around the shoulders with one arm like I might fall over, "You were just across the street. He came straight up to me. Hell, he was wearing a general's uniform. You couldn't have missed him."

Warner said, a little plea in his voice, "Will, right behind us is a damn curious crowd. They don't know what happened but they are sympathetic for the time being. Let's keep them that way. You could be in bad trouble here."

"But I saw Les!" I reached up to pull off my eye patch, but he was faster than I was and jerked my hand down.

"Let's keep things as they are for the time being," he said.

Ahead, I saw a big, gray automobile backing toward us. "What the hell is that?"

"That's Justa's Cadillac. We come up in it."

I tried to slow down. "I ain't getting in that damn thing."

He jerked me on. "Are you drunk? Have you lost your mind? We got to get you out of here. So far nobody knows you are Wilson Young, but it wouldn't take much for them to find out."

"Where is Sergeant McMartin?"

"Doing whatever in hell you ordered him to do. Don't hang back, Wilson. We got to get you in this automobile."

He was opening a door, the rear one. There were two on each side and I noticed that the car was really white, but had been grayed over with road dust. I said, "Why in hell did you wave Lauren off?"

From inside I heard Justa yell, "Hurry up. Get him in." I could smell the awful fumes of the infernal machine.

Warner was pushing my head down, forcing me to duck under what appeared to be the black canvas top of the thing. He said, "I thought you was trying to go unrecognized. Don't you reckon folks would have put two and two together if they had seen her come up and hug you?"

I could hear crowd noise behind me, but Warner had already shoved me into the damn horseless carriage. Once inside I was surprised at how big it was. It was as big as a wagon. From the left front seat Justa said, "I'm going."

Warner jumped in and slammed the door after him just as Justa made the engine roar. We shot away so hard it pushed me back against the seats, which were soft leather. There were glass windows on each side with little curtains. From the front Justa yelled back, "Pull them damn curtains down. And, Will, get that damn hat and uniform top off. Help him, Warner. He's still acting like somebody hit him between the eyes with a rifle stock."

I could not understand what was happening. I knew we were racing along at great speed, skidding around corners and screeching to sudden stops and then blowing out again like a high wind, but I couldn't get the feel for it. Sometimes Justa would blow the horn, and it made me think of the first time an automobile had honked at me. My hand had jerked the revolver out of my shoulder holster and I'd stopped myself just in time from putting a hole through the damn thing. It had been two young women and it had scared the hell out of them. They'd raced away, both white-faced and crouching down inside the little open car.

I couldn't understand why Warner and Justa didn't say anything about Les. Maybe they just saw the uniform and couldn't believe it was him. Maybe Warner hadn't gotten a good look. But they both should have seen the tall, slim general who'd come up to me. And why had Sergeant McMartin waved them over to help me? I shook my head. It was all a muddle.

Warner was trying to unbutton my tunic. "Damnit, Wilson, give me a little help here. People can still see in through the windshield."

I knocked his hands away and finished undoing the rest of the buttons. Then I shrugged my way out of the tunic and threw it on the seat beside the campaign hat. After that I started in on the tie. It was a hell of a lot easier to get undone than it had been to tie. I said to Justa, "Which direction you heading?"

Without turning his head he said, "Mostly south. I'm just trying to get us out of town. I never realized this city was so damn big before. Warner, look out that back window and see if anybody is following us."

I could see myself that we were hitting the outskirts of town. The houses were getting smaller and poorer. I had always wondered why the poor people always seemed to live on the edge of town. I said urgently, "I got to get to Three Wells. And in a hurry."

Justa glanced back. "Three Wells? I never heard of it."

"It's only a train watering stop. It's this side of Hondo. Take the Hondo road and see if you can see the railroad."

"What the hell do you want to go to Three Wells for?" Warner asked. "We're going to drive you to Del Rio."

"No, you're not," I said. "I don't think this machine could get over that road. Besides, I've already got a plan. I got two horses waiting for me at that watering station."

Justa turned and looked at Warner.

Warner shrugged. "I don't know."

"He's about half off his head."

"I heard that," I said. "You don't worry about my head." I got the tie off and started unbuttoning the shirt. Justa had quit turning so often and had lit out on a dusty and bumpy road. I caught glimpses of open prairie, rolling and hilly with cedar brakes and mesquite trees. We were clear of town.

"How far is this Three Wells?"

"Twenty-five, thirty miles. Little more, little less. I have never stepped it off. I cannot understand why neither one of you has anything to say about that officer who came up to me. Not the captain or the lieutenant, but the general who came later. Had one star on each epaulet."

I saw Justa glance up at a little mirror over the dash. I knew he was trading looks with Warner. Warner said, "You don't got to take the shirt off, Will. It just looks like a khaki shirt."

"I got a change of clothes with the horses at Three Wells," I said. "I don't want any part of this uniform on me. I got to find a place to hide it. And by the way, you two can quit talking about me like I was loco. I know what I saw. How fast we going, Justa?"

He glanced down. "Not quite seventy."

"*Seventy* miles an hour?"

"Yeah."

I turned to the window and tried to work the curtain. It was some
kind of velvet. "What gets this out of the way?"

"It's like a window shade, Will. Pull down a little and then let
go. It'll go all the way up."

I did so and immediately got a view of the countryside whizzing
by faster than I'd ever seen it, even on a runaway train I'd been on
once. "Heaven help us! Justa, you'll get us all killed!"

As it was we were jouncing and bouncing all over the place. Occasionally we'd hit a bump and I'd rise up so that my head struck
the soft top of the canopy or whatever it was called. "Hell, have we
got to go this fast?" I yelled.

From the front seat Justa said, "You're the one ought to know,
Will."

Warner said, "I still don't think we ought to let him out on his
own. You sure we can't make it to Del Rio?"

"Not in this automobile. When we were coming up a few days
ago I thought of driving and I asked about the roads. They get
mighty bad once you get much south of San Antonio and there practically ain't no road all the way to Del Rio. And you know how rough
that country is. We could run off in a *barranca* as easy as not."

I was starting to come back to myself. The experience of seeing
Les again was still very much with me and had produced an effect
on my mind and my heart that I could not explain.

Warner said to Justa, "I hate like hell to leave him on his own.
Why don't we drive to Hondo and take him on the train the rest of
the way?"

Over his shoulder Justa said, "You're forgetting about the ladies.
They're waiting for us at the Menenger Hotel. At least I hope they
are."

"All right. What say you let me and Will off at Hondo and then
you go back and see about them? I'll take him on the train. Do you
think it might be better to get him across the border? Just to be on
the safe side?"

"Now that you mention it, it couldn't hurt."

"Will you two yahoos quit talking about me like I wasn't here!" I said. "What in hell is going on? What is all this about?"

Justa laughed. "If you don't know I don't reckon I can tell you."

"Tell me what?"

Warner snorted. "Hell, Will, you just stopped a federal gold shipment and sent it the other way. I don't think Uncle Sam is going to be tickled to death with you."

"I wasn't going to steal that gold."

Justa turned his head completely around and looked at me. "We're your friends. We believe you. But I wouldn't try and tell that to anyone else."

"You are the same two who refuse to admit that a general officer come walking up to me. Warner, hell, you ought to have recognized him. You saw Les at least a dozen times."

In a louder voice than was necessary, Justa said, "Will, that man you say you saw was the—"

Warner broke in. "Leave it be, Justa. Let his head alone. He's confused right now. That's why I don't think we ought to let him on his own."

"Have you two been drinking?" I howled. "What in hell is going on here? You talk like I'm crazy or something. You get me to Three Wells and I'll take it from there. If anybody is crazy around here it's the two of you. And what am I doing in this damn automobile that I swore I'd never ride in? Two thousand dollars for a piece of junk. Hell!"

Warner laughed and Justa said, "Try closer to four thousand. And Warner has got a silver Pierce-Arrow that cost more."

"You're both crazy. You got a bottle in this tin lizzy?"

They found a bottle of whiskey and I had a drink and watched the countryside flying backward. That was the way it looked, we were going so fast. Then, suddenly, I spotted a trail of smoke up ahead, and as we gained, I could see it was a train. It was going slowly, perhaps twenty-five miles an hour. When we were abreast of it I could see, by the number of cars, that it was the special train that had brought the gold. I pointed out the window. "There's the gold train. Look at it. Justa, how far have we come from San Antonio, you reckon?"

He glanced out the side. The train was about two or three miles across the prairie. "Oh, I don't know," he said. "I didn't look at the odometer when we left. I was a little busy."

I didn't know what the hell he was talking about and didn't much care. "Guess. Ten miles? Fifteen?"

Warner said, "I'd reckon about fifteen. No more than that."

I took another drink from the bottle. "I wonder what the hell Rollie is doing. I couldn't have been wrong about him. I explained how easy it would be to take that gold straight into Mexico."

"I bet you did," Justa said.

I said, "Cut it hard left. We got to intercept that train."

He turned around and looked at me. "Are you crazy? This ain't a horse, Will. I can't drive over that kind of country. Besides, you better stay the hell away from that train and act like you never heard of it."

Warner suddenly laughed.

"What in hell is so funny?"

He shook his head. "I don't know. Just the sight of you strutting around up there in that uniform, giving orders. You gave those two old boys hell."

Justa started laughing, too. "Especially that fat one. What were you saying to him?"

"I was explaining to little boys what happens when they disobey orders," I said grimly.

"Anyway," Warner said, "it was funny. At least until you turned white in the face. He went all over pale, didn't he, Justa?"

"As white as those bandages he was wearing. Even some of the crowd noticed it. Thank heavens."

I had been wearing the bandages so long I had forgotten about them. I had taken off my eye patch and the sling, but I was still sitting there in the gauze and adhesive tape. I reached up and worked a thumbnail under a strip of the tape and started to pull. It hurt like hell. It felt like I was pulling my skin off.

"Will," Warner said, "you probably put that on fresh shaved. Your whiskers have growed since then. Likely you will need to get some alcohol or something and kind of work it off. Unless you like to hurt."

"Ol' Will likes to hurt, don't you, partner?" Justa piped up.

I said, "Was I you I wouldn't be making them kind of remarks with my back to me." He laughed. I went on, "And I ain't the damn fool laid out the price of two damn good racehorses for this rattletrap."

"Oh, yeah? Would you have rather taken the time to ride a horse to this place we're going?"

"I was planning on taking my own train."

"Yeah, I know. All the way to Mexico."

"Justa," Warner said sharply, "you ought not to be saying that to Will. Ain't either one of us would have had near the nerve to pull off what he just did."

"I know. And I can only hope the idiot gets away with it. Seriously, Will, you ought to go on over to Mexico and hang around for a couple of months. Maybe you weren't recognized. Maybe you covered your tracks with a foot of sand. But these things have a way of getting around."

"Damnit! Get it through your head I didn't do anything." I had been fiddling around with a knob on the door at my side and finally figured out how to roll down the glass. The front windshield was so dusty you could barely see through it. I stuck my head out the opening and the wind hit me like a big fist. If I'd been wearing a hat it would have ended up in Oklahoma. As it was it felt like my hair was being torn out of my scalp. Looking ahead, I could barely make out the outline of the water tower in the distance. The road was curving around toward the tracks. I turned my head around and looked back. We were throwing up a cloud of dust that could have been seen from Oklahoma or maybe even Ohio. I looked for the train but it had either fallen so far behind it was out of sight or had started back for San Antonio. I truly had no idea what the sergeant was doing. If he was going to try to steal the gold, that would make me an accomplice. But since there was nothing I could do about it I was determined not to worry. I pulled my head back in and rolled up the window and told Justa that the water tank didn't appear to be more than two or three miles away. He said that he could see it and was heading that way as fast as the road would permit.

"I want to know one thing," I said. "Whose bright idea was it that brought y'all into that plaza where you knew some serious business might be happening? Was it Lauren talked you into it?" Nobody said anything. I glanced at Warner. "Laura?"

"If you have to know, it was Warner's idea," Justa said.

I looked at him again and wrinkled my brow. "You? The horse trainer? Did you lose your mind?"

Justa said, "Get off his back. We were in it together. He said it first is all."

I shook my head. "Of all the dumb damn ideas. What possessed y'all? What would you have done if something had gone wrong?"

"We'd have thought of something, Mr. Young," Justa said. "You ain't the only one can think."

Warner said quietly, "Lauren told us that the sergeant had promised to be with you."

"We didn't figure we could do any less," Justa added. "We are supposed to be your friends, you know."

Warner said, "Justa and I got to counting up the number of times you'd helped us out of tight spots. We didn't see how we could let you go it alone."

From the front seat Justa said drolly, "Course, we didn't know you had other help on the way."

"Justa!" Warner snapped. "Shut up!"

"I was just going to say that we wanted to be there to explain to the authorities that Will was protecting the gold from that band of robbers that were lurking nearby, ready to snatch it. Hell, when they ask me what we were doing on this drive I'm going to say we were chasing them so Will could make them see the error of their ways." He laughed.

"Justa, are you confused?" I said. "This is not a real bandage on my face. I ain't hurt. You want to remember that before you keep on with such remarks."

Then the automobile began slowing and we bore straight at the water tank. Justa brought it to a stop in a great slewing cloud of dust. I stepped out the door, choking in the white fog of caliche. In a glance I could see the water station was deserted. There had never been a caretaker, and my vaquero had departed. But I saw my horses immediately. They came running over to the north side of the corral as soon as they saw us get out of the car. They both looked rested and fit and I could see feed and water in both troughs.

Warner walked over to the fence and leaned on it. "Morgan cross," he said. "Good traveling horses, Will. You ought to make it in two days, switching off. Both look in good shape."

"I know," I said. But you might as well try and stop the flow of the Mississippi with a straw as to stop Warner from talking horses when one was in sight.

We located a little shed where my gear had been stored. While I took off the rest of my uniform and put on the clothes I had sent along, Warner and Justa saddled one horse and packed the other. I suddenly realized that I had forgotten to bring a revolver. All I had was the .45 the sergeant had given me. Well, likely I wouldn't need a weapon. I knew that neither Warner nor Justa were armed, since it was against the law to carry a firearm inside the city limits of San Antonio.

Justa packed my uniform and boots and the other stuff in the trunk of his Cadillac. He said, "I'll hold this for you. One day you may want to show it to your grandchildren and tell them about the time you made the biggest fool of yourself."

"Listen, tell Lauren I'll be all right," I said. "See that she gets on a train, and I'll be home quick as I can."

"Don't get in no hurry, Will," Warner said. "Rough as the country is between here and the border, ain't likely nobody is going to spot you. You going to your ranch in Mexico?"

"Likely. I'm wondering what the sergeant is up to right now."

Justa spit into the dust. "You know ain't a damn thing you can do about that."

Then there wasn't nothing left for it but to shake hands all around and mount up. I slipped the .45 into the left pouch of the saddlebags of the horse I was riding. He was a big, long-legged roan that could cover territory. The other was a smaller bay, but he was deep-chested and determined.

Warner said, "Watch their feet, Will. That's the only thing can stop you is you get a lame horse."

I gave them a wave and rode out through the open gate of the corral and turned toward the southwest. I had some miles ahead of me but it wasn't the kind of trip I hadn't taken before. I turned once in the saddle and waved again. "Thanks!" I yelled.

They waved back and then I rode into the brush that I knew would get thicker and thicker. I had no intention of going through any towns. Not that there were any on the route I'd chosen between me and the border. Just bad, mean, rough country.

THE BRUSH and cedar brakes and mesquite thickets were so thick that sometimes a man on horseback couldn't see over them. The only way to travel through such country was by following cow trails. It was difficult to hold a direct course as the trails wandered, but I did the best I could. After I'd been traveling for about half an hour I got out my watch and was astonished to see that it was after two o'clock. I didn't know where the time had gone, but it had certainly flown. I resolved that the next clearing I came to I'd get down, loosen the horse's cinches, and make myself some kind of meal and even have a drink of whiskey. But as I rode I realized I could do that anytime. I reached around with my left hand and unbuckled the pouch on that side and found the bottle. I also felt the Colt .45. I would have liked to stick it in my belt, but it was too heavy. Besides, I didn't figure to need any help in such barren country.

I rode on, making pretty good time when the trail would permit and then having to slow as it narrowed and I had to drop the other horse in behind me and go single file. I comforted myself with the knowledge that there was only about thirty more miles of the *brasada* before I could break out into open country and really cover some miles. It felt good to be back in my own clothes again and back in my own self. The relief I felt at having the whole business behind me was almost overwhelming. And, of course, I was feeling the best because I was heading for Lauren and home.

I was deliberately not letting myself think about Les Richter. The very idea of it left me slightly dazed. But I knew what I had seen and I knew that I had been in my right mind. Once I had confronted the captain, matters had slowed down like they always did in times of danger and I had been aware of every sight, every sound, every movement. Les Richter had walked up to me on that plaza and had spoken to me, and I had spoken to him. And nobody was going to ever convince me it had all been in my mind. Of course, I'd gone white and felt faint; who wouldn't after seeing a long-lost friend that was presumed dead? No, not presumed—I knew he had died. But I wasn't going to search for any explanations about that, not then, not until I got home and could talk it over with Lauren.

Finally I saw a big clearing ahead. The trail had broadened to some ten yards across and I could see a big open space about half a mile ahead that appeared to be ringed with post oak trees and some good grass. That would give me a chance to let my horses graze a bit, and there might even be water. Little underground springs ran all through that country and occasionally surfaced. A spread of good grass was a likely sign of a small spring nearby. I touched my horse with the heels of my boots and urged it forward in a canter. I was ready to take a rest myself. It had been a long, jumbled-up, odd kind of day.

The clearing appeared to be about fifty yards across. I was about halfway into it and pulling my horses up when three horsemen suddenly emerged from the trees and headed straight toward me.

I jerked my horse up instantly and watched as they came. There was no doubt in my mind that they were *brasaderos,* a particularly low form of outlaw who hid in the thick bush and ventured out to rob and even murder.

As they neared they came together. The one to my left looked to be the oldest. I could see sprinkles of gray in the stubble of his beard. The other two were younger, but no less hard looking. I was acutely aware of how defenseless I was. All I had was the .45 and it was in the saddlebag.

They stopped about six or seven yards from me. The oldest leaned his arms on the pommel of his saddle and spat tobacco in the dust. He said to the other two, "Well, now, boys, look here what we got us. Man with two horses. You reckon he need two horses?"

The middle one said, "I don't reckon he need none."

"I got money," I said. And I did. I figured to have about a thousand dollars in my wallet. "Suppose I drop it on the ground for y'all and I'll ride on through and be on about my business."

The old man spit tobacco juice again. "Well, right now we're about *our* bid'ness an' I reckon we'll conduct it as we see fit." He suddenly drew a revolver out of his belt. I could see it was a big old

Navy Colt .44, what they called a thumb buster. "Now," he said, "you just step out of that saddle an' set yoreself down on the ground and we'll tend to our bid'ness."

I knew that once they had me on foot I was done for. They could deal with me then at their leisure. For a second I considered trying to make a break for it, either to the left or right or straight at them, but I was unsure I'd spot a trail in time, and the brush was so thick as to be almost impenetrable. Then a thought occurred to me about the .45. It was not much of a chance, especially against three drawn revolvers, but it was the only chance I had.

The old man slowly cocked the hammer of his big revolver. The gun he was carrying was an advantage to me. Those big .44s packed a lot of wallop but were not particularly accurate. He said, "You a-goin' to git off that horse, 'r do I got to git you off?"

I let the reins drop to the ground so that my horse would stand and slowly brought my right leg over. As I did I acted like I was hanging on to the saddlebag for balance. But what I was doing was letting my hand slip in under the flap until I found the reassuring hardness of the big semiautomatic.

"Hurry up!" one of the others said. "Hell, I never seen a man git off a horse so damn slow."

"I'm injured," I said. "I'm hurt. Can't you see these bandages?"

One of them said, "You fixin' to be a hell of a lot more hurt you don't get a move on."

Finally my hand closed around the grip of the .45. As my right foot touched the ground I cocked the weapon while it was still inside the saddlebag. They could not see because of the angle I'd pulled my horse around to. As I took my left foot out of the stirrup I pulled the .45 out and down. In that instant I heard the sound of a shot and a burning sensation seized my right cheek. It caused me to stagger a step backward from my horse. I swung to my left, bringing up the .45. The old man was closest to me but he hadn't as yet seen my gun. I heard several shots and then as many thuds. I knew I hadn't been hit and then realized that, in their haste to shoot at what little of me they could see, they'd shot my horse instead. I ducked low as my horse began to stagger. The old man swung toward me. I extended my arm and fired. I missed. The automatic jumped up and to the right, kicking like a twelve-gauge shotgun.

I heard a shot sing over my head and then I carefully squeezed off another round, allowing for the .45's barrel deviation. The old man went backward out of his saddle as if he'd been swept by a giant hand. I turned toward the others. But by now my horse was down on his front knees and about to roll over. I had no cover.

I sighted on the one in the middle and fired two rapid rounds. The second one slewed him around in the saddle, but he didn't fall. I felt something slam into my right thigh and could only hope it hadn't broken the bone.

The third man, the younger of the two, was having trouble with his horse. It had turned him sideways to me. I fired at his shoulder and knew I'd missed. Then his horse jumped back around to face me just as I fired a second shot. I saw it go home and saw him twist in the saddle and fall forward, landing facedown on the ground.

I came back to the one that had been in the middle. He had switched his revolver to his left hand; his right arm was hanging useless. I figured my bullet had broken his arm. I knelt, aiming carefully, not sure how much ammunition I had left in the gun. Before I could pull the trigger he fired and I felt a hard tug at my right side. It burned for an instant and then went numb. I ignored it. The man was trying to get the hammer back for another shot. I steadied my hand and squeezed the trigger. He went straight backward over the rear of his horse. It startled the animal so that he kicked back, catching the man in midair and kicking him a few yards farther than he would have landed. Then the animal went bucking and pitching off into the underbrush. I slowly sat down, fearful of finding out how badly I'd been shot. I was holding the .45 in my lap, the hammer still back from the previous shot. I carefully let it down with my thumb, thankful that the clip had held enough ammunition to dispatch my attackers.

Before I did anything else I looked at each one of them carefully. They were dead. Each looked like a big wad of old clothes tossed on the ground. There ain't nothing looks as dead as a dead man. It made me shudder to think of the risks I had run in the plaza only to be set upon by a trio of common bandits.

I reached up and felt my cheek. I could feel the blood and feel the furrow through the bandages and the skin, but the bullet did not seem to have broken my cheekbone. Next I looked at the wound in my thigh, about six inches down from my right hip. I felt the back of my leg where the bullet would have exited had it been a through-and-through. I could feel a hard object. It felt like the bullet hadn't had quite enough force to go on through. Of course, it might have hit the bone and shattered. If that was the case I was in bad shape. To find out I extended my leg. It worked fine except that it made a fresh gush of blood bubble through the hole in my jeans.

Then I came to the shot that had taken me in the side. I carefully unbuttoned my shirt, afraid of what I was going to see. The hole was just below my ribs and about six inches in from my right side. I didn't know if the bullet had hit any vital organs, but I was bleeding like hell. I felt around to the back with my left arm, hoping there wasn't an exit wound. There was, and by the slippery feel of my fingers I knew it was bleeding badly also.

Moving as slowly as I could, I took my shirt off and ripped it into strips. It was a clumsy effort but I managed to stuff a square of my shirt in the exit wound. Then I did the same for the one in front and took several strips of my shirt, tied them together, and wrapped them around my waist in the hope that would stanch the bleeding a little. I was already feeling faint—whether from loss of blood or the shock of getting shot, I didn't know. My thigh wasn't bleeding near as bad as the hole in my side, but I tore off a little square of my shirt and poked it into the hole and tied a makeshift tourniquet around it.

I knew I had been weakened, but I didn't realize how much until I tried to stand. I made it, but I had to get to my knees and slowly work my way up. Then I stood and surveyed the scene, wondering how to get to help. The outlaws' horses had all run off. The roan I'd been riding was dead. The horse I had used as a pack animal was standing some ten yards from me, the halter rope trailing on the ground. All my horses were trained to ground rein, consider themselves tied to something solid when their reins were dropped on the ground. But I didn't know if that horse considered the lead rope a rein or not. Besides, I figured he'd been badly spooked by all the shooting. But I had to lay hands on him. I knew I wasn't going to be able to walk very far, not bleeding the way I was. I started toward him, humming low. He turned and pricked his ears at me. Horses don't like the smell of blood and I'm sure I fairly reeked of the stuff to his big nostrils.

He let me get within five yards and then moved away a yard or two, still watching me. There was feed to entice him with, but unfortunately it was on the packsaddle on his back. So was the bottle of whiskey I badly needed a drink of, and the food that might give me some strength. There had been food and a bottle of whiskey in the saddlebags of the roan, but he had fallen on that side and I knew I couldn't have retrieved it even if I'd been well and twice as strong.

It took longer than I could afford to catch the horse, but finally I was close enough to reach out and take him by one of the prongs of the packsaddle. I grasped the wooden stock and leaned against the horse, breathing heavily. After I had recovered a little I fumbled open one of the saddlebags and found a bottle of whiskey, got it open, and took a hard drink. After it had bit deep into my stomach and some of the fumes had chased away the fog in my brain, I leaned my head back and took a deep breath. I looked down at my side. Blood was running down my bare belly and down my jeans to join the blood flowing from the wound in my thigh. I thought of pouring some of the whiskey on the wounds but decided the hell with it. I was going to bleed to death long before I could die of any infection.

I didn't know what to do with the horse. I knew I could get the packsaddle off, but I didn't see any way of climbing on his back and then riding him with nothing but a lead rope. It seemed a better idea to lean on the saddle and support as much of my weight as I could that way. One thing I knew was that I needed to hurry. I needed a doctor and I needed one bad. I reached out and got the lead rope and wrapped it around my left wrist and made a knot. If I dropped it and fell I didn't want to have to catch the horse again.

Holding the lead rope with my left hand and curling my right arm around the front horns of the packsaddle, I urged the bay ahead. I could tell he was confused. He was used to two reins and a man on his back. But I got him started, and after a few minutes we had crossed the clearing. I found a pretty wide trail that seemed to be the only way out. But it was leading due south and I wanted to go east, toward Hondo. There was no help for it. I had to go the way the trail led and take my chances. I took the heavy .45 out of my waistband and put it in the saddlebag and started the horse down the long trail.

I had no idea how far it was to anywhere. All I knew was that I couldn't go back because there was nothing to go back to. Hondo was the only town around and it was somewhere to the east, how far I had no idea. When you follow cattle trails through the thickets you lose your sense of direction because sometimes you can't even see the sun. So all I could do was lean against the packsaddle, keep the horse in a slow walk, and hope the trail I was on would take me somewhere, anywhere, even to the cabin of a squatter who might have a wagon he could use to haul me into a town.

Time had lost its meaning. I was judging the passage of my life by how weak I was growing. I could now look back and see I was leaving little spots of blood on the dusty trail. Occasionally I would pull the horse up and eat a little cheese or beef jerky and wash it down with whiskey. By now all three wounds had begun to pulse and throb but I welcomed the pain. It meant I could still feel something, and it helped me fight the impulse to sit down and give up. Ahead, the trail was beginning to look darker and narrower. I knew it wasn't. I'd been in the same shape a time or two before and I knew my vision was constricting from loss of blood.

I trudged on. Now I was growing so weak that every step was an effort. I almost wanted to weep. It seemed so senseless to have been shot by three two-bit outlaws. I had a thousand dollars in my pocket and if they'd held their fire I'd have been more than willing to give it to them. But of course the thousand wouldn't have satisfied them. It would have surprised them, yes, but if there was that much they'd have wanted to see how much more there was. And there were my two horses, either of which was worth the price of their three put together.

I thought of Lauren. Hell, if I died in the middle of this big thicket it might be weeks, months before anyone found me and she'd have all that time to grieve and worry. *Oh,* I thought, *I wish I hadn't pulled that stunt in San Antonio. If it hadn't been for my arrogance I would never have ended up in such a spot.* My arrogance. I hated to think of the troubles it had caused me.

The trail stretched out like a long, dim hallway. I could tell my mind was starting to go away from me because sometimes I wouldn't be there and then I'd come to with a start and realize I was still hanging on to the packsaddle, still trudging, still trying to get somewhere. Once I thought I saw Les just ahead. He was sitting his horse sideways across the trail. He was wearing one of his favorite shirts, a red-and-white checked one. And he had on his pearl-gray western hat with the wide brim that he'd paid eighty dollars for. Les always had been a man to take pride in his appearance. I heard him say, "C'mon, Will, you can do it."

But I knew I was just making it up in my head—hallucinating, I think it's called. I had *seen* Les Richter on the plaza. This one was just a mirage.

And then I seemed to dream that I broke out of the brush and was on a wide stretch of bare ground that looked like a road. I stood there, swaying. I could see heat waves rising. The road appeared to run east and west. Ahead, the brush had thinned out considerably, but I didn't push on. The horse waited patiently. I heard a noise and, looking over the packsaddle, thought I could make out a buggy coming down the road toward me from the west.

As I grimly hung on to the packsaddle, feeling the strength draining out of me, I looked around at the country in the hazy, dim sunlight. It was all too familiar. It was the scrubby brushland west of Corpus Christi where I had committed my first act of robbery by stealing, at gunpoint, some fourteen dollars forty-two years ago. And as the black object neared I had no doubt but that it was that same rancher and his wife coming to get their money back and take me in to the kind of justice I deserved.

With the last of my energy I tried to reach around and pull out my wallet. It seemed stuck in my back pocket. I was going to try to see if they would take what I had and call it quits. I knew there was interest owed on the money after so many years, and interest can mount up. I could only hope that I had enough on me to somehow make it right. I would promise them any amount, whatever I possessed, if they would only forgive me for the shameful thing I had done.

The world seemed to be getting grayer and grayer. I felt myself slipping down the side of the horse. I knew I had to stay conscious to tell the rancher about the three dead bandits. I had killed them. I had to make him understand that they might have robbed him if I hadn't come along. Maybe then he would forgive me.

I suddenly felt the dust of the road in my mouth. I raised my head slightly and looked down the road at the buggy that was nearing. It was making some kind of strange noise. I couldn't place it. All I wanted to do was close my eyes and sleep.

CHAPTER
17

WHEN I first opened my eyes I thought I'd gone sun blind. Everywhere I glanced it looked white. I could tell I was in a bed, but even the foot railing was white. The ceiling was white and the walls were white. I felt groggy and so weak it was an effort to keep my eyelids up. Then I realized I was wet. I could feel a wet sheet under me, and the thin shirt I was wearing was soaked. For the life of me I couldn't think what was going on. I couldn't remember anything and didn't feel like trying. All I knew was I was in an all-white room and I was soaking wet. I didn't know what I was doing there or how I'd got there, and I didn't much care.

My eyelids drooped down and I coughed slightly. My mouth felt dry as dust. From some far-off place I heard a voice. It sounded anxious, but it irritated me. I didn't want to be bothered. I wanted to sleep. The voice said, "Will! Will! Honey, are you awake? Will?"

I got my eyes about half open. Standing at the foot of the bed was Lauren. Damned if she wasn't dressed in white too, except her hair was still golden. The glow from the bare light bulb in the ceiling shone around her hair like a halo. I wondered if she'd finally made it all the way to angel. I tried to smile or say hello or something, but I was so tired. Finally I moved my hand a little under the covers in a kind of wave. I didn't know if she saw it or not. I thought she looked as beautiful as ever but awful tired. I vaguely wondered why she wasn't in bed with me. When my eyes closed by themselves again, I heard her say, sounding relieved, "That's right, honey, get some more sleep. Rest. Just rest. I'll be right here."

I WAS unconscious for four days. I almost died from loss of blood and then infection set in and I nearly died from that. The night I'd woken soaked to the skin had been the night my fever had broken. The next day I was better and the day after that I was able to sit up in bed and take some light nourishment. To my astonishment, I was in a hospital in Hondo. I'd have given you ten-to-one odds that Hondo didn't even have a doctor, much less a ten-bed hospital. That was why the room was so white. It turned out that it was a railroad hospital, maintained by the Texas & Rio Grande Railroad for its employees, who were always getting hurt on the job.

Lauren told me the rest. I had been found on a little ranch road by Mr. Dan Stubbs and his wife. They had been on the way to Hondo in their Ford carryall to pick up some supplies. Instead they had found me and rushed me to the hospital. It had been a near thing, Lauren said. "Mr. Stubbs said you kept talking about robbers. That they'd better hurry because robbers were about. Then you started worrying about fourteen dollars. He said he found that kind of strange since you had your wallet half out and there were hundred-dollar bills scattered all over the place. Do you remember any of that?"

I shook my head. "No, I don't. But how did you get here?"

"They got your name and address off a card in your wallet and one of the doctors wired to Del Rio and Mrs. Bridesdale told them where I was staying in San Antonio, at the Menenger. I got word just as I was going to leave to go back to Del Rio." She gave me a frown. "I suppose it doesn't matter that you scared me to death."

"Of course it does, honey. Hell, when I got in that gunfight with those bandits it was you I was worrying about because I'd promised there wouldn't be a gun fired, and there I was blazing away. I figured to catch hell if I got myself hurt or killed."

"Well, you nearly did. I ought to be very angry at you, but right now I haven't got the strength."

One of the nurses had told me Lauren had stayed up watching me for three days and nights. It was really the first time we'd been able to talk. I'd woken that morning feeling considerably stronger. To my great embarrassment a nurse had come in and given me a bath and then I'd eaten for the first time in all these days. Other than feeling weak, I hurt in several places. My side was the worst, but my cheekbone was a good second. They were giving me laudanum but I hated to take the damn stuff even if it did kill the pain because it made me so groggy.

"So you got on the train?" I asked Lauren.

She shook her head. "No, we all came. Justa and Warner and Laura. Nora couldn't come. And then there were the newspapermen."

"The who?" I raised my head slightly.

"The reporters. The gentlemen of the press. By the time I got word, Sergeant McMartin had returned with the gold and told them all about how you had saved it." She gave me a look and shook her head slowly. "I don't know why I worry about you, Wilson. You could slip out of a broom straw."

"What are you talking about, the press, reporters?"

"They followed us down here. Warner and Justa gave a statement. They can lie almost as good as you can. You're a hero, believe it or not." She shook her head. "Why don't you stick to gambling, lucky as you are?"

"Listen, honey, I'm weak. Don't josh me like that."

"Josh you?" She reached down beside her chair and picked up a paper and held it in front of me. Below a line of EXTRA EXTRA EXTRA, a headline said: "EX-BANK ROBBER FOILS GOLD ROBBERS."

"You want to read it or you want me to read it to you?" Lauren asked.

I held out my hand. "I think I'm strong enough. I still think this is some kind of joke." I got hold of the paper and found the main article. It said:

San Antonio (Special)—Famed former bank robber, pardoned 26 years ago by a Governor's decree, was today instrumental in preventing a robbery attempt of the quarter of a million dollars in gold bullion that was to have gone on display at the Federal Reserve Bank.

Wilson Young, masquerading as a United States Army colonel, was successful in having the gold reloaded on the special train and sent far enough out of town to be out of harm's way until the situation could be set right by local authorities.

First Sergeant R. C. McMartin, recently retired from the United States Army, helped Young in the ruse.

Former Sergeant McMartin said that Mr. Young had gotten wind of the robbery attempt some several days back and was determined to stop it in such a fashion as would present the least danger to the large crowd that had gathered in the Military Plaza.

Sergeant McMartin, who said he'd long been an admirer of Mr. Young, said he'd been willing to take part in the ruse also because of the danger of a gunfight amidst the large crowd.

"If that gang of thieves and gunmen had tried to take the gold by force, there is no telling how many innocent people could have been hurt or killed with the number of bullets that would have been flying."

Sergeant McMartin went on to add, "Mr. Young had given me strict instructions to take the train about 25 miles out of town and to bring it back only when I got word that the robbers had dispersed."

Information is still slack at this point as to all that transpired since Mr. Young apparently departed in pursuit of the robbers.

Mr. Justa Williams, well-known rancher from Matagorda County, and the famous horse breeder Warner Grayson said they drove Mr. Young to the Three Wells water stop where he had two horses waiting. They said the last they saw of him he was riding west in hot pursuit.

Bexar County sheriff W. C. Slocum said he was aware of the attempted robbery and that plans had been made to prevent it.

He declined comment as to whether he and Mr. Young had acted in concert, though he did commend Mr. Young for his civic-mindedness.

More details will be provided as they become available to this newspaper.

I put the paper down. "Am I dreaming?"

She shook her head. "No. You're a hero." She picked up another paper. "There's more. This was day before yesterday's. You want me to read it to you?"

I nodded. "Yeah. That is kind of tiring work. A man can only bear up under so many lies."

"This is the *San Antonio Express*. It says,

"It was learned early today that former bank robber Wilson Young, who was responsible for preventing an attempt at the theft of the Federal gold to have been displayed Saturday, lay in critical condition in a railroad hospital in Hondo after a heroic attempt to apprehend the gang believed to have had designs on the gold. Dr. Clarence Bond, the physician attending Mr. Young, said the former gunman was suffering from three gun wounds and was unconscious and running a high fever.

"Mr. Young had been found by a rancher and his wife, a Mr. and Mrs. Stubbs, on a road about four miles outside of Hondo. They said as critically wounded as he was, he still made an attempt to alert them that there were outlaws in the area.

"A later search by Sheriff W. C. Slocum of Bexar County and Sheriff Tom Matts of Hondo turned up the bodies of three men whom Sheriff Slocum described as well-known desperadoes who could well have been part of the gang. It is believed that Mr. Young dispatched all three in a one-sided fight. Sheriff Matts said he saw evidence of quite a few horses at the camp and he speculated that there could have been as many as 12 to 15 men in the gang.

"Dr. Bond refused to speculate on Mr. Young's condition, but he said that Mr. Young's wife was with him as well as several friends."

She put the newspaper down. "There's more, but that's about all I can stand to read."

I shook my head in amazement. "How did this happen? By the way, how did they know it was me?"

She laughed a little. I reckoned it was the first time she'd had a real laugh in quite a while. Lord, she looked beautiful. She was sitting in a little armchair near my bed. She was wearing a pale green silk dress that looked outstanding on her and a small gold necklace and some emerald earrings I had given her. She said, "Honey, your disguise was great at a distance, but then Warner and Justa went up and got you and brought you back through the crowd and there were at least a dozen people from Del Rio and some that knew you from other places. First thing I heard was, 'That's Wilson Young, ain't it? Don't tell me he's back to robbing banks again!' And Justa and Warner both called you by name. Why, there was even a man came up and asked if I wasn't your wife."

"Did you know what was happening?"

She shook her head. "No, and it scared me to death. All I saw was you go pale as a ghost and then the sergeant was motioning for Justa and Warner to come get you. After that I had no idea what was happening until Justa and Warner got back. Of course, after that, the telegram came." She sighed. "How many times can a body be frightened out of their wits and still stay sane?"

"Aw, you knew I'd be all right. I'm always all right, honey. You shouldn't worry about me."

She said grimly, "Well, now you've got a real bandage on your face. Wilson, I swear, if you have messed your face up I am never going to forgive you."

That alarmed me. "Is it bad?"

"It's going to leave a scar about two inches long. The doctor told me the bullet cut a groove you could have laid your little finger in. He said your cheekbone was showing. He said you were going to look like one of those Prussian noblemen with a dueling scar."

I looked at her for a long minute. "How are you managing to stay so beautiful in this damn hospital?"

"I've got a room at the hotel next door."

I nodded at a little bed against the wall. "But they told me you've been sleeping here every night."

"I go and take a bath while you're resting in the afternoon and relax." Then she got a wry look on her face. "I have to keep myself fixed up. Being married to you I never know from one day to the next when I might be back on the market."

I grimaced. "Aw, it ain't that bad."

Before she answered, a nurse came in and said the doctor was coming to see me and then they wanted me to rest. Lauren got up and leaned down and kissed me softly. She whispered, "I love you."

"I don't blame you. Hero like me."

She gave me a little slap on the arm. "Oh, you. I hope it hurts when they take your bandages off." As she went out I watched her every step of the way.

I wanted to laugh out loud—I needed to laugh—but I couldn't. At least not yet. I had been fortunate way beyond lucky and I could not shake the feeling that seeing Les had had something to do with it. It felt like some kind of second chance, what kind I didn't know; but I knew I was never going to be the same after what I had been through. So far I had not mentioned seeing Les to Lauren and I wasn't sure I was going to. Maybe she'd be like Warner and Justa— not having seen anything, convinced I had been hallucinating. What I mainly wanted was to get out of the hospital and go home and do some thinking.

Lauren came back that night after I had been fed supper. "Fed" was the right word because I damn sure wouldn't have eaten the stuff given a choice. But I knew I was weak and the doctor made certain I got nourishment to build my strength back up. So I ate everything they gave me. It was good food; it had just fallen into uncaring hands on its trip into the kitchen and then to my plate.

Lauren had changed into a peach-colored chiffon gown. I said, "How many dresses did you bring?"

"Enough." She'd pulled her chair close enough so that she could reach out and touch me from time to time. "You look like you've lost twenty pounds, and you didn't have much to spare."

I gave her a stern look. "I thought I told you to stay home. What were you doing at the plaza? And you conspired with the sergeant. Wife goes behind a man's back and conspires with his friend. By the way, where is Rollie?"

She laughed. "I would expect he's back at the Mexican ranch waiting to see what position the army is going to take on his part in the business. He hung around until he was sure you were out of danger and then left. I am very fond of him, Will. And I felt a great deal safer for you with him at your side."

"By the way, what *is* the army's attitude toward this business?"

She reached down to the pile of papers. "There's a short article in here somewhere. There have been so many I can't keep up with them."

"Just what you remember."

"They were rather guarded in their comments. They almost said they were grateful for your help, but didn't quite. They made it clear that the detail of soldiers would have been more than able to handle any trouble. They did point out that it was illegal to wear a uniform and impersonate a ranking officer."

"I guess if they were coming for me they'd already have been here."

"Oh, by the way," she said, "Sheriff Slocum has identified those three men you killed as part of the gang they had been watching carefully." Her brow furrowed. "Honey, was there really a gang going to try a robbery in that plaza? With all those people around?"

I shrugged. "You wouldn't believe me if I told you."

Her brow was still puckered. "You mean this was really the reason you did all this? To stop a robbery, to keep innocent people from being hit in the cross fire?"

"I'll say this—you like and trust Sergeant McMartin. Ask him if those soldiers guarding the detail could have handled a dozen robbers. He'll tell you they were from the Quartermaster Corps and mainly didn't know anything about fighting. They count boots and hats and hand out uniforms. The two officers were from Finance. Did that captain look like he was a combat leader?"

She shook her head slowly. "Why didn't you tell me?"

I looked down at the bedclothes and said, trying for humility, "Some loads a man has to carry for himself." I could only hope I didn't suddenly get struck by lightning.

She sighed and said, "Then I guess you deserve your reward."

"Honey, I ain't quite sure I'm ready for that yet. Wait'll the stitches come out."

She made a face. "You shouldn't even be thinking about that. No. It was announced a few days ago. They have called off the gold tour."

My mouth fell open and I stared at her. "Well, I'll be a son-ofabitch." I sat there thinking about it. I didn't know what to say. I doubted that my actions had really had anything to do with the decision. More likely the government realized they were making fools out of themselves by trying to make fools out of the common folk. Still, there had been quite a crowd turned out to see that quarter of a million. Maybe the thought had occurred to them that a robbery could really happen and they'd be a hell of a long time wiping the egg off their faces. It wouldn't exactly be good advertising for recruiting. Finally I shrugged. "Glad to see they come to their senses."

Lauren looked at me in some amazement. "Is that all you've got to say? After a month and a half of railing and ranting and then damn near getting yourself killed, that's it? They've come to their senses?"

I flicked a hand. "You know me. I'm not a man to go in for over-statement."

"Ha!" Then she said, "Oh, by the way, you got a telegram from the Secretary of the Treasury thanking you for your good citizenship and bravery."

"That all? Just thanks? Didn't send a bale of new money?"

"And you got one from the governor and the mayor of San Antonio saying about the same. And, oh, you got one from Sheriff Slocum. It was a little different. He thanked you for your help but he said, in future, he'd appreciate it if you'd mind your own business since they already had plans made to handle that gang."

I came within a breath of telling her there was no gang, that the three men I'd killed were just common brush bandits who wouldn't know how to hold up a grocery store, much less a government bullion detail. But that would have given the game away, so I kept my mouth shut. Instead I said, "Any idea when I can get out of here?"

"The doctor said in a day or two. He said you could recuperate at home just as well and maybe you'd take all the reporters with you."

"Are they still here?"

"Oh, yes. At least one or two."

I laid my head back on the pillow and sighed. "Honey, you can't believe how anxious I am to have this over and be back home."

She said quietly, "Oh, yes, I can." Then she reached out and took my hand. "In a few more days it will be over. And you're going back in the saloon and casino business."

I suddenly raised my head. "Say, didn't that article say that Rollie was retired from the army?"

She nodded. "Yes. A couple of weeks ago. Maybe longer."

"But how? Why? When?"

She patted my hand. "I'll let him tell you about it."

I gave her an accusing look. "Did you make him do it so he could go to San Antonio with me?"

"Of course not. You'll see him soon and he'll tell you all about it. Now I'm going to go. You go to sleep."

She leaned over and kissed me, and even as weak as I was, I felt a faint stirring. But then she was gone and a nurse came bustling in to take my temperature and see if I wanted a bedpan. A hospital, I had decided, was the most humiliating experience a man could go through.

I WAS sitting on the side of the bed, still in my hospital gown. I had been up and walking around a little. We would be catching the train for Del Rio in about three hours and I wanted to tell Lauren about Les Richter before we left. I was still weak but I felt I was up to the ride home. They would take me to the depot on a stretcher and then get me settled in a double seat that had already been arranged for. The hospital had wanted to send a nurse with me for the trip but I had said no to that idea. It was going to be embarrassing enough to be hand-carried onto the train; I didn't want to call any more attention to myself.

The doctor had allowed me a little whiskey and I had a glass in my hand. Lauren was sitting in the corner of the small room with all our gear around her. My saddle was there. She told me how Warner had gone out and caught up the horse I'd been using as a pack animal and then had brought in my saddle and other gear. He'd already seen to shipping the horse to Del Rio, but he'd left the saddle and the two sets of saddlebags at the hospital, so it was the same whiskey I'd brought from Del Rio that I was drinking now. I didn't know if it going through a gunfight had made it stronger or me weaker, but it sure seemed to pack a bigger punch than usual.

There was no point in putting off the matter any longer. I said, "Honey, did you see a man come up to me there on the plaza? I don't mean that fat little captain or the lieutenant. And certainly not the sergeant."

She nodded. "Yes." She looked at me kind of funny. "I've been curious about that, but I didn't want to ask. It was less than a minute later that you went pale in the face and the sergeant waved for Justa and Warner to come get you."

I felt a flood of relief. "You saw him, then?"

"Of course. But you never seemed to look at him. I could see you talking but you weren't talking to him. And you walked backwards a few steps."

My mind clouded. "Wasn't he wearing a uniform?"

She looked blank. "A uniform?"

"Yes. Like mine, only where I had an eagle he had a star, the star of a brigadier general."

"No, Will." She shook her head. "The only man I saw was the bank manager."

"What? How do you know?"

"Because I heard someone say. They called him by name. What was it?" She studied on that for a moment. "Gilbert. The manager of the Federal Reserve Bank."

My heart sank. I had so been counting on her seeing what I had, maybe even hearing what I had. This was her line of country. It didn't matter that Warner and Justa hadn't seen him; it only mattered that Lauren had. I knew I hadn't been seeing things. I *knew* I hadn't. I knew I hadn't imagined it. I *knew* I hadn't. And I didn't believe in ghosts.

My face must have reflected my feelings because she got up suddenly and came and sat beside me on the bed. She put her arm around me. "Honey, what's the matter? Sweetheart, talk to me."

All I could do was shake my head. "It doesn't matter. I thought something mighty important had happened, but I guess not."

"What? What? Tell me. You are scaring me out of my wits, Will. What did you think happened?"

I sighed. It really didn't matter. In a flat voice I said, "You know about Les Richter. You know what he meant to me. You know what kind of man he was."

She nodded. "Yes. You told me you'd been thinking about him a lot lately."

Matter-of-factly I said, "He came up to me on the plaza. He was dressed as a one-star general. That part is important. I guess that's the reason the sergeant explained all the ranks to me. A brigadier general is the next rank up from what I was, a full colonel. Les even said he came that way so he'd outrank me and I'd have to listen." I looked around at her. She was listening intently, getting that little crease in her forehead. It was a second before she realized I had stopped talking and was expecting something from her.

She looked up into my eyes. "Are you sure it was him?"

I nodded. "He looked about the same age as when I saw him last, though there was a tiredness in his face."

"And he spoke to you?"

I nodded.

"And you could hear him?"

I nodded.

"What did he say?"

The whole scene and every movement and every word had been engraved on my mind like someone had put it there with a hammer and chisel. "He told me that I didn't want to be doing what I was doing. He said we hadn't even wanted to do it in the old, bad days, that it had been against our nature." I paused and searched my heart for a second. "I told him I wasn't going to rob the gold, that it was just a stunt."

Her eyes were intent upon my face. At that instant I didn't know what the truth was within me. After a long pause she said, "What else did he say?"

I paused myself. Finally I said, "He said that wasn't the kind of gold that counted and he said I already knew that." I looked at her. "I don't know what he meant by that. Do you?"

Her face got calm. She nodded. "I think so."

"Then he said I'd always been a fair man and an honest man but I could be more than that. He said I could be rich but not with that kind of gold. Then he said I had eyes and ears and I ought to use them. He said he wouldn't be able to help me again." I looked around at her.

She got up and walked back to her chair. She had a strange look on her face. "And then what?"

I shook my head. "Nothing. He walked past me and when I turned around to watch him he'd disappeared." I took a drink of whiskey.

She studied me for a long moment. "And you feel like you saw him? You don't think it could have been brought on by the danger or the excitement?"

"Lauren, for more years than I care to remember I've exposed myself to danger and I never saw people who weren't there before."

"You're satisfied that you saw him?"

"I *know* I saw him."

In a soft voice she said, "Convinced of things not seen."

I nodded. "That was the first thing that came to my mind after I got over the shock. But it has shaken me to the roots that you didn't see him."

She said quickly, "Oh, no. That doesn't matter. I wasn't intended to see him."

"But you believe in that sort of thing."

She smiled. "That's not the way it works, Will."

"Well, do you believe I was seeing things, imagining things?"

She shook her head. "No. I don't. If you saw him, he was there."

I was frustrated. I had hoped to get some explanation from her, some insight. She was the Christian. "Well, what in hell does it mean?"

She shook her head. "Only you can decide that, Will. You were the only one to receive the message."

"Then does what he had to say mean anything to you?"

She nodded. "Yes. But it's only important what it means to you."

I shook my head. "Damn, Lauren, that ain't a hell of a lot of help."

She smiled. "What you are asking for is a very personal matter. It's all in you."

WE HAD been riding for about two hours. I had lain down on the seat most of the way, but now I was sitting up. The doctor had put me on a pretty short lead rope when it came to the whiskey and had put Lauren in charge of the bottle. It had finally come time for me to have another one and she'd poured me a little in a glass. I said, "Hell, Lauren, the man said I could have a drink, not a drop. You didn't put enough in that glass to drown a fly."

She grudgingly added a few more drops and handed me the glass. I took a sip, savoring it. I figured we had about another hour and a half to go. I couldn't wait to get in my own house and in my own bed. I'd been gone eight days, and it was the longest eight days I'd ever experienced.

Lauren, sitting across from me, said, "Well, now that it's over, how do you feel?"

I thought for a moment or two. I'd been giving the subject considerable thought as I'd lain in the hospital. I didn't know if I'd accomplished anything or not. With the exception of Les, I didn't know that a whole lot had happened. They had canceled the con job they were running, but they'd been nearly through anyway. "Before I can answer that," I said, "I'd like to sit down with Willis and compare notes and see how we each feel about what the other has done. Sort of get his insight."

Her face brightened. "Oh, Will, that makes me feel so good hearing you talk about your son like that again."

I took another little sip. "Maybe I'm closer to seeing his point. Maybe not. I don't know. We'd have to talk. Listen, when I get well why don't we take the train to that New York City and then get on one of those ships and go over to France and have a visit."

She clasped her hands together like a little girl. "That would be wonderful! Oh, Will, do you mean it?"

I nodded. "Even if he has got the clap."

She reddened. "Wilson Young, how dare you talk about my son like that. His last letter said not to worry about him for a while because he had the flu. The flu! Damnit!"

"That's what they call it in France."

"You had better stop that kind of talk." She held up the bottle and made a gesture as if she was pouring it out.

I put up my hand in surrender. "All right, all right. He's got the flu. And he's a virgin. I know, I used to get the flu myself back when I was a virgin. Before you came along with your lustful ways and led me astray."

She gave me a dry look. "Now I know you're getting better. You're starting to sound like your old, mean self."

CHAPTER
18

THE SERGEANT and I were sitting out on the front porch of an afternoon drinking lemonade with rum in it. The days had run on into August and the iced drinks tasted mighty good in the heat. I'd been home almost three weeks and was nearly back on my feet, though I didn't plan on entering any rodeos. I knew one thing, though. The next person who said to me, "You don't heal near as fast the older you get as you did when you were young," was going to get an earful from me to the effect of, "Listen, you go and get shot three times and get an infection in every wound and see how damn fast you heal. The doctor said if it hadn't been for my constitution I'd've never made it."

I had seen the sergeant a number of times since my return—in fact he'd been at the station to meet us and help me home—but this was the first time we'd had a chance to have a private talk. I'd given him a job. In fact, I'd given him my job. I'd made him the general manager over both the saloon and the casino. It had near harelipped the managers of each establishment, but there wasn't much they could do about it. When I'd told Rollie what his job was he'd been shocked. But then I'd explained it was the one job that didn't require any ability. All he had to do was keep an eye on the other two managers and look suspicious all the time. I'd said, "That's all I ever done, Sergeant, and I reckon you can handle it. While you are getting your feet wet bring the books to Lauren and she'll keep you straight. And have a visit with my lawyer about the law and the rules that go to running a place like that."

Of course I'd paid him an amount equal to the position, which was five hundred a month. It had left him shocked and nearly breathless. All he could say was, "Ah, Your Honor, you shouldn't be after joshing a poor old Irishman."

There'd been other changes, too. Once I was home I'd sent for my lawyer and had him handle some matters for me. I'd had him buy two Cadillacs from an automobile dealer in Houston. I'd gotten Rollie one like Justa's except it was black. I'd gotten Lauren a little red roadster where you could put the top up and down. It was now in the carriage house, where, no doubt, Mr. Bridesdale was cursing it soundly. He'd told me he'd rather curry a horse than shine a damn piece of iron. I didn't blame him.

The automobiles didn't belong to either Lauren or Rollie. Taxes, I had discovered, had suddenly taken on an ominous presence, and the corporation that owned the saloon and the casino owned the cars.

I'd also had a phone installed and electricity brought into the house. That had meant one of those hotel-size electric refrigerators. I would have gotten Mrs. Bridesdale a gas stove to cook on but she wouldn't give up her old cast-iron wood-burning one.

I had absolutely no intention of riding in either car, I wasn't going to use the damn telephone, and I imagined that the illumination of the light bulbs was coming from kerosene lanterns. Lauren, naturally, was thrilled to death, especially with the telephone.

Rollie was overcome. The Cadillac that had been assigned to him was sitting in the driveway that I had constructed out of asphalt. It curved around in a semicircle through the front yard just like all the carriage drives I'd seen in front of those stately homes in Virginia.

The reporters had finally caught up with me and I'd said a lot of things. I'd said that I felt bad about not working closely with the sheriff of Bexar County, but there hadn't been time. I'd had some inside knowledge of the gang and a certain amount of past experience (that had got a laugh from the reporters) and I was desperate to keep the gold from getting far enough onto the plaza for an attack. As it was, I said, I was nearly too late because of an attack of flu which I'd been suffering from for several days. I said if there was a hero it had been Sergeant McMartin, who had taken over and averted the disaster. I exonerated the sergeant by claiming to have shown him a false and forged set of commission papers so that he had no reason to think I wasn't a regular army officer on reserve. I had applauded the quick work and cooperation of Captain Bell and Lieutenant Wood and had said I was very sorry that the people of San Antonio and the towns farther west didn't get a chance to see what good care the government was taking with their hard-earned dollars. In short I said exactly the opposite of what I had meant to say by what I'd done. The newspapers still called me a hero, only now they called me modest as well. I had claimed to have had my friends hurry me to what I knew to be the gang's rendezvous point so that I could track them and get word back to the sheriff. I had said it had been my own foolish blunder that had caused my wounds. I had said that I considered myself as lucky as a man could get.

I had said all those ridiculous words because it seemed the easiest and least painful for everyone involved. A great deal had changed in my mind since I had seen and heard Les. Matters that had once seemed important no longer did, and matters I had paid little attention to now loomed large in my mind—matters like letting those I cared for be certain of it. I had, in Lauren's words, taken off the hard parts of myself and thrown them away.

There was no doubt in my mind about Les. The man I saw on the plaza was as real as the bricks beneath my feet. It was easy to distinguish between him and the figure I'd seen sitting a horse and urging me on when I'd staggered down the cow trail. That Les had been conjured up by my fevered brain, shocked by the bullet wounds and the loss of blood.

I glanced to my right. The sergeant was lounging back in his chair, looking very dapper in a light gray poplin suit with matching vest and a gold watch chain stretched across his middle. He was also wearing at an angle a black plug hat that he insisted on calling a derby.

He caught my eye and smiled. "Ah, it's to laugh, ain't it, Colonel?"

I nodded. We had never discussed what had happened that day and damn little of what had gone on before because there had always been someone else around, and what had happened between us was for us alone. I didn't even want Lauren to know the whole story. I said, "Yeah, Rollie, one hell of a big laugh."

He shook his head. "I'm still after not believing how it turned out. We all told the same story with no chance of consulting one with the other. Even your friends, after you were shot, was the same. Ah, it was a rub o' the green and no mistake."

"We got lucky," I said. "So damn lucky I can't believe it. At least I did."

He gave me a sardonic look. "Aye, sir, only shot three times. I guess if you'd caught four you'd have thought yourself all the more fortunate."

I grimaced back. "That's not what I mean. Listen, something I never quite understood. The papers said you had retired. I thought you were on leave? What happened to your thirty-year retirement?"

"Technically, Your Honor, I was still in the army. But I had thirty days' leave coming to me, so I made my retirement to come at the end of the thirty days. I knew I'd need to go back and forth to the camp for the various little items we'd need in our grand adventure. But, aye, I had retired."

"What about the thirty years and the pension talk?"

He smiled. "Seems I heard a gentleman tell me he'd give me a job paying twice what I was getting in the army. Three times. Even one such as I knew that was the best hand to play."

"How could you know I meant it?"

"Sir, a man don't have to be around you for long to know you don't make statements lightly. If you told me my pants was afire I wouldn't bother to look, but would jump in the nearest water. And, sir, may I say that was a handsome statement you made to the newspapers about you having forged papers of commission." He chuckled quietly. "Aye, they was forged, but not by you."

I shrugged. "It all worked out."

He took his plug hat off and looked inside it and then put it back on his head. "Sir, I still don't understand this job you've given me. It's a monstrous responsibility. Why would you want to go and trust such a one as me with your very own business?"

I took a drink of the rum and lemonade. "I trusted you with my life, didn't I? Wouldn't you expect me to trust you with my money?"

He nodded. "Aye, you are a thinking man, sir, and no mistake. I've been doing just as you've said, walking around, looking wise, and keeping my mouth shut."

"That's the ticket. The two men who report to you don't know how much you know. You've handled men most all of your career in the army. That's all you're doing now. You're not handling money, but people. Keep your mouth shut, and none the wiser."

He smiled ruefully. "I'm after noticing that I worry more about your money than I ever did my own."

His divorce had been handled easily. My lawyer had done it for him by mail and telegram and telephone. Fifteen hundred dollars had been sent to his wife, and back had come a decree of divorce.

"Rollie, you were coming with me all the way, weren't you? It wasn't the vow to my wife that put you there. Answer me."

He rubbed the back of his hand across his mouth. "Colonel, I never had no choice once I'd drawn cards in the game. I knew you couldn't do it alone. You had to have me with you, a proper soldier who knew the scheme of things. I knew you didn't want anyone else running the risk, that you wanted to do it alone, but I couldn't let you because you didn't know enough. But, ah, Colonel, we made a lovely pair."

"I'm not a colonel anymore, Rollie."

He shook his head. "You'll always be the colonel to me, sir." He suddenly got a big smile on his face. "Ah, sir, sure and you were grand up there on that plaza. Grand! Stalking about, slapping your stick! Ah, you dressed down that plump little captain something proper, sir. I tell you, you looked and acted more like an officer than any I've ever seen in my days. You had the look of it, the sound of it, the very presence of it. Aye, you was grand." He paused. "Of course until you saw him and went all pale."

My head snapped around toward him. "What? Went pale when I saw who?"

He looked at me for a long moment, a smile stealing across his face. "Why, your old friend, Les Richter."

I stared at him, my heart beating like a drum tattoo. My voice faltering, I said, "You saw him? You saw him come up?"

He looked toward the horizon. "In a manner of speaking, Colonel. I saw him in your eyes. I heard you talking to him." He grinned. "That man from the bank had come up and you were confusing him for certain, sir. He didn't know who or what you were talking about."

I was feeling faint again. "Could you hear him?"

He shook his head. "No, but I knew what he said to you."

I swallowed and looked down at the ground. "Uh, do you think it had anything to do with, uh, church, uh, or religion?" My mouth was very dry but I did not move to relieve it with the drink in my hand.

He smiled slightly and took off his hat and twirled it between his hands. "Do you mean do I think it was of the good Lord Jesus?"

"Yeah." My mouth was so dry I could barely speak.

"That would be for you to decide, sir. Whatever is in your heart."

"That's what my wife said."

"There is no other answer, sir. The matter is personal between you and Him."

"But if you didn't hear Les speaking to me, how do you know what he said?"

He touched his chest. "Maybe I heard it in here. He was after telling you in so many words that there was more gold in heaven than was ever dreamed of on earth. And he wasn't speaking of the kind you can ring on a bar to get the barkeep's attention."

I took a quick drink. I was nearly breathless. "Sergeant, this is making my head swim."

He looked over at me. "And why would that be? Sure and didn't you ask for it, Colonel?"

"What? Ask for what?"

He put his hat back on. "Would you be remembering sometime back when I asked you how you fancied your chances of bringing this business off clean and complete?"

I was puzzled. "Well, yes, I guess so. Why?"

"You're not remembering what you answered?"

I shook my head slowly. "No, not right off."

"You said it would take a miracle."

I looked away. Something had happened I hadn't realized. "But I told Les I wasn't going to rob the gold, that it was only a stunt."

"And what did he say to that?"

I was beginning to sweat, and my mouth was dry again. "He

passed it by, said something else. Said it wasn't the kind of gold that counts." I looked at the sergeant. "You were right. He did say that. I guess it *was* a miracle of some kind. I don't know, Rollie, I just don't know."

Rollie took a sip of his drink and looked at the horizon. "Maybe you're after looking at the wrong miracle. Maybe you're thinking the miracle was you decided not to steal the gold."

I felt uneasy. "I don't know. I don't think I meant to steal it."

"They be all kinds of miracles, Colonel. Maybe this was a small wee miracle that had nothing to do with the gold or the government or the bank or any of those reasons you said put you in that plaza. Maybe it was one of those miracles the good Lord does can't no one else see. Only the one person." He looked over at me.

For a second I couldn't speak. Then I cleared my throat. "There's always that chance."

The sergeant smiled. "Chance? I thought you weren't a gambling man, Colonel?"

"I'm not."

He stood up and put his glass on the porch railing. "Well, I'm after going down and seeing about the business."

I stood up, too. "Yeah, go on down and make us some more money."

He smiled. "Ah, Colonel, darlin', I think we're rich enough."

WHOLE STORY

 4/ '00